The Bounce Back

OTHER TITLES BY ADDIE WOOLRIDGE

The Checklist

The Bounce Back

Addie Woolridge

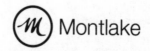

Montlake

Text copyright © 2021 Alexandra Massengale
All rights reserved.

Published by Montlake, Seattle
www.apub.com

Amazon, the Amazon logo, and Montlake are trademarks of Amazon.com, Inc., or its affiliates.

ISBN-13: 9781542030342
ISBN-10: 154203034X

Cover design and illustration by Liz Casal

Printed in the United States of America

To CoCo and Marshall: I know what being a sister means because of you two. I love you.

CHAPTER ONE

"Don't clap for that."

The harsh whisper shattered Neale's concentration. Looking up from the photo she'd just lit on fire, she searched the sparse crowd for the whisperer but saw only a few bored-looking patrons over by the bar. Objectively, she knew not everyone was going to like her art, but did they have to whisper so loudly about it? Her piece had just started. They could at least give her five minutes to warm up. Hell, everyone had given Sarah's giant papier-mâché dog's head in the next room nearly an hour, and that didn't even have a multimedia element to it.

Flames from the photo in her hand licked her fingertips, and she dropped it into the burn bin she'd painstakingly lugged into the gallery earlier that morning, belatedly realizing that she hadn't recited the line from *Return of the Jedi* before she'd let it go.

Picking up another picture, Neale waited for the flash of pink light from the projector overhead to tell her that it was time for the next photo. When the mutilated makeover scene from *Grease* began playing, she seized the image of the March for the Equal Rights Amendment, clicked her lighter, and said, "Upgrade yourself. He's a stud."

Neale waited for the audience to react. Over by the bar, a woman clapped half-heartedly into the silence. Maybe the audience didn't realize the film and the march had happened at the same time? Darin might have been right. The piece needed show notes. At least she'd remembered her line this time.

"I swear, Americans will clap for anything," the bored-looking white man by the bar said, putting his hand over the woman's to silence her claps. "This is not good."

Definitely should have done show notes, Neale thought as she began to wilt under the heat of the sparkly white sequins on her majorette uniform. How could something without pants be so warm and itchy?

This was not going the way she had anticipated. She had imagined this piece being met with awe. The kind reserved for great artists like Lorraine O'Grady or Tehching Hsieh. Instead, she was getting crickets.

Shaking the thought off, Neale reached for the next picture as she watched the art features editor for the *Seattle Times* walk into the gallery and saunter over to her parents. Of course he was here. The Wootherford Collective shows were always covered. After all, it was known as the Seattle showcase to find up-and-coming artists. Knowing her dad, he'd probably emailed the guy weeks ago, just to be sure he saw Neale's name on the flyer.

Overhead, Julia Roberts bought clothes in *Pretty Woman*, and Neale was painfully aware that her video loop only had a few more seconds before she needed to give up on the picture and prepare for the next clip. A little bubble of panic began to rise in her. Hoisting the cover of *The Beauty Myth* to waist height, she clicked her lighter and shouted, "Money is his power, baby."

In the corner, her sister Dylan clapped as if she could inspire the entire room to follow her lead. Next to her parents, the *Times* critic tilted his head to one side and then the other, as if getting a better angle on the piece would provide additional clarity. Neale reminded herself that art was meant to make people uncomfortable. She just hadn't expected herself to be one of those people.

"I don't think she made it into the Collective on her own merits," the formerly clapping woman said, tipping her head toward Neale's parents.

That stung. Gasps of delight over the dog head came from the next room, further highlighting the perplexed audience reaction in front of her.

The screen flipped again, and *The Birds'* infamous schoolhouse scene began to run in a flickering loop; the sounds of Tippi Hedren and a pack of schoolchildren running and screaming from a murder of crows echoed around the gallery. Scanning the crowd, Neale found Dr. McMillan, director of the Wootherford Collective, watching her, followed by Jenna, her assistant, filming on her phone.

In that moment, every critique Neale had ever received ran double time through her scattered thoughts, causing her anxiety to spike and little beads of sweat to form under her giant smelly hat. Why hadn't the company dry-cleaned the outfit before renting it out again? That seemed like a thing they should have done.

Neale watched a less-than-congratulatory smile creep across Jenna's face as if she was enjoying the lukewarm reception. Neale needed to wipe that silly smile right off her face and get everyone's attention. It was time to go big or go home.

Reaching for the photo of the March on Washington, Neale thrust the image over her head along with the lighter and took a deep breath. "Better to fear pretend monsters than face the real ones."

"Oh!" the woman by the bar shrieked, covering her mouth. Next to her, the face of the rude whispering man went slack with surprise.

Neale tried and failed to suppress a grin. That was the reaction she was looking for. Dropping the photo into the burn bin with panache, she waited for the color from the projector to change again and reached for the next image. She had just started to recall her line for *The Godfather Part III* when a strange smell caught her attention. Almost like burnt plastic.

Neale flicked her eyes toward the bar to see if they had started creating some sort of fancy cocktail. No. No flaming cocktails. But the bartender did look at her with complete horror, which was an unexpected response. The strangeness of it made Neale hot. Like, her head was starting to sweat. And the burnt-plastic smell was getting—

"Shit," Neale yelped, reaching up and yanking the flaming hat off her head. Chucking the hat into the burn bin with a force to rival an NFL quarterback, Neale ran her hands over her head to check for singed hair. Lucky for her, the hat was so tall and so furry that the fire hadn't managed to do any real damage . . . unless she counted the damage to her ego.

Looking around, Neale took in the puzzled faces of the crowd, all of whom seemed to be grappling with what they'd just seen, unsure whether Neale had intentionally lit herself on fire to make a statement or if something had gone wrong. Scanning her family's reaction, she was confronted by the enthusiastic nods of her father, the wincing of her mother, and Dylan's holy-shit-this-is-bad smile.

Okay, maybe the mistake was more obvious than she'd realized. But her battleship hadn't sunk yet. Sure, Dr. McMillan's mouth was wide open in a potential scream of terror, but she hadn't stepped in. Maybe Neale could keep going.

Neale coughed and reached for the next image. Her eyes were watering, but she refused to give in to tears or sniffles. Although those could have been caused by the burnt-plastic smell—

"Oh dear."

Dylan's polite remark rocked Neale just as the bin next to her began belching flames. She watched in anguish as the bartender grabbed a bottle of San Pellegrino and began sprinting toward the billowing black smoke coming from the bin. But he wasn't fast enough. Someone in the next room squealed, and then the space was filled with the sound of breaking glass.

Out of the corner of her eye, Neale could see her father quickly snatching a red fire extinguisher from the wall, as if this were something he handled all the time. He was so dramatic. Neale choked in a breath of chemical fumes and began, "Dad, I don't think that is going to be—"

And then the ceiling began to rain blood.

Or at least Neale thought it was blood, until rusty water from the fire sprinklers got in her mouth. Around her, people screeched and made for the exits as Neale stood watching her sparkly white cowboy boots slowly turn a sad, stale brown.

"Come on, Neale. Time to go." Her mother's stern hand wrapped around her forearm. Half-conscious, Neale let herself be marched into the next gallery, where Sarah's papier-mâché dog head was slowly turning into sludge in the middle of the room. Something inside of her snapped as she watched the Lisa Frank–colored mess on the floor, and Neale found herself closing her eyes to fight the giggles.

If this was real—and Neale struggled to believe that this wasn't an absurd fever dream—then all she could do was hope the company wouldn't charge her for the damage to the majorette suit. Her mother's grip on her tightened as she tripped on the soaking floor mat that protected the entryway to the gallery. Wrenching her eyes open, she barely righted herself in time to prevent her face from being the second casualty of the night.

As she stood outside the gallery, with the damp March Seattle air wrapped around her, it finally dawned on Neale just how bad things were. To her right, Sarah stood sobbing into Lo's shoulder, who stopped comforting her just long enough to look at Neale like she was the Antichrist. Behind her, Darin was staring at her as if she had grown a second head. Looking down at her stained, sparkly uniform, Neale guessed she looked a little rough, although the uniform still showed off her legs nicely. She completed her rotation just in time to catch Jenna grinning like a kid on Christmas, holding up her phone like she was still taping the show. Somewhere in the distance, a fire truck blared.

"Neale? Honey?" Her father's voice sounded like it was coming from underwater, not three feet away. "Do you think the trauma damaged her hearing?"

"What? No, Dad. She is just taking it in," Dylan said, her voice sounding like the eye roll that Neale was sure her sister was too polite to display publicly.

"Okay, Neale. Blink if you can hear me," her father said, reaching out.

"Maybe we give her a bit of space? Let the fresh air help." That was from Dylan's boyfriend, Mike, who gently backed away, trying to give her the inverse amount of space to her father's hovering.

"Oh, poor Neale," Henry said, pulling her into a hug as her mother exhaled.

"Henry. She nearly burned down a gallery. I think it's okay to give her a moment before expecting her to respond—"

"Everyone okay?" Dr. McMillan's voice boomed, causing Neale to jump.

"Oh, good! You are in there." Her father squeezed her even tighter, causing the fabric of her unitard to squelch uncomfortably as a volley of *yes*es and *over here*s went up around her.

"Dad, don't hover," Neale heard herself say, her voice scratchy from the smoke and the fact that her father was squeezing all the air out of her lungs.

"I'm not hovering," her father said, looking affronted behind his Coke-bottle glasses.

"You are, darling," her mother shouted over the wail of the approaching sirens. Not for the first time, Neale marveled at her mother's ability to project. Bernice Delacroix could probably sub in for a siren if the fire department needed an extra one. Which it appeared it did not, seeing as it had sent not one but two ambulances in addition to a truck. The sirens shut off as the firefighters disembarked and walked toward a drenched Dr. McMillan, ostensibly to understand what exactly had happened and what help the gallery actually needed.

"On the upside, the gallery doesn't have to worry about whether or not their sprinkler system works," Dylan said, a little too brightly, stepping strategically into Neale's line of sight so that she couldn't see the gallery door. Dylan was so not subtle. Under normal circumstances, Neale would be irritated by her babying, but right now, standing outside her ruined show in a disgusting uniform, she was grateful for it.

"Good point. You never really know how safe these kinds of places are," her father said, seizing on the idea as if Dylan had set him up for a touchdown.

"Henry, you had a show here two years ago. What are you—" Bernice caught a glare from Dylan and stopped short. Attempting to redirect her honesty, she said, "But you're right. You never know when management has changed."

"Mom. It's okay; you don't need to lie. The piece has some lumps. But I'm sure I can smooth it out next week. Maybe add show notes and rethink the costume." Neale rummaged around in her head for some additional positive spin that she could put on this. "My horoscope did say that fire was a 'do' today, so who knows? This might be a good thing."

"Neale, maybe you shouldn't plan to attend the next Collective workshop," her mother said gently, as if it were normal for someone to skip a workshop after a failed show.

"Why not?" Neale asked, trying to read the pained look on her mother's face.

"Maybe we talk about this once you've had a chance to shower?" Dylan's diplomatic big-sister tone was back.

"Yes. Let's talk about this after—"

"Neale. May I have a word with you?" Dr. McMillan appeared from behind her parents. Although she was a foot shorter than the family, her voice carried, and the sea of Delacroix parted to let her pass, anxiety rolling off each of them.

7

"Yes." Neale blinked at Dr. McMillan, whose white tuxedo shirt was stained the same repugnant rust color as Neale's boots. She watched as the formerly immaculately dressed Dr. McMillan walked a few paces away before stopping, irritation written on her face. Neale belatedly realized that she was supposed to follow her away from her hovering family. "Oh. Sorry, I didn't realize you meant now."

"That is generally what the phrase *May I have a word* implies," Dr. McMillan said, propping one hand on her hip. This was not a good sign.

"I just want to say how sorry I am. I know—"

Dr. McMillan held a hand up. "I'm sure your intention wasn't to devastate your colleagues and the showcase." Her diction was so crisp that the *t* in *wasn't* nearly gave Neale whiplash.

"Yes. Yes. Exactly. I had no idea the hat was—"

"Nonetheless," Dr. McMillan interrupted, this time with a glare that would blind freeway drivers, "I think it is wise for you to step back from the Collective."

Neale heard a ringing in her ears that had nothing to do with the fire alarm. Logically, she knew the meaning of Dr. McMillan's words. But cognitively, they did not make any sense. Feeling her face get hot, she stammered, "It was one bad show. Bad shows happen."

"My dear, this is beyond one bad show," Dr. McMillan said, her tone softening a little as she watched Neale's confusion. "I've already got board members hounding me left, right, and center about your removal."

"But the whole point of the Collective is to refine our craft. Clearly, this needs refining," Neale said, gesturing to the gallery, where the fire-fighters were ambling out of the front door, probably grateful the damage was to a papier-mâché dog and a fuzzy majorette's hat.

"And that's the problem," Dr. McMillan said, her hawklike eyes watching as Neale checked to see if her heart had fully shattered yet or if there were still a few pieces of it intact. *Nope. No pieces of it*, she thought, only pulling herself away from her physical check-in when Dr. McMillan began to speak again. "Even if I could find a way for the board to reinstate you and to insure you after this, which I cannot imagine is possible, your work wasn't ready for the cohort's show tonight."

"That's okay. I have other ideas for pieces that are stronger than this. I've been thinking about something for the June show. And—"

"Neale, you are consistently late to Collective meetings, and you rarely have your materials ready for critiques. Not to mention that when you do put in even a modicum of effort, it is often derivative. For whatever reason, you just aren't fully committing to your work." Neale felt her jaw drop as Dr. McMillan continued with a shake of her head that reminded Neale of a deeply disappointed basketball coach whose team lost a playoff game on a technical error. "Now, I know there is tremendous pressure on you to perform, between your parents and your sister's recent success. But I recommend you take this opportunity to reevaluate what you want."

Neale fought to suppress a whimper. She was sure her lower lip was quivering, and she pressed her mouth into a straight line until it lost feeling altogether. Bringing up her middle sister, Billie, felt like a low blow. It was wonderful that after years of toiling away in New York art-scene obscurity, Billie had finally found a way to transform her paintings into a variety show that had taken off like a rocket. And all right, Neale's piece wasn't perfect. But wasn't burning down your own show and ruining your friends' night enough? Did Dr. McMillan have to do the whole family-comparison thing too?

"My advice is either get serious or retire. Right now, you just aren't at the level you need to be to be a contributing member of the Wootherford Collective. Or the larger art world, for that matter."

Somewhere in the distance, Neale could hear the sound of Sarah still sobbing and wished she could do the same. In fact, if Dr. McMillan said anything more, Neale might not have a choice in when or where she took up Sarah's new favorite pastime. Neale threw up a silent prayer to whatever star or satellite was twinkling overhead, begging it to end this conversation soon, please.

Dr. McMillan sighed heavily. "Honestly, Neale, I'm just not convinced that you're going to go further in the art world." With that, she turned to face Neale's parents and said, "Henry, Bernice, good to see you both. I wish it were under more fortunate circumstances."

Her mother's arms were crossed in a defensive position over her favorite fleece vest, while her father's mouth hung slightly ajar. Next to them, her sister looked like she was getting ready to take off her spiked heel and drive it into Dr. McMillan's clavicle. Motioning to the still-filming Jenna that they were leaving, Dr. McMillan strutted away to the nearly unrecognizable sound of speechless Delacroix.

"Oh, honey. What does she know?" Bernice said, breaking the silence after a beat.

Neale appreciated the thought, even if just two months ago her mother had celebrated Dr. McMillan's work, pushed her to apply, and said that the Collective was the perfect first step to truly taking her art and business acumen to the next level. The memory nudged what little restraint Neale had, and she burst into the kind of tears that made Sarah look like an amateur.

"Aw, no, no. Don't cry. Come here," her father said, holding his arms out wide for yet another sequined-sprinkler-water hug. Neale shook her head, not wanting to be publicly comforted by her family when her peers were still staring daggers into her side. Unfortunately, neither her mother nor father was subtle, and Bernice reached her first, wrapping her in a hug that felt more like a yardstick trying to bend than a gesture of comfort—which, of course, did not stop her father from layering on his own hug.

There were only two saving graces in that moment. One was that Billie was too busy to fly out for the show. The other was that Dylan had managed to keep the rust off her sleeveless white blouse, which meant that a true Delacroix group hug was out of the question. Against her better judgment, Neale leaned into her parents' soothing coos for a moment, letting herself soak up their shielding until she could stop shaking.

Eventually, she lost track of the five deep breaths she was supposed to be taking. Clearing her throat, she began shaking her parents off. "All right. Let's just go home."

"Of course. We can work through all of this tomorrow. And I just want you to know that your feelings are—"

"Dad, let's validate feelings at home. I think everyone's tired," Dylan said, using the tone Neale had come to recognize as her polite this-isn't-a-discussion voice. Her sister was not an artist, and nowhere was it on clearer display than when she was trying to herd the family into some sense of normalcy. It never worked, but Dylan would try all night on Neale's behalf if needed.

"I'd like that," Neale said to the sidewalk, preempting whatever addendum her dad would try to add to the moment.

Keeping her eyes down, she started walking toward where she'd parked her car. It was pointless to try to go back into the gallery to salvage anything. If Dr. McMillan was going to kick her out of the Collective, then the least she could do was find a home for Neale's failed burn bin. Reaching her car, she began fishing around the weird, tiny sequined pocket of her majorette uniform for her car key and realized the pocket was still full of rusty water. Removing her key, she sighed. She was definitely going to have to buy the stupid majorette suit.

CHAPTER TWO

Neale rolled over in her massive pile of blankets and searched for her phone. At some point in the last fifteen hours, she had chucked it away from her when the string of I-don't-want-to-work-with-you-anymore messages related to the Great Sprinkler Disaster had started rolling in. The only person who hadn't reached out was Darin. She'd called him last night to cry and debrief, but he hadn't picked up. While ignoring his phone wasn't atypical of Darin, Neale still felt like her not-boyfriend should have called her back by now, given that he'd been there for her literal meltdown. Locating her phone, Neale was about to send another sad text when Milo, the family's giant perro de presa, started to whine at her bedroom door. From downstairs, she heard the sound of Dylan pretending not to shout at her parents. If she didn't let the dog out to terrorize her eldest sister soon, he would lose his little dog mind, which would mess with her ability to fully engage in self-pity.

"Keep your shirt on," Neale mumbled, pushing herself into a seated position. The act meant that she caught sight of herself in the mirror, a thing she had been avoiding like the plague. Her naturally fine-boned body that her mother liked to call "delicate" looked just plain bony. Neale could deal with being knobby. What she couldn't deal with was the sad, ashy pallor that had taken the place of her bronze skin. Unlike Dylan, she'd never be caught wearing an uncomfortable outfit, pressing her hair into submission, or stuffing her feet into shoes she didn't love.

Neale was committed to being exclusively herself, no matter what the world thought. Her one vanity was her skin. She loved the way it used to glow like she had been sprinkled with actual Black-girl magic. Now, she looked like someone had shut off her internal lamp and left her face with a flickering light bulb from a 7-Eleven right before closing time.

Running her nails over her hair to try to push a few of the more unruly dyed-blonde strands back into her braid, she shoved her covers off and pushed herself into standing, feeling her stiff muscles stretch and strain in protest. Throwing a faded orange hoodie on in place of a bra, she turned to Milo, who had begun wagging his tail so hard it was practically throwing him off balance. As soon as she twisted the door handle, Milo forced his bulky frame through the crack she had opened and took off down the stairs.

"Ungrateful," Neale mumbled. She was turning to go back to bed when the sound of her family's not-whispers reached her.

"It's not like she can live here forever," Bernice hissed.

"I agree. But should we still do this now? She's never been independent," her father said quietly.

Neale's blood stopped cold. Were they talking about her? They couldn't seriously be considering making her move after she had shattered her entire career and paid $375.62 for a destroyed majorette costume.

"Mom has a point, Dad. Besides, did you ever think that propping Neale up all the time is the reason why she isn't independent?" Dylan actually whispered.

"She's not like Dylan, Henry. We know she doesn't plan or think ahead. This isn't something we can wait for her to do on her own."

Neale sucked in her breath and her stomach at the same time, then closed her eyes against the sting of tears as her mother's words dented her heart. She wanted to be independent. Really, she tried to make a living off her art every day. It just wasn't working out lately. She glanced back over her shoulder at her bed, then gave the idea up. She knew she didn't want to hear what her family thought, but the threat of her imminent demise was serious, and she was too afraid to stop eavesdropping now.

"That's my point. How do we know she can do this? Neale's never really been responsible for anything."

Neale winced as her father's true feelings chipped off another piece of her heart. Did he actually think she was a failure? *No*, Neale reasoned. He didn't think she was a failure. Just irresponsible. Not that being irresponsible was much better. Neale frowned, hoping Dylan would come to her defense.

"It's time, Dad. You have to let her learn to fend for herself. Maybe she will surprise you?"

"I know we hoped the show would launch her, but it's Neale. She's always fifty fifty when it comes to hard work." Her mother's alto snaked its way upstairs, and Neale desperately wished that she hadn't let the dog out. She leaned into the door and scrubbed a hand over her eyes as they began to sting. How could her family say that about her? Sure, she hadn't exactly won the day or anything, but the one thing she'd always counted on was her family's faith in her. Apparently, they had just been pretending.

"We're all nervous for Neale, Dad. But this is the best set up she has ever been. She has to have saved money living with you two, and she's made all kinds of friends who can help her navigate this. Hell, didn't you introduce her to a job prospect? Honestly, if she can't move out now, y'all are basically going to die of old age with her still in the house. The show was a setback, not the end of the—oh! Hello, Milo. Ew. Please don't jump on me—" Dylan broke off, sounding tormented.

For a brief moment, Neale set her pain aside to enjoy the fact that Dylan's precious, expensive wardrobe was probably covered in dog slobber. Her schadenfreude lasted exactly three seconds before her mother shouted, "Neale, are you up?"

It took everything inside of Neale not to shout *NO* and dive back into bed. She didn't want to see those Brutuses right now. Gritting her teeth, she swallowed the feeling of betrayal as she began her slow descent toward the kitchen. Each step reminded her of her failure and triggered a flash of some bad review, cruel text, or gallery cancellation from the past fifteen hours.

The blaze was, frankly, a blessing. Even before the fire actually started, Ms. Delacroix was going down in flames.

Have you considered showing at a roller rink? That may be more your speed.

Unfortunately, the 4th Street Gallery is not in a position to stage your work at this time. Financially, the insurance is simply too high, and the likelihood of attendance so low that the show does not have an obvious benefit to the gallery.

Look, Neale, the idea was bad from the jump. People want to work with your family. They don't want to work with you.

"As I live and breathe, Neale Delacroix back in the land of the living," Bernice said, interrupting her spiral as she reached the bottom of the staircase. Neale looked at her mother, who was standing casually on one foot, like a flamingo of doom with a coffee mug in hand, the contents of which had likely gone cold hours ago.

Pulling her shoulders back, she tried to put on her best face, as if she hadn't just heard all her most beloved family members—minus Grandmama—talking about her like she was an incompetent loser. Sure, her sweatshirt had a ketchup stain on it from God knew when, but that was no reason to give them confirmation of her inability to care for herself.

"It's me, indeed," Neale said. Taking a deep breath, she tried to wince out a smile.

"Dylan, are you and Mike coming by for a drink after dinner with the Robinsons?" her mother asked innocently.

"That was the plan," Dylan said a little too brightly as she eyed Neale. Of all her family members, her sister was the most likely to have been aware of their conversation volume.

"Neale, do you think you might want to . . ." Bernice paused as if considering delicacy, then brushed it off before adding, "shower before they arrive?"

"Not really," Neale replied, giving her shoulder a sniff and tilting her chin up defiantly. She could decide when she needed a shower, despite what her parents seemed to think.

"Oh." Only Bernice could pack that much judgment into one syllable.

"All right. Well, I'm going to head over to the Robinsons'. Don't want to be late," Dylan said, giving her parents meaningful looks. Turning her pitying gaze on Neale, she added, "See you all in a few hours. Of course, Mom and Dad, you can text me if the plan needs to change."

Her sister added extra emphasis to the word *change*, as if she expected Neale to throw some kind of tantrum that Dylan and her boyfriend wouldn't want to witness.

"See you later," Neale said, sounding chipper as a bird in the morning as her sister made her way to the door. No way was she going to give her parents any reason to text Dylan anything other than *Do you know where the wine opener is?*

As soon as the door clicked, her mother said, "Why don't we all talk in the kitchen?"

Neale felt her dad look at her sideways, tension rolling off him as she followed Bernice. The fact that her father had absolutely no bounce in his step was a bad sign. Neale reassured herself that she could get through whatever was coming next. Really, if she could survive all the rust water in her majorette suit, this was nothing.

Settling onto a barstool to face her ruin, Neale watched her parents exchange a loaded glance. Bernice narrowed her eyes at her husband, who shrugged and widened his gaze for a moment, making his eyes appear to pop behind his thick glasses.

Sighing the sigh of a woman deeply put upon, Bernice ran a hand over her graying low ponytail and said, "Neale, your father and I have been talking. Before the show you had some really wonderful plans to move out and spread your wings. We both think it is time for you to pursue those dreams."

"Umm . . ." Neale had known this was coming. She should have been able to muster something better than *umm*. And yet, here she was blinking and smiling like her world wasn't coming down around her ears, lest she reaffirm her parents' belief that she was a twenty-eight-year-old baby.

Mistaking her silence for disagreement, her father collapsed onto the stool next to her and exhaled heavily, his eyes darting between the two women sitting with him. Filling up his lungs, he said, "Now, Neale, we know the Collective show was a setback. But that is no reason why you can't live your dreams. You and that young man dressed in that weird jumpsuit—"

"Darin," Bernice interrupted, narrowing her eyes at her husband.

"Yes. Darin. Why should the show stop you and Darin from starting that artists' co-op?"

Neale started. She had forgotten that she'd told her parents about their idea to turn the ramshackle house where many of the Collective members crashed into a real artistic co-op. Now that they'd brought it up, she realized there'd never been a better reason for the house to happen. She just needed a bit of time to get Darin on board. Adding a pinch of brightness to her tone for good measure, she said, "I understand, but Darin and I thought of the house as more of a future venture. You know, when the time is perfect."

"Who can control for timing? When an idea is good, it's best to capitalize on the moment." Bernice shrugged her shoulders blithely as if she couldn't solve the timing problem by not kicking her out. "You're in a rut, dear. Sometimes you need a kick in the ass to pull yourself together," her mother said in what Neale suspected she thought was a caring tone.

"It's not a rut. And I just got my ass kicked," Neale said, still trying to smile as if she were perfectly fine. "I just don't know if I'm emotionally—I mean, financially—ready," Neale amended quickly as her father's face fell. Whether or not she was emotionally ready, she would be damned if she'd admit it now. Redirecting her father's concern, she added, "How can I even afford this right now, after the costume and the papier-mâché-dog replacement? I'll have to sleep in my car . . . and that's assuming I can find a way to afford the insurance on it."

"Don't be dramatic," her mother said, rolling her eyes with a grand dismissive gesture. "It isn't like we are pushing you into the world at age twelve with nothing but our love and a five-pound bag of potatoes."

"What your mother means is that we are here to help you as you get on your feet," her father offered, narrowing his eyes at her mother. Reaching out across the table, he took Neale's hand. "Here is the thing, Neale. Everyone has to fight for their art. Maybe you need to consider a day job." Her father said the words gently, but they hit her as if he had screamed them with gale force. "Did you follow up with Vikram or Carmindy about those gallery job openings I connected you to?"

"I . . ." Neale's face went numb as she searched her memory. She remembered receiving the introduction emails last month. She also remembered deciding that she would respond to them later—a date that never actually came. It was clear that neither of her father's friends had bothered to tell on her, so her parents had no idea that she hadn't followed up.

Neale knew she should tell them. It was in her own best interest to come clean about her failure. But if she did that, it would be further confirmation that she really was as helpless and irresponsible as they thought she was.

"Baby," Bernice said, clearly mistaking her hesitation for something else. "I know you know this, but there is no shame in working to support your art. Your father and I both had day jobs when we were getting started and—"

"I was an excellent courier back in the—"

"Henry, now is not the time for that interruption." Bernice cut him off, her tone nothing like the one she was attempting to use with Neale. The exchange was so jarring that it would have been funny to Neale if her eyes didn't feel like they were going to start melting into puddles of tears at any moment. "As I was saying, sometimes you have to be practical just so you can do the things the world deems impractical."

"I know," Neale said, her voice sounding small. She knew her mother hadn't meant to insult her or suggest she give up. But a nine-to-five had always felt like quitting in a way that living at home hadn't. It wasn't that she enjoyed living with her parents or that the safety net of her childhood bedroom was so alluring. She'd just assumed that eventually she would start earning money and move out. With a day job it was so much harder to actually find time to create art. A day job was what artists got when they were ready to give up on being artists but not ready to admit it. In five years' time, she would be running around calling her career her "passion" and asking Dylan for tips on how best to wear gray, slim-cut slacks. The whole idea was dreadful.

"Every artist has had to balance what makes them money and what makes them whole," Henry said, giving her hand a squeeze. *If he's angling for a family hug after this, he's going to be sorely disappointed,* Neale thought.

"Even when you are successful, you'll make this choice," Bernice said, stopping to try to make eye contact with Neale again before adding, "I could probably keep painting *Icebreak #4* over and over and we'd be billionaires. But my heart doesn't want that. So I balance a successful piece of my business with the concepts I haven't explored."

Neale wished her mother had painted fifty thousand variations. Then she could be a trust fund baby, and they would not be having this discussion. Deciding it was time to put an end to this unbearable conversation, Neale forced a lie out of her mouth: "Don't worry. I totally get it. In fact, I reached out to them, and I think the thing with Carmindy is going to come through."

Even in her tragic state, she couldn't bring herself to give up the last shreds of her dignity. She would figure out a way. And Darin would probably float her some cash or forgive a bit of her rent until she could truly get on her feet. Once she had gotten herself together, she would tell her parents the truth about the jobs, and they could all laugh about it.

"You did?" Her mother stopped short, sounding as surprised as her father looked.

"Yes. In fact, I had just been thinking it was time for me to get a day job before Dad suggested it," Neale said, digging into her lie and forcing herself to sound as light as possible given the fact that her entire family thought she was as useless as a single sock with a hole in the heel.

"Well, that's very good news," Henry said, sounding excited. "Did Carmindy mention when she might like you to start?"

"No, that didn't come up," Neale said, holding her chin high and leaning into the farce. Henry and Bernice exchanged loaded glances, their disbelief in her follow-through etched in the lines on their foreheads. Neale couldn't let that happen, so she doubled down. "But I'll bring it up soon. And actually, Darin is really antsy to get the house up and running. He texted me about it last night, so I could probably move out as soon as the timing lines up."

Her mother's eyebrows shot toward her hairline, and Neale was momentarily delighted to think that she had surprised her parents with her capability. At least she was until her mother asked, "So when do you think the timing will line up?"

"Ah, yes. Possibly a week . . . or a week and a half. Depending on the state of the house and whether or not it needs . . ." Neale cast about for some random excuse to not move in and spotted a clump of Milo's fur stranded in a corner. "Cleaning. You know how houses can be dirty."

"Right," Henry said, nodding as if this were the most reasonable thing he had ever heard and not a description of the living conditions in his own home.

"Well, I'm glad you have a plan," Bernice said, standing up to get more coffee.

Taking her mother's departure from the table as a sign that she was dismissed, Neale stood up and beamed at her parents. "You know me. I can plan in a pinch."

"Well, good for you. Let us know once you and Darin have settled on a date next week. You can always borrow my small sculpture van. Although you may want to put something down on—"

"Thanks, Dad, but I can do it myself," Neale said, cutting her father off with a side hug before making her way out of the room. She made it all the way up the stairs before she let the smile fade from her face. Sure, she hadn't planned to do anything herself. But now that she thought about it, she was perfectly capable of proving her family wrong. And she would, just as soon as she talked to Darin.

Taking a deep breath, Neale turned toward the bathroom, deciding that she did need a shower. While she was fine with ketchup stains for her parents, she wasn't about to turn up at Darin's place in a dingy sweatshirt. Not when she was about to start her new life as the director of Seattle's new preeminent art commune with her nonlinear life partner by her side.

CHAPTER THREE

Neale pulled on the parking brake of her old Honda CR-V but didn't get out right away. The silence of her car was the perfect place to think. Since she'd had "The Talk" with her parents yesterday, she'd cried, prayed, and finally readjusted her attitude. Yes, it was hurtful that her family thought she was incompetent, but she could prove them wrong, just like she'd proved Mrs. Kirkpatrick wrong in the second grade when she'd said Neale couldn't color a map with exclusively pink and purple crayons. In fact, she had colored that map in beautifully. This was just another example of people underestimating her.

She and Darin would turn the Collective's scraggly crash house into something much greater and grander. With the two of them working side by side, they would build a place where artists of all stripes could flourish. This was going to work itself out. Her horoscope had said as much, as had that little slip of paper crammed inside a fortune cookie at Panda Express.

Taking a deep breath, she got out of the car. With her head held high, she marched toward the front door, refusing to acknowledge that several people in the house had watched her try to burn down a gallery a few days ago. It would be the perfect environment for her to get on her feet. Very *La bohème* and all that.

Neale knocked, then pushed open the door, knowing that it was unlikely anyone would actually answer. The smell of weed, sweat, and spray paint washed over her like a tidal wave, and Neale instinctively began breathing through her mouth. It was fine, though; when she and Darin took over, they would air the place out and institute an only-spray-paint-outside rule.

Hearing the sound of a bass overhead, Neale relaxed a little as she started toward the stairs. It had been hard to pin Darin down about a time for her to come by. Finally, she'd just texted him that she would come over in the afternoon and hoped that he'd gotten the message. From the sound of rumbling speakers, she was fairly certain he was awake. Plus, it was 2:35 p.m.

She reached the second-floor landing and smiled. It looked like Morrigan had redone the hallway mural, and as usual, they had outdone themself. Floating past the bright whirlpool of colors overlaid with gold designs, Neale reached Morrigan's cracked door.

"The hallway looks amazing," she called, unsure if Morrigan could hear over Darin's bass.

"Thanks! Good to hear your voice," Morrigan yelled back, not coming to the door. This was standard for Morrigan, and Neale didn't take it personally. In fact, this was one of the great things that she hoped to preserve about the house when she and Darin took over management. Everyone was always working on something, so no one really took offense to you just doing your own thing.

Making her way down the hall, Neale reached Darin's room and pounded on the door. In theory, he knew she was coming over. But in practice, Neale was never really sure how much he kept track of time.

"Who is it?" Darin called over the vibrations of the music.

"It's Neale. We were going to talk today, remember?"

Neale heard the music shut off, followed by a thudding and a scraping sound, and wondered if Darin had fallen out of a chair or something. But then he opened the door partially, offering just enough space for her to slide through.

"Hey, Neale," Darin said, holding a stack of laundry that he had clearly just yanked off a chair.

"Hey, stranger. How have you been?" Neale decided it was best to skirt around the obvious for a moment. She hadn't seen him since the show, but he had a good excuse. The Collective took up a lot of an artist's time.

"Um. Good. Do people know you're here?" he asked, peeking into the hallway before closing the bedroom door and chucking the pile of clothes in a corner.

"No. I wanted to talk to you first. Then we can say hi to all of our friends."

"Right . . . ," Darin said, the corners of his mouth turning down slightly.

Leaning herself against his desk, Neale did her best to seem casual as she said, "After leaving the Collective, I started thinking—"

"Wait. Weren't you kicked out?" Darin asked, interrupting her carefully planned speech. In their six or eightish months together, depending on how one counted, Darin had never been a stickler for details. Of course her membership in the Collective would be the one social construct he would buy into.

"I mean, in a manner of speaking." Neale waved her hand to brush the detail aside. "However, I think—"

"Because the video made it look like Dr. McMillan kicked you out." Neale went completely still, watching Darin's brown eyes scrutinize her. After a moment, he said, "You know there is a video, right?"

"What video?"

"Oh," Darin said, his lips drawn into a perfect circle as his shoulders bunched toward his ears in an uncomfortable-looking hunch. "I wouldn't have brought it up if I'd known you didn't know."

"What's in the video?" Neale hated that her voice sounded like she was afraid. She wasn't afraid. She was terrified.

"You can look it up later. We don't have to watch it right now," Darin said, rocking his shoulders back and forth before dropping himself on a corner of the bed and patting the space next to him.

Neale ignored the invitation and took out her phone. "Better to know now. What do I google?"

"*Fire fail art girl.*" Darin sucked a noisy breath through his teeth and hissed, "Or you could just google your name."

"Oof," Neale said, shaking her head as she typed. "Someone really doesn't like me."

"Might be a couple someones," Darin mumbled, then caught sight of Neale's face. "Sorry. There are some remixes out there too."

"Good to know," Neale said, as several iterations of her horrified face popped up on YouTube. Exhaling, she leaned farther back against the desk, pointedly ignoring Darin's meaningful glances at the spot next to him on the bed. Pressing the play triangle, she held her breath.

Her first thought was that if she ever saw Jenna again, she would beat her ass into the ground. Neale's second thought was that Jenna must have put tremendous energy and a considerable amount of sadistic glee into creating this video. If it weren't about one of the worst moments of her life, Neale would be impressed by the graphics, sound effects, and voice-over that accompanied her shouts, the screams of patrons, and Sarah's loud sobbing. As it was, it made her want to cry. Or be sick. Maybe both.

It was also a pitch-perfect, humorous recap of contemporary art gone wrong. No wonder so many people had watched it. Jenna had edited her work so that it looked like every awful scene from a movie with a stereotypically pretentious artist.

"How dare Jenna?" Neale blurted out as the video finished. Shutting the app before the next video could play, she added, "I'm not pretentious."

"No . . . but the piece was a little—"

"What a betrayal! And you want to work with her after she posted this?" Neale asked, consciously shouting over whatever opinion Darin was going to level about her piece. After all, his big idea had been to wear a jumpsuit, hold a tray, and see how many patrons tried to hand him their trash, like some basic commentary on American capitalism and the Black man. As if *that* one hadn't been done before. He'd just been smart enough not to use fire in his piece; otherwise, he'd be in this video and she'd be way nicer to him.

Darin looked uneasy for a moment, then said, "Well, it isn't as if the piece is about anyone in the Collective." Catching Neale's death glare, he rushed on. "Think of it more as a commentary on art . . . that just happens to feature you."

"It did feature me. And she filmed it before I left the Collective," Neale said, gesturing around the room as if this were obvious.

"Technically, you were kicked out," Darin said again.

"I know how I left," Neale snapped. Darin shrugged, and she realized that her opinion didn't matter, because as far as he was concerned, Neale and the Collective were two separate things. That stung just as much as realizing that 1.7 million people had watched her in a stupid majorette uniform slowly turn into a rust-covered mess and get fired. Sighing, Neale tucked the negative thoughts into a pocket at the back of her mind and said, "Whatever. That's not why I'm here."

Darin looked up, a gleam in his eye as he patted the bed again. "Have a seat."

Neale looked at the spot next to him but decided it was better to sit in the chair that had only recently been serving as a dirty-clothes hamper so she could see him while they discussed their future. After all, this was serious, especially if she was going to mend fences since she'd left the Collective. Flopping into the chair, she leaned back, stretching her long legs out in front of her so she could see her scuffed-up combat boots with the fraying sparkly laces. She had worn these shoes specifically because they made her happy, and if going viral for an epic fail wasn't a reason to need happiness, Neale wasn't sure what was.

Eyeing Darin, she cleared her throat and forced herself not to back away from her intended topic. "So anyway, before we got sidetracked,

I was going to talk to you about our plan to turn this house into an artists' collective of our own."

"What?" Darin asked, his mouth open a little.

"You know, our plan to reinvigorate this house and make it a place for artists to flourish. We came up with it at the boba spot a few months ago. Then we talked about it again at the Collective venue walk-through. Remember?" She paused, staring deep into Darin's eyes as if she could telegraph a meaningful moment to him with her gaze.

Darin quirked a perfectly manicured eyebrow at her. "Kind of . . ."

"It's okay; I'm sure as we talk about it, the idea will come back to you," Neale said. A yawning pit in the bottom of her stomach had started to open up, and she did her best to ignore it. Surely Darin couldn't have forgotten their plan. This wasn't like when he'd forgotten her birthday plans. They had been talking about this plan for months.

"Anyway, it's just that I've been reflecting, and I'm ready to move out of my parents' house. And now that I don't have the Collective scaffolding me, I realize how important independence is to my artistic process," she said, doing her best to channel her oldest sister. Dylan would be so proud to know that Neale retained at least a sixth of whatever consultanty, jargon-type things she said. Drawing in a deep breath to go with her smile, she finished with, "So I think it is time for us to act on our plan and start our own artists' house."

"I'm sorry. You want to move out of your parents' house?" Darin asked, drawing out the vowel in *you* as if he wasn't entirely sure where Neale was going with all of this.

"Yes. And then I would like for us to move in together and start our future," Neale said, excitement tingeing her voice as she put two and two together for him.

After a moment of intense blinking, which made Neale wonder if he was trying to send her an SOS with his eyes, he said, "Neale, that thing about the artists' house . . . that wasn't serious. I thought you knew that was just a daydream. You do know that, right?"

The sparkling hope inside of her began to whimper and melt as the confusion on Darin's face shifted into something more like distaste. "What? No . . . I mean, our plan was so detailed. Who comes up with detailed daydreams?"

"I daydream for a living, Neale," Darin said, pointing at his chest and looking befuddled.

"But we could do it," Neale said. "We work great together, and it would support our longer-term goals that—"

"No, we couldn't," Darin cut in, his tone harsher than she was used to hearing. "Neale, do you have money to buy a house? Because last I checked, you were too broke to pay for parking at the poke bar on Market. And I sure don't have the cash."

Okay, this was about money, a thing she hadn't really thought through. But that was why she and Darin worked well together. She could imagine great things, and he brought an element of realism. Luckily, they were both creative enough that they could work their way up to house ownership.

"Maybe we don't need to buy the house. We could just get started sprucing things up here. Maybe help guide people?" she said, forcing some brightness into her tone.

"And how do you suggest we do that? We just waltz downstairs and announce ourselves as king and queen of the Collective house? A Collective which you no longer belong to, remember?" Darin snorted, sounding like an indignant bull in a china shop.

Neale's gaze dropped to an abandoned shoe on the corner of the bed as she thought. This was not going as smoothly as she'd imagined. The pit in her stomach began to expand again and turned over, as if it were excited about the prospect of consuming her hopes and dreams. Darin might have a point about their de facto taking over the house, but she couldn't just give up. Not after she had told her parents that she would be moving out at the end of next week.

Maybe Darin thought this was a pipe dream, but she could make it work. All he needed to do was trust in their ability to capitalize on the energy of the moment. And he could do that. She would help him see that it was possible. Usually, Darin was a spontaneous kind of guy. It was part of why they never made plans for conventional dates. They just sort of rolled with whatever energy brought them together or pulled them apart.

Taking a steadying breath through her nose, Neale changed tactics again. "You're right. That isn't the way to do this. But maybe I could move in here with you, and over time, we could—"

"I'm sorry, what?"

"Well, if we want to make an artists' lifestyle together, I could move into this room with you, and over time we could find a way . . ." Neale's voice trailed off as Darin's face became inscrutable.

He shifted uncomfortably on the bed and put a hand on her knee, attempting to look into her eyes from an odd angle, like an actor in a B-level holiday movie about to have a heart-to-heart with his aging grandma who was secretly Mrs. Claus. "Look, Neale. I like you. I thought we were on the same page about us not being together. I just have too much going on with my art. And I'm starting a DJ business. Now really isn't the right time for me to be serious—"

Not serious. Neale's brain shut off as she let the words spin in her mind. She understood that they were above labels. After all, the term *boyfriend* for a thirty-year-old man seemed downright puerile. But that didn't mean they weren't committed to one another. Their commitment just didn't look like other people's. Hell, she would say that any person who was willing to sleep with someone who left shoes on their bed was pretty serious. Not to mention the countless hours she spent listening to him recount RPG video game achievements.

Did he think their relationship was a joke? Who joked about moving in with someone over boba? Going out to get tapioca in sweet tea while wearing pajamas was basically the most serious a relationship could get. Yet he was acting as if she were not his nonlinear life partner, or whatever other bullshit title he decided to give her.

". . . and really, I shouldn't be mixing personal and professional, so—"

"What?" Neale said, pushing his hand off her knee as her brain tuned back in. "We've been together literally the entire time we were in the Collective. We met at a Collective show before either of us were accepted into the group. And now—what, six months later?—you are worried about mixing personal and professional?"

"Aw, Neale, don't be like that."

"Be like what? Feeling a little betrayed? I should have known you were in a jerk mood when you didn't answer my texts after the show. What kind of nonlinear life partner does that?" Neale let the words slide out of her mouth, tilting her head to the side.

"Ah." Darin stopped and scrubbed a hand over his face for a moment. "Well, the thing is . . ." He paused, widening his eyes and shrugging like the gesture should mean something to Neale.

She was tempted to tell him that she had recently tried the meaningful-gaze method of communication and could 100 percent confirm that it was deeply ineffectual. Instead, she let her eyes go wide and shrugged back at him like they were in a grade school fight.

"I mean, the thing is, we were just having fun. We talked about labels. You remember?"

"Just like you remember us talking about the house?"

Darin looked around the room hopelessly, as if searching for some sort of communication lifeline, before sighing, "Neale. At the end of the day, I need to surround myself with people who are serious about their art. The house is for people showing their work. A relationship with me is for someone who is fine-tuning their talent. I deserve serious people. Talented people. And that just isn't you."

The ground shifted beneath Neale's feet, and she gripped the side of the chair to remind herself that she was sitting down. Her ears began to ring, and blood rushed to her face as soon as she watched Darin close his mouth with an uncomfortable grimace. The moments ticked by as she tried to collect her thoughts, failed, then tried again. It was one thing for Dr. McMillan to think she didn't have talent. It was another for her nonlinear life partner to think she didn't have it. He had watched her work before, during and after the Collective workshops. But here he was acting like he hadn't seen her do the work with his own two eyes.

"Neale?" Darin asked, hesitation on his face.

"Uh, yeah," Neale said, swallowing back the lump that had lodged itself in her throat.

"You understand, right? Like, it's about the integrity of the art."

Integrity of the art. Something about the phrase jogged Neale's mind back into gear. That was not something Darin would think of on his own. Neale doubted he even knew what the phrase meant. He'd probably taken it from Dr. McMillan or Jenna or Sarah or one of those other pretentious jerks. What he was actually saying was that he didn't want to be publicly associated with her. As if her failure were contagious.

Taking a deep breath, Neale attempted to force a lid on her hurt. Right now, the goal was just to get out of this smelly frat house in disguise. Screw Darin and his bullshit, borrowed vocabulary. "I understand that you're breaking up with me because you think I'm not talented enough."

Darin relaxed as if he hadn't just gutted her. Leaning back on his elbows, he smiled and said, "Technically we weren't dating, so we don't need to break up. Really, this is just expectation management. What I'm saying is that my personhood is a community, and if I bring bad energy—"

"You know, I'm good. I'm gonna go." Neale held up a hand to cut him off. She could feel the nicks that her family had put on her heart starting to crack into something more terrible, and she did not want to be in Darin's messy bedroom when it finally split in two. Ignoring the look of surprise on his face, she said, "I have somewhere else to be now."

"Oh," Darin said, sounding surprised that Neale would want to leave after he'd just tried to distance himself from her. "But did you want to . . ." He trailed off again, nodding at the spot next to him on the bed.

"Are you actually suggesting we have sex? After you broke up with me?" Neale blinked at him, debating whether he could possibly be implying what he seemed to be.

"Again, we didn't technically break up, since we weren't actually together. And you said you wanted to talk in your text." Darin seemed genuinely confused, and Neale became more convinced that he absolutely had not come up with the phrase *integrity of the art* on his own.

"I literally meant talk. Like we just did," Neale said, standing up.

"I thought it was a euphemism," Darin said, leaning off his elbows and throwing his hands in the air.

"When have I ever used a euphemism for sex? I'm very direct about that," Neale said, incredulity pushing aside her hurt for a second. She was vaguely aware that the volume of her voice was increasing, but she didn't care. Now that she wasn't focusing on feeling hurt, she had room for mad. And as it turned out, she was incredibly mad. "Even if I wasn't direct, why on God's earth would I want to sleep with the guy who just told me I wasn't talented and who doesn't want to be publicly associated with me?"

"I didn't say it like that," Darin sputtered. "Not all mean and insulting."

"Ah yes. Because tone really matters when telling your partner of six months that you think they are a joke." Neale absolutely refused to cry over this. Or at least she refused to cry while she was still in shouting distance of the house. Pulling her shoulders back, she started a semi-dignified march to the door.

"Neale, are you seriously mad?" Darin asked from behind her.

Leveling her very best Bernice glare at him from over her shoulder, she watched as Darin sank back onto the bed and closed his mouth.

Satisfied that she'd had the last word, Neale hustled down the hallway and stairs before blowing through the living room and wrenching the door open. She let the gray late-March mist wash over her as she fumbled to find her car key in her numerous pants pockets. This had to be why people hated cargo pants. *How does anyone remember where the important things are when they need to make a quick exit?* Neale thought before finally locating her keys down by her left calf.

Turning the key in the lock and wiping away a tear, Neale got in the car, mumbling, "Panda Express is a liar. So much for *La Bohème* . . . unless I'm Mimi. But then Darin would come back as I lay dying like a tubercular waif, and I don't want—ah!"

Neale squealed, clutching a hand to her chest as a pounding on her car window pulled her attention. Morrigan stood on the other side of the car door, looking equally surprised, their shoulder-length, puffy red hair sticking out at odd angles under an Ampelmännchen ball cap.

"Sorry, Neale," they said as soon as Neale calmed down enough to start the car and roll down her window.

"It's okay," Neale sniffed, trying to appear as if she hadn't been on the verge of sobbing her eyes out.

"I didn't mean to chase you, but you flew out of the house so fast. Like, were you on the track team in high school? Because that was incredible." Morrigan shook their head at the digression. "Anyway, I heard you and Darin talking about you needing to find a place," Morrigan said, looking momentarily guilty before adding, "Sorry, thin walls. Anyway, screw that guy. He's the worst. Also, fuck the establishment art haters. You were onto something."

"Okay. Thank you?" Neale said, her voice sounding watery. She wasn't sure where Morrigan was going with all of this, but she was grateful for the encouragement, even if it could have been better timed.

"You're welcome," Morrigan said in their usual direct but dreamy manner. After a moment, they shook their head and said, "But that's not why I'm out here. It sounds like you need a place, and I have a friend who is looking for a roommate. If you're interested, I can give you Corinne's email address."

"You would?" Neale asked, still trying to shake off the malaise of Darin breaking off their not-relationship.

"Of course. You need a place, and I like you. Corinne needs a roommate, and I like her. I think the two of you would get along," Morrigan said, as if this were the single most obvious statement in the world, then laughed and added, "Plus, I really hate to see Darin succeed in thwarting your plans. I never understood why you dated that guy."

"I guess I don't know why either," Neale said. Her giggle sounded wobbly, but she was glad that there was someone in the world who thought she was good enough for Darin, art, and housing. Taking out her phone, Neale carefully navigated the plastic bag she had placed over her cracked screen—an unfortunate accident from a misguided game of catch with her mother—and said, "What's her email address?"

"It's Unicorn.CorinneP@SeattlePets.com. And that's Corinne with one r and two n's," Morrigan said, adding the spelling.

"Was just plain CorinneP already taken?" Neale asked, typing the address into her phone.

"Nah. Corinne is just passionate about animals. Anyway, let me know how it works out, yeah?"

"I will. Thanks, Morrigan."

"Don't worry about it. And keep your head up," Morrigan said, tapping the hood of the car twice before walking back toward the house.

Neale rolled up her window, then sat in the car for a moment longer. Not three minutes ago, she'd been contemplating sleeping with the troll under the bridge in Fremont rather than admitting to her family that her art house dream, and apparently her not-boyfriend partner, were a farce. Now she had a lead on a place, just like her horoscope and the Panda Express fortune cookie had promised.

Taking a deep breath, Neale wiped the remaining moisture from her eyes and whispered, "Guess I'm not Mimi after all."

CHAPTER FOUR

Neale stood outside an unimpressive apartment building in the Central District and exhaled. She wasn't sure why she was nervous. When they'd exchanged emails, Corinne had seemed normal enough, but now that Neale might be standing outside her potential new apartment, she wasn't so sure of her path.

It occurred to her that she didn't know Morrigan all that well, and the promise of cheap rent might not have been the only factor she should have taken into consideration. What if this woman turned out to be a monster? Or one of those weirdos who went through your drawers when you weren't home? Neale wished she hadn't told her parents she'd move out so fast. If she hadn't picked such a ridiculous deadline, she'd have more than four days to find a roommate who wasn't a cult leader. Maybe it would be better for her to just endure admitting defeat to her parents until she could find a job and afford her own place.

"Neale. I don't get it. Why aren't you moving to the artist house?" Dylan asked, squinting up at the building. Her face was as enthusiastic about the place as Neale felt. Which was to say, not excited at all. A small part of Neale wished she hadn't asked her sister to come with her, but she'd seen enough scary movies to know that visiting a stranger's house without a friend was a surefire way to be murdered.

"I just don't think it's right for me." Neale shrugged her hands into the pockets of her overalls, hoping the answer would be enough for her older sister to drop the subject.

"What do you mean? You talked about you and your undercommitted life partner and the art house idea nonstop for like a month," Dylan said, narrowing her eyes at her.

"Nonlinear life partner," Neale corrected. For a moment, she considered leaving out the rest of the story. As much as it hurt to talk about Darin, she also knew that her sister was not going to let something like this go. Exhaling the rest of her words quickly so she wouldn't lose her nerve, Neale said, "And we broke up."

"*Quelle surprise*," Dylan said, her tone flat as she tried not to laugh. "How could you have seen that coming from a nonlinear life partner?"

"Don't be a jerk, Dylan. I wasn't mean when you and Nicolas broke up." Neale turned her gaze toward a scraggly tree in someone's front yard down the block. "He called me unserious and talentless."

"Oh, he is trash. I'm so sorry, Neale," Dylan said, reaching a hand out and pulling her into a squeeze. Part of Neale wanted to headbutt her sister for saying something mean, but another part of her was enjoying the comfort that came from a hug and someone else's righteous indignation. "It wasn't my intention to rub salt in the wound. Fuck that guy. He's the talentless one. What does he know?"

A small piece of Neale wanted to point out that he seemed to know exactly what Dylan and her parents knew. In fact, since yesterday's breakup, she had been turning his words over in her mind, and they really weren't all that different from her family's. They all boiled down to the idea that she had no talent and no way of surviving on her own.

Feeling a lump rise in her throat, Neale decided that she wasn't ready to pick a fight with her sister right before she saw her new apartment, so instead she let it slide, saying, "It's okay. I know you love me," which, for the record, she thought was true.

"So you are aware that you have a pattern of dating these kinds of guys?" Dylan said, releasing Neale to arm's length.

"Technically we weren't dating," Neale said as Dylan rubbed her arm like she was still a little kid.

"You can call it whatever you want, but you changed his sheets, drove him to get haircuts, and remembered his pizza order. That is what girlfriends do."

"Maybe . . . ," Neale said noncommittally.

"All of your relationships seem to go south at about the same time. It's like clockwork. Sixish months in, you break up; then you mope for two months and meet someone new but equally bad," Dylan said, her voice officially shifting into lecture mode.

Neale pulled away, wishing she had opted to headbutt Dylan. "Okay, I don't need a laundry list of every failed relationship."

"It's not a laundry list. I figured it was just better to get it all out on the table before you go and find someone new."

"I can make my own decisions about who to date," Neale said, bristling as her sister tilted her head in skepticism. "In fact, I'm giving men up. They just screw up my life."

Her sister cocked her head to one side and pursed her lips, as if studying Neale's sincerity. After a moment she said, "Giving up men altogether feels a tad draconian to me."

"Well, you aren't giving up men. I am," Neale said, pulling herself up to her full height and looking her sister directly in the eye. "Don't smirk at me. I'm serious about this. Darin was the last straw. After I sign this lease, I'm going to be a New Neale. No more bad boyfriends. No more failed art projects. No more living with Mom and Dad. And no more stealing your expensive snacks when I'm broke."

"What do my organic granola fruit bars have to do with this?" Dylan's face scrunched with surprise.

"I'm going to be so reliable that I won't need your snacks anymore," Neale said, putting her hands back in the pockets of her overalls.

"That doesn't make—" Dylan cut herself off. Shaking her head, she crossed her arms and said, "Actually, that doesn't matter. I feel like this is extreme. But frankly, if becoming New Neale means paying your own bills and no more loser boyfriends, then I'm all for it."

"The only thing that is extreme is how *extremely* good this decision is." Neale smiled and was tempted to hug her sister again despite Dylan snorting at her pun. Instead, she settled for, "You're skeptical now, but you'll see. New Neale is a badass."

Dylan drummed her perfect pale-pink manicure on her arms for a second as if debating saying something more, then let it go. Dropping her arms, she rotated to face the building and said, "Are you ready to do this now?"

Glancing up at the ancient building across the street, Neale bit down on her lip and said, "I guess so."

"All right, then let's go. I've got to catch a Lyft back to the office after this, so we should hurry," Dylan said, already walking toward the front of the building. "It's number 205, right?"

"Uh, yeah," Neale said. As they reached the reinforced glass door, she watched as Dylan squinted at the buzzer box and began tapping out the apartment number. Instinctively, Neale stepped back a foot, feeling nervous about whoever would be on the other side.

"Hello?" crackled a man's voice through the aged speaker box.

Neale's eyes were wide. She was absolutely not expecting a man. Maybe Corinne had a boyfriend? Apprehension rolled off Neale, and she crept toward her sister, who looked between Neale and the box like something slimy might pop out.

"Hello?" the voice came again, and Dylan glared at Neale, gesturing for her to speak to the box.

"Hello?" Neale called, staying a yard away from the box as if someone could reach through it and shake her. Dylan grabbed her and dragged her back toward the box. Clearing her throat, she tried again. "Hello. I'm looking for Corinne."

"Wrong apartment," the man groused before the box clicked.

"Neale." Dylan's voice cracked with exasperation. "Are you sure that is the right number?"

"No!" Neale shouted, not even bothering to try to lie.

"Well, can you check? And why are you acting scared? You're making me nervous."

"I don't know. Horror movies about roommates made me scared," Neale said, pulling out her phone and carefully tapping at the broken screen.

"Wait, you are acting scared because of movies?" Dylan said, looking irritated, then added, "Not because you are in any way, shape, or form actually seeing, hearing, smelling, or even Spidey-sensing anything to be afraid of?"

Neale shrugged, offering her sister a half smile.

"Oh my God." Dylan rolled her eyes and tossed her hair over her shoulders.

"Sorry," Neale said, trying to look contrite as she held up her phone. "It's apartment 305."

Dylan squinted at the phone to verify, then stepped away from the box, saying, "You dial this time."

"Fine." Taking a deep breath, Neale pressed in *#305* and waited, praying not to get another cranky, crackling man voice this time.

"Hello."

Neale grinned at the box. This could be Corinne. Realizing the box couldn't see her smile, she said, "Hi, this is Neale Delacroix. I'm here to see Corinne Park."

"Hi, Neale. Hang tight. I'll buzz you in."

Two seconds later, Neale heard the door click and watched as Dylan's arm shot out to grab it. Stepping into the brightly lit entryway, Neale took a moment to gaze up at a very 1970s light fixture. Sure, the building was dated, but it was clean and not nearly as drab looking as the outside suggested.

"Elevator is this way," Dylan said, pointing to the left. Walking past a short corridor of mailboxes, the pair crammed into a small blush-pink elevator.

Using her elbow to push the third-floor button, Neale said, "So far, not murdery."

"Says you," Dylan said under her breath.

Exiting the elevator, the two sisters walked down the hall, the industrial-grade carpeting muffling the sound of Dylan's three-inch sling-back heels as they went. Finding the burnt-orange door marked 305, they stopped. After a quick exchange of glances with her sister, Neale took a fortifying deep breath and knocked.

The sound of someone tripping over something behind the door floated toward them, followed by a yelp and someone shouting, "Just a moment."

Dylan had just enough time to make a slightly concerned face and position herself a few inches in front of Neale when the door ripped open, revealing a full-figured woman who would have been about six inches shorter than either of the Delacroix sisters if not for her tall and impressively messy topknot.

"Hi, I'm Corinne. Which one of you is Neale?" The woman fairly vibrated off the floor, extending a hand toward the two of them.

"I am." Neale reached around Dylan's protective stance to shake her hand. "Nice to meet you. This is my sister Dylan."

"Nice to meet you both. Come on in." Corinne turned around, leaving the front door open for them to follow, then stopped abruptly. Gesturing to her right, she said, "Sorry, I forgot. Korean household—shoe rack is right there."

Grateful she never bothered to lace up her boots, Neale toed off her shoes and popped them in the rack by the door, trying not to feel impatient as Dylan carefully removed one shoe, then the next. As soon as her sister straightened up, Neale hurried to catch up with their energetic tour guide. "First stop on our fabulous tour, the living room."

While Dylan closed the door, Neale looked around for potential threats. In the common area, she supposed most people would have had a couch and maybe a TV. Instead, Corinne had doubled down on the 1970s vibe, throwing large cushions, low tables, and big shaggy rugs all over the floor. Everywhere she looked there was some hint of avocado, burnt orange, or dark brown. Apart from a very mod-looking dining set, a tall stack of cushions, and a large bookcase that held a bizarre and impressive collection of unicorn figurines, there was no real furniture.

Mistaking Neale's silence for misunderstanding, Corinne looked up at her and said, "It's a 1970s theme."

"I like it." Neale shrugged, feeling her shoulders relax a little as it became clear that she was not in immediate danger of being kidnapped.

"Can we see the kitchen?" Dylan asked, her tone less bright than Neale's as she gave the living room a cursory glance.

"Of course." Corinne turned to a doorway hung with beads and said, "It's also seventies themed."

Neale grinned. This was clearly a sign. She had only recently fallen down the rabbit hole of classic TV reruns and was now firmly obsessed with the *Mary Tyler Moore Show* spin-off, *Rhoda*. And just like the eponymous Rhoda's home, her new apartment had beads in a door-way. Neale was sold.

At her side, Neale could feel Dylan tensing at the sight of nowhere to sit and ultrakitsch decor. The three of them walked into the kitchen to find modern, albeit dated, appliances, including a fridge covered in drawings of different unicorns.

"You sure have a lot of unicorns hanging around here," Neale said lightly. Deep down, she was dying to know why Corinne had covered every free inch of an otherwise gloriously themed apartment in unicorn pictures.

Corinne stopped in front of the oven, her face deadly serious. "Unicorns are conduits for the soul. Their many lives represent human-ity's second chance."

41

"Right." Neale nodded. She wasn't entirely sure how many lives a unicorn had or how they provided a second chance for humanity, but Corinne seemed to have done the math on the premise, and it made sense to her, so Neale let it go. As a firm believer in aliens, who was she to poke holes in someone else's belief system?

From over by the microwave, she could feel Dylan buzzing with some kind of follow-up question that Neale was fairly certain Corinne would entertain with as much enthusiasm as a child receiving a toothbrush for Christmas. So instead, she asked, "You are a vet tech, right?"

Corinne relaxed. "I am. I wish the building allowed pets, but we just aren't that lucky." With that, she turned out of the kitchen, leaving Neale and Dylan to follow. Her sister threw Neale a meaningful look, then tilted her head toward the fridge of unicorns, eyes wide with alarm. Neale shrugged. As long as this woman didn't require Neale to dress as a unicorn and the bathroom wasn't disgusting, she could make this place work.

Walking down a long hallway, Corinne pointed to a door on the right. "So this would be your bedroom and bathroom. Mine is just down there."

Both rooms were shockingly plain after the visual feast that was the 1970s reincarnated. Neale's walls were white, and the carpet was a basic beige. But the room was big enough and had lots of light coming through a quirky, extra-long rectangular window.

"This is nice, isn't it, Dyl?" Neale said.

"Yes. Very . . ." Dylan looked around the bedroom and frowned at the carpet before settling on, "Airy."

Neale shook her head. Her sister had no poker face. Stepping out of the bedroom, Neale examined the bathroom for a moment. It was equally sparse. There was a small bathtub-shower combo that had clearly been put in some time in the nineties and was slightly off color when compared to the rest of the amenities. The counters were also lower than her five-foot-ten frame would have liked, but that was to be expected.

"So I know we talked a little bit over email, but I just wanted to get a sense of who you are as a person and how you like to run a house," Neale said, recalling one of the questions Dylan had tried to drill into her head on the drive over.

"Well, I'm not a big partier, anymore." Corinne added the "anymore" as an afterthought, half smiling as she continued. "These days, I'm pretty self-contained. I like to have my book club over once a month. My family is local, so my sister is around sometimes. But it seems like yours is too." Corinne gestured to Dylan and grinned. "Maybe we could have a sister dinner?"

"That would be fun," Neale said, bouncing on her toes. So far, no red flags. Of course, Dylan was tutting behind her. Neale ignored that. She probably just wanted to hurry up and leave so she could get back to the office.

"Then that is settled. What else?" Corinne asked, tapping her chin with her index finger. "In terms of chores. I'm probably messier than my mom would like, but I have a housekeeper who comes every two weeks, so we would be splitting the cost on that."

"I can live with that," Neale said, thinking of her own childhood home and the dust that had lived on the floorboards since Dylan had gotten her own place. Best not to mention that bit when trying to convince someone to let you live with them. "What about—"

Neale was interrupted by a cough from nowhere, startling both her and, by the looks of it, Dylan, who was scanning the room with hawk eyes. Squinting toward a corner of the living room, Neale practically jumped through the roof as what she'd mistaken for a pile of pillows moved. Grabbing her sister, Neale looked between the woman-pillow, Corinne, and Dylan, who, to her credit, was already crouched in a fighting stance they had learned in their week-and-a-half-long stint in judo class during elementary school.

"What is going on?" Dylan had technically phrased this as a question, but to Neale's ears, it was a demand.

"You didn't see me when you came in?" the woman-pillow asked with the exact same level of demand as Dylan.

"No. Why didn't you introduce yourself?" Neale asked, emboldened by standing behind Dylan's solid frame.

"Sorry! That is my sister," Corinne said, her hands held up in a cease-fire gesture.

"Does she always lurk like that?" Dylan said, remaining in her crouch.

"Who says I'm lurking?" the woman-pillow shot back.

"Chloe is just here to keep me company for my potential-roommate visit," Corinne said, eyeing her sister with a shut-up death stare that Neale was all too familiar with.

"Wait. Did you invite your sister here in case I was a serial killer?" Neale asked, desperately trying to keep the humor out of her voice.

"I mean, I wasn't thinking of a serial killer, more like . . ." Corinne looked at the ground for a moment, then back at Neale, and said with a shrug, "A cannibal?"

"I brought Dylan in because I was worried you might be an ax murderer," Neale said, stepping out from behind her sister, unable to hide her amusement. In between giggles, Neale watched as Corinne went from nervousness to peals of laughter.

"Still doesn't explain why Chloe didn't announce herself," Dylan grumbled over the sounds of their laughter.

Neale ignored her sister and the unhappy harrumphs of Chloe, instead focusing on what must be the preordained, perfect alignment of the moment. Sure, Corinne was a weirdo with an inexplicable unicorn obsession, but the rent was cheap, and Neale could not think of a better roommate than one who also used her sister as a potential ax-murderer shield. Silently sending a big thank-you to Morrigan and even a little drop of gratitude to Darin for this serendipitous meeting, Neale let her laughter die down.

Refocusing her attention on Corinne, Neale was about to resume her line of questioning when Corinne started speaking. "So what do you say? You want to move in?"

"I do." Neale grinned, despite Dylan elbowing her side.

"Yay! This is going to be great." Corinne clapped, bouncing on her toes. "So I guess I can send you all of the sublease details, and you can let me know when you want to move in?"

"Works for me." Neale shrugged.

"Cool," Corinne said, walking them both to the door. She waited as the pair of them slipped into their shoes, then said, "Talk to you soon, roomie."

"Talk soon." Neale waved as Dylan practically pushed her out the door and toward the blush-colored elevator.

As soon as she heard the door click, Dylan hissed, "You cannot move in there!"

"Don't be absurd." Neale sighed heavily.

"Absurd? That Chloe is terrifying. What kind of stealth pillow-ninja nonsense was that?" Dylan said, gently shoving Neale into the elevator.

"Well, Chloe doesn't live there, and I think the apartment is great," Neale mumbled, jabbing the first-floor button.

"Neale. It's ancient. I didn't see a dishwasher, and there is nowhere to sit."

Her sister would think that anything that didn't gleam and smell like new industrial construction was subpar. Biting back the urge to shout, she sighed. "We can wash dishes by hand. Really, I couldn't find a single flaw."

"Well, I can think of a few more if you need them," Dylan said, sounding irritated that her little sister wasn't giving in. "Neale, what are you doing? Surely the gallery will be paying you enough to find something better than—"

"There is no gallery job," Neale blurted.

"What?" Dylan's question had the exact same grinding tone as a spoon left in a garbage disposal.

"You heard me. There is no gallery job," Neale said, slipping out of the elevator. She began hustling through the lobby toward her car. If she had any luck at all, she should be able to out–speed walk her sister.

Of course, Neale had forgotten that her sister was basically a champion high-heel sprinter until Dylan matched her stride and said, "What do you mean? Dad said you were going to work with Carmindy."

"I lied. I never actually emailed Carmindy after Dad connected us, and by the time I got back to her, the spot was gone."

Out of the corner of her eye, Neale watched as Dylan's jaw dropped. "Neale. Have you lost your mind? How do you think you are going to pay for an apartment? Monopoly money? Beanie Baby sales? Magic?"

"I have money," Neale said, slowing down just enough to glare at her sister. Dylan's laugh was derisive, and Neale almost stopped to strangle her. "I do. I still have Grandmama's emergency money."

"You expect me to believe that you, who regularly scrounges in the couch for change, really hasn't spent Grandmama's emergency-fund money that she gave you like ten years ago?" Dylan asked, sounding like the claim was dubious at best and an outright lie at worst.

"Yes. Mostly because I can't remember the security PIN to the savings account she put it in, and the bank needed my Social Security card, and at the time, Mom had no idea where Dad put the card," Neale said. Watching as her explanation did little to satisfy Dylan, she changed tactics swiftly and added, "But also because I didn't need the money and I was saving it for a rainy day . . . because I can plan ahead."

"This is hardly planning ahead," Dylan said, eyes wide.

"Dylan, back off. I'm not nearly as incompetent as you think." Neale stopped in front of her car and rounded on her sister.

Dylan held her hands up, blinking in surprise. "I never said you were incompetent. I just think—"

"I heard you and Mom and Dad talking. I know you don't think I'm capable of surviving on my own." Neale cut her sister off. A small corner of her mind enjoyed watching her sister's superior expression falter as the color drained from her face. "Seriously, I'm trying here. Can that be enough for you? Just for today at least?"

"Neale, I'm sorry about that. Honestly, but really, this plan doesn't make sense. That money won't—"

"Are you going to let me sleep on your couch?" she said, fishing around in her pockets for her car key as Dylan blanched, opening her mouth and then closing it. Neale's heart dropped an inch. Logically, she'd known her sister was not about to let her move in. But somehow, the visual confirmation that she was a burden to her loved ones made it worse. Swallowing her pride, she said, "That's what I thought. The truth is, Corinne seems nice; Morrigan says she is a good person. Yes, the place is old or whatever, but I can afford it."

"But, Neale—"

"First you want me to move out; then you pick apart how I do it. You can't have it both ways, Dylan. So what's it going to be?" Neale asked, locating her key in her front chest pocket as her sister stared at her, speechless. Heat flooded her face as both she and her sister waded through different forms of humiliation. Dylan for being judgmental, and her for being unwanted. Turning her back to Dylan, she unlocked the car and said, "That's what I thought. Now, if you will excuse me, you should call your Lyft, because I need to pack."

CHAPTER FIVE

Neale glared at her closet and wondered how she had this much stuff to pack. Chucking a pair of spray-painted sneakers into the box, she tried not to focus on the strange grief she felt. She wasn't going anywhere far away, but in an odd way, it felt like she was packing up her childhood and her dreams all in one fell swoop. If she hadn't had roughly twelve hours left before her parents threatened to charge an extortionary rent, she could easily have spent six months sobbing over her dead dreams, broken heart, and childhood toys. As it was, most of her stuff was going in a box with a bit of heartache and only a few second glances.

Neale had just picked up a sweater that had more holes than she wanted in a sweater when her phone buzzed. Glancing over, she saw a message from Billie roll across her phone screen. Avoiding the shattered pieces of plastic, Neale unlocked her phone and read the message.

Sister mine! Dylan says you are moving out?

Looking at her stack of unpacked boxes, Neale decided she could take a small break to text her sister. Smiling at the phone like it was a puppy, she typed,

Sister! I miss you. How are you?

And, yes! I've got a great place in the CD. Very 70s mod. You'll love it.

PS Since when do you and Dylan talk?

She set the phone down and shrugged. Billie could be slow to respond, so it was a better use of her time to continue packing. Neale had just decided to toss out the sweater when her phone interrupted her again. Reaching over with lightning speed, she read Billie's reply.

Since Dylan insisted we set up a weekly call. LOL!

Neale frowned at the phone, reached for a fuzzy pink sweater, and tried to shrug off feeling bad about not being in the Billie-Dylan loop. After all, Billie's time was limited since her show had been hailed as a "dark and twisted commentary on society" by every underground art critic who'd managed to get a seat in the little off-off-off-Broadway theater in New York. She could see where the life of a "creative mastermind" might be just busy enough to match Dylan's whirlwind high-achieving energy. Really, the more she thought about it, the two of them were just different sides of the same badass successful coin. A currency, Neale felt with a pang of sadness, she was deeply unfamiliar with. Searching for a lightheartedness she didn't quite feel, Neale typed back,

Weekly call. That is the most Dylan thing ever.

I know. I laugh, too, but it's cool. Otherwise, we get busy.

Before Neale could respond to the first set of messages, the next wave came rushing in as if Billie was trying to do all her catching up in one two-minute burst.

The new place sounds awesome.

Gotta go. I need to figure out how to get out of this LA show before Marceline murders me . . . aka stops giving me money.

Talk soon. Love you!

Neale frowned down at the screen and wondered why Billie was trying to get out of her LA show. And why her art dealer would want to murder her for it. Granted, Marceline wasn't exactly typical for the art world. As far as Neale knew, her parents' art dealers had never bankrolled a massive multimedia show, but still . . . how much money was Billie walking away from? And why was she doing it?

She wished she could ask Billie, but she seemed to have so little free time these days. Of course, Dylan probably knew, but there was no way she was going to ask her right now. Maybe once she found a job and could gloat fully, she'd ask her about it, but—

A soft knock on the door pulled Neale's attention away from her success fantasies. She paused, her pulse beating hard, unsure of what to do. Her general procedure with the front door was just to scream, "Come in!" at whoever was on the other side. But this was her bedroom door, so that seemed like a questionable policy. Moreover, she knew it couldn't be her parents, because they'd never met a closed door they respected in their nearly forty-year marriage.

"Who is it?" Neale asked, clutching her phone and wishing she had Milo to protect her.

"It's Dylan. Can I come in?" Her sister's voice floated gently from the other side of the door, the sound of it acting like a swift kick to her subconscious. Stewing on her sister must have caused Neale to manifest her unwelcome presence. The problem was, she had no idea how to unmanifest her. Accurately interpreting her silence as reluctance, Dylan called, "If it influences your decision, I'm here to apologize by way of helping you pack."

Looking around the room, Neale conceded that she did need a fair amount of help. She made sure to sound grouchy about it for good measure. "Come in."

"Hi, Neale," Dylan said, as she cracked the door open and tentatively inched her way through. "I brought you Cruise coffee."

"Thanks," Neale said, crushing any note of gratitude in her voice as her sister walked through the door and handed her the warm beverage.

"I'm sorry I was mean to you yesterday. I shouldn't have made fun of your boyfriends or tried to tell you where to live or freaked out about you not having a job," Dylan said, moving a pile of jeans with the toe of her ballet flat before sitting down across from her.

For a brief moment, Neale considered holding on to her grudge a little longer, but one sip of coffee changed her mind. Dylan might be judgy and bossy, but she also had excellent taste in coffee and a willingness to drop eight dollars on a pour-over by way of an apology. "It's okay. I forgive you."

"I don't like fighting with you." Dylan sighed, reaching for a box, despite the fact that Neale had already stuffed it to the brim. "I understand your plan and why you feel like you have to do it this way."

"Thank you," Neale said, tilting her chin up and dropping a mostly folded sweater into the little space Dylan had managed to create with her rearranging.

After a moment's hesitation, her sister said, "I'm wondering . . . Grandmama's emergency money won't last more than a few months—which I'm sure you know," Dylan added hastily, after reading the look of annoyance Neale shot her. "Anyway, what do you plan to do for a job? Try and put up another show?"

"No." Neale sighed and shook her head hard enough that her freshly styled puffs wobbled. "I meant what I said—I'm done with art now."

"Okay. So what will you do?" Dylan asked gently.

Neale paused for a moment. Admittedly, she hadn't thought that far into the future. All the day jobs she'd had in the past had either fallen into her lap or come to her via some half-hearted stint working with a temp agency. As she eyed her sister, her brain snapped a few puzzle pieces together. Putting on her most winning little-sister smile, she said, "You know what a great way to apologize to me would be?"

"The coffee I already gave you?"

"In a manner of speaking, yes," Neale said, making puppy dog eyes. "Couldn't you just get me a job with you? Maybe running coffee at Technocore or something?"

Dylan paused mid–sweater refolding and arched an eyebrow at her as if waiting on Neale to tell the punch line to a questionable joke. When nothing happened, she said, "Could I get you a job? Possibly. Would I? Hell no."

"What? Dylan, come on. People use their connections to get friends jobs all the time."

"Neale, this is about you standing on your own two feet. Me getting you a job is the opposite of that," Dylan said, sounding indignant.

"So much for sisterly support."

"I will support you. I just won't do the work for you," Dylan snapped back, so fast that it stunned Neale. Dylan must have sensed her hurt, because she softened as she added, "Despite what Mom and Dad may fear, I know you are capable of doing this. If you're really serious about being on your own, I will help you get a résumé together and practice for interviews. You can even borrow my clothes."

When Neale didn't immediately respond, Dylan began wiggling her eyebrows and nudging Neale with her elbow playfully. Finally, Neale gave up on guilting her sister and sighed. "Well, it was worth a try. And for the record, I was going to take your clothes anyway, so that isn't much of an offer."

"How about this: I'll make you a deal," Dylan said, smiling at Neale.

"If it involves selling my soul to Satan, you should know that is off the table," Neale said, reaching for a pile of mismatched socks.

"No devil . . . unless it's Prada." Dylan snort-laughed at her own joke before pulling it together. "If, and I mean only if, you are actively looking for jobs, my closet is your closet. But no safety pins in the designer stuff. Got it?"

"Really?" Neale's chest expanded.

"Yes, really," Dylan said, half smiling at her. "I mean it, though, Neale, like applying for three jobs a week. No goofing off."

"Thank you, sister." The warm feeling in Neale's chest spread, and she launched a sneak hug at Dylan, nearly knocking the two of them sideways.

"I love you, Neale, and I want you to succeed," Dylan said, batting some of Neale's hair away from her face as she returned the hug. "So do we have a deal?"

"Of course."

"Good, because when you check your email, you'll see I've sent you several job postings, as well as a few articles on interviewing best practices. Let me know when you have read them, and we can discuss. Sound good?" Dylan said, picking up a green woolly cap and folding it with expert precision.

Neale turned her attention to a pile of books to hide her smile. For today, Neale was okay with Dylan making the plan. Come tomorrow, New Neale was taking over.

~

"See, Neale? That wasn't that bad. Our workout took less time than the dentist!" Dylan said, completely ignoring the fact that Neale was basically half-dead in the seat next to her.

Taking her time, Neale turned her neck to stare at Dylan, just in case moving fast tweaked an already exhausted muscle. "If you are smothered by a pillow in your sleep, I want you to know it was me."

Dylan's eyes darted away from the road briefly to look at Neale before she began cackling. "You won't be able to smother me. You're too sore to move that fast. You can't even turn your head."

"That's why I'll murder you in your sleep. I won't have to catch you."

"Don't worry. You'll survive."

"What part of *drink coffee and talk about my job search* sounded like *torture Neale through fitness?*" Neale asked under her breath.

"I did say wear workout gear." Dylan shrugged, her hands still on the wheel, then added, "Besides, you are getting coffee as soon as we get home and make it."

"I thought we were going for a walk *with* coffee . . . ," Neale grumbled.

"Any word on any of the jobs we applied to?" Dylan asked, ignoring her entirely.

"No." Neale huffed as much from the exhaustion as from the stress.

"Okay, no need to sulk," Dylan said in her characteristically upbeat manner. "I just thought you did a really good job on that application for the front desk position at Starstrike Press."

"Sorry," Neale mumbled. She knew Dylan was trying to help, but she also didn't feel like she needed a reminder that she remained undesirable in both the art world and the working-stiff world. It just stung, because she really had tried on some of those applications, and she hadn't heard a peep from any of them. Not even the dog-food place with the weird social media accounts featuring snakes.

"It's okay. I know looking for jobs is stressful. And really, three weeks would be incredibly fast. It takes most people months, so don't let this get you down. We'll get there."

Neale couldn't decide if she wanted to punch Dylan in her overly optimistic face or if she was comforted by the thought, so she went for,

"Thanks. I'll check my email again when we get to your place. Best to do disappointment with coffee."

"That's the spirit," Dylan said, turning into her building's upscale parking lot. Neale watched as her sister shut off her car and bounded toward the ultramodern elevator as if they hadn't just endured thirty-five minutes of Pilates-themed agony.

"I'll hold the elevator for you," Dylan called, shaking Neale out of her thoughts with a not-so-subtle reminder to stop lollygagging.

Neale took a deep breath and got out of the car, speed shuffling toward the elevator as fast as her already aching muscles would allow. "You can hop in the shower. I'll make our coffee and check my email."

"Sounds like a fantastic plan," Dylan said, letting go of the door and sending them rocketing upward at about three times the speed of Neale's building's rickety elevator.

Following her sister out of the elevator and down the brightly lit new-construction hallway, Neale felt her mood lift. Once she left Dylan's place, got home and showered, napped, and ate a reasonable number of cookies, New Neale would kick in for good. Today was the day she was going to get it together, with or without a job. As Dylan unlocked the door to her apartment, Neale continued her line of positive thinking all the way to the kitchen, making plans to do her laundry.

While her sister's fancy coffee machine sputtered, she flopped down on Dylan's designer couch with her phone in hand. Smiling as she looked for her email icon, Neale decided that this moment was her cocoon moment. She was on the precipice of hatching into some astonishing butterfly; she just had to be patient and enjoy the ride while—

"Oh my God," Neale said to no one as she looked down at her email. There in black and white was an email from Happy Hearts, with the subject line *Scheduling an Interview*. Neale's heart skipped a beat as she tried to remember which company Happy Hearts even was. Not that it mattered. After weeks of crickets, someone wanted to meet Neale and potentially give her a job.

"What is it?" Dylan opened the door, a billow of steam following her out of the bathroom. Trotting toward her in a towel, she said, "I heard you shout. Everything okay?"

"I'm fine," Neale said, still grinning. "I got an interview."

"Woo-hoo! Way to go, Neale. I'm so proud of you!" Dylan bounced over to Neale's side of the couch and launched a bear hug at her sister.

"Thanks," Neale said, overlooking the fact that Dylan was still dripping wet and in her shower cap. "Do you remember Happy Hearts?"

"Was that the greeting card place?" Dylan said, releasing her.

"Oh," Neale said. What she really thought was *please no*. That job sounded so deeply boring that she had considered not applying at all. If Dylan hadn't been hovering over her shoulder saying silly things like, "You love poetry!" and "This ties nicely with art!" she would have just closed the browser and walked away.

"I had a good feeling about that one. Didn't I tell you?" Dylan said, still bubbling with pride.

Neale looked back at the email from someone named Rich and began a prayer to whatever god was floating overhead that Dylan's otherwise excellent memory was wrong and this wasn't the card place. When she clicked on the link in Rich's signature, a familiar and deeply sad website from roughly 2001 began its creaky attempt at loading on her phone. Oof. This was the singing greeting card licensing firm. Workplace dread filled Neale, even as she tried to puff up her chest and act excited for Dylan's sake.

Dylan leaned in to look at Neale's phone, then smiled up at her sister. "Once you have the job, I'm sure you can suggest a website upgrade." When Neale didn't smile back, Dylan added, "This is a good thing. You're already seeing places where you can add value."

"At a greeting card company? Dylan, I don't think—"

"Okay, first, let's celebrate the fact that your résumé and cover letter are attracting attention," Dylan said, putting a hand on her hip and adopting a no-nonsense tone. "And second, no one's first job is all glamour, okay? Think of this as a stepping-stone."

"I don't even have the job yet," Neale mumbled.

"You're right; you don't," Dylan said, her tone softening just a hair before her wild, upbeat joy returned. "The good news is, I still have forty-five minutes before I need to meet Mike, so let me just throw on some clothes, and then we can start interview prepping."

"Now?"

"Yup! The more time we have to get you ready, the better. Now, you start drafting a yes-response email while I get dressed."

"I mean, the guy just sent this; I think we can wait a few minutes to—"

"No excuses. Chop-chop. You are getting this job, or my name isn't Dylan Delacroix."

With that, Dylan turned and dashed into her bedroom, leaving Neale to wonder how attached to her name her sister really was. Sighing, she clicked the reply button. Best to answer Rich before Dylan came back and tried to write the email herself.

CHAPTER SIX

Neale stared up at the dingy two-story office building and wondered exactly where in her life she'd gone wrong. She knew there had to have been missteps, since she was in Northgate wearing something so drab only Dylan would find it fun and interviewing for a job at a company that licensed music for the kind of greeting cards that made people wish they'd never gotten a birthday card at all.

Walking toward the building, Neale reached a hand into the pocket of the gray, wide-legged trousers she had borrowed from Dylan and touched the list of interview tactics her sister had attempted to drill into her head over the last few days. After Neale had made the double mistake of not making eye contact with her sister as she'd shaken her hand and accepting a job offer on the spot without asking about the salary or benefits, Dylan had decided Neale needed a proper set of rules if she was to have any hope of landing this job. In classic Dylan fashion, she had even typed up the list and printed it out for Neale, just in case she forgot anything and needed to sneak into the bathroom for a refresher at some point.

"I am a self-directed worker who likes to interact with colleagues." Neale mumbled Dylan's catchphrase as she reached for the door, practicing her I'm-likable-but-no-nonsense smile in its grimy reflection. The inside of the building was as gray as the outside, with a hint of fluorescent lighting just to hammer home the cog-in-the-machine experience.

Neale shook her head, then reminded herself that no lobby looked appealing. Just because the building was sad didn't mean that she wasn't on a new path to greatness. Looking around to make sure the hallways were empty, she whispered as she walked, "I am detail oriented. I like the job done right."

Pausing briefly at the building directory to find Happy Hearts' suite number, 107, Neale continued her recitation: "I like a collaborative work environment." She had messed that one up in practice. Apparently, *I like crystals on my desk* was not what businesses wanted to hear in response to *What kind of work environment do you like?* Passing suite 105, Neale looked down at the drab green industrial carpet. "I do wish I could bring in crystals, though."

"Well, Susan keeps plants at her desk, so I don't see why you couldn't bring a crystal," said a voice from behind Neale, almost making her jump out of her borrowed, pointy-toed heels. Clutching her chest, she spun around and found herself face to face with a demigod dressed in a pair of perfectly creased khakis and an equally well-starched pastel-purple button-up. Looking up at the man's face, Neale experienced several colliding thoughts. The first was that she knew he was a demigod because only a demigod would not have wrinkles in his clothes after 11:00 a.m. The second was that he had absolutely flawless rich-brown skin and the kind of smile that could power New York City at midnight.

Dark eyes sparkled with humor as the man looked at her. Catching sight of the surprise on her face, he frowned. "I'm sorry—it wasn't my intention to scare you. Are you Neale?"

For a moment Neale remained silent, wondering if the man was a mind reader or if this was part of his demigod power. How else could he know her name? She also wondered if he even had pores.

"I'm Anthony. I work at Happy Hearts. Rich mentioned that he had an interview today," the man said, interrupting her thoughts and nodding encouragingly at her. Then he paused, placing a hand over his broad chest, and smiled again before adding, "Unless you aren't Neale. In which case, Calhoun Orthodontia is across the lobby in suite 108."

"Sorry, you surprised me," Neale said, finally finding her words. So much for the shoulders-back first impression Dylan had planned for her. "I'm Neale Delacroix."

"Nice to meet you, Neale. I was just headed back from the mail room when I spotted you," Anthony said, holding out his hand.

"Nice to meet you, Anthony," Neale said, trying very hard not to focus on the feel of his hands. Job interviews were not a dating service; it said so on Dylan's list. She couldn't fix the thing about the crystals, but she could get the rest of her interview right. Demigod or not, she still needed a job. Neale forced herself to make eye contact with him as she let go of his hand, ignoring that his bone structure was so unusual that it almost hurt to look at his face.

"Let's get you to your interview. Wouldn't want you to be late," Anthony said, smiling as he reached around her and held the door open with an after-you gesture. "I believe you are meeting in the conference room."

"Thank you," Neale said, unable to hide her smile at his oddly chivalrous behavior as she walked through the door and into the reception area. Inside, the office was less drab than the rest of the building, which was promising to Neale. Yes, there was a giant banner, like the kind hung on freeway overpasses, attached to the office wall that read, HAPPY HEARTS . . . SHARE LOVE IN AN ENVELOPE. However, the walls weren't gray, and Susan's plants brightened up the place.

"May I offer you a drink before you meet with Rich? Perhaps some water?" Anthony asked, gently steering her toward a small, windowless conference room.

"I'm fine. Thank you very much for the offer," Neale said as they entered the conference room. His question was so formal that she found herself responding in kind, as if they were two people at a society lunch.

"In that case, I'll let Rich know you are here. Good luck, Neale," Anthony said, unleashing his smile again before turning to leave and gently shutting the conference room door behind him so she had some privacy.

Neale exhaled, then gave herself a shake, releasing some of the nervous energy that came with meeting an unexpected, good-looking person. Then she gave herself another shake to rid herself of the preinterview jitters that were starting to set in, before choosing a seat at the overly large six-person table. The thing was so big Neale couldn't help but wonder how Happy Hearts had gotten the table inside the room. They'd probably had to build it in there.

The door clicked open, and Neale's attention was pulled to a warm-looking middle-aged Asian man with freckles sprinkled across his nose. Smiling down at her, he said, "Welcome, Neale, I'm Rich Wong."

"Nice to meet you, Rich," Neale said, shaking his hand.

"Anything I can get you before we get going?" Rich asked, gesturing over his shoulder at the door.

"Oh no, thanks. Anthony already offered."

"Of course he did." Rich smiled as if he should have guessed, then took a seat across from her. "Okay, then—we'll just get started."

This is it, she told herself. Reaching into the purse Dylan had insisted she carry, Neale extracted a leather folio and withdrew a copy of her résumé, secretly pleased that she had remembered this detail from her practice sessions. "Would you like a copy of my résumé?"

"Sure, thank you," Rich said, glancing down at the résumé she had passed him. "So, Neale, tell me about yourself."

Neale grinned. Dylan had said this question would be first. Her method was working. Neale just had to stick to the plan. Taking a deep breath, she began, "Well, I grew up in Seattle and spent a few semesters at DePaul University, in Chicago, before returning home to pursue a career as an artist." So far, so good. Rich didn't even lift an eyebrow at her leaving school without a degree. Exhaling out the rest of her answer, she quickly continued, "I've spent the last few years working as an artist, and I've learned a ton, but I'm ready to move on."

"Interesting. Who's your favorite artist?"

Neale blinked for a second. Was this a trick? Nowhere in Dylan's rehearsal had this come up. Rich was supposed to ask something like, *What drew you to this position?* not make small talk.

"Living or deceased?" Neale asked, mostly to give herself time to think through how to make this answer reflect her skill set.

"Let's say living." Rich shrugged and leaned back in his chair as if these kinds of questions were standard while interviewing.

"Lorraine O'Grady."

"I don't know her. I'll have to look her up," Rich said, smiling.

"Oh, you have to. She works across several mediums, and each piece is powerful. I really appreciate the form as much as the content. Every decision she makes feels deliberate." Neale could feel herself slipping into an art diatribe and forced herself to redirect. No matter how this interview turned out, she was leaving art behind—and all the pain that came with it. Smiling, she offered her best New Neale tie-in: "Which is what I liked about art. It allowed me to make deliberate, creative choices to communicate with an audience."

Good pivot, Neale congratulated herself.

"Are you still working on your art, though?" Rich asked.

Apparently, it wasn't quite as good a pivot as she thought. Neale felt like a deer in headlights. She did not want to explain that she lacked both talent and drive, at least according to Dr. McMillan, Darin, and roughly two million people on YouTube. Feeling her stomach churn, she tried to change the subject again. "Not anymore. I'm ready to take the skills I learned being an artist and do . . ." Do what, exactly? What was this job again? Neale could practically hear Dylan shouting at her to get back to the basics. "Something new." She repeated her prior sentiment and hoped that Rich suffered from sudden amnesia or something.

"Well, I hope you will continue to work on your art. I like all of our employees to have rich outside lives. It makes work more fun." Rich nodded as if this was an important piece of information.

"Art will always be a part of my life. I just need a break from it," Neale said, putting on her best no-nonsense smile. This whole interview was starting to feel a lot more like talking to her dad than talking to her potential boss. If Rich started playing choral reproductions of Gregorian chants, she was out. Neale would rather sleep on an air mattress and wear borrowed clothes for all of eternity than have another Henry in her life.

"Right. Well, I will say that this job isn't as creative as you might be used to. Although we work with some pretty creative products," Rich said, good-natured smiles rolling off him.

"I'd love to learn more about how you think someone would be successful in this position," Neale said, seizing the opportunity to bring the conversation back to the plan.

"Well . . ." For a moment, Rich looked surprised by the question, as if people applying for Data and Licensing Coordinator II positions didn't usually ask how they could be successful. "I think the first thing to know is that the role requires a bit of creativity and a lot of organization. Most of the tracking is done on a spreadsheet, so learning that software quickly would be a benefit."

"Right. I like technology," Neale said, nodding with more enthusiasm than she felt. Spreadsheets had never sounded appealing to her. Then again, neither had braces, and she was glad she had gotten those now.

Rich smiled and looked down at her résumé as if his next interview question were written on it. When nothing appeared, he looked up and said, "So if you were going to be a house pet, what kind of pet would you be, and why?"

"Excuse me?" Neale said. It wasn't that she hadn't heard the question; it was that she truly didn't understand it. What did house pets have to do with greeting cards?

"If you could be any house pet in the world, which would you be and why?" Rich asked, not batting an eyelash at the abrupt turn the interview had taken.

Abandoning all hope of sticking to the plan, Neale said the first thing that came to her mind. "I'd be one of those outlandish poodles that people have shaved and dyed bizarre colors."

Rich's eyebrows shot toward his salt-and-pepper hairline as a grin crept across his face. "Why is that?"

All her careful preparation, and this guy was playing the interview equivalent of Mad Libs. *Thanks for nothing, Dylan,* she thought. Smiling at Rich, she said, "Well, if I am going to be a house pet, I may as well go all in. Plus, I figure that anyone who spends that much time and energy on their dog must really love and care for the pet. I bet a poodle like that gets filet mignon every night and sleeps on a California king mattress with a pillow top."

"That is a very elaborate answer," Rich said, smiling as if he weren't just as quirky for asking a weird question as Neale was for answering it.

"Well, if I'm going to dream about being a house pet, I may as well shoot for the moon." Neale did her best to not laugh as she doubled down on the absurd.

"Fair enough." Rich lifted one shoulder in a half shrug, then said, "Tell me, what is your greatest failure?"

"My greatest failure?" Neale croaked, wishing she'd taken Anthony up on that glass of water. Her mouth went dry, despite the fact that her body seemed determined to sweat through the armpits of her shirt in twenty seconds or less. Dylan had prepared her for the chance that someone might ask about the video. She had not prepared her for someone who hadn't seen the video but apparently wanted to hear about it in gory detail with a job offer hanging in the balance.

"Yes." Rich nodded like this was a reasonable thing to ask someone, then added, "It could be anything. It does not have to be work related."

"Right," Neale said, wishing for the first time in her life that she had worn a watch. How much longer did she have to spend in this tiny room? Would a buzzer go off after a half hour? Maybe she could just sit here and wait until someone else came to—

Neale cut the thought spiral off. No one was coming to save her. And in all likelihood, Rich would google her sooner or later. She had to answer Rich honestly, but that didn't mean she had to watch as he reacted. Looking down at the table, she said, "I accidentally ruined my own art piece in the middle of a show. Like, really ruined. I mean, fire was involved, and it was so bad that it went viral."

"Oh. How did the fire start?" Rich asked.

Neale looked up, catching sight of Rich's nervous expression. "It was part of the show. But I forgot to check if my costume was flame retardant. Turns out it wasn't, and—"

"You set yourself on fire?" Rich blurted out, interrupting her painful retelling.

"Only my hat. But it set off the fire alarm and the fire trucks had to come and . . . yeah. It was in the papers." Neale looked at a black-and-white photograph just above Rich's head. It was of some abstract sculpture. Not that it mattered. Frankly, she would look at the ugly green carpet again if she had to. Just so long as she didn't have to see anyone's face.

Rich exhaled loudly and drummed his fingers on the conference table before saying, "Well, that is a pretty impressive failure."

"Thanks."

"I can't say as I've ever failed that publicly before," Rich continued.

"I wouldn't recommend it." Neale half laughed, forcing herself to look at Rich again, who seemed to be considering her response carefully.

After what felt like eons, he said, "Well, we'll just have to keep you away from the birthday candles."

"I promise I don't make it a habit to play with fire. Especially after the papier-mâché dog melted."

"How do you melt a papier-mâché dog with fire? Is it the glue?" Rich asked, his concern transforming into genuine curiosity.

"Sprinkler system," Neale said, a little joy creeping into her heart as Rich snort-laughed. If nothing else, she was glad the incident was out in the open and she wouldn't have to dread it coming up during the rest of the interview. "If you google the video, you are looking for the one by Jenna. Although there are some pretty good remixes out there too."

"Duly noted." Rich smirked. "I don't think I have any more questions for you. Is there anything else you would like to share?"

Taking a deep breath, Neale decided she had nothing to lose and made her final pitch. "I know I don't seem like a great, traditional candidate and that admitting to being an unwitting arsonist is not a good look. However, I really believe I can do this job and do it well."

Rich's eyes narrowed as if he were studying a specimen he'd found in the back of a cupboard. Neale's heart began to pound as her face got hot. She was surprised by how much she wanted this job. Or rather, how much she was craving good news. Anything to prove that she was on the path to New Neale and not some screwup.

The way Rich was looking at her reminded Neale of Dr. McMillan firing her from the Collective all over again, and she began dreading having to explain how the interview had gone to Dylan, who'd probably told their mom, their dad, and possibly Billie about her potential job. Neale's eyes began to sting as she thought about enduring another round of poor-Neale-can't-even-get-a-boring-job pity hugs. And then there would be the strangely vague but encouraging text messages from Grandmama, as if Neale didn't know that her dad told Grandmama everything. Her grandmama wasn't even good at texting, but she—

"All right. Here's the deal. I have one more question for you," Rich said, blocking her running thoughts.

"Yes," Neale said, hating how hesitant she sounded.

"If offered this position, when could you start?" Rich asked.

The question nearly stopped Neale's heart. Was this a trick? *The last few questions weren't, so maybe this isn't either*, Neale thought. Smiling, she answered, "Well, my old gallery is currently sitting in three inches of rusty pipe water, so basically anytime."

"Good. Let's have you come in a week from next Monday. Assuming you want the job." Rich grinned at the shock on her face.

"I don't understand. I just admitted to lighting my gallery on fire," Neale said, feeling joy bubble up in her chest as if she had a bubble machine going full tilt in her rib cage.

"Well, yes. And you don't seem to have any typical nine-to-five experience." Rich nodded as if this were a fact and not the insult it sounded like, then continued, "But I appreciate your candor, and we like creative thinking at Happy Hearts, and you've got that in spades. You just need someone to give you a chance."

"And you are going to give me one?" Neale asked, hardly hearing him over the blood pounding in her ears.

"I'm trying to. So what do you say? Do you accept?"

"Yes!" Neale shouted, reaching a hand across the table to shake on the deal before Rich changed his mind. A small voice that sounded a lot like Dylan chastised her for agreeing to the job without so much as seeing a benefits package, but Neale ignored it. Dylan would be a lot less disappointed once Neale was no longer counting on sleeping on her couch as a backup plan.

"We're delighted to have you on board. I can't wait for the team to meet you. We are small but scrappy. You'll see when you start."

As she released his hand, it took all of Neale's limited willpower not to throw her pretend hat in the air and jump up and down. As far as she was concerned, this was her Mary Tyler Moore moment. It really was a pity that Dylan wouldn't let her wear a hat to the interview.

CHAPTER SEVEN

Neale parked her car at the back of the small lot and waved her hands in the air. Her palms were sweaty. In her past attempts at desk jobs, she hadn't really cared one way or the other how she performed. But this felt different. One, because she wasn't there on a temp agency placement, and two, because despite how deeply boring the idea of working a nine-to-five sounded, she wanted to do well. If she wasn't going to be an artist, then she needed to get serious about building a new career. Even if that career started with her being the Data and Licensing Coordinator II. Whatever that meant.

Getting out of the car, Neale tried to steady her shaking hands by grabbing the strap on her flower power tote bag. Dylan had nearly sat on her until she'd agreed to wear the snoozefest of a forest-green dress that she'd picked out for her. Neale had argued that Rich wanted everyone to bring their full selves to work. Her sister had maintained that did not mean he wanted them to dress like their full selves. The tote bag had been their compromise.

Stepping through the lobby, Neale made an effort to think positive thoughts. As it turned out, a new job was the only way to get out of Dylan's sister workouts, so at least she wasn't sore. If she was lucky, maybe she could stretch that into a full week off. The whole idea made her smile as she pulled on the office door handle.

"Good morning," Neale said, in her best approximation of Rhoda Morgenstern.

Neale waited for someone to answer, rocking back on her heels as she surveyed the little front desk area. When no one answered, she tried again. "Hello?"

Was she alone? Rich had said to come at 8:00 a.m., and the door was unlocked. Surely that meant someone was there. They probably had headphones on or something and couldn't hear her. Neale shrugged and decided to look around, praying that this wasn't the zombie apocalypse and that her new job wasn't the walking dead's first target.

The small front desk area was still shrouded in tall green plants, like a tiny jungle, complete with special lights to provide a particularly unfriendly-looking fern with enough fake sunlight to thrive. Ignoring the small conference room down the left-hand hall, she crept past the desk and the little frosted-glass divider wall, then stopped short.

She wasn't sure what she had expected, but it wasn't four cubicles, two doors with nameplates that suggested offices, and a massive copy machine. In the back corner there appeared to be a small coffeepot burbling away next to a microwave that had managed to survive the early nineties. The place was tiny and retro in the not-good way.

"Hello," she called again, this time without expecting an answer. Neale was about to go sit in one of the two chairs in the waiting area by the front desk when something shiny on one of the cubicle walls caught her eye. Throwing a careful glance over her shoulder, she sneaked toward the desk to get a closer look.

Neale hovered at the entrance to a meticulously tidy cubicle. Whoever sat here would rival her sister in organizational skills. A penholder with exactly five of the same pen sat near a neatly color-coded Post-it pallet. The shiny thing on the wall was a gold-leaf calendar with carefully constructed abstract figures in motion. Sneaking into the cube, Neale leaned in closer to the calendar and squinted. It was beautiful in its own strange way. As she stepped all the way in, she could see that the figures blended into April as if their motion created the month. Each day leading up to the twenty-sixth was carefully crossed off, as if the person doing the crossing did not want to ruin the calendar's exquisite detailing by marking the passage of time.

Turning her attention to a neat stack of rainbow-colored file folders, Neale jumped as the office door slammed and voices filled the room. Frozen in horror, she looked up to find four people walking down the hallway. For a small second, Neale considered hiding as a tan woman holding a bakery box said, "Honestly, the plot of the show is so convoluted. I don't—"

Neale's heart stopped as the group walking through the hall spotted her. If she hadn't been panicking, she could have come up with some clever response. Instead, she simply blinked at the group and said, "Hello."

"Good morning. I'm afraid that is my desk. Yours is just across from me," Anthony said, although he did not sound particularly bothered that she was hovering in his space. As he came closer, Neale could see the angular features of his face. It was the sort of face that was so unusual to look at that she couldn't decide if it was beautiful or strange. High, sharp cheekbones and a strong, square jaw should have made his features seem boxy, but full lips and dark-brown eyes gave him just enough softness to appear friendly.

Giving her head a shake, Neale realized belatedly that she didn't need to decide if he was beautiful or strange. She needed to explain what she was doing poking around his desk. Pulling herself up to her full height, all she managed was, "I'm supposed to start today."

"Hi, Neale," Rich called from behind the woman with the bakery box. "Sorry we weren't here to greet you, but we thought doughnuts would be a good first-day welcome treat."

"We also thought Susan would be here, but it looks like she is running late. I'm Melissa," the bakery box said.

"Nice to meet you," Neale said, almost forgetting that she was standing by a stranger's desk.

"I'm Travis," the small, pale man next to Rich said.

"I think we've met before. Shall we go to the conference room? Unless you want to eat at my desk too." Anthony smirked.

Refusing to feel embarrassed, Neale tilted her chin a little higher than she would normally hold her head and said, "Anthony, you have a lovely calendar."

Rich, Melissa, and Travis laughed as Neale strutted out of his cubicle. Anthony's smile was unhurried, as if he was amused by her gumption.

"Susan tends to come in when she wants, so we won't wait for her," Rich said, a hint of laughter still clinging to his voice. He had warned her that the group would be small, but she hadn't realized just how small he meant. As it was, they couldn't even field a soccer team.

As they settled down around the table, Melissa opened up the box to reveal a dozen doughnuts, and Neale grinned. While the office might not be able to form a soccer team, they acted like they were feeding one. If this was their food energy, Neale could learn to like this job. Reaching for an old-fashioned glazed doughnut, she grabbed a thin diner napkin and leaned back in her chair, waiting for the group to settle. Once everyone had a doughnut, she asked, "So what does everyone do here?"

"Well, I dabble in a bit of everything, so I'll let everyone else talk," Rich said, taking a big bite of an apple fritter.

"You're letting us talk so you can eat. Don't pretend." Melissa smiled, holding something chocolate covered. "Like I said, I'm Melissa Vargas. I handle all of the printing, manufacturing, and shipping logistics for our in-house line of cards. Fun fact, I had one line in a Chris Rock film when I was five."

Neale felt her smile spread. "You were a child star? Any other movies of yours we should look for?"

"Oh no. I got cast exactly once. Hated the costume they put me in and never acted again. In hindsight, that may have been foolish. I could have paid for college with that."

"Yeah, but child stars always turn out to be weirdos." Travis grinned, then added, "Not that you aren't weird now."

"I'll take that as the compliment I'm sure you meant it to be," Melissa said with mock indignation, shaking her wavy hair over her shoulders. "Go on and tell her what you do, Travis."

"Why, thank you for that kind introduction, Melissa. I'm Travis Deal . . . last I checked, anyway."

Neale bit into her old-fashioned as Travis explained his role, something to do with supporting logistics for other larger greeting card firms. Sitting in the conference room, she was struck by how familial the office felt compared to the cold and calculating place she had pictured in her mind. As the team joked with one another, Neale relaxed as her first-day jitters worked their way out of her system.

"All right, all right. That is enough out of you two," Rich laughed, waving off Melissa and Travis, who had gone down a rabbit hole over that TV show again. Turning toward Anthony, he said, "Why don't you tell her what you do?"

The familiar slow smile spread across Anthony's face. "Not much to know, really. I'm not a child star like Mel or anything."

"This guy," Melissa said, interrupting Anthony to roll her eyes.

"Mr. Shy is deflecting. But we won't let him, will we?" Travis said, hitching his thumb at Anthony. "Go on, artist. Tell her what you do."

"I used to handle song licensing for our musical card clients, which I guess is your job now. And I help with the IT and draw our in-house cards," Anthony said, looking down at his hands. "It's not a big deal."

"It is a big deal. You are the reason the company is expanding," Rich said, giving Anthony a smile coated in pride. "Two years ago, this guy comes to us with an idea for a card. Before Anthony started sharing his artistic skills, we solely handled song licensing for bigger companies.

Now, we are expanding. We launched our first card line this year, and some of the local grocery stores, like QFC, are carrying our cards right next to the big card makers, like Hallmark. We even have plans to pitch a line to a national chain like Target."

"Wow. That is amazing," Neale said.

"It is. In fact, the two of you should talk, because I know you are an artist as well and—"

The sound of the conference room door thudding into the wall cut Rich off and saved Neale from having to explain why she was not an artist anymore. Sure, her coworkers would probably google her and find out about the video. But if they hadn't already, she didn't really want to tell them about it. Besides, even if she wanted to go back to being an artist, she wasn't an artist like Anthony. She very much doubted that Happy Hearts would want her manifestos on a card.

"Hello, Susan. Glad you could join us," Rich said, drawing Neale's attention to the dour-looking woman standing in the doorway. If Neale had to guess, she was in her late forties, but her expression made her seem like she was one million. Her strange, dead-center part and jet-black dye job didn't do much for her curb appeal, but it did remind Neale vaguely of the girl from *The Ring*, so Susan had that going for her.

"I see you all started without me," she said, opening the lid to the bakery box and sniffing at the doughnuts. Frowning a little, she dropped the lid, then looked over at Neale's half-finished old-fashioned and scowled.

"We were just wrapping up," Rich said, looking down at his watch. "My apologies. Anthony and I have a nine a.m. meeting, so we have to dash off."

Turning to face Neale, Anthony said, "You are sitting next to me. I left your computer log-in info on a Post-it by your keyboard, along with your email-address instructions."

"Thank you," Neale said, trying not to stare too hard at his face. She could decide if it was beautiful or not when she got home. It wasn't as if she was going to forget the angles of it anytime soon.

"Oh," Rich said, shaking Neale from her musings on beauty. "Also, I sent your HR forms to your work email so you can print and fill them out. We can meet after ten to get you all set up with payroll and all that. Once that is done, Anthony can begin training you."

"Sounds good. Thanks for the warm welcome, everyone," Neale said, standing up and taking her doughnut with her. She wasn't sure what Susan's deal was, but there was no way she was letting her snatch her breakfast.

"Welcome aboard," Rich called, halfway out the door.

Neale would never admit it to anyone, but she was secretly a little glad to be there.

~

Neale glared at the ancient Canon machine and wondered if the combination printer-copier was older than she was. Not that its age would have changed the fact that she hated the machine with her entire being.

She had been delighted to spend the first forty-five minutes of her morning getting settled into her new work space. Unlike in temp jobs, Neale actually had her own everything, and it was oddly fun. Yes, she had messed up recording her voice mail roughly twelve times, and when she'd finally gotten it right, Travis had gently informed her that she had spelled her email address wrong. She didn't mind. Neale even thought reading the employee handbook was fun in a weird sort of desk-life kind of way. If this was her new reality, she was determined to make the most of it.

Or at least she had been until she'd tried to print and sign her employment forms.

Neale glared at the printer, which flashed a combination of warning and incompetent-user lights. Bending down, she squinted at the base of the machine and saw a little square icon that, if she tilted her head sideways, could possibly be construed as a stack of paper. Next to it was an odd button. Taking a deep breath, Neale pressed the button and prayed nothing exploded.

Instead, a terrifying, spring-loaded drawer shot out at her like a demon-possessed jack-in-the-box. Neale was so surprised she knocked herself backward, landing awkwardly on her butt. Glancing quickly over her shoulder, she took comfort in the fact that absolutely no one had seen her. Melissa and Travis were on the other side of her and Anthony's cubicles, each wearing headphones to catch up on the podcast everyone listened to. Pulling herself back into her crouch, Neale looked down at the drawer. The machine had paper, which meant that she had officially exhausted her knowledge of what could go wrong with printers. Pushing the drawer back into place, she stood up and checked the flashing lights again. No change.

Racking her brains, Neale thought about next steps. She could either find someone to ask or just wait until her meeting with Rich, thereby not completing her very first and possibly easiest task on the job. She didn't want to do that. Accepting that she was going to feel foolish admitting that she didn't understand a printer, Neale took a deep breath and began her slow walk to Susan's desk, hoping that as the office manager, she would know what to do.

Carefully approaching the jungle that served as Susan's work space, Neale cleared her throat and said, "Hi, Susan."

Susan jumped, looking up from the news site she was scanning, and angled her head slightly to the left to see Neale past a massive fern. Her eyes flicked back to whatever she was reading, then up at Neale again. Sighing, she said, "Hello."

Okay, so Neale wasn't sure what she had done to piss Susan off, but she was sure they could get past it with a little of her patented charm. Putting on her best smile, Neale tried again. "We didn't get to chat much this morning, but I just want to say that based on your plants alone, I'm super excited to be working with you."

Not a total lie, Neale thought. She did in fact like the plant energy. Susan's energy, on the other hand, Neale wasn't as wild about. After an awkward series of heartbeats, Susan raised an eyebrow but didn't say anything, forcing Neale to continue. So much for her charm. "Right. I'm struggling with the copy machine. There are a bunch of lights going off, and I have no idea what they mean. I thought maybe, as office manager, you might know how to fix it. Or if not, maybe who I should talk to?"

Neale let the sentence trail off as Susan sighed, then pushed herself out of the chair. Walking past Neale and some sort of spindly not-cactus plant, she said, "Let me take a look."

"Thank you so much," Neale said, attempting to make her words sound as gracious as possible. Trailing behind Susan, she searched her mind for office-appropriate small talk and landed on, "So how long have you been working here?"

"Nine years," Susan said, her tone flat as she rounded the cubicle to the copy machine. Neale glanced sideways in time to make eye contact with Travis, whose eyes went wide at their passing. The look didn't exactly inspire courage in Neale.

"You are out of blue ink," Susan said, sniffing down at the copy machine and sounding bored.

"Oh. Thanks," Neale said, feeling a little silly, since it had taken Susan all of three seconds to figure that out. Hoping to never have this conversation again, she said, "Could you show me which light is for the toner?"

"This one," Susan said, tapping vaguely at all the flashing lights. Jabbing a button on the side of the machine, Neale watched as the entire front sprang open, revealing its guts. "There is toner in the cupboard over there." Susan gestured to a wall, then began walking away without another word.

"Thank you!" Neale said after her, then realized that she had no idea how to even change toner. Pulling her shoulders back, she called to Susan, who was slowly making her way back toward the front desk, "Hey, Susan. Would you mind showing me how to change the toner?"

"You have a few semesters of college under your belt. You are a smart girl. I think you can read the box and figure it out," Susan snarled, then kept walking without so much as a backward glance.

Neale's jaw dropped, and she looked over at Melissa and Travis, whose headphones had apparently kept them from hearing so much as one unhelpful word of Susan's condescension. Looking over her shoulder at the open copy machine door, she decided it was for the best that the other two hadn't heard Susan. No need for her to get a reputation as a needy diva on her first day. Yes, Susan had meant Neale's not finishing college as a jab, but hey, Neale had gotten into college, so Susan wasn't wrong. She was smart, and she could figure this out.

Neale walked toward the cupboards and did her best to think through her current situation. Thanking her genetics for her height, she reached up and stood on her toes, her fingers inching a toner box out of its place on the shelf. Bringing the box down, she studied it carefully, then felt her heart sink. The instructions on the outside were not in English, but it did have a picture of a printer on the front, and the package was blue, so this seemed like a good sign.

Carrying the box back to the printer, Neale removed about fifty layers of packaging and a sheet of instructions that she couldn't read. Unwrapping the toner, she found the thing covered in various tags and an orange bit of plastic. Neale looked at the new toner, then bent down until she identified the corresponding part on the machine. Taking a deep breath, she set the new toner on top of the printer, then found a similar orange knob and tugged gently at it. Nothing happened. Looking down at the drawing on the instructions, Neale squinted. It seemed like she was supposed to pull the orange tab to change the thing. Maybe she just wasn't pulling hard enough?

From somewhere over her shoulder, Neale heard Rich's voice fill the room. "Thanks, Anthony. Neale, I'm going to run to the restroom; then I'll be right with you."

"All right," Neale managed to call, her voice sounding shaky. For a moment, her blood stopped running. An hour should have been sufficient to complete the forms. In fact, it would have been if it weren't for the stupid printer and how carefully she had read the HR policy on internet usage. Neale willed herself not to panic. Rich was in the bathroom; that was more than enough time to change the toner and print out the forms for her first meeting.

"Okay. You can do this," Neale said, reaching down to give the toner a hard yank, right as Anthony's voice floated over her shoulder.

"Do you need help?" he asked.

"I think I got it," Neale said. The toner didn't give way. Perhaps she needed to twist and pull, like a light bulb? Putting even more force behind the movement, she gritted her teeth and yanked again.

"Are you sure?" Anthony's voice sounded closer as he added, "Oh, you don't want to pull—"

CRACK!

Neale slammed her eyes shut as her airway was flooded with dust. Coughing and blinking furiously, she backed away from the machine. Looking down at her hands, she felt horror course through her as she realized they were covered in strange blue dust. She looked farther down. Her legs were covered in dust. Touching the dress she'd borrowed from Dylan, she felt grainy dust. Her sister was going to throw a fit. Coughing again, Neale felt her cheeks and realized that if there was dust on her face, there would also likely be dust in her hair. Still coughing, she looked up and froze.

Next to her, Anthony's formerly pale-yellow dress shirt was also covered in blue dust. As was his face and his freshly pressed dress slacks. In fact, all of him was covered in dust, as if someone had tried to make him a blue ghost in a 1970s movie.

"Oh my God." It was all she could manage to say after blinking at him for a minute.

Anthony did not look up at her; rather, he continued to brush at his pants as he said, "I was trying to warn you. That was the ink valve."

"I . . . I am so sorry . . . ," Neale stuttered, watching the ink dust on his pants smudge and get messier. Instinctively, she stopped swatting at her own outfit. If she was lucky, the dry cleaner might be able to save this. Not that they had been much help with the majorette uniform, but still.

"It's okay," Anthony said, looking up. As his eyes ran over her, an inscrutable expression crept across his face. "You, um . . . you may want to . . ."

Anthony's words trailed off as his shoulders began to shake. He closed his eyes and pressed his lips together, then crossed his inked arms as if hugging himself.

Was he . . . crying? Neale's heart dropped. In all her temp jobs and even her food-service jobs, she had never once made a coworker cry. Now, on her first day, she had destroyed a copy machine and made a grown man sob.

"Holy cow!" Melissa's voice rang out.

Neale turned to look at her right as Travis popped out of his chair, the wheels squeaking, to take a look. His mouth falling open, he said, "Oh, wow."

"I . . . ," Neale said, her gaze turning back to Anthony, whose shoulders were still shaking. "I'm so sorry. Susan said I would be able to figure this out, and I really thought I could, but I guess . . ." Her voice trailed off as her gaze jumped wildly between her three new coworkers. Melissa was holding a box of Kleenex and walking toward them, her face alternating between shock and humor. Travis's mouth was still open, but he had begun to smile. Anthony's eyes were still glued to the ground, his hand over his face. Neale shuddered and reached out, almost touching his arm before pulling her stained hand away. Taking a deep breath, she added, "Please don't cry. I'll pay for your shirt."

Anthony looked up and blinked at Neale, his eyes dry. Then he began to laugh. A deep, rolling sound that seemed to warm up the whole room. Grinning, he tried to say something, but a fresh round of giggles caused him to double over.

"You may want these," Melissa said, shaking the box of Kleenex at her.

Anthony righted himself and took a deep breath. Forcing a straight face, he said, "Your teeth. I have—" He began to choke on a chuckle. Taking another deep breath, he tried again. "Toothpaste, and there—" Laughter claimed him again, and he doubled over, managing to wheeze out, "One moment. So sorry."

Neale blinked between him and the other two. Melissa pressed her smile into a straight line and looked over her shoulder, away from Neale.

"What's wrong?" Neale asked, taking a tissue.

"Teeth," Travis coughed out, pointedly looking at the floor before doubling over like Anthony.

If Neale hadn't enacted the greatest art show meltdown of all time, she wouldn't have known what the sensation was that filled the pit of her stomach. As it was, she had gotten good at identifying the emotions running through her—existential dread and utter humiliation. Putting the pieces together, she realized that the explosion made her look like she had tried to eat a Smurf.

"Okay, Neale, ready when you are." The sound of Rich happily calling out to the office as he walked down the hall stopped everyone. Looking at the commotion, he froze. "What happened?"

"Printer mishap," Anthony said, careful not to make eye contact with Neale.

"It looks like it," Rich said, his shoulders tightening as he looked between Neale and Anthony.

"It's my fault," Neale blurted, as she swiped a hand in front of her teeth. "Susan's instructions made changing toner sound so simple."

Watching Rich's lips press into a thin line, she waved her hands around at the copy machine and added, "I wanted to print out the forms for our meeting, then Anthony tried to warn me, and yeah . . ."

Rich's eyes squinted. Taking a deep breath, he put his hands on his hips and looked around. "It's okay. I have some T-shirts left over from a trade fair if you want to change."

"I'm so sorry. I'll pay for the printer. And your dry cleaning," Neale said, gesturing to Anthony, who had stopped laughing, although a hint of a smile still clung to his face.

"No worries. We have a vacuum for a reason," Rich said, walking over to the cabinets and pulling out a Happy Hearts T-shirt. "We'll get this sorted out in no time. Maybe just . . ." He stopped short, still holding the T-shirt in one hand, the cupboard only halfway closed. He blinked a few times at Neale, then dropped his gaze. "Maybe just go to the bathroom and give your face a scrub first. You have ink all over your mouth."

CHAPTER EIGHT

Neale wove around the slow-walking date-nighters crowding the Ave and kicked herself for agreeing to Dylan's first-day-of-work celebration. Had she known just how exhausting her first day of work would be, she would have insisted on takeout instead of trying to brave the deeply quirky and oh-so-hip crowds that packed the U District at happy hour—now dinnertime. But Neale had known Dylan wouldn't take no for an answer, so instead she'd driven home and rinsed the unintentional *Avatar* costume off herself before she'd gone out in public.

Neale blew air through her lips like she was a horse and tried to relax as she reached the trendy bar and restaurant that Dylan seemed to think was low key. Of course, her sister's idea of low key would involve mood lighting and sleek decor with just the barest of nods toward kitsch and the college scene around them. Neale just hoped their portion sizes were bigger than the average fancy places that Dylan dragged her to. Nudging the restaurant door open, she stopped to get her bearings as the buzz of the after-work crowd filled her head. She had just commenced diving into a deeper level of regret over agreeing to drinks before someone shouted, "You're here!"

Startled, Neale dropped the plastic bag containing Dylan's ink-stained clothes on the floor with one hand and pushed her heart back into her chest with the other. Looking up from the sack, she had just enough time to brace herself as Billie came barreling toward her from the bar, where she and Dylan had evidently been waiting.

"I'm so freaking happy to see you," Billie growled. Feeling her sister's arms wrap around her, Neale blinked in the midst of a bear hug as she was squeezed and rocked back and forth in one overpowering motion. Neale grinned despite her crummy day. As close as she and Dylan were, she and Billie shared a special younger-sister bond. She had missed their inside jokes and weird little-sister acts of rebellion since Billie had gone away to college. Their occasionally tempestuous, mostly loving, us-against-the-grown-ups relationship just wasn't the same over long distances. Especially since they were all grown-ups now. Neale took a deep breath, the familiar scent of her sister's lotion filling her senses and calming her nerves.

When Billie finally let go, Neale took a step back to observe her sister and was floored. Unlike Dylan, who screamed *professional*, everything about Billie radiated *cool*. Not so long ago her sister had been the queen of old plaid and faded jeans, but not anymore. From the black, wide-brimmed hat to the thin-framed, cat-eyed glasses and the gauzy dress that floated around her as she spread her arms wide, Billie was undeniably edgy. Even her long box braids seemed cooler than average to Neale. In truth, she looked, walked, talked, and generally gave off artist vibes of the highest level. Meanwhile, Neale thought that all she did was give off *mess* energy.

Dylan emerged from behind her sister balancing three champagne flutes. "Congratulations on your first day!"

"I didn't know Billie would be here," Neale said, her cheeks warming as a group of patrons closest to them turned to spy on their celebration.

"Dylan didn't tell you? I'm here for a couple of months to put on a new show," Billie said, stepping back and appraising Neale, her brow furrowing slightly. "I find that hard to believe."

"I did tell you. Didn't I? Billie texted me about it right before I went to the house to help you pack, and I could have sworn I mentioned it." Dylan stopped, then shrugged the oversight off, champagne flutes outstretched. "Oh well. Double surprise!"

Neale quirked her eyebrow at her older sister as she accepted her glass. Why hadn't Billie just texted the whole sister chain or mentioned it when she'd texted her?

"Let's get out of the doorway," Billie said, grabbing Neale's arm and pulling her toward the three chairs that she and Dylan had been guarding for the better part of the last forty-five minutes, if the spread of half-finished hors d'oeuvres plates was any indication. Neale was so hungry she couldn't even be mad at them for eating without her.

"So tell us all about—" Dylan started, then stopped as Neale reached across her to grab some sort of bacon-wrapped something. "What are you wearing?"

"I . . . things . . . ," Neale said, looking down at her *Ghostbusters*-inspired romper, complete with a hole in the knee.

"You didn't wear that to work, did you?" Billie asked, settling into the high-backed chair on the other side of her.

"No, of course not," Neale said, dropping into the middle chair and avoiding her sister's gaze. She really didn't feel like starting off the story of her first day with the Great Ink Mishap. And since when did Billie care how she dressed? Probably around the same time she'd become all successful and Dylan's bestie. Remembering the plastic bag holding Dylan's ink-stained clothes in her hand, she said, "There was a mishap. Don't worry about it."

"You didn't light the place on fire, did you?" Billie laughed, quirking one eyebrow as she took a drink.

"No," Neale said, managing to sound only half as hurt as she felt. That comment was a little too close to home given the day she'd had.

"Be nice, Billie," Dylan said, taking a sip of her drink.

"What? It was a reasonable question given your track record." Billie grinned wickedly, as if she hadn't just touched the nerviest of Neale's nerves.

Looking gently at Neale, Dylan asked, "Did you get fired?"

"No! Why do the two of you always think the worst?"

Neale watched as her sisters exchanged loaded glances. Billie smiled. "No reason. If you didn't get fired and you didn't set off the smoke detector, then we're still celebrating. Tell us about the mishap."

Neale sighed. She was happy to see Billie, but the force of her two sisters together was a lot when all she wanted to do was sleep and pretend today had never happened. Looking between the pair of them, who were still rapid-fire communicating with meaningful glances, Neale tried to adjust her attitude. Yes, sometimes it felt like the two of them were hovering or ganging up on her, but it also felt like love under all their questions and concerns. Just a slightly annoying love that was very loud and liked champagne and hugs too much.

"Okay, fine," she said, reaching for some sort of cold puff pastry and cramming it into her mouth, enjoying the look of anticipation on Dylan's face as she waited almost as much as she enjoyed the look of irritation on Billie's. Stretching out the moment, Neale picked up her glass of champagne with an exaggerated nod of gratitude toward Dylan and took a long, slow sip.

"Spill," Billie demanded.

"Well, there was a mishap and—"

"Wait, what's in your hair?" Dylan interrupted.

"Yeah, it looks like you tried a spray dye job, but it got weird." Billie reached up to touch her hair, and Neale swatted her hand away.

"Don't touch it, or you'll have to wash your hands. And I was trying to tell you what happened," she said, glaring at Dylan, irritated that she'd managed to miss the ink around her ears despite scrubbing like a fiend.

"Sorry. Sorry. We won't interrupt anymore," Dylan said, taking a sip of her drink and eyeing Billie.

Neale very sincerely doubted that her sisters wouldn't talk over her, but she started her story again, this time making it to meeting all her coworkers before Billie interjected, "So this Anthony. What's he look like? Is he cute? Guys named Anthony are always cute."

"Not the point of the story," Neale said, rolling her eyes.

"Oh, he must be cute if Neale tried to change the subject," Dylan said, grinning. "What's his last name? We can google him."

"That's not why. I need to get to the important—"

"Cute Anthony is important," Dylan said.

"We don't need his whole name. *Happy Hearts* plus *Anthony* should bring up his LinkedIn," Billie half teased, taking out her phone.

"Can you two google him when I'm not here? I need to get to the devastating part of my day."

"More devastating than how handsome Anthony is?" Dylan asked, wiggling her eyebrows. Neale rolled her eyes. The champagne was clearly making her sister silly.

"He isn't devastating. If anything, he is unusual—"

"Found him," Billie shouted. "Well, damn. Neale really buried the lede on this one."

Her sister tossed the phone over Neale's head to Dylan, who made an impressive one-handed catch without spilling a drop of her drink. Taking one look, Dylan said, "Neale, he's cute. It doesn't say if he's married or anything, but people don't put that on LinkedIn. Did you see a ring?"

"What? No. I didn't even look," Neale said, sticking her nose in the air. As a matter of fact, she had noticed that he didn't wear a ring, but she didn't need to admit that to her sister. Instead, she added, "I'm a secular nun now, remember."

"What?" Billie said, her smile spreading from ear to ear.

"Don't get her started on it." Dylan rolled her eyes. "Neale. Trust me. You are not cut out to be a nun."

"Oh, you are one hundred percent not going to be a nun," Billie snickered into her champagne glass as if the idea of a celibate Neale were the most laughable thing she'd heard in a week.

Neale bristled. "Why is that funny? I'm turning over a new leaf."

"Sure," Billie said, raising her glass and draining it. She sounded like she believed Neale about as much as she believed in the Easter Bunny.

"On the upside," Dylan said, leaning into the bar counter to get a better look at both of her sisters, "this one has to be better than Darin. At least he isn't a DJ."

Neale held her breath at the mention of Darin. She had been doing a decent job of not thinking about him, her shattered plans for the future, or her destroyed art career today. *Really*, Neale thought, *it's amazing what ink dust can do for a broken heart.* Leave it to her sisters to disrupt the only good thing that had come out of her first day at work.

"Who said she needs to date? She can just sleep with An-thon-ee." Billie drew out each of the syllables in his name like it was in an R&B song, drawing Neale back into the conversation.

"I will be doing no such thing. I just want to focus on me."

"I can respect self-care," Billie said, nodding wisely. For a brief moment, Neale felt comforted by her sister's agreement, until she started leaning past her to look at Dylan. She braced herself right as Billie shouted, "But I can also respect getting it."

"Don't encourage that," Dylan said, leaning into Neale's space to slap Billie's arm good-naturedly as the two of them cackled. "For once, I think Neale is right. She finally has a good job, which she has been working for all of five minutes, and what? You want her to just jeopardize it for a one-night stand? Neale can find someone who isn't a coworker to date."

"Why would it be in jeopardy? Neale's mistake with the fire wasn't because she was sleeping with the Collective guy." Billie offered her counterargument as if Neale weren't right there listening to her sisters joke about her heartbreak.

"Neale, ignore her. Be responsible with—"

"I'm being responsible about this," Neale cut in, trying to forget the sting. "That is why I'm not out checking for a ring on Anthony's finger or googling him like you two weirdos. Like I said, I'm New Neale now, and New Neale has her life together. New Neale does not hunt for a boyfriend fifteen seconds into her new job."

"Right," Billie said, a giggle threatening to creep into her voice at any moment as she eyed Dylan, who pressed her lips together in a flat line, ostensibly to keep the same giggle off her face.

"I mean it, you two," Neale said, a little bit of hurt coloring her voice. "I'm breaking the cycle. This job may be boring, but I'm serious about it. I'm finally getting my life together."

"We know you're serious," Dylan said. She attempted to sound supportive, but her voice was still tinged with amusement.

"Do we, though?" Billie said, outright laughing as she unsuccessfully attempted to catch the bartender's eye to get another drink.

"Whatever. I have to tell you what's in my hair." Neale huffed, and both her sisters stopped smirking.

After a second Dylan said, "Okay, Neale, we're sorry."

Squinting at her, Billie must have registered Neale's hurt feelings, because she nudged her with her shoulder and said, "We know you are going to be a really good New Neale. We'll be quiet. What happened to your hair?"

This time, Neale made it through Susan's being weird about the doughnut before they interrupted ("That bitch," from Billie, and "Buy your own damn doughnut," from Dylan). Then they let her continue to Susan and the toner incident, where they stopped her again ("I told you about her," from Billie, and "How does she even have a job?" from Dylan). Finally, Neale made another plea to finish, and after extracting another round of useless *we'll be quiet*s from them, she got to the horrible part.

"Anyway, it turned out that the tissue I used to wipe my teeth ended up smudging my lipstick and the ink together, so I basically had Bozo the Clown's mouth. So yeah. I still have a job. But also, I'm mortified, and I do not want to go back there." Neale shrugged as she wrapped up the traumatic story, then looked up from the bubbles she had been watching float to the top of her glass.

After a moment, Billie blinked at her, then shook her head and said, "So you have ink in your hair? No big deal. At least you weren't covered in bird poop."

"I think the one who should feel embarrassed is Susan," Dylan rushed. "I bet she probably tampered with the printer just to make you feel bad."

"Someone that petty off a one-dollar doughnut. I wouldn't put it past her," Billie said, tilting her empty glass at Dylan and nodding. "And joke's on her, 'cause you still got a job, and you have a meet-cute story for your future husband."

"Not my future husband. Not even looking for one." Neale rolled her eyes.

Billie snorted. "Oh, right. I forgot. Secular nunnery. Whatever that means."

"You're such a gremlin."

"Why, thank you." Billie opened her mouth to say more when her phone began buzzing. Looking down at the phone, she sighed. "It's Kelsea. She is still upset over my canceling the LA show. I have to take this. Want me to order more drinks while I'm up?"

"Yes, please, Gremmie," Neale said, wondering exactly how bad the freak-out was that Billie needed to take a call from her business manager after what had to be 10:00 p.m. East Coast time.

"Are we calling her Gremmie now? Like, short for *gremlin*?" Dylan chuckled, drawing Neale back into the conversation. "Love it. I would also like another glass, please, Gremmie."

"Whatever," Billie said, shaking her hair over her shoulders play-fully. Pressing a button on her phone, her sister adopted an ultraprofessional tone and said, "This is Billie Delacroix."

As Billie walked toward a quiet corner of the bar, Neale and Dylan went back and forth over what to order for dinner. Eventually, Billie returned and immediately tried to change their order, the three of them poking and prodding at one another until a compromise was reached. As the evening wore on, Neale began to let go of the inauspicious start to her job. There was something so familiar about being with her sisters that it was comforting. Sure, they bickered and bossed and interrupted. And they had a questionable grasp on the definition of both *personal space* and *personal life*. But as Neale listened to them, she had to admit that if she was going to have a bad day at the office, she couldn't think of any two people she would rather confess it to than her sisters.

~

Neale set her coffee mug and her tote bag down on her desk in one motion before settling herself into her chair. After a debrief with her sisters, two glasses of bubbles, and some delightful orzo with seasonal vegetables, she had managed to talk herself out of quitting. By the time she had rinsed the remaining ink out of her hair and then rinsed it out of her shower, she had even convinced herself that the job and the printer mishap might be good things. After all, it was unlikely that Susan would ever skip showing her how to do something again.

Sipping on her coffee, Neale took advantage of a moment alone in the office to collect her thoughts. After the printer debacle, the rest of her first day had been rather mundane. Rich had managed to remove the old cartridge and install a new one, and although her forms were a little ink smudgy, she had been able to print them out and turn them in. Now that she was officially set up on the payroll, today was all about getting her trained. Or at least it would be whenever Anthony arrived.

She was just starting to think that this 8:00 a.m. start time wasn't as hard and fast as Rich seemed to think it was when she heard the office door click open. Glancing up, Neale watched as Melissa and Anthony strolled down the hall, each clutching their own large travel coffee mug.

Noticing Neale, Melissa chirped, "Good morning."

"Hello," Neale said, trying her best to imitate Melissa's chipper tone.

"Good morning, Neale. Have you settled in okay?" Anthony asked, his voice gentle for someone she had only recently assaulted with a copy machine. When he turned to face his cubicle, Neale's brain stopped functioning for a full thirty seconds as she watched him bend over to reach his computer monitor.

That booty. It was the first and only thought that came to Neale, although she felt a little guilty about it. Yes, she was a secular nun now. But also, she could appreciate a butt. It wasn't like she was dead. It was the kind of perfectly round backside that songs were written about. Hell, if she wanted to, Neale could probably write a song about his ass right this moment. The thing was a masterpiece.

"Neale?" Anthony said, rotating around to face her, causing Neale to jump as her mind snapped back to attention. Wrinkling his brow in mild concern, he clarified, "Were you able to get into your computer? Email still working okay?"

"Uh, yeah. Thanks for asking," Neale said, attempting to shake off the remnants of her guilt by reassuring herself that a little slipup was okay for novices in the celibacy department. After all, she still had her job, and it wasn't like she would ever make the mistake of associating one good-looking man with her future plans again. It was just that his butt even looked good in workplace khaki, which was strategically designed to ruin asses around the world . . .

Okay, maybe not such a little slipup, Neale thought, interrupting herself before she could get any further down that rabbit hole. Attempting to act like a responsible working adult who respected her coworkers rather than lusting after them, Neale clicked over to her calendar so she could look at the exactly two meetings she had scheduled today. First, a training meeting with Anthony, and then a welcome lunch with Travis and Melissa.

Well, Neale thought, *there's no way around it*—she was just going to have to get used to working with the best butt in the greater Northgate area. She could do that. After all, New Neale was all about personal growth, which learning how to work with good-looking people and doing absolutely nothing about it completely qualified as. Turning halfway in her chair so she could see Anthony's face, she said, "I know we have our training meeting at eight thirty, but I don't have anything else on my calendar, so just let me know when you are ready."

There. *That sounded exactly like what a working adult would say*, Neale thought.

"Sure. Let me get my notes, and I'll come over to your desk," Anthony said with a smile. Looking at the small stack of neatly organized notebooks behind him, he selected a burgundy one, then grabbed a pen with equal care, despite the fact that every pen in his penholder was the same. Then he began pushing his chair toward Neale's cubicle. Instinctively, she wheeled herself a little off center so that he could also access her screen.

Settling himself next to her, Anthony said, "Ready to do this?"

"As I'll ever be," Neale answered, taking a big sip of her coffee.

"All right. Today we'll start with the basics of clearing a song for card usage."

"Okay. Our use? Or an outside vendor?" Neale asked, feeling just the tiniest bit proud that she remembered a detail from yesterday's breakfast. A feeling that was only exacerbated by Anthony smiling at her.

"Good question. Outside-vendor use. Although if we had the capability to produce a musical card, in theory we could also use this system. But that is another story." Anthony shook his head at the digression as if the idea frustrated him. Taking a clipped breath, he shrugged. "Anyway, let's start by opening the server."

Biting back curiosity about what it took to actually make a singing card, Neale dutifully clicked on the internet browser icon, then waited.

For a moment, Anthony looked confused, then sheepish, before saying, "Ah. We still host our shared drive on an internal server. Go back to your desktop."

Neale didn't claim to have any great knowledge of computers, but even she had to question what a company was still doing using internal servers decades after the birth of the internet. Even her mother, analog queen that she was, used an internet shared drive. Deciding now was not the time to ask for an explanation, Neale clicked back to the desktop and selected the only folder that was currently on her home screen.

"Well done," Anthony said, genuinely sounding pleased that she had done the most basic step. Neale was loath to admit it, but after months of the Collective critiquing her every choice, she was delighted to receive any workplace praise at all. Even if it was for clicking something. "Now we are going to click on the 'Clearance' file."

As Neale proceeded to move through click after click, she had two thoughts. The first was that she liked Anthony's speaking voice; in contrast to the sharp angles of his face, his voice was melodic and gentle. Like a living version of the New Agey encouragement podcasts that Billie would never admit to listening to publicly, although her podcatcher was full of them.

The second was that literally every step of what was shaping up to be a fairly boring task was the most manual and time-consuming version of what could possibly be done. By the time Anthony had finished with the second copy-and-paste-the-date-and-time-into-a-spreadsheet-then-hit-save explanation, Neale had wanted to scream, *Please get a tracking software.*

Instead, she quietly sat clicking and growing increasingly anxious that she wouldn't be able to read her fifteen pages of notes, which basically amounted to sending a request to the music publisher, getting a form signed and countersigned, and confirming the payment method so the song could go in a card. The whole system was a mess of details that should come together much more elegantly than they did.

"So those are the basics. Any questions?" Anthony asked, clapping his hands together and drawing Neale's attention away from the screen. Looking closely at his hands, she could see the hint of a tattoo peeking out from under his cuff. Neale squinted at it, trying to make out what the delicate lines of black ink against dark-brown skin could be. "Neale?"

She forced her attention away from his arm, mentally berating herself. Neale had almost completed the entire training session without letting her mind wander, only to have her attention span snatched away at the last second by a tattoo she shouldn't even be interested in. Blinking twice, she said the first thing that came to mind. "Why is every task so manual?"

"Oh." The single syllable sounded like a laugh as Anthony's eyebrows shot up unexpectedly. He leaned back in his chair to see around Neale, then popped up quickly, looking left to right, before sitting back down. Leaning toward her, Anthony dropped his voice to barely above a whisper and said, "A few years ago we had a liquidity scare."

"Liquidity scare?" Neale asked.

Anthony held up a hand, motioning for her to bring her voice down as he looked around the room to make sure no one else was listening. "We should whisper. I'm probably not supposed to tell you this. But one of the big vendors stopped using us for rights clearing, and we almost didn't, you know . . ." Anthony stopped talking and used his shushing hand to make some sort of circular gesture.

As a matter of fact, Neale didn't know. She also didn't really know how good she was at whispering, so she made her eyes wide and shook her head hard enough to make her hair fall over her shoulder. Leaning in toward him, she shrugged, hoping he'd understand her miming.

Anthony sighed, "We almost didn't make it."

"I see," Neale mouthed. Catching Anthony's paranoia, she looked over her shoulder to make sure Rich's door was still closed before attempting to whisper, "But what about now?"

"What? You are just moving your mouth," Anthony said, still leaning in conspiratorially, laughter playing with the edges of his full lips.

"Sorry, I'm bad at whispering." Neale tried to say this in a soft voice.

Anthony blinked at her for just a moment, then straightened up and tilted his head back, letting out a bark of a laugh.

"Don't laugh. It's a skill I never developed. You don't know. If you had my parents, you wouldn't whisper either. It is basically impossible—"

"Sorry, sorry," Anthony said, his laughter dying down to a half-hearted chuckle. "I mean, it's just . . . who doesn't know how to whisper?"

"You only think that because you haven't met anyone related to me. Even my grandmama can't whisper. It makes going to church a mess," Neale said, rolling her eyes. After popping up to make sure Melissa and Travis still had their headphones on, she sat back down quickly. Raising one eyebrow, she attempted a meaningful nod and added, "Tell me what happened."

Leaning back in as if they hadn't just established that Neale wasn't capable of whispering, Anthony said, "We survived, but barely. Now, Rich is more careful. He scrimped on every penny to start this new line. It's a big gamble, hiring you to take stuff off my plate so I can draw, plus the actual investment in the cards, but if it pays off, Happy Hearts will have a better diversified income stream and be more secure. Hence all the manual stuff. He is afraid to invest and have us come up short if it doesn't pan out."

"I get it." Neale went silent, letting Anthony's words sink in. As she glanced down at her lap and back again, a question snagged on the edges of her mind. "Are our in-house cards the ones on the fridge?"

"Yes." Anthony's smile was fleeting, as if he had tried to swallow it rather than let Neale see its light. But too late: Neale knew pride when she saw it, and Anthony was secretly proud of those cards.

"Did you draw all of those? They are very pretty." She watched the smile try to escape its container once more.

Anthony looked down at his hand. "They're no big deal."

"Yes, they are. No one wants my art on their fridge," Neale said, the self-deprecating joke halfway out of her mouth before she realized how much the truth of it stung. Truly, no one wanted her art. That was why she had this job in the first place. Shaking off the hurt, she added, "Your work is lovely. Do the cards sing?"

"No. I wish," Anthony said, looking wistfully over at her.

"You wish?" Neale said, fighting to keep the horror out of her words. Secretly she wondered why the high-pitched versions of disco songs that jumped out of those cards were so desirable. But given Anthony's reaction, she was clearly in the minority. Apparently, a screeching golden oldie in paper format was something to aspire to.

"Well, yeah. It's the most unique kind of card. Everyone remembers getting one of those. It would be fun to have my art on something like that."

"Right." Neale hoped she was better at sounding convinced than she was at whispering.

Anthony looked at her, his head tilted slightly to the left as if he were about to say something, when the sound of Susan shuffling down the hall caused both of them to jump, eyes wide at the prospect of being heard. Anthony laughed as Neale tried her best not to side-eye Susan. Clearing his throat, he said, a little too loudly, "So anyway. That's how clearing songs works."

Neale grinned. Anthony might have been able to whisper, but when it came to sneaking around, he was about as subtle as any Delacroix living. Which was to say, not subtle at all.

"Thanks for showing me how to do this," Neale said, placing extra emphasis on *how* and making sure her voice would be loud enough for Susan to hear even if she were located in the Grand Canyon and not over by the supply cupboard.

"Glad to see you recovered from the ink . . . ," Anthony said, his smile sly as he stood up, his gaze flipping delicately between her plain desk space and Susan as he searched for a polite word to use.

"Fiasco?" Neale offered, cheerfully. If she had learned anything from the fire incident, it was that she was better off just telling it like it was. No amount of cute branding would save her ink-covered face on this one. "I've also been calling it the Smurf-blender incident."

Anthony coughed, belatedly trying to cover a laugh.

"I can admit it: I looked like a Smurf. You just looked like the guy standing next to a Smurf when it suffered some sort of unfortunate kitchen accident."

This time Anthony didn't even try to hide his laughter. Neale grinned up at him as his joy filled the room. Pulling himself together, he turned his smile back on Neale, and she fought the urge to tell him to point that thing somewhere else. Preferably at someone who wasn't trying to get their life together.

"Well, I'm glad the Smurf-blender incident didn't send you packing." Grabbing the back of his chair, Anthony began rolling it back toward his desk, before stopping to add, "Let me know if you have any questions about what I just showed you or about anything else in the office."

"Will do," Neale said, smiling against her better judgment. Sure, this job seemed like it might be boring as hell. But at least one of her coworkers had a sense of humor. And a tattoo that she was curious about.

CHAPTER NINE

Neale rolled over, the rubber of her air mattress groaning as she fumbled for her phone on the floor. Cracking one eye, she looked at the time: 6:11 a.m. Whoever thought they should text her at the crack of dawn could rot in the special part of purgatory that was reserved for jerks who disrupted sleep patterns and people who got antsy in line at the bank. Objectively, Neale knew she needed to get up. But she also knew that she had roughly fourteen more minutes of sleep before Corinne's alarm clock blared out Pachelbel's Canon at decibels that made the classical music piece feel like the soundtrack to a horror movie.

Ignoring the text, she mentally committed her next paycheck to buying some furniture and ear plugs, before rolling over on her squeaky mattress and drifting back to sleep until the aggressive theme of brides everywhere assaulted her ears and sent her heart rate soaring. Neale listened to the sound of Corinne grumbling as she slapped at her bedside table, loudly missing the offending clock's snooze button. Forcing herself out of bed, Neale shuffled to the bathroom to take a first pass at waking up. After using the toilet, she washed her hands and splashed water on her face, getting halfway through drying it off before she realized that she had never actually used her face wash. She needed coffee.

Drying off for the second time, Neale felt her thoughts start to assemble. Who had texted her anyway? Noting that Corinne was still in the grousing stage of her morning routine, she shuffled back to her room and reached down for her phone and the offending text message. Blinking at the screen, Neale read the name and felt detestation slip into her bones. *Darin.*

Clicking on the little text icon, Neale let her eyes adjust to the phone's glow, then read,

Hey! I heard you moved in with Morrigan's friend? Glad that worked out for you.

For a moment, Neale froze, unsure of what to do. She hadn't expected to hear from Darin again—after all, calling someone talentless did feel like a great way to end a nonrelationship—but there he was, his benign text glowing up at her, as if they were still friends. How did she even respond to that?

Her heart ached. The text felt a little like an olive branch, like the move someone would make before they launched an apology at you. Maybe now that he'd had a little time to reflect, he felt differently about her art . . . or maybe just her in general. They did use to have fun together.

Not that it matters, Neale reminded herself. Darin was a symptom, not the cause of Neale's current problems. No olive branch in the world was going to send her back to Old Neale with the ruined career and the broken heart. Exhaling, she opted for what she hoped was a polite dismissal.

I did. Thanks for checking in.

Letting her phone fall to her mattress, she forced Darin from her mind and tried to focus on the day ahead. Shuffling toward the kitchen, she was pleased to find Corinne, clad in leopard-print jammies, already fussing with the coffee maker.

"Morning," Neale mumbled, edging her way toward the fridge.

"Good morning," Corinne singsonged. This was a marvel to Neale. Her roommate spent a solid five to ten minutes every morning cussing out her alarm clock, but as soon as she left her bedroom, she was bright and happy as a summer day. "Want some coffee?"

"Yes, thank you," Neale answered, yanking some half-and-half out of the fridge.

Since leaving the comfort of her parents' house, Neale had discovered that while she enjoyed not hearing her father's collection of obscure funk records at all hours of the day and night, she did miss the fancy coffee. Unlike Dylan, neither she nor Corinne was making Cruise Coffee House Blend money, and so she was forced to explore the world of whatever was lower on the shelf than Don Francisco. Neale didn't consider herself much of a coffee snob, but she could safely say that the last month of spending all her own money on food had taught her something new about her tastes.

So much for being part of the proletariat, Neale thought, throwing a heavy dose of cream into her coffee mug as Corinne began pouring. Grabbing a PowerBar out of the cupboard, she took her coffee and padded over to the table, her roommate trailing behind.

"I heard you grumbling to yourself," Corinne said, sipping her not–Don Francisco. "Everything okay?"

"Sorry," Neale said, swallowing her first sip of coffee as quickly as she could. Her current theory was that the coffee was palatable if she could drink it while it was still hot enough to scald her taste buds.

"No need to be sorry. I know I say all kinds of silly nonsense when I wake up."

Neale thought that calling Corinne's alarm clock word choice *silly* was an understatement but decided that two months into her new roommate situation was not the time to point out that a sailor would blush if they heard her language.

"Just this guy I used to hang out with texting me. I don't even know why."

"Predictable. Dudes always do stuff like that," Corinne said, taking a much slower sip of coffee than Neale would have advised, then shook her head and said, "So how was dinner with your sister?"

"It was fun. Turns out my middle sister is back in town. Apparently, she decided that the Los Angeles show she was working on was 'a giant, tacky, goth version of the Museum of Ice Cream' or something like that." Neale rolled her eyes and used air quotes around her sister's description of her abandoned show before continuing. "Anyway, it was wild because someone actually recognized her from an interview that she did with *Art Wire*, and they paid our tab."

"Nice," Corinne said, wiggling her eyebrows at Neale's luck before pausing. "Wait, your sister is famous? Like, famous how? Which sister?"

Neale smiled. She had to appreciate that Corinne's first thought was about Neale's free food and not her sister's fame. "Billie. And she is art-world famous. Not, like, Hollywood famous. In fact, basically my whole family is. Except for me. And my sister Dylan, but she is a weirdo."

"That's cool. So your whole family is famous? For what kind of art?" Corinne asked, her speech getting faster with each question.

Wincing down another sip of coffee, Neale gingerly picked her way through her jumbled morning thoughts and said, "My mom is mostly known for painting. My dad is known for factory art—think like Warhol or Koons, or Michelangelo but with less religion and only four assistants instead of thirty. He is the guy who did the large-scale pocket watch outside of the Columbia Center—the tower on Fifth," she added, as if that were the detail Corinne would need more than the fact that her dad's work was literally in every corner of the city. "Then Billie started out as a painter like Mom, but she didn't blow up until she started collaborating with other mixed-media artists, like me. Or like I used to be." Neale stopped to wave her hand in front of her face as if she could push her confused words and her old identity away, before finishing, "Anyway, now she puts together these variety shows inspired by her work."

"You aren't an artist anymore?" Corinne said, leaning forward like she was watching a soap opera instead of her groggy roommate slugging down medium-bad coffee.

"I just decided to move on after I left the Collective." Neale softened the blow to her ego by leaving out the video. She could mention that later. Like, right before she walked out the door. Or sometime next week. Or maybe never.

"I don't understand. You can't make art because you were fired? It's not like the Collective controls you," Corinne asked, her tone implying that she was offended on Neale's behalf.

"Eh, it's more complex than that," Neale said, sinking into her chair as she searched for a way to explain the labyrinthian world of making a living in fine art. She considered stalling with another sip of coffee but decided it was better just to try talking through it. "Early-career artists survive off of group shows. Some of these shows are arranged by an art dealer, others by nonprofits, like the Collective. Artists do this until there are enough potential buyers to merit their own show. In this case, the Collective was sort of like a combo employer and peer group, since they gave me a small stipend to live as well as a place to start. No one is going to commission me, show my stuff, or buy serious works without their blessing."

"Well, I say forget them. Can you be a solo artist? Like when Beyoncé left Destiny's Child?"

Neale smirked. She didn't have the heart to say that in real life, she was less like Beyoncé and more like the singers that had gotten kicked out of Girls Tyme after losing on *Star Search*. Standing to put her half-empty coffee mug in the sink, she said, "I mean, technically yes. But it was a bad enough experience that I'm pretty sure this was God's way of getting me to see the light."

Corinne frowned, following Neale's lead and standing up, coffee mug in hand. "Or maybe it was God's way of telling you to move on?"

"Yeah, do yourself a favor and google *Bad Art, Big Fire*. I think you'll understand then." Neale tried to smile, but the muscles in her face felt frozen in something closer to a grimace.

"I don't know anything about art," Corinne said, taking Neale's mug from her hand, dumping the remaining coffee out, and leaving both mugs to soak in the sink. "But I bet you just need a new idea."

"Nah, I'm done making art. Really, I'm okay with it," Neale said, reading Corinne's skepticism. "It's time for me to grow up." Neale's laugh sounded hollow as she grabbed a banana off the counter. Looking over at the clock, she said, "I better get ready for work. Trust me—watch the video on your break or something. Do it when you need a laugh."

Shuffling down the hall, Neale waited until she was safely in her bedroom with the door shut before she let her shoulders drop. A small part of her wanted to believe that Corinne was right. That all she needed was a new idea. But the truth was, Neale also needed talent. And if that video proved anything, it was that she was long on ideas and very short on whatever talent made the rest of her family so successful.

Walking over to the moving boxes she was using as a dresser, she began rifling through the deeply boring wardrobe she had liberated from Dylan's closet. Pushing aside the bright, off-kilter clothes she used to love, she settled on a short-sleeved black blouse and an equally black skirt. Giving up neon knits and fun plaids for button-downs was a good thing. In fact, if dreary clothes were the only price to pay for becoming New Neale, she could live with that. No matter how dull it sounded, Neale would rather be boring five times over than be the girl in the video again.

~

Neale carefully typed the date and time on the licensing form into the master spreadsheet. If it was possible to die of tedium, she was likely to keel over at any minute. The first two weeks on the job had been so new that Neale was able to sort of look past the extreme boredom that accompanied entering data into a spreadsheet all day. In week three, she had managed to convince herself that walking to and from the copy machine and the filing cabinets was better than the gym because she could listen to podcasts. But now, almost a month into the job, Neale had run out of ways to convince herself this was anything other than drudgery. A small but vocal corner of her brain suggested that she missed being an artist, but Neale ignored its words, as usual. After all, anytime she even sketched a piece out, traumatic memories washed over her like cold, salty waves in the Pacific. It was still too soon to think about art as far as she was concerned.

Really, a day job was better for her. She liked her coworkers, minus Susan, and surely there had to be some way to make this less terrible. Otherwise, no amount of short stories read by LeVar Burton could possibly keep her from losing her mind. Or what was left of it, anyway.

Stealing a glance at Anthony, she watched as his left hand danced lightly over some sketch, careful not to smudge whatever he was working on. She had realized that the arm that had the tattoo was also his writing hand, and it made her smile. Lefties were rumored to be sinister, and the idea of an evil greeting card designer amused her to no end. In fact, over the course of the last week, she had been trying to find a way to bring up an idea of Halloween cards that played dirges, just to see if he'd go for it.

Not that dirges were possible, since singing cards were out of their price range. Talk about irony. Neale snorted and tried to turn her attention to the spreadsheet. Using the soothing tones of LeVar Burton as her anchor, she began. Left-click. Type date. Right arrow to the next column.

It was just . . . why were the cards so expensive to produce? How hard could it be to find some sort of singing mechanism and cram it between two pieces of paper? Surely someone on the internet had already figured this out. She could just—

No. Neale cut the thought off, abruptly. Her job was to serve as a go-between for music companies and card companies. That was it. It had taken her weeks to find a place that would even hire her. She wasn't there to get new product lines going. Her job was to type the date into a box. *To be fair*, she thought, *this process could honestly be automated.* Probably with an app on her phone, which would leave time—

Nope. She shook her head. Neale did not need to be creative in this job. Look where creativity had gotten her. Recognized in the grocery store for all the wrong reasons. For years, she had been so careful with her art. Never sharing herself with the wrong people or in the wrong place. Neale had guarded her talent like it was gold until her parents encouraged her to apply for the Collective. And when she'd finally, truly put her creativity out there, she'd had her heart stomped into a zillion glittering pieces.

No, she reasoned. She wasn't going to change a single thing. Neale would stick to the plan. She was good at putting numbers in a spread-sheet. She should just leave it that way.

Neale took a deep breath and forced herself to focus on the next piece of paper that needed entering. Exhaling, she looked over her shoulder, then clicked to YouTube. She would just watch a video of how they put together those cards. Once she knew that, she'd probably know why this was so hard, and she could let the singing cards go.

"Hey, Neale."

Swallowing a startled cry into a squeak, she glanced over her cubicle wall to find Rich, looking as surprised as she felt. Neale tried to coax her heart out of her throat while flipping away from the video. Managing a breathy exhale, she said, "You scared me."

"Sorry. I should have known. You did look laser focused." Rich nodded solemnly. "What are you doing?"

For a moment, Neale wondered if there was any way she could lie and say that she was pecking at spreadsheets. She had lost track of time and watched at least five card videos, and the actual manufacturing didn't seem that difficult. If only she knew how long her boss had been standing there. According to Dylan, the first rule of a workplace fib was that it had to be within the realm of possibility. She had meant it in the context of telling Neale she couldn't call in sick with the excuse that aliens had abducted her, but it probably applied here too. Sighing, she gave up searching for a realistic excuse and said, "Trying to understand how singing cards are made."

"Oh. I have a diagram in my office if you want to take a look." Rich shrugged, and Neale realized that his understanding of why she was researching the cards and her reason for looking into how they were made were two different things. She could just shut her mouth and go back to being a spreadsheet drone. No harm done.

Except that she had more questions burning a hole in her mind. Had they tried to make their cards sing? If so, did they just not sell? Or was there some sort of Hallmark conspiracy keeping the little man out of the card game?

"I'm just trying to figure out if there is a way we could make our own cards sing." Neale heard herself say this before she realized that she had given her brain permission to speak.

From over at his desk, Neale saw Anthony start listening to their conversation. He was too polite to turn around and openly eavesdrop, but his hand had stopped moving, and he had tilted his head ever so slightly to catch her and Rich's words better.

"Well," Rich said, his eyebrows slowly retracting down his forehead in surprise, "mostly because the volume of cards we'd sell wouldn't generate a significant enough discount on the card parts that we'd need to be competitive at market rates. Let alone the cost of licensing."

"But what if there was a way to do it? I'm not saying we have to be in every store across the country, but what if we just started small?" Neale said, worrying her bottom lip with her teeth.

At this point, Anthony stopped pretending to have qualms about listening to other people's conversations and began to rotate his chair around.

"I mean, if there was a way, that would be great." Rich shrugged.

"It seems like it'd be worth looking into," Neale said, clasping her hands behind her back to keep from fidgeting. From over Rich's shoulder, Melissa wrinkled her nose while Travis arched one eyebrow. Neither look was very encouraging, but it was too late for Neale to back out now.

Rich pursed his lips to one side as if trying to think through how to respond to Neale's suggestions. Her heartbeat sped up to double time, and she kicked herself. What on earth had made her feel like she needed to start suggesting things a month into a new job? She had a perfectly good, albeit deeply boring, setup here, and now she was about to blow it just because she was tired of the copy-paste function.

Relaxing his face, Rich opened his mouth, but Anthony was faster. "We haven't looked at the numbers in a year."

In that moment, Neale could have hugged Anthony. Sure, she knew almost nothing about him except that he looked good in pastel button-ups, but that didn't matter as she watched Rich return to his thinking face.

"Now that I am getting the hang of this job, I can see a few places where I might be able to make things speed up. You know, like process improvements," Neale rambled, waving her hand in a circular gesture and wishing she'd read more self-help books on communication in the workplace. Or at least the job tips in the magazines at the nail salon. Shaking the thought away, she continued, "Maybe with my extra time, I could, you know, look into the whole singing card manufacturing . . . thing."

Neale let her hand fall to her side and watched as Rich mulled the idea over. Glancing from Rich to Anthony, she made momentary eye contact. Just enough to catch Anthony's quiet smile and nod as the seconds ticked by slower than hours.

"I could help her out," Anthony said, his smile widening as he neatly folded his hands in his lap, rocking ever so slightly in his swivel chair.

Rich shrugged again, the tension leaving his face as all the good-natured dad energy returned. "All right. Let me know what you find. And I'm excited about these process improvements."

"Wonderful. We can go over them in our one-on-one meeting next week," she said, forcing herself to sound excited as Rich walked back toward his office. She hadn't really thought past *there has to be an app for that* when she'd made up the thing about process improvements, but now that she'd committed to it, she guessed she'd better spend some time in the app store tonight.

Oh God, Neale thought, cutting her wandering mind off. She was turning into the kind of person who took work home, and it had only been a month. She shuddered. Operation New Neale was working a little too well.

"Excited to work with you, partner." Anthony's gentle voice floated toward her, interrupting her newfound work-life-balance spiral.

"Me too. Time to get started on your singing card dream." Neale smirked, turning to see how her joke about his dream landed, and stopped.

Something in Anthony's demeanor had changed from helpful coworker to sex god. From his desk, his gaze roamed over her, and a thrill rushed through her body. Her mind clouded over as she watched the gleam in his eyes, the intensity of his single hot up and down making her pulse race. As his full lips parted, Neale gave up on keeping her more base urges at bay, letting every naughty thought she'd ever had about his mouth run freely through her mind.

"It's not the only dream I have about Happy Hearts, but it's a place to start," he said with a naughty smile, before he turned to face his computer without another word.

Just like that, the spell he had her under was broken. Neale paused in front of her computer screen as she tried to process whatever had just passed between them. She'd been out of the game for a minute, so there was a chance her imagination had run away with her, but a not-so-insubstantial part of her also thought that Anthony had been checking her out. And that, just maybe, his dreams about Happy Hearts weren't the innocent kind. She wondered if they involved her, because it seemed like they might. Or at least her dreams about Happy Hearts involved him, whether or not she wanted them to.

Then again, would someone that polite really be checking out a coworker and using double entendres?

Shaking her head, she exhaled and turned her attention back to her computer. She knew where this line of thinking was headed. Hell, she'd just gotten a text from an old "coworker" this morning. She didn't need to let her imagination run away with her. If anything, she needed to get her head on straight and keep it there. She would just have to get used to Anthony's looks. In fact, if she was going to make the whole singing card thing happen, she had to get used to them.

CHAPTER TEN

Neale stared at the photo of her two deeply sweaty sisters on social media and felt a pang of jealousy. When she had declined to go to what Dylan insisted on calling "sister workout" at 6:00 a.m. this morning, she hadn't realized that Billie was going to be there. The Billie of old despised gyms. She wouldn't even consider stepping foot in one. As far as Billie and Neale had been concerned, the gym was all Dylan's domain. And yet, here was photographic evidence that Billie had been there . . . in chartreuse spandex, which would have been awful on anyone less cool. Neale wrinkled her nose at her two older sisters, who grinned back up at her, looking like stylish spin-class goddesses who'd just won the success lotto.

Reluctantly, Neale double tapped to like the picture, then set the phone down. She knew it was unreasonable to feel left out of the successful-sister club, especially since she had been invited to the workout and declined because only monsters chose spin over sleep. Of course, that didn't stop her from feeling miffed.

Neale drummed her fingers on the countertop as she waited for the ancient office microwave to work its tired magic on her diet freezer meal. At the grocery store, a three-for-six-dollars special had seemed like a good deal and a way to save time making lunches. Now that she was faced with the scrawny reality of a frozen delicacy, Neale was beginning to think that she was owed at least three dollars back from that sale.

The sound of her silenced phone vibrating against the plastic counter-top summoned Neale, and she was grateful to whoever had texted her for distracting her from the inevitable disappointment that awaited whenever this meal finally finished heating up.

Opening the next message, Neale frowned as Darin's name came up.

I've been thinking, and I feel bad about our miscommunication. Want to get coffee and talk about it?

So much for giving him the polite brush-off, Neale thought. What did he mean, *miscommunication?* As far as Neale was concerned, there was no miscommunication. He'd been perfectly clear about her being "talentless" and them "not dating." In fact, she would say that when it came to crushing her dreams and breaking her heart, he'd been top-shelf-crystal clear. The guy was basically Waterford. Where he hadn't been clear was deceiving her into thinking that they'd had a real relationship built on mutual respect in the first place.

"Nope McNopersons!" Neale said, looking back down at the text and deciding she would just not answer. *How's that for miscommunication?* she thought, letting a smug smile cross her face.

Neale decided her food was likely hot enough and pressed the button to release the latch door before carefully removing the little plastic tray with the tips of her fingers. She had learned the hard way earlier in the week that those little black trays tended to be hotter than the food inside, and she was not eager to burn her fingers again. Popping the tray on top of the cardboard packaging for her Spicy Red Enchilada with Fiesta Rice, Neale fished a fork and knife out of the communal silverware drawer and carried her tray to the conference room. She'd noticed that Travis and Melissa tended to eat at their desks, but she found that after several hours of copying and pasting, if she didn't get a brain break, the rest of her day went from foggy to downright invisible after lunch.

Pushing the conference room door open, Neale hesitated as Susan looked up from her lunch box and a section of the newspaper. For a brief moment, she thought the woman was going to move some of the newspaper out of the way so that she could have a seat. After an awkward heartbeat in which Susan did more glaring than moving, Neale got the hint.

"Sorry. Didn't realize you were in here. I'll go."

Susan grunted something that could have been a curse, a word of thanks, or a made-up language as Neale closed the door, unsure of where to go next. There was a sad little picnic bench next to a scraggly bush by the side of the building that was closest to the freeway. Neale assumed that people didn't eat there because watching trucks whizzing by wasn't exactly an appetizing ambience, but the alternative was either trying to sweep Fiesta Rice off her keyboard or having her car smell like red sauce for the next forty-eight hours. She decided to give the old picnic bench a try. If all else failed, she could always put on some music to drown out the traffic and breathe through her mouth so she didn't have to smell the exhaust.

Holding her head up, Neale marched out into the watery May sunlight, carefully making her way to the shady corner of the building. Giving the picnic table an appraising look, Neale did her best to step over the bench seat in her pencil skirt before setting her food down. Sure, it wasn't exactly fancy, but it wasn't covered in bird poop, either, so she'd take it.

Neale began poking at the tough exterior of her enchilada and tried not to stew on Susan. It wasn't like she had been rude to the woman. Or at least, not rude as far as she knew. Maybe Susan had some special thing where she was offended if people mentioned her plants too soon, or maybe she—

"Hey, mind if I join you?"

Neale's head shot up; she was startled to find Anthony standing in front of her, backlit by the sun as if he were some sort of beautiful god in a Renaissance painting. Heat flooded her senses, and somewhere in the back of her mind, Neale was vaguely aware that she needed to either speak or close her mouth while she was ogling.

Not that she was ogling. People recovering from epic life melt-downs didn't ogle. This was basically scientific curiosity. Closing her mouth, she cleared her throat to make sure her vocal cords still worked, then said, "Yup. Yes. Sure. Of course. Have a seat."

Anthony smiled as he sat down, and Neale began kicking herself. How many words did she need to answer affirmatively? And did one of them need to be *yup*?

"I rarely see anyone eating at this table, but today's weather is nice, and I saw you, and I thought, *That's a good idea. I should join her*," Anthony said.

Neale was grateful that he was looking down to unwrap his sand-wich. Better to have those brown eyes pointed elsewhere until she could pull the smile off her face. "Someone was already eating in the confer-ence room, so I thought I'd try outside."

"Someone?" Anthony asked, raising a skeptical eyebrow before tak-ing a bite of his sandwich.

"Don't look at me like that," Neale said.

"I'm not looking at you like anything," Anthony said, looking mischievous.

Neale exhaled loudly, giving in to his questioning brows. "Okay, fine. Someone is Susan, and I don't know why, but she hates me. Do you know what I did to her?"

"Don't feel bad. Susan hates everyone. She is just extra grouchy with the new people. She'll get used to you eventually."

"How long did it take her to warm up to the last new person?" Neale asked, cautiously optimistic that her torment might end sooner rather than later.

"It took Travis about two years, so you don't have too much longer to wait." Anthony smirked.

"Wow. That's reassuring. Thanks, friend," Neale said, making sure to add a sarcastic smile to her words as she pushed her rapidly cooling food to the side.

"What are friends for?" Anthony's features relaxed into a smile as he turned his attention back to his sandwich.

Taking another bite of her now-lukewarm food, mostly to avoid staring, Neale wondered about the mystery man in front of her. Outside of the fact that he was a talented artist, she really didn't know much about him. Not how he'd started drawing. How he'd even found this job. Where he was from, or—

"Did you make the calendar on your desk?" Neale said, half surprising herself as she asked the question that had been rolling around in the back of her mind for weeks.

Anthony looked up, blinking a few times with the abrupt turn of the conversation. Unhurried, he swallowed his bite of sandwich, wiping his mouth in an oddly genteel fashion before speaking. "No. It's from this parkour nonprofit I volunteer for."

"I'm sorry?" Neale said, in case she'd misheard him over the freeway traffic.

"Do you know parkour?" Anthony asked, brushing crumbs from his hands.

"You mean the French sport where people launch themselves off of park benches and buildings?" Neale asked, trying not to let skepticism creep into her voice.

Apparently, her attempt wasn't that successful, because Anthony smirked. It was the kind of face people wore when they knew you were trying your best, but you were way off course. "That is one way to think about it."

"I.e., not how anyone who actually does the sport thinks about it?" Neale said with a chuckle as she scooped up the last of her Fiesta Rice. She was going to be hungry again in an hour; she could feel it.

Anthony laughed. "The word comes from the French phrase for *obstacle course.*"

"Which is different from a park bench how?"

"Well, there are a lot of different ideologies around the activity, so we could talk about this all day."

"Okay, give me the CliffsNotes. How do you approach parkour?" Neale asked, playfully batting her eyelashes. She was vaguely aware that her demeanor might have been construed as flirty.

"You really want to know?" Shrugging with his full body, Anthony said, "All right, then. I like to think of parkour more as a fitness philosophy where everyday objects are your gym. My goal, when I practice, is to imagine new ways to interact with my environment."

"Can you give me an example?" Neale asked, still smiling. She reasoned that there was no world in which anyone could plausibly think she was being flirty about running at a wall.

Anthony's smile began to spread as he talked about different ways to get from point A to point B in any given space. The more he said, the more animated he became, his naturally soft-spoken words rushing to get out of him as if they were doing backflips off his lips. As he wove through the intricacies of his fitness routine, Neale found herself leaning in. She had no intention of climbing up a wall, but she couldn't help enjoying his enthusiasm as he described the training method.

Taking a deep breath, he slowed down his explanation of how the military had incorporated aspects of parkour into its training—because the spatial-navigation techniques had proved particularly useful for soldiers in combat situations—and looked around as if he were surprised to find Neale still sitting there. Looking a bit sheepish, he added, "Anyway, that is a little bit about it, I guess. If you want to see what it looks like, the organization I volunteer with is putting on an event next weekend."

Was he asking her out? Neale's heart rate spiked with her thoughts, her face getting hot. She liked Anthony. Thought he was cute, even. Okay, *cute* was downplaying what was in front of her. He was a stone-cold fox.

But she wasn't about to give up New Neale just when she had finally managed to stop being a screwup. Workplace romances always went sideways, and if this one did, she would absolutely have to find a new job. And then she probably wouldn't be able to make rent, and she would have to beg to sleep on Dylan's couch and live off eating Girl Scout Cookies, all because of her inability to make wise dating choices, and—

"I mean as friends. Melissa and Travis will be there too," Anthony added, furrowing his brow and interrupting her thoughts.

Spreading a smile tight across her face, Neale felt her heart rate plummet. "I'd be delighted to see what 'the philosophy of engaging with the environment in new ways' looks like." Neale used air quotes so Anthony knew she wasn't taking herself too seriously, then smiled, pushing aside the twinge of disappointment that prickled at the back of her mind. Sure, she hadn't wanted the trouble of a workplace romance, but did she really scream *friend zone* that loudly? On the upside, she had been doing her very best to come off as Normal Workplace Person for a month now, and this was confirmation that it was working.

For a moment, Anthony looked surprised. Sputtering slightly, he said, "Okay, then. I'll, uh . . . I'll text you the information."

"Cool," Neale said, feeling slightly awkward. Looking around, she realized they had been outside for quite some time. She stood up and said, "We should probably head back inside."

"Yeah. Time to get back to the grind." Anthony rose and began neatly rolling up the paper that had wrapped his sandwich. Neale watched the gesture with a half smile. Just like his desk, Anthony cleaned up sandwich paper in an organized and detail-oriented manner, as if it were normal to treat the disposal of wrappers with such care. Looking up, he made eye contact with Neale, his lips matching the half smile on her face. "What?"

Trying not to stare, she squinted at the cars whizzing by on the overpass, giving her mind time to think of an excuse for watching him so closely. "Do you need my number?"

"I do," Anthony said, letting the other half of his smile catch up with the first as he retrieved his phone from his pocket. Looking down to unlock his phone, he said, "Whenever you are ready."

Neale doubted she would ever be ready for that smile, even in friend form, but she gave him her phone number anyway.

CHAPTER ELEVEN

Neale pulled up to the front of her parents' house and put the car in park, giving herself a second to breathe before she went inside. When she'd agreed to have dinner with Billie, she hadn't realized that her sister meant, *Come over and eat whatever is in Mom and Dad's fridge with me.* If she had, she might have suggested another location. For years, it felt like she and Billie had been a matching set as far as their parents were concerned, and all of a sudden they were being treated like different people. It wasn't that Neale was still upset about being forced to move out, but it did sort of feel like her parents had hustled her out of the house to make room for her sister. Billie was being given free rein while Neale got the boot, and that stung.

Stumbling her way up the overgrown path, Neale tried the door handle and found it locked. That added to the hurt. Since when did her parents lock the doors? She stared down at the keypad and racked her brain for the code until she could hear Milo whining on the other side of the door, accompanied by the sound of Billie asking the dog to pipe down. Billie swung the door open wide and grinned, pulling her sister into a warm hug before half dragging her across the threshold and into the dog-hair-covered hallway. "Neale!"

"Sorry. Got stuck in the five-o'clock traffic like all the other working stiffs," Neale said, peeling off her navy-blue cardigan and sinking down into her favorite armchair.

"I'll bet you get to listen to a lot of audiobooks, though," Billie said brightly, as Neale watched her try to suppress a shudder. Until recently, the idea of a day job had elicited the same response from Neale, but it was weird to see it on someone else's face.

"I do. I just finished that new biography on Thurgood Marshall," Neale said, pushing aside the feeling that she was being judged.

"I'll check it out," Billie called over her shoulder as she made her way toward the kitchen. Neale heard jars knocking against one another as her sister searched for something in the fridge. With a triumphant grunt, Billie returned, dropping down on the couch across from Neale with a plate full of their mother's nice cheese and crackers. "Don't worry; I left enough of her camembert in the fridge. She'll never notice we ate some."

Neale looked at the giant half wheel of cheese on the plate dubiously, then realized that the upside of Billie living here was that Neale wouldn't be the suspected thief of Bernice's snacks anymore. Shrugging, she picked up a cracker. "Eh, what Mom doesn't know won't hurt her. So how are you? It's nice to finally hang out; I feel like I haven't seen you in ages."

"I know! It's been weird, but I think I'm finally starting to make progress on the show after the whole LA mess, and—"

"Wait, what's the deal with that?" Neale interrupted, earning herself a sideways look from her sister.

"Like I said at dinner, the show just felt wrong. It was too big, and I was surrounded by all these strangers, and it just didn't feel like the magic was there." Billie stopped and shook her head, a gesture that looked oddly like a shiver. Whatever had gone wrong, it seemed like Billie wanted to talk about it almost as much as Neale wanted to throw a viewing party for the Fire Incident. "I just want this Seattle show to recoup Marceline's initial investment. Anyway, that's all behind me."

"Okay, but what actually happened?" Neale pushed.

"Dylan didn't tell you?"

"Tell me what?" Neale said, feigning interest in a cracker to hide her irritation. Just because Dylan knew something didn't mean that Neale did, as evidenced by the fact that Dylan had forgotten to mention that Billie was even coming home.

"It's not as big a deal as Marceline and Kelsea think it is." Billie rolled her eyes and reached for another cracker. "But basically, after a few weeks of talking to the LA assistants, I finally got inside of the venue, and . . . Neale, it looked like a Macy's gone wrong. I realized that I'm not ready to do a show like that. Or to manage fifteen assistants. I get that Marceline has a vision for my career, and mostly I agree with her."

"I don't get it. Marceline fronted all that money, and now it's just . . . gone?" Neale asked, trying not to panic as she thought about how outlandish Billie's choice must have seemed.

"Okay, well, that part was bad. But, Neale, it was too big. And the theater company we were partnering with wanted to add mirrors to my work—"

"Mirrors?" Neale said, wrinkling her nose.

"Yes. Gross. I know," Billie said, shrugging as if the whole thing were so obviously tacky that she'd had to back out. "Anyway, luckily Kelsea got me out of there, and Marceline gets it, but I can't go back to my New York venue because they are already staging something else, so I figured I'd come home and try and stage something in short order to bounce back."

"Wow." Neale managed to get the word out, despite the fact that she had nearly choked on a cracker. She couldn't imagine backing out of a paying gig, let alone one that massive. "Billie, how are you being so chill about this?"

"Trust me, Neale—if you saw that venue, you'd have walked away too. My work isn't meant to be supersized and stuck to a ceiling. But I'm okay now. You know how it goes; there are bound to be bumps and bruises in this life." Billie smiled, then stopped just long enough to scoop up a cracker before adding, "Anyway, enough about me. How goes it, sister mine? Are you running away to the tropics with the cute guy from work?"

Neale rolled her eyes at Billie, who gracelessly crammed a cracker into her mouth and grinned at her. "No. I haven't run off with Anthony, because I'm not running off with any man."

"Right. The whole New Neale thing."

"I'll have you know that I'm putting off such a great volume of disinterested vibes that he invited me to some parkour event and was very clear about it being a friendship invitation," Neale said, careful to keep her earlier bewilderment out of her tone.

Billie snorted and picked up a bite of cheese. "I believe he's as sincere about friendship as you are about leaving men behind."

"So, deeply committed, then?" Neale said, half laughing as she reached for the cheese knife. "I'm not joking. I'm done with men and art and—"

"Actually, about that," Billie said, rolling her eyes. "I've been thinking about it, and I don't think you should be done with art. I wasn't gonna mention it just now, but since we are already on the subject, I found a venue for my show, and I need help making decisions about stuff like projectors, lighting, and concessions. You keep texting me about how much you hate that stupid spreadsheet at work, and it got me thinking that you'd be perfect for the job of my assistant. Plus, it would give us a chance to hang out while we work."

Neale's eyes went wide with surprise before beginning to water, and she cleared her throat of the phantom cracker crumbs that attempted to choke her. Her armpits started to sweat, despite the fact that it was not more than sixty-three degrees outside. Just the idea of going anywhere near a performance venue made her nervous. She wanted to spend time with Billie, but hell, she didn't even think she could go to a concert for at least another six months. The whole idea made her want to break out in hives. "Why can't you ask Marceline? I thought you two were cool now."

"One, because she is still in LA cleaning up; two, because I am not her only client; and three, because she isn't my little sister."

Glancing carefully at her sister, Neale said, "Look, Billie, I'm super excited about your show, and I'm glad you are past the whole LA thing, but I don't think I can help. I'm already swimming with a new project at work—" Her speech was punctuated by her sister's derisive snort, and Neale fidgeted, hastily adding, "And besides, I'm pretty sure I'm performance art poison."

"I think you mean you are treading water at work. But in either case, I hardly think a fire mishap is poisonous. Come on, Neale, please. This venue is still so much bigger than the last one, and I could probably get Marceline to give you a cut of the ticket sales, so there'd be money in it for you. Please help me out. I don't want to work with strangers, and I promise it'll be fun."

"Okay, maybe not poison. But I'm certainly persona non grata around the Seattle art scene."

"Everyone already knows we're related. If your fear is causing my failure by association, I'm not entirely dependent on more good press to survive, so that's not a good reason to say no either."

"I don't know, Bill. I'm just not ready to be back on the art scene yet. I need time to heal."

"You've had plenty of time to heal. What you need to do is get back on the horse. And I need you. There's no way that I can pull this off without help. I want more creative control for this show, and I don't trust anyone else to help me execute my vision. Please, Neale. Please consider it." Billy dragged the word *please* out until it had about fifteen extra syllables.

"I never want to see a horse again. I'm considering not even going to Mom's show next month."

Billie glared at her. "Don't even think about skipping Mom's show. In fact, I'm going to pretend you didn't say that." Covering her ears, she sang *la la la*s over the sound of Neale's frustration. Billie glanced at Neale to be sure she was done talking, then put her hands down and said, "So anyway, what I'm hearing is, you want to sleep on it before saying yes. Correct?"

"No, you jerk. What I'm saying is no," Neale said, putting extra emphasis on *no*.

"Right, so we'll negotiate this later." Billie grinned, completely ignoring her little sister's vexed growl. Looking mischievously at her, she said, "We're out of camembert and crackers. Want to see what else we can scrounge up for dinner? I think Dad still has some of that expensive gourmet Thai food left over from his work lunch yesterday."

Neale weighed her options and decided to let Billie's insistence on her joining the show slide for now. Why fight when she could eat expensive Thai food she couldn't afford? Shrugging, Neale pushed herself out of the chair and reached for their empty appetizer plate. Looking at her sister, she said, "I hope he ordered some of that spicy larb."

"He didn't," Billy sighed. "But there is some pad see ew, some soup, and a spring roll. Split it with you?"

"Works for me," Neale said, pushing her concerns aside to focus on spending time with her sister. Nothing said family like plotting to steal someone else's leftovers.

~

Sadists invented spreadsheets, Neale thought, pushing a chunk of hair back over her shoulder and half swallowing a groan. They had to be the creators. Otherwise, the stupid formula would work. Instead, she was going to go into her time-saving process meeting and have nothing to show Rich but—

"Hey, Neale." Rich's voice interrupted her burgeoning internal diatribe. "I finished my call a little early. Any chance you'd want to start our meeting now? That might give me just enough time to go outside for lunch today."

Neale was on the verge of saying no when Rich chuckled at his own chained-to-his-desk joke. She cringed inwardly and hoped that even as New Neale, she never got to the place where eating at her desk and never seeing daylight were the norm. Incomplete spreadsheet or no, she should at least give him a chance to see the sun.

"Sure, just let me grab a few things," she said.

"Thanks. I'll be in my office whenever you're ready." Rich smiled, then walked with jaunty determination back to his office.

Sighing, Neale grabbed her battered phone and a bright-green file folder off her desk, then shuffled toward Rich's office. Out of the corner of her eye, she saw Anthony smile and give her a thumbs-up. Throughout the course of the week, she had been bouncing her singing card ideas off him, each one met with encouragement, enthusiasm, and a few well-placed questions. Now, she just hoped she could make all that hard work pay off.

After closing Rich's office door, she plopped down in the chair in front of him and tried not to stare at the myriad hokey greeting cards he had plastered to his office's back wall. Literally, the guy had so many that he had nearly wallpapered the place in *#1 Grandma*, *Happy Golden Anniversary*, and *My Deepest Condolences*.

Looking down at his desk, Neale spotted a photo of a French bulldog posed in a sweater under a Christmas tree and couldn't help but relax. It was the most dog-dad thing she had ever seen. In fact, a dog in a sweater was basically Rich's entire energy—loving and a little absurd. In her short time here, he'd remembered Melissa's mother's birthday and offered to proofread Travis's essay on Tolstoy for his classic-literature night class. Now that she knew him better, it wasn't a surprise that Rich had bet on Anthony's art to help rebuild his business despite its being risky. The guy was so friendly and encouraging he probably thought Susan was going to turn around and be good at her job any day now.

"So what can I do for you?" Rich said, leaning back in his chair and smiling affably, his question drawing Neale into the conversation and reinforcing the idea that she didn't need to be nervous.

"I was thinking we could start with those process improvements I mentioned. I'm hoping this will save all of us a lot of time and enhance the quality of our work so that we could consider pursuing the card-expansion idea you, me, and Anthony talked about."

"I'm all for better work. Tell me about your ideas." Rich smiled the exact sort of smile that her father used whenever she mentioned a new idea to him, as if he was concerned but too kind to show it.

Neale took a deep breath and sent out a small prayer to the gods of technology, then said, "So I've been thinking about the process of getting licensing agreements into the spreadsheet and documented and how manual that all is. Turns out there is software to track this stuff, so I've been testing apps out all week."

Neale watched Rich's forehead crinkle as he prepared to respond, then remembered the convincing evidence Anthony had helped her develop. Pulling out a sheet of paper from her file folder, she said, "To determine the likelihood of computer error versus human error, I went back through submission logs from seven years ago, and it looks like the computer is about fifteen percent more accurate than someone who's typing. See, here somebody used the publishing date 1973, but the year couldn't possibly have been 1973 because Luther Vandross didn't even put out 'Never Let Me Go' until 1993. So clearly that's a typing error. Then you can see here, the form was kicked back, and it delayed final payment on our end by nearly a month."

Neale paused to take in Rich's face, which had gone from dad encouraging to flat-out dad concerned. She couldn't believe she was anxious about this; it wasn't as if her new job required her to use fire. Beating back nerves, she squeezed her hands together in her lap and started again. "It would require an investment, but if we paid the twenty-four dollars and ninety-nine cents per month for the Dash Write app, we could map the form fields to the tracking spreadsheet, then scan the forms so it autoenters the information, and we'd be more accurate. And if we got a company iPad, we could just take pictures, so we wouldn't have to walk back and forth between the printer and the filing cabinet, so we'd save ourselves a boatload of staff hours, which saves money in the long run too."

Rich studied her for a moment, probably checking to make sure she was actually done speaking before trying to get a word in. Finally, he said, "It seems like you have done an impressive amount of research. Is this something anyone could learn to use?"

"Absolutely. Especially if we get one device that is designated for the app so we don't have to purchase multiple licenses right away. Further down the line, it might make sense for us to look at an entirely digital signing process. Our partners would have to be comfortable with the software we use, but that would save us even more time, plus the cost of ink and paper, and almost entirely eliminate error."

Neale tried to keep her excitement in check. She was this close to not spending eight hours a day being bored to tears. Silently, she vowed to do the absolute best she could to make the singing card thing happen. If she could succeed at that, who knew what else Rich would let her do with her day. She couldn't wait to tell Dylan about her success. Her sister would be delighted that she'd gotten her first workplace project green-lighted. She'd probably even tell her parents, although they likely wouldn't care. She could tell Corinne. And Anthony. He'd actually care . . .

Rich squinted at a corner of the office, probably working out the numbers in his head, and Neale tried to slow her whirling mind down as a little happy well burbled inside of her. She needed to put the brakes on her excitement just in case she didn't get Rich's final approval for her new project, or she risked being crushed by disappointment and doldrums. Just like with her art, it was better if she didn't get herself too wrapped up in this. The only thing sadder than having Darin and Dr. McMillan sit on her dreams until they cracked would be having her soul crushed by a spreadsheet.

"It's not cheap, but I can see the benefit. I say we get a year's trial of the time-saving software and see how it goes. If at any point it isn't working for us, we can just get rid of it and go back to the old way of doing things," Rich said, sounding tired but optimistic.

"Somehow, I don't think we're gonna want to go back," Neale said, trying to hide a smile.

"Why don't you have Susan order a used iPad; that way everyone can have access. Sound good?"

"It sounds amazing." Neale grinned, packing up her folder.

"Fantastic. Any other projects you want to talk about?" Rich asked, his face brightening now that he had finally committed to spending some money.

"Not right now. I'm just ready to get going on this project."

"All right, then. I look forward to a progress report," Rich said, standing up.

"I look forward to giving you one." Neale beamed as she stood up to follow Rich to the door.

Reaching for the door handle, Rich asked, "Unrelated, but how is the artwork going? Any new pieces you are working on?"

For a moment, Neale felt like the joy bubble inside of her had burst, leaving a weird, sticky mess in her throat that prevented her from making anything other than a gagging noise. Her eyes flipped toward the hall, where Travis, Melissa, and Anthony all stood huddled, temporarily silenced by their boss opening his office door. Internally, her mind spun and landed on the book that Dylan had given her, *The Successful Woman's Guide to the Modern Workplace*. Scanning her mental map for any helpful advice, Neale's brain landed on the chapter about personal lives. Clearing her throat, she said, "Nothing new from me.

However, my mom has a show coming up in a week. If you all are interested, I'd be happy to bring in the information. My mom loves meeting new people."

Neale cackled inside. There was nothing Bernice hated more than meeting new people. Except for maybe new people at her shows. But her coworkers didn't need to know that. She just needed a good deflection technique. Whoever Victoria Blake, PhD, was, her book did have some good advice around avoiding talking about oneself.

"I'd be interested," Anthony said, shaking Neale out of her self-congratulatory stance.

"Okay," Neale croaked as she watched Melissa and Travis nod along without offering a verbal commitment. When she had employed Dr. Blake's strategy, she hadn't actually thought through what would happen if someone wanted to attend. Rearranging her surprise into a smile, she said, "Great. I'll bring in a few gallery postcards so you all have the information."

Neale intentionally amended that thought. She would bring them in, assuming she could steal a few postcards without her mother noticing.

~

Neale stared at the can of paint in front of her, then at her roommate, and wondered if she'd made a mistake. When Corinne had suggested that the pair of them paint her room, Neale had been all for it. But now, at 8:00 p.m. on a Friday night, she was having second thoughts. Especially since, now that she was watching her roommate closely, Neale wasn't 100 percent convinced Corinne actually knew what she was doing, despite her reassurances.

Next to her, Corinne was practically vibrating off the floor with excitement, alternating between trying to cram her ratty Bob Marley T-shirt into some sort of social-media-worthy knot and poorly covering all of Neale's worldly possessions with plastic. Catching Neale's eye, she said, "Smile, Neale!" before busting out her phone and attempting a long-armed selfie.

Neale was fairly certain her grin looked more like a grimace. A suspicion that was only confirmed when Corinne looked at her phone and shook her head. Pulling her dark, shoulder-length hair into an effortless, chic, messy bun on the top of her head, she said, "We'll try again later. You ready to do this?"

"As I'll ever be," Neale said, staring dubiously at the roller brush in Corinne's hand. She wasn't usually a stickler for rules, but years of watching her mother paint had taught her that they needed to lay some primer down before they attempted to put this robin's-egg-blue paint on the walls, or the results would be the opposite of fantastic. This would take them forever. Dumping some primer into her roller tray and replacing the lid on the can, Neale picked up a roller brush and smiled. "Thanks for doing this with me."

"Of course. This place has to feel like your home too."

Neale didn't bother to hide her grin. There was something wonderful about hearing a new friend tell her she belonged. Here, in her soon-to-be-bluish room, she could be a recovering artist who was trying to find herself without any social expectations. That kind of acceptance was just what she needed, whether or not Corinne knew it.

Still smiling, Neale decided it was time to bring up another mystery. After the strong reaction to her query about the unicorns, Neale had left other home-decor questions to sit idle, but since she was facing hours of painting, now seemed like as good a time as any.

Angling her face toward the open bedroom window, Neale breathed in and cautiously asked, "So I noticed that you have a Glitter Cat mug. Is that a cartoon you're into, or did someone give you that as a gift?"

"Oh no. I love Glitter Cat almost as much as I love unicorns."

"Me too! I was obsessed with that show in the fifth grade. Like, I am pretty sure my parents were worried about me."

"I almost added a Glitter Cat poster to the living room when I first moved in. It's just that three themes in one apartment feels like a bridge too far. Like, if it's the seventies and unicorns, throwing Glitter Cat in feels like too much."

"I mean, I went as Glitter Cat for Halloween . . . in high school. So I can't judge." Neale laughed at herself and felt some of the tension from the workweek leave her shoulders.

Corinne giggled. "That is so much better than my Glitter Cat manicure."

"That's a thing?" Neale asked, excitement welling in her chest.

"It is if you do it yourself." Corinne snorted. "It looked awful."

"I can see where that would be a bad idea." Neale nodded sagely, then looked over at Corinne, the two of them falling into giggles again.

"I was just expressing myself artistically," Corinne said, smiling and waving her hand in some sort of relaxed, pseudoartistic gesture. Letting the smile fall from her face, she added, "Speaking of art, I watched that video, and . . ."

"Yeah." Neale hissed the word through her scowl.

"Yeah . . ." Corinne blinked at her for a moment. "Like, the fire was bad, but I didn't think your idea was all that bad. Whoever made that video was mean."

Neale shrugged. "If it weren't me in the video, I could see where someone lighting their majorette hat on fire is kind of funny."

"Oh, for sure," Corinne laughed as she rolled an uneven splotch of primer on the wall. "But I wouldn't be doing that to any of my coworkers. Even Mona, and I can't stand her."

"That's 'cause you're a good person. I bet Mona probably would do it to you."

"See, that's why I wouldn't do it. 'Cause it's snaky," Corinne said, stopping her work to roll her eyes.

Neale laughed. "It was really hurtful at first, but you know, I'm okay not doing the artist thing now. Like, it's kind of nice having a steady job."

"I mean, I love what I do. But even then, sometimes it can feel like a grind. I can't imagine slogging away at something that I don't completely love."

Neale's pride smarted. Corinne hadn't meant her words to be a dig, but they sort of felt that way. Happy Hearts might not be glamorous, but Neale wasn't half-bad at the work. Hell, she had convinced Rich to invest in infrastructure again. Melissa said the guy hadn't even bought new pens in a year before Neale had come on board. That had to be a sign that she was onto something.

Pushing aside the unintentional sting, she focused on the roller brush in front of her for a moment before responding. "You know, I used to feel that way. But I'm finding out that I might be good at more than one thing. I thought I would hate the nine-to-five life more than I do."

"Well, that's good for you. Although I got to say I'm kind of sad I'm not gonna be going to any of your fancy art shows."

"You mean you're sad you don't get to see me set myself on fire? And here I thought you wanted me to feel like I belong," Neale joked.

Corinne's laugh echoed against the half-painted walls. "That's not what I meant, and you know it."

"Sure. That's what every serial-killer roommate always says. If Dylan comes down here and finds my body in the freezer, this will be the moment that people point to and say, *Neale should've known.*"

"I wouldn't put your body in a freezer," Corinne cackled. "I do a way better job of hiding a body."

"For my sake, I hope not." Neale laughed, reaching up to get some primer close to the ceiling.

"Don't joke. The government is probably listening to this right now, and they're going to be digging through our fridge when we go to work on Monday."

"I guess I'll just have to take the bodies out of the freezer, then. Or find a way to pin my murder victims on you." Neale grinned.

"If you're going to pin a murder on me, could it be after my birth-day? I have big plans for turning twenty-eight."

"When are you turning twenty-eight?"

"Next month. July fifth, to be exact," Corinne said, her bubbly demeanor inching closer to bubbling over.

"And what do these big plans entail?" Neale asked, hoping her roommate didn't plan to try to rent a unicorn or something.

"I haven't gotten to that yet, but I know it's going to be fabulous," Corinne said, pretending to toss her hair over her shoulder.

"I think we should throw a party. We just need a good theme," Neale said, the excitement of celebrating a birthday causing her to lose her focus on the task at hand.

"It could be like a joint Neale-just-moved-in-and-Corinne's-fabulous-at-twenty-eight party." Corinne clapped her free hand against the handle of her roller and bounced on the balls of her feet. "We could do it the weekend before. That way we don't get stuck with the required Fourth of July party theme."

Casting about the room for inspiration, Neale felt as though she'd been struck by a lightning bolt, like a cartoon character with a good idea. Squealing, she said, "What about a Glitter Cat party?"

"Oh my God! Yes. This is genius. New roommate bonding project. Let me get paper so we can start an invite list."

Neale could almost feel the glitter-drenched excitement rolling off her roommate. "Yes to all of the roommate projects. But first, we have to finish this. Because tomorrow I have to go to some sports event for a coworker, and I'm not trying to sleep on the couch all weekend."

"Fine. We can finish this. But you know I'm coming back to the Glitter Cat party. It's the only way I can turn twenty-eight," Corinne said, smiling so hard that it looked like it hurt. "Anyway, why are you going to sports tomorrow?"

"It's a long story," Neale said, picking up her roller brush and sighing. "It involves a terrible coworker, a copy machine issue, and park benches. Really, I don't even know where to begin."

"Well, this is going to take a while, so you may as well start from the top." Corinne grinned, and Neale thought that painting her room all night might not be so bad.

CHAPTER TWELVE

Neale bit her bottom lip as she circled the block, looking for parking. Despite the fact that it was 8:00 a.m., there were already tons of people flooding Jefferson Park. A car pulled out of a spot, and she let out a squeak of triumph as she threw her car in reverse, backing up a full fifty feet to reach the spot, beating another eager driver to it. Carefully, she eased the car into the spot, feeling a deep sense of pride as she parallel parked.

Hopping out of the car, she made her way toward the park, keeping an eye out for the landmarks Anthony had given her. Locating the lawn bowling area, Neale grinned at a giant blue-and-white balloon arch and began wandering toward a massive green banner that read PARKOUR FOR THE PEOPLE strung between two precariously placed umbrella poles.

She spotted Anthony in a bright-red T-shirt, his muscles flexing as he hefted a flat of water onto a folding table. Neale's mind froze as she watched him. He had all the same quiet confidence as he did in the office, but somehow, out here in the sunlight, joy just seemed to radiate off him. It was almost magnetic. A blonde woman with a sleeve tattoo began unpacking the water bottles. She said something, and Anthony tilted his head back, laughing into the sun. As he righted his head, he noticed Neale, smiled, and waved.

Neale jumped, heat flooding into her cheeks at the thought of being caught staring. The reasonable corner of her brain reminded her that it didn't really matter if she was staring because she wasn't interested in dating right now. For all Anthony knew, she just liked standing at the entrance to things and taking in the general ambience for longer than was common. Taking a deep breath, Neale sided with her logical brain and began walking toward him.

"Hi," Neale called, with a short, nerdy wave at Anthony as soon as she stepped within hearing distance.

"You made it," Anthony said, turning away from the table and walking toward Neale with the same easy smile. He stopped in front of her just outside arm's reach, and Neale wondered what the protocol was for social activities with coworkers. Did she hug him? Was this a fist-bump situation? She wasn't entirely sure, so she kept her hands on the strap of her cross-body bag and made a note to check Dr. Blake's book when she got home.

"I'm on time too. Are Melissa and Travis here yet?" Neale asked, feeling like a fish out of coworker water.

"I haven't seen them yet. But I'm sure they are on their way. Travis is a stickler for time." Anthony shrugged.

"Parking was a nightmare. I had no idea parkour in the park was so popular," Neale said, searching for small talk topics and wondering if she was destined to feel awkward around good-looking men for the rest of her life. Then again, she'd felt immediately comfortable around Darin, and look where that had gotten her . . . deleting pictures in her phone and putting duct tape over her heart.

"It's only crowded because the weather is nice, so that means everyone and their mother is in the park today. I don't think most of these people are here to learn the basics of parkour. I suspect most of them are here to spread out their picnic blankets and try and sneak sips of wine out of a water bottle."

"Honestly, I wish I'd thought to bring wine in a water bottle. It's a perfect day for rosé," Neale laughed.

Anthony had opened his mouth to say something when Melissa's alto shot across the park, causing both of them to jump.

"There you two are!"

"Sorry we're late. Speed Racer over here jacked our parking spot." Travis grinned and pointed at Neale.

"I'm not Speed Racer," Neale said, refusing to feel embarrassed that the car she had evidently beaten out for a spot was Travis's. "And I didn't know that was you all trying to get to the spot. Otherwise, I wouldn't have beaten you to it."

"Don't let him make you feel bad," Melissa said, approaching Neale with her arms wide. As her arms wrapped around her, she added, "Travis drives like an old man."

Okay, so this was a hugging crowd, Neale thought as Melissa released her.

"She backed up like seventy-five yards at fifty miles per hour, then parallel parked like it was nothing to get that spot," Travis said, laughing as he gave Neale a hug. Turning toward Anthony, Neale hesitated. Had she missed her hug window earlier? Why hadn't she just leaned in and done it when she'd had the chance?

Anthony blinked at her for a moment, then smiled and held his arms wide, solving the hug dilemma by saying, "We missed our hug earlier."

Leaning into him, Neale did her best to hug Anthony in the same fleeting manner as her other coworkers. She deliberately did not notice that they were the same height, so their bodies lined up perfectly, or how his strong arms felt comforting around her back. She certainly didn't pay attention to the spicy smell of his body wash. Nor did she wish she could linger and get a sense for how his muscles felt under that T-shirt.

Or at least that was what she told herself when she let go after the appropriate three seconds of coworker hug time.

"Neale, you are new to this, but this is not our first parkour park rodeo, and I'm dying to break the bars in before the kids get ahold of it," Melissa said, grinning and pulling Neale's attention away from the lingering feel of Anthony's body against her own.

"Pull-up contest, anyone?" Travis asked.

"You're on," Melissa said, laughing. "Especially since you lost the last one."

"Only because you had Anthony tag in for you," Travis said, gesturing to him as if it were obvious that Melissa had cheated. Still looking a little incensed, he turned to Anthony and said, "You in this time? Or are you going to bail Melissa out again?"

"I'll pass on embarrassing you both," Anthony laughed, with the easy confidence of someone who could absolutely win a pull-up contest.

"Neale? Want to join?" Travis asked, smiling.

"I have the upper-body strength of an aging kangaroo, so no thank you."

Melissa's laugh echoed around the park, then she shrugged one shoulder and said, "Suit yourself. Let's go, Trav. Coffee on Monday is at stake."

"My money is on Mel," Neale called as she watched her shove Travis and make a run for the pull-up bar.

"Thanks, Neale," Travis said over his shoulder as he regained his balance. Rolling his eyes, he turned and jogged off after Melissa.

Smiling, Anthony turned to face her and said, "It's pretty early, so a lot of the demonstrations haven't started, but I could show you around. Maybe tell you a little bit about what's going on? If you're interested, that is."

Neale shrugged. "I'd love for you to show me around."

"All right. Where to start?" Anthony rubbed his hands together like a little kid with a bad idea, looking eager.

"How about you start by explaining what Parkour for the People is?"

"Good question," Anthony said, dropping his hands. "So Parkour for the People is a local nonprofit that strives to make parkour accessible to all communities. They do that by building parks, like this one that we are celebrating the opening of today, and by offering free classes around town. I teach a volunteer class on the weekends."

"Hence the calendar on your desk," Neale said, studying his expression.

Anthony nodded solemnly. "Yes. The foundation made it for me in celebration of my having taught one hundred free courses for the seven-and-unders, which I'm teaching today, in fact. We are partnering with a youth center so the kids can try out something new."

Suddenly, the funny calendar made sense to her. Parkour wasn't just a hobby; it was his way of giving back to the community.

"That is really sweet. How did you get into this?" Neale asked as Anthony steered them toward a small set of wooden platforms and low-to-the-ground bars.

"It's a long story," Anthony demurred.

"I've got time, obviously," Neale said with a chuckle, then added, "Only if you want to tell me, of course. No pressure."

"I don't mind sharing," Anthony said. His smile was still warm, but there was some reluctance in his eyes as he began. "My father passed away when I was seven years old. Prostate cancer," Anthony added, his gaze fixed on the padded park ground.

"I'm so sorry," Neale said, trying to catch his eye.

"It's okay. It was a long time ago. It was a surprise. Prostate cancer isn't really considered a young man's disease. Anyway, I had a lot of energy, and my mom and grandma weren't really sure what to do with me. I was always bouncing off the walls and that sort of thing. A friend at church suggested my mom find an activity for me, and my grandma thought gymnastics might be good."

Anthony chuckled softly at the memory of his younger self, and Neale's heart ached for him. Taking a deep breath, he looked up from the park surface and said, "Turned out I loved gymnastics, and I was good at it. I stuck with it all the way until my freshman year in high school, when I had a growth spurt, and it made me realize that I needed to be about a foot shorter if I was going to continue in the sport competitively."

Neale laughed. "I'm familiar with that disappointment. No one told me that racehorse jockeys were like a hundred and five pounds until way too late into my Career Day presentation."

The sound of Anthony's true laugh reached her ears, and Neale felt herself smile. She hadn't realized how much she enjoyed the sound until now.

"Adults just let us down." Anthony shook his head as the last of his laughter died away. "Anyway, it was right around then that my mom got a new job. It was super long hours, but it paid really well. My grandma thought it'd be good if the two of us could spend more time together on her commute, so she started looking for other things for me to do and found a climbing gym. So I started going to the gym after school to fill time until my mom finished up at work. The people there became like a second family to me, and they happened to offer classes in parkour. When one of the instructors went out on maternity leave, they started training me to fill in for her classes, and I've been teaching ever since."

"That is the warmest and fuzziest way to acquire a hobby. I feel like that is how Hallmark pretends like people in Christmas movies get into volunteering. Spending time with your mom. Adorable," Neale said, fighting the urge to give him a real hug this time. For a moment, Neale tried to imagine Darin teaching a pack of sweaty seven-year-olds anything and almost laughed. The idea was so absurd. He didn't even have the patience to teach Neale how to play a video game. Trying to teach kids would have made his head explode.

"If you had to smell me after I spent hours a day at a gym, you'd think it was less adorable," Anthony chuckled.

"I'm sure little Anthony's hygiene wasn't that bad. You smell good now."

"Thanks," Anthony said, snorting. His mouth twitched up at the corners. "That is very reassuring."

"I do what I can." Neale shrugged, feeling herself relax in his company. "What is happening with all this?" she asked, gesturing to the various park components with her mint-green manicure.

"So there are really three movement categories in parkour: jumping, vaulting, and climbing. What you see here is constructed to facilitate one or more of those movements. We try and make each piece have multiple solutions, since part of the fun of parkour is problem solving," Anthony said, looking over his shoulder briefly as if he'd just remembered why they were there.

Neale nodded along as Anthony explained the various elements of a course that encouraged prosocial behaviors and how people worked together at a park. Every so often, he would stop and show her how an element might work, and that was when Neale's mind really started to misbehave. She really had come there in a friendly capacity, but it was hard not to be curious about someone when she was watching him hoist himself up a wall, muscles flexing through the cotton of his T-shirt. She'd never really given much thought to anyone's back muscles, but watching Anthony climb, she began to wonder what his back muscles actually looked like.

"This here is a good place to start." Anthony hopped down from the low-level wall he was standing on and grinned at her, shaking her out of her wandering thoughts. "Want to try it?"

Neale laughed. While Anthony might have the back muscles for this, she absolutely did not. And more importantly, she had no interest in developing those muscles today. Or any other day, really. "Ha. No. You just hopped up there looking all cute and thought you could convince me to break my neck. No thank you."

"You think I'm cute?" Anthony asked, his big goofy grin stopping Neale in her tracks.

"I . . . ," Neale sputtered, trying to pull herself together. She had not meant to say that out loud. This was why hugging coworkers should be in the off-limits column. It did humiliating things like this to her psyche. Grasping at the first excuse that came to mind, she said, "I just meant that you were like the Black Spider-Man."

Anthony's laugh seemed to fill up the entire park; the sound was so warm that it felt like the sun at high noon. "I'm definitely not. I feel like that title belongs to the French guy who scaled a building to save a kid."

"In the Marvel universe, there can be more than one Spider-Man. Just saying." Neale shrugged as Anthony continued to chuckle.

"You're cute too. Maybe you could be Spider-Woman?" Anthony gestured to her, his smile highlighting his high cheekbones. For a moment, Neale's heartbeat jumped as a silly smile spread across her face. He seriously thought she was cute too? She stilled, trying to think of an appropriate response, when Anthony added, "Hop up here and give it a try, Spider-Woman."

"I'm pretty good on the ground," Neale said, trying not to interrogate her disappointment. He didn't mean cute like that; he was poking fun at her. On the upside, for the first time in her life, she hadn't rushed to fill the silence, so at least she didn't have to backtrack on a second awkward slipup. After all, the only thing that could make a slipup like *you're cute* worse was backtracking to say, *I think you're cute, but only if you think I'm cute.* Best to leave the whole idea alone before she had to have some kind of talk with Rich wearing his HR hat.

Anthony smiled. "Fine. I'll let you off the hook, but only because you think I'm cute. I can live off of a compliment like that for a year."

"I'll bet you can," Neale said, hoping her flat tone was doing a better job of hiding her embarrassment than her cheeks were.

"If you change your mind, I better be the first person you call," Anthony said, the warm glow of his full smile still shining directly on her. "Since parkour isn't your hobby, I'm curious—what do you do for fun?"

Neale felt her mind twitch as she thought through her hobbies. For a moment, she considered leaving art out altogether but then decided that she might as well be honest with Anthony. "Well, until recently my hobby was also my profession. Now, I guess it's just a hobby."

"Your art?" Anthony's voice was gentle.

"You guessed it. For so long everything that I did contributed to my art in some way. Every book I read, every movie I watched, other artists' shows—all of that was really toward the end goal of making something new. Saying something in a different way."

"But you don't do that now?" Anthony's forehead was wrinkled by a scowl.

"No," Neale said, wishing the conversation would turn. Thinking about who she used to be still made her sad, despite how well she was doing with her new job.

"I like to think that art evolves with the artist," Anthony said, optimism lacing his tone. "Maybe this is just the next phase in your evolution?"

Neale felt her heart tug. She desperately wanted Anthony's words to be true. But she also knew that wishing didn't make it so. She was evolving into someone who appreciated art but did not make it. Still, she let the thought turn over in her head. It was nice to have a daydream. To his credit, Anthony did not rush to fill the silence, instead slowing his pace to let Neale take in more of the park as she thought. Out of the corner of her eye, she watched as children began to flood the area, their eyes wide with wonder. Neale envied them. The world was still so big and easy in their eyes that a few wooden boxes held magic for them in a way boxes never could for a grown-up.

Aware that she had let the silence stretch for a little too long, Neale laughed quietly and said, "Maybe you are right. Or maybe I'm evolving into the kind of woman who knits sweaters for trees. I've been thinking about joining some sort of knitting circle or something."

Anthony's expression was quiet for a moment, and then he said, "Do you even know how to knit?" Neale laughed and watched as a grin spread across his face. "It's fine if you don't want to pursue art, but at least pick a more believable hobby."

"You got me. There's no way I'm learning to knit just so I can dress up a tree."

Anthony had opened his mouth to say something when a small, curly-headed streak of light came running at him full tilt, nearly knocking him into Neale. A very excited kindergartener wrapped his arms around Anthony's legs and looked up to shout, "Hi, Mr. Anthony, I'm here. Are we going to start soon?"

Taking a moment to regain his balance, Anthony threw Neale an apologetic look before turning his focus to the child wrapped around him like a vine. "Hi, Marcus. I'm glad you're here. We will get started in about ten minutes. But if you want to warm up now, you may."

"Okay. I've been practicing at home. I'm gonna show you all my jumps," Marcus said, still clinging to his leg as he looked up at Anthony, stars in his eyes.

"I'm so excited to see your jumps. Go ahead and get warmed up over there. I'll see you soon." Anthony gave the back of Marcus's head a pat as the boy let him go and bolted back toward the new park. "Marcus is always *very* excited to show me his jumps."

"Well, jumping is pretty exciting," Neale chuckled.

"That's the great thing about teaching the little ones; they are pretty much excited about anything we do. And honestly, they're too little to do much vaulting and not really coordinated enough to do a lot of climbing, so we spend pretty much every lesson jumping. It never gets old for them." Anthony shook his head.

"If I was in kindergarten and knew someone who wanted to watch me jump up and down for forty-five minutes, that would be like winning the six-year-old lotto," Neale laughed.

"You have no idea. Half the parents who drop off their kids tell me that they just want me to run them ragged. The more jumping, the better," Anthony laughed. Glancing down at his watch, he winced and said, "Class starts in seven minutes; I'd probably better go get ready. Thank you for coming to check this out. I had fun."

"Me too. I feel like I just learned about a whole new world."

"Next time, we'll have to get you out there to actually try some moves," Anthony said, smiling his quiet smile.

"Not going to happen, Spider-Man." Neale shook her head and chuckled.

"Sooner or later, you're going to try it. I'm a patient guy. I can wait."

"You're going to be waiting awhile, my friend. There is a reason I managed to light that majorette hat on fire, and it's called absolutely no coordination."

"It's going to happen; you'll see." Anthony grinned at her good-naturedly. He paused for a moment and looked toward the park before turning his focus back on Neale. Making eye contact, he said, "Anyway, I should probably go, but you have my cell number if you ever want to hang out or just talk. No parkour required."

Neale paused for a fraction of a second. Maybe Anthony was flirting with her? It did sort of feel like a flirty offer. Then again, telling someone to call you didn't seem like an overtly flirty act. Really, most of the guys she dated didn't do phone calls.

Another impressive mental leap made by me, Neale thought, giving herself a shake before answering matter-of-factly with, "Will do."

"All right, I guess I'll see you on Monday. Unless you want to talk sooner. Then you could just text me."

Is this flirting? she asked herself again, then paused. She hoped not. Neale liked Anthony. And she did think he was cute. But she was in no place to be with anyone right now. Not when she still couldn't bring herself to unfollow Darin on social media. Besides, her judgment track record wasn't exactly spotless.

In fact, her judgment was probably the number one reason Anthony wasn't flirting. Again, she reminded herself that this was in her traitorous heart. Better to give Anthony a little distance so she couldn't humiliate herself. The last thing she needed was another misunderstanding à la Darin and the artists' house. Only worse, because she would still have to see Anthony at work every day. *No*, Neale told herself firmly. Dylan was right about her dating cycles. It had been over two months since she and Darin had broken up, and now her mind was just trying to trick her into her old habits. This was not flirting; this was Old Neale trying to creep back into her life.

Giving herself a shake, she smiled. "Well, I guess I better go find Travis and Mel. Talk to you on Monday."

"All right," Anthony said, putting his hands in his pockets and looking down at the padded park surface before looking back, his smile hitting her square in the chest. "Bye."

"See ya," Neale said with a short wave, practically tripping over her own feet to get out of that smile's tractor beam. Turning away with an awkward stumble, Neale hurried to find Melissa and Travis, reminding herself the whole way that she was New Neale, who didn't trip over herself or succumb to tractor-beam smiles. New Neale only cared about getting herself together. And the best way to do that was not to trust her treacherous instincts . . . and to avoid all her favorite bad decisions, including flirting with coworkers.

CHAPTER THIRTEEN

"Are you actually parking the car, or are you just saying you are parking?" Billie asked, her irritation barely masked by her nerves.

"Umm . . . I'm parking . . . in like four minutes," Neale said. When Billie had interrupted her Sunday with her sad-sack, overwhelmed-sounding phone call about visiting the venue, she couldn't refuse helping her sister. After all, Billie had a point about getting back on the horse. It wasn't like she could avoid all art forever.

"It is paid parking, so you might want to look for something on the street."

"I have a job, Billie," Neale balked. If Billie wanted her help, treating her like she was still in diapers wasn't going to get her any points.

"Sorry, I'm just looking out," Billie said.

"It's all right." Neale felt a twinge of guilt tickle the back of her mind as the Black Spot came into view. She had never staged a show this big, and she could imagine that Billie was stressed. Especially since the clock was furiously ticking toward opening night with little more than a month to go. Sighing, she asked, "How much is parking?"

"It's like twenty dollars."

"Okay, no. That's exorbitant. I'm glad you mentioned it; I'll look for street parking."

"That's what I thought," Billie chuckled with her usual spunk. "I'll wait for you outside the venue."

Neale circled the block twice before she found a spot on the crowded Belltown street and whipped into it, causing several other cars to honk. Jumping out of the car, she approached a bland-looking two-story building painted a rather uninspiring shade of dark gray. Outside its movie-theater-like double doors, Billie stood, hopping from one foot to the next, her usually mellow demeanor replaced with agitation amped up to the highest volume.

As soon as Billie caught sight of Neale, she said, "I'm so glad you are here. I hate talking to the venue alone."

"What do you mean, you hate talking to the venue? You've done this before," Neale said, wrapping her arm through her sister's and pulling her in close.

"Yeah, and I messed it up. What if they don't agree with what I want? I can't break two contracts, or Marceline will literally stab me, and Kelsea will probably hold me down for her. So instead, I'll be stuck in a contract that is going to produce something . . . ," Billie rambled, waving her free hand in the air in search of the word she needed, before finally settling on, "dreadful."

"Billie, that is not gonna happen. Calm down."

"I should've just gone with a regular old gallery space. Why did I choose a theater? I've made a tremendous mistake, haven't I?" her sister asked, panic tingeing every third word of her impending spiral.

"No, you haven't made a mistake." *But I did when I answered your dramatic call,* Neale thought. "Billie, the only reason you think you need a gallery is because Mom displays at galleries. You know damn well that a gallery is absolutely the wrong venue for your work, and Marceline agrees. Now stop it," Neale said, surprised by the firmness in her tone. She was pretty sure she hadn't sounded this decisive since her two-week stint as an au pair when she was nineteen.

"You know what? You're right. This is just first-day jitters. I always get these." Billie blinked at her for a moment, her arm still looped through Neale's, and said, "Look at you, little sister, getting all good at taking charge."

"Oh, please." Neale rolled her eyes.

"See, I knew my gut was right. I need you!"

"I'm not a chicken; you don't have to butter me up," Neale said, trying her best to sound put upon despite feeling flattered by her sister's attention. In a way, the two of them huddled together made Neale feel like they were back in the dynamic-duo days that she missed so much. She would never admit it, but Billie was right. It was fun to hang out and talk art in a low-pressure way again.

"I don't think *chicken* belongs in that expression," Billie laughed as she dragged her through the theater doors.

While the exterior of the building was completely nondescript, the interior was altogether fabulous. Old-world theater glamour wrapped its arms around them as the doors closed. Letting her eyes adjust to the dimly lit hallway, Neale saw vintage movie posters and long red-velvet curtains draped at intervals along the corridor. Crown molding drew the eye up toward the tall ceilings, highlighted by the hazy light that came from the fine alabaster sconces dotting the walls. The whole place had a soft, eerie vibe.

"I see why you picked this venue. I love it," Neale whispered, leaning into her sister. The theater had an unsettling feel to it, as if the person entering the space needed to stay on their toes. In short, it was the physical embodiment of her sister, soft and sharp all at the same time.

"You don't think it's too much? My plan is to replace the movie posters with my pieces, then to make the bar look like an old-school movie-theater concession stand but stylize the staff so that it maintains the weirdness. And then wait till you see the theater space. This is where I need you, because I really don't have a sense of the multimedia stuff that the other artists will need and—"

"Hello, Billie, good to see you again." A completely average, middle-aged woman in a summery blouse appeared from behind one of the velvet curtains, causing Neale to jump a good three inches off the ground.

"Good to see you too," Billie called to the woman, clearly recovering from the shock faster.

As Neale took a steadying breath, the woman turned to her and said, "Hi, I'm Nhi Hoang, house manager for the Black Spot."

"Nice to meet you. I'm Neale, Billie's sister," Neale said, still stuck on the fact that Nhi looked so normal that she almost seemed out of place at the venue.

"Nice to meet you, Neale." Turning her attention back to Billie, Nhi asked, "Did you want to head into the theater to talk about your tech needs? I'm happy to walk you through what the house has and what vendors we can partner with to bring in any other items you may want."

"Great," Billie said, following Nhi into the theater and dragging Neale with her. "I was just telling Neale that I want her opinion on the set."

Neale stopped hearing her sister's words as they walked into the theater. In many ways, it was a standard stage setup, only so much bigger and odder. The ceilings looked like the arches of a cathedral painted in different shades of black and gray. The heavenly-dome feeling was only enhanced as Nhi walked behind the booth to bring up the house-lights. The second story had amber-glass-covered windows, and if she squinted, Neale could see crown molding and little rosettes at the joints of the arches like in a gothic church. As if in a dream, she let go of her sister's arm and began to wander around the theater, taking in the stage from every angle. Her heart rate picked up as she watched small specks of dust float down in the white lighting of the stage as she imagined everything that an artist could say in a place as unusual as this.

"Hey, Neale. Can you come over for a sec?" Billie's voice seemed to push against the walls, and Neale almost had to catch her breath. The way the theater played with sound made her want to cry. Giving her head a shake, Neale ambled over to her sister. She was not going to fall in love with this place. She was just here to weigh in about screens or seat cushions or whatever.

Finally reaching Billie and Nhi, she asked, "What's up?"

"The house has two projectors, and you know projectors aren't my thing. The venue in New York only had a crappy little projector on a wobbly cart." Billie held out a clipboard with a list of equipment on it. "Which would you use?"

Neale looked down at the list for a moment. "They are both good pieces of equipment, so it really depends on what you envision them doing and how you want them to work with sound."

"Well, what would you do with them?" Billie asked, looking only slightly put out that the answer wasn't a quick yes or no.

"Hmm . . . if it were me, I'd probably want to do some sort of big wall at the back of the stage and project a set onto that. That way you're not changing the set with every act. You'll have flexibility, so you could even show the pieces that tie to each act before the performer starts. It'll also let the artists select their own media. The stage is big enough that if you mounted the projector, you could probably do it without the projections running across their faces. Unless that is the look the artist is going for. Maybe you want the mounting system to be on a remote-controlled tray so you have options."

"We can have the projectors mounted so that a tech can control them from the booth." Nhi nodded helpfully at Neale.

"Walk me through what you are imagining. Is a beam of light from a zillion miles above going to feel like divine lighting as opposed to vintage film? If we project it head on, it would give the stage that medieval-movie-theater quality, wouldn't it?" Billie asked, her voice hinting at a combination of skepticism and nerves.

"Bill, trust me," Neale said, nudging her sister. "It won't look like the Rapture. You want the continuity a mounted projector will provide."

Her sister sighed, then let her shoulders drop. "I think you are right. Actually, I know you are right. It's just that the setup in New York was different."

Neale watched as Billie rocked back and forth on her heels, her indecision making everyone else anxious. Using a projector wasn't rocket science. No wonder LA hadn't worked out. Her sister was just too exacting. Then again, it was her show, so Billie being picky shouldn't really bother her.

It occurred to Neale that maybe if she had been this picky about her own show, the fire wouldn't have happened. Of course, she could have been exacting within a centimeter of her life, and that wouldn't necessarily have stopped her show from being a disaster. The idea that she couldn't have prevented failure threatened to swallow her up like a black hole, and Neale shivered. Reminding herself that she had no plans to stage a show again, she pushed the threatening thought aside.

Attempting to look like she was thinking about projectors, too, she redirected her thoughts to making plans for her and her sister. Maybe after they were done here, the two of them could go to dinner. Neale could eat sushi—

"Okay, I want to go with the mounted Christie projector," Billie finally said.

As Billie and Nhi began rambling around the theater discussing other changes, Neale let her mind wander. Maybe Anthony was right. Perhaps she was evolving. Not into a performance artist, but into someone who helped foster art. She could just be Billie's shadow. Helping fill the gaps in her sister's creative vision.

"Hey, Neale," Billie called again, forcing her to pay attention once more. As Neale wandered toward the pair, Billie started speaking rapidly. "I need to run. Would you mind going through the rest of this checklist with Nhi? It's mostly for the reception area and snacks."

Neale's heart sank. "I thought we were getting coffee or dinner or something to catch up. I still don't know anything about your life in New York and—"

"Totally hear you; it's just that I forgot I agreed to do this podcast interview, and Dad is letting me use his studio space later, so now I need to run back to the house to prep for it," Billie said, throwing on her wide-brimmed hat and giving Neale an apologetic smile. "Next time, I swear. But right now, I gotta go. My Lyft is here."

Neale bit down on a small wedge of irritation. It wasn't like Billie was intentionally blowing her off. Sighing, she said, "Happy to help."

"Thank you both," Billie called, already halfway out the door.

So much for quality sister time, Neale thought, as she turned to Nhi and said, "Sorry, you're stuck with me."

"Nothing to be sorry about," Nhi said, gracefully sidestepping the sister argument that had just unfolded in front of her. Neale had to hand it to her: this woman was good at her job. Which was lucky, because Neale had no idea what she was doing and no interest in doing it without her sister.

~

Neale grabbed her file full of musical card research and headed to the conference room, strangely excited for her meeting with Rich and Anthony. Sure, if anyone had asked her six weeks ago if she would ever be excited about the high-pitched squeals of a singing greeting card, she would have laughed in their face. But now that she had spent the better part of the last two weeks trying to think through the actual logistics of making a card, she had a whole new appreciation for them, *in a word-problem-on-a-math-test sort of way*, Neale thought as she rounded the corner into the conference room.

"Hi, Neale," Rich said.

"Good morning," she singsonged to her boss as she took a seat on the opposite side of the conference room table and began arranging the papers in her file so that each handout was in its own distinct pile.

"Hello. Sorry I'm late," Anthony said, hurrying into the room and turning to shut the door.

Neale's pulse began to race along with her thoughts. She hadn't texted Anthony after the park. In fact, the more she thought about it, the clearer it became that she should just give him and his cute Black Spider-Man self a wide berth. She couldn't tempt fate if she didn't give herself an opening.

"Don't worry about it. We just got here," Rich said, smiling at Anthony as he took a seat next to Neale at the conference table. Using his best I'm-the-boss tone, he said, "Neale, would you like to walk us through what you've learned?"

Clearing her throat, Neale forced herself to focus on the task at hand. "Sure. I've spent the last couple of days getting familiar with the elements of a singing card, how they are created, what timelines look like, and what potential stumbling blocks could be, et cetera, so I thought I'd bring you all up to speed on what I learned, and then we could decide on the next steps together."

"Sounds good," Anthony said, as Rich nodded in affirmation.

"First things first. We know Anthony can handle the design, but I thought it would be good to go over the specific elements that he will want to take into consideration as he thinks about the artwork." Neale began passing out her handouts that outlined the actual components of a card. As Rich and Anthony studied the handouts, she went into the details about the different options for card sizing and paper weight, along with annotations on what the card sizes would mean for customers who also had to consider postage, as well as costs for engaging their freelance copywriter for the interior. Then she followed up with a note about the actual mechanism for printing, folding, and gluing the cards together.

"So are there printers in the area who could do this?" Rich stopped her to ask, which thankfully gave her a moment to take a breath and a sip of water.

Swallowing, Neale said, "Yes. And if we can make this work, I'll look into pricing tiers for bulk orders and that sort of thing."

Pricing tiers for bulk orders. Neale nearly shuddered as she replayed the workplace jargon in her head.

"I know we have more to cover, but can I just say that this is excellent research," Rich said, derailing Neale's personal disgust.

"Well, thanks," Neale said, feeling herself inflate just a little bit. Deep down, she knew she was on the right track letting art go. Cards might be less exciting, but she was safe from failure at Happy Hearts in a way she couldn't be with art. Giving herself an inner high five, she said, "Maybe don't get too excited about my research just yet, because there are some big hurdles we need to clear, including cost to get the project up and running and the singing mechanism. On the retail market, those recording devices are like ten dollars a pop." Neale paused as Rich winced and Anthony bit down on his bottom lip. "Basically, we'd need to find a manufacturer who can get us a hefty break on those things; otherwise, our cards will need to retail for twenty-five dollars for us to make a profit."

"Maybe if they were printed in gold," Anthony chuckled, shaking his head.

"Hmmm," Rich said, pursing his lips and scowling. After a moment, he asked the question Neale had been dreading most. "All right, so the singing mechanism is a problem, but tell me, what type of investment are we looking at to get this off the ground?"

"Well . . . ," Neale said, wrinkling her nose and eyeing Anthony. When they had talked about the number back at their cubes, he had told her it was a long shot but that he would back her up. She just hoped she could talk fast enough that Rich wouldn't shoot them down before he got the chance. "To get us up and running, we are looking at a low-end investment of about seven thousand dollars."

"Ouch," Rich said, wincing visibly. "I don't know that we have—"

"Yes, ouch, but as you know from the line you just launched, once the infrastructure is built, this stuff is easy to maintain," Neale jumped in, smiling and nodding as if she were presenting good news. Out of the corner of her eye, she saw Anthony lean in to get Rich's attention.

"Here's the thing. I think it might make sense to take the hit all at once. We have already invested in Neale and launched the other card line, so we are going to be running at a deficit anyway. Why not double down and really invest in our expansion?"

"When you frame it like that, Anthony, I can see where an additional seven thousand dollars is a drop in the bucket." Rich laughed, nodding at the two of them, before his expression sobered and he added, "But realistically, we won't see that money back—or our return on investment for beefing up the staff and launching the new line—for another year or two, if we are lucky."

"I thought you might say that," Neale said, smiling and reaching for her stack of papers. Finding the chart she was looking for, she passed around the projection Dylan had helped her make. "I made us a chart. As you can see from the different scenarios below, it makes sense for us to start with the smaller popular holidays, for example Halloween and birthdays. That way we can benefit from the seasonal bump without having to compete with some of the bigger card makers. Similarly, if we do this right, people pick up the Halloween card, like it, and think of us for the next birthday card they need. Birthdays happen year round, so we could recoup our money faster."

"There is less crowding at Halloween," Rich conceded, looking down at the chart.

"Timeline-wise, we know Halloween would be tight, but it is doable," Anthony said, giving Neale a smile.

"Especially if we keep all of the manufacturing pieces local," Neale added, knowing that supporting local business would be the cherry on top for her boss.

Looking up at the two of them, Rich sighed. "All right. In for a penny, in for a pound. You've convinced me."

"Awesome! I think you are really going to be happy you did this in the long run," Neale said, smiling so hard her cheeks hurt.

"I sure hope so. Good work, everyone," Rich said with a worried smile, before standing up and cruising toward the conference room door.

As soon as he left, Neale audibly exhaled and began gathering the papers she had spread out around her. Next to her, Anthony took his time standing up, then carefully placed the meeting handout in his leather portfolio. Neale did her very best not to notice the fit of his slacks or what parkour thighs looked like in otherwise drab material. Instead, she forced herself to get organized. After a moment, he said, "Thanks for doing all this research. I'm so excited to try this out."

"My pleasure. Besides, now that Rich knows that an app can do my job in half the time, I needed to find some other way to be useful." Neale smirked, standing up with her file in one hand and pushing in her chair with the other.

"I'm still shocked you convinced him to buy that iPad and the software."

"I'm not special, trust me. Rich is just really practical. Once I made the case for potentially making more money by saving staff hours, it was easy."

"Don't say that. You are special," Anthony said, his words as soft as they were flattering. "Seriously, Rich can be so stubborn. It took me years to convince the guy just to get a scanner. You launched a new card in an hour. You have some impressive powers of persuasion."

"That is the most mundane skill anyone has ever accused me of having. Thank you," Neale chuckled, feeling her cheeks warm over the compliment.

"Laugh if you want, but I think it's a good skill to have," Anthony said, smiling at her with appreciation.

"Right. Sure," Neale said, attempting to deflect some of the attention away from herself. She wasn't used to this kind of praise, and it was a little embarrassing.

"No. I mean it. It's a valuable, practical skill. Not everyone can convince people to do what is in their best interest. Especially if that person has some trauma around an action."

Neale just smiled at him for a few heartbeats, letting the friendly tension build between them as they walked down the hall. She wasn't entirely sure how to respond to the world's most boring and simultaneously flattering compliment. *Practical* was never a thing she'd wanted someone to say about her. But now that they had, it felt sort of nice.

"Anyway, you should be proud of yourself." Anthony looked down at the carpet, then back at her. Finally, he said, "Hey, so what time should I stop by your mom's show?"

The conversation shift was so abrupt it took her by surprise. Blinking, she tried to remember how he knew about her mom's show. Had he googled her whole family? Not that she was in a place to judge. Her sisters had googled him after her first day on the job.

"The gallery postcard said *Three Souls* was running from six to nine p.m. on Saturday. Is it like a be-on-time thing, or like a drop-in-whenever thing? I've never really been to a serious art opening before," Anthony said, sheepishly tucking his hands into the pockets of his gray slacks.

"Oh. I forgot about the postcards," Neale said, remembering that she'd placed the stack of gallery cards on the filing cabinet in front of his desk. As if on cue, they both turned to look at the neat little stack she had left obviously sitting in front of them. Turning back to Anthony, she laughed. "It's a drop-in kind of thing. And really, you don't have to come if you don't want to. It just seemed mean not to invite people. I won't hold it against you. Pinkie promise."

"No, I want to come," Anthony said, his body language relaxing as his laughter faded away.

The little voice in the back of her head started making all kinds of noise again, asking questions that Neale really didn't want to think about. Like, why did he want to go to the show? And what did it mean if he did come to the show? Mel and Travis weren't coming. At least she didn't think they were. Was he trying to hang out . . . or *hang out*?

Anthony blinked at her, waiting for a response, and Neale crammed the voice back into its corner of her mind, along with the thoughts about the fit of his slacks. She had gone to his parkour event; it was only natural for a friend to return the favor.

Shrugging, Neale said, "In that case, I wouldn't get there before six forty-five. Only the art weirdos get there early. And my mom hates those people."

"All right. It's a date," Anthony said, turning and dropping into his desk chair casually as the little voice of anxiety tried to make its way back into the forefront of Neale's mind.

This is not a date, she reassured the little voice. No one over the age of thirteen considered something a date if their parents were there.

CHAPTER FOURTEEN

"Twenty bucks says Mom murders that guy if he doesn't go away," Billie whispered, hiding her grin behind her plastic wineglass.

Over in the corner, Neale watched her mother grow more agitated while a pretentious-looking man in tortoiseshell glasses spewed a steady stream of words at her. Turning back to Billie, Neale said, "Twenty-five bucks says that she eats him alive in the next three minutes."

"We should go over there and save her," Dylan said, her brow creasing as they watched their mother, in her most professional and therefore least comfortable clothes, eyeing the exits.

"You are no fun, Dylan," Henry said, a sparkling water in his hand and a big, mischievous grin on his youthful features.

"Dad. Shouldn't you be the one watching out for Mom tonight? You know how much she despises these things," Dylan tutted.

Neale made eye contact with Billie to try to secretly work out the terms of their bet. She was in the middle of using her eyebrows to tag on an extra five dollars if Dylan broke up the fight, when Billie leaned around Neale's head to get a look at someone walking through the door.

Interrupting Dylan and their father's argument, Billie said, "Neale, is that the guy from work?"

"What?" Neale said, as fear crept through her.

"Is it?" Dylan asked, sounding excited.

While her father said, "Who's he?"

The four of them all managed to turn and stare at the door at the exact same time. The only thing that could have made synchronized gawking with her sisters and father more awkward was Anthony spotting Neale and making eye contact, which of course he did.

"I didn't think he'd actually show up," Neale hissed to her family under her breath as heat washed over her.

"Well, he's here now," Billie said, her tone laden with implied meaning.

"I don't know him," her father said, too loudly for a space that was intentionally designed to echo. Even if he had said it at a reasonable volume, Anthony was all of four feet away. He could absolutely hear them talking about him. Neale wished she could melt into the floor. How was it possible that absolutely no one in the Delacroix family had any chill at all, including her?

"Hello," Anthony said, stopping in front of the group and eyeing them all. Neale got the distinct impression that he was debating whether a hug would be appropriate in front of people whose very essence seemed to scream, *We are related to Neale and we want to humiliate her!*

"Hey," Neale said, stepping forward with her arms wide, determined not to let the presence of her family change her behavior. "Thanks for coming."

More than anything, Neale wished her family wasn't standing right there. For once, she wanted to hug Anthony without having to think through the social implications of physical contact. The parkour park had been a first hug, and those were never that satisfying. And now, all she could do was acknowledge that he smelled delicious—like spices and a forest all at the same time—and that she was pretty sure his arms gave way better hugs than what she was getting before she had to step away for propriety's sake.

Turning to face her family, Neale smiled and said, "Family, this is my friend Anthony from work. The one who does the artwork for the greeting cards. Anthony, that is my sister Billie and my dad, Henry, both artists as well, so you have something in common with them. And that is my sister Dylan, who is a consultant."

"Nice to meet you all. Neale has told me so much about you." Anthony smiled politely, while Billie and Dylan made wide eyes at each other and Neale in an alternating fashion.

"Nice to meet you too," Henry said, moving his sparkling beverage to his left hand and offering his now-condensation-sweaty hand to Anthony, who, much to Neale's dismay, shook it without so much as batting an eyelash at the moisture. Henry released his hand and scowled a little at him, a gesture that Neale suspected was meant to look intimidating but mostly came off as silly thanks to the Coke-bottle glasses he wore. "So, young man, Neale hasn't mentioned you before. Tell me about yourself."

Neale needed lightning to strike her now, please. Her dad was attempting to interview Anthony like this was a high school date. He hadn't even done that when she was in high school. Did he have to start now?

"Sure," Anthony said, his expression serious as he thought about Henry's question. "Well. I'm originally from Seattle. I have a degree in marketing from Santa Clara. I work with Neale at Happy Hearts, and this is my first art show."

Henry narrowed his left eye at Anthony as if he were trying to mimic the People's Eyebrow but hadn't gotten the gesture down yet. Neale felt her skin prickle with sweat as she waited for him to respond. Finally, he said, "Bucky the Bronco. Good education. Do you want to hear a joke?"

"I'd love to," Anthony said.

"Dad, no," Neale said, whatever dread she had been feeling now multiplied tenfold. If Anthony knew her family at all, he would have politely declined a joke, because half of her father's jokes didn't make sense. Hell, his version of a chicken crossing the road ended with the chicken eating grapes.

"It's a good joke. You never want people to know how funny I am." Henry pouted at her.

"That's definitely not why we don't want you to tell jokes," Billie mumbled under her breath as she watched the impending familial train wreck.

Undeterred, Henry's smile broadened to cartoonish levels. "A rabbit, a cow, and a bronco go to a disco. The rabbit walks up to the bartender and asks for a carrot, and the bartender says, 'We don't carry those.' Then the cow walks up and asks for some hay, and the bartender says, 'We don't have that either.' Then the bartender looks at the bronco and says, 'If you are looking for alfalfa, you're outa luck.' To which the bronco says, 'Nah, double whiskey is fine.'"

For three agonizing heartbeats, Neale watched as Anthony processed one of the corniest jokes she'd ever heard, her thoughts racing. First off, what were animals doing in a disco? Second, did discos even exist anymore? And third, why on God's earth had she invited a coworker to her mother's show? She would have to see this man every day, and—

Anthony's face cracked into a smile, and he began to chuckle. Not the polite chuckle of someone humoring a man in his sixties but the laugh of someone who actually thought dad jokes were funny. To her great surprise, Anthony's laughing made her father laugh harder at his own joke. Neale glanced at her sisters for help. Dylan's face looked like she had found a stain on her favorite blouse, while Billie seemed outright disgusted that anyone would laugh at such a bad joke.

"That's a good one," Anthony said as he pulled himself together.

"I got lots of jokes. These three don't think I'm funny. But I keep telling them that people think I'm really funny," Henry said, still basking in the glow of someone laughing at his jokes. "I've been thinking

I should do an open mic night. I got other jokes. You want to hear another?"

In that moment, if Neale could have set a second majorette hat on fire, she would have, just to escape the extreme humiliation of her father reenacting the role of dad on some sort of mid-2000s teen show.

"Sure. Why not?" Anthony said, as if there weren't an entire gallery full of more interesting things to see and do.

"All right. So there is a rooster on the side—"

Neale's brain screamed, and she felt horror cross her face. This was going to be a bastardization of a Popsicle-stick joke; she could just feel it.

"Hey, Dad," Dylan said, putting her hand on her father's shoulder. "It looks like Mom is going to eat that Gary Puglisi guy alive. Maybe Neale and Anthony should go interrupt?" She put extra emphasis on Anthony's name to show Neale that she was trying to make an opening for them to get away. The whole thing was so unsubtle that Neale was sure her face was hot sauce red. The only thing that could have made Dylan's bailing them out worse was if she'd added a wink.

"Yeah. We don't need another fistfight," Billie jumped in helpfully. Or at least it would have been helpful if she hadn't been grinning like a cat with a mouse.

Turning his attention in the direction the Delacroix daughters were looking, Anthony watched Bernice forcefully telling the man something. Wincing slightly, he said, "Is that your mom?"

"The one and only," Neale said, shaking her head. Giving her sisters a sideways glance, she added, "We should bail Gary out before Mom snatches what's left of the hair off his head."

"Okay," Anthony said, looking wary. Turning back to her father, he said, "Tell me the rest of the joke later?"

"All right." Henry shook his head in resigned disappointment, as if whatever was going to happen with the rooster was a real knee-slapper.

"Right," Neale said, starting a saunter toward her mother, Anthony at her side. Dropping her voice, she said, "Thank you for laughing at my dad's jokes. He will probably make it to New Year's off of your validation alone."

"He seems cool. Besides, who doesn't like dad jokes?" Anthony asked, looking Neale directly in the eye, causing her heart to skip a beat. She wished they weren't the same height. It made unintentionally staring into his dark eyes much easier than it should have been.

"I think most people would take a hard pass on dad jokes," Neale chuckled, dropping her gaze to the floor quickly. She felt herself smiling and tried to suppress it. She did not want to be goofily grinning in front of her mother. On a good day, Bernice was mildly intrusive. On a day like today, she would hit Anthony with every nosy, too-personal question she had in her unfriendly-Canadian repertoire.

"Why? That was actually a pretty good one. I mean, you have to know something about the different food preferences of farm animals to get it, so admittedly, it may not be the stand-up material he thinks it is," Anthony said, shrugging along with his defense of her father. "But overall, I think it holds up."

Neale laughed and shook her head. "Promise me one thing."

"All right." Anthony's voice was gentle against the bebop the gallery was piping through the space.

"Do not tell my dad you think his jokes are passable."

"I can't promise that." Anthony smiled, his expression half-scandalized.

"Oh, you have to. It's in your own best interest. Otherwise, he is going to 'bring me lunch,' but really he will be at the office with a full comedy set for you." Neale put *bring me lunch* in air quotes so Anthony knew exactly what he was getting into.

"I don't see what's wrong with that," Anthony said, holding up his hands.

"Trust me, you will," Neale laughed, loosening up as they eased into a friendly conversation. Unfortunately, this newfound comfort arrived right as they came within earshot of her mother, whose rant had really built up steam.

"Look, Gary. You come to every show, you hem and haw, and then you ask me some sort of silly question like 'Is your work political?' As if, being a Black woman and a mother, I have the luxury of being separate from politics? Now, I don't know what you—"

"Hi, Mom." Neale bounced over to her mother's side and grabbed her arm. Turning to Gary, she said, "Hi, Gary, so good to see you again. Sorry, I just have to steal my mom for a bit."

"Of course. I completely understand. Congratulations on another fantastic opening, Bernice. Truly visionary stuff here," Gary said. For his part, he did not look the least upset at being read by Bernice. *Shows what a fool he is,* Neale thought. If he understood her mother's work at all, he would have started to back away the moment she'd called his question silly. As it was, he would be lucky if Bernice let him walk out of here with so much as a flyer advertising her art. Neale just hoped the gallery moved fast on selling whatever it was Gary was interested in. Otherwise, Bernice would pry the little red *sold* dot out of his cold, dead hands.

"Right," Bernice barked as Neale dragged her toward where she had left Anthony, next to one of her mother's early bronze pieces. Without checking to see if they were out of hearing range, her mother said, "That man is the definition of failing up. And we are all forced to put up with his rudimentary understanding of—"

"Mom, I want you to meet a friend of mine from work," Neale said, hoping to cut her mother off before she started a second rant. "This is Anthony. He designs the artwork for our greeting card line."

"Oh," Bernice said, letting the rage in her tone melt away as she gave Anthony a once-over. "Hello, Anthony. Nice to meet you. Neale did not mention that she had a friend coming." To anyone else, her mother's words would have seemed perfectly normal, but Neale knew better. In the back of her mind, Bernice was scanning for any mention of Anthony. Any hint that Neale knew a man, and that that man was very attractive. Unluckily for Bernice, Neale hadn't said boo to her mother, so she did not have much to go on. Luckily for Neale, that meant her mother couldn't embarrass her nearly as much as her father had.

"Nice to meet you, Ms. Delacroix. I was telling your husband this is my first real gallery show, outside of the stuff you go to in college, and I am blown away. Your work is incredible," Anthony said, oozing polite sincerity. If Neale hadn't known he had been raised by his grandmother, she would have guessed it in this instance. No one was this polite when faced with a raging woman in her midsixties who clearly only cared enough about what others thought to make a quarter of an effort. Indeed, her mother was wearing some sort of mock-neck sweater and floor-length skirt that were only brought out for occasions like this. Glancing down, Neale could see the telltale sign of her mother's "fancy" hiking boots peeking out from under her hem. Yet here Anthony was, treating her like she was a queen and not like he hadn't just watched her nearly consume someone's soul in something from 1987 she'd found in her closet. Neale had to hand it to his grandma: the guy was gold in awkward social situations.

"Why, thank you, Anthony. Has Neale given you any context?" Bernice said, eyeing Neale. The look should have been innocent, but Neale knew her mother had at least three questionable racy jokes lurking in her mind, waiting for the right moment to be said.

"We haven't had a chance to walk around yet," Anthony said, folding his hands nicely in front of him. "I just arrived and wanted to meet you first. I did do a bit of background research before I came. Just looking up the mediums you work in, gallery history. That sort of thing." Anthony's glance flickered toward Neale, his face revealing a hint of a smile. Her mother would never know that they had come to bail her out. The joke could stay between the two of them.

He is good, Neale thought as her mother's face transitioned to a much softer expression. "Well, that is lovely of you. So you know a bit about art."

"Just a little from college. I'm not an artist like you."

"Who says you need to be?" Bernice smiled, completely flattered. "If you produce something that evokes an emotion, then that is art enough. The whole gallery thing is overrated. Trust me," Bernice said, waving a disinterested hand at the walls, as if she hadn't achieved something most people spent a lifetime wishing they had. "Anyway, I'm sure you know that this is really an inflection moment for me. You'll see pieces here from all phases of my career. Please don't judge the work from twenty-five years ago too harshly. I had three small daughters," Bernice said. Her tone was meant to be a joke, but Neale knew there was love behind it.

"Anyway, I'd be happy to . . ." Her mother paused, and her lip curled as she spied someone walking through the door. Sucking in a deep breath, she said, "I'm sorry. Neale, Brett just arrived. You will have to show Anthony around. I need to hide in the restroom. Lovely to meet you, Anthony. You are welcome anytime." With that, Bernice turned on her heel and began a double-time march toward the bathroom.

"Nice to meet you too," Anthony called over his shoulder in the general direction of her mother.

Neale waited until her mother was safely tucked into the bathroom before she uttered so much as a groan. Unlike her father, her mother would hear literally any word anyone said within three hundred yards of the restroom. Her hearing was legendary. "And now you have met the whole family."

"You have a great family," Anthony said, beaming around the room.

"Do I?" Neale asked skeptically.

"Yes. Everyone has their own thing, and you all show up for each other."

"I guess so," Neale said. And she supposed it was true. What Anthony didn't know was that bickering like old men playing pinochle came with the always-being-there-for-one-another part. Neale decided it was best to leave him to his delusion. There was still plenty of night ahead to disabuse him of the notion. Risking a glance at him, Neale asked, "Do you want to grab a drink, then take a look around?"

"Sure," Anthony said in his characteristically comfortable manner. Neale marveled at this. He wasn't a big talker, but he was never uncomfortable in his silence. Usually, Neale felt compelled to make conversation for someone. But this silence wasn't Anthony leaning on her to do the emotional labor of maintaining a friendship. Instead, it was like the quiet was part of the friendship. Its presence had as much to say as their words.

Reaching the bar, they each selected a drink—Coke for her and water for him—before Neale decided it was time to play guide again. Reflecting back on Anthony's introduction to her mother, who, as far as she could tell, was still hiding in the bathroom, she asked, "So did you really google my mom?"

Anthony looked up at her with surprise. "Of course I did. I googled your dad and Billie too. Had to be prepared. Didn't want to embarrass you."

"Embarrass me how?" Neale asked, suddenly aware of how close they had to walk with one another in order to navigate through the crowded space.

"You know." Anthony shrugged, looking down casually as his arm brushed hers. "Like your coworkers are the kind of folks who only show up for the free appetizers."

A half smile crossed Neale's face before she could stop herself. It was adorable that Anthony thought he could embarrass her . . . the girl who'd made herself internet famous for creating bad art. The fact that he had prepared, as if going to her mother's art show were an exam, struck Neale as possibly the sweetest thing anyone had done for her since Nick Englin had paid for her lemonade in the seventh grade.

Aware that Anthony was watching her out of the corner of his eye, she took a sip of Coke before saying, "The only way to be that guy is to have shown up and instantly crammed seventeen puff pastries down your throat."

"Oh, do you have those? Because I thought this was just a cheese-cube situation," Anthony said, looking around the room and bouncing on his toes with mock enthusiasm.

"I'll let you know when the waitstaff passes by with a tray," Neale said, letting her voice go deadpan as Anthony chuckled.

"Seriously, though, I do have questions for your parents. Like, I want to know how your mom used knives to create the texture I saw in this one painting. The whole texture was so even and fine that I can't figure out how she did it. Also, I want to ask your dad what it was like to meet George Clinton."

As Anthony continued talking, all Neale could think was *oh no*.

This could not be happening. She was grinning like someone had handed her a puppy as her heart melted into a gooey puddle somewhere in her chest cavity. Anthony really had googled her parents, and he genuinely had come with questions for them like this was some sort of friendship pop quiz. The whole gesture was too endearing. He was cute. And quirky. And thoughtful. And she had a crush on him.

"Neale?" Anthony said, interrupting her thoughts.

"Sorry, I was just, uh . . ." Neale racked her mind for something other than *I was just freaking out over having a crush on you* and came up with, "Checking to see if my mom was out of the bathroom so you could ask her your questions. She's not out yet."

"She'll have to come out eventually. And I'll be the new Gary when she does." Anthony smiled at her, and Neale felt her heart thud in her chest like a bass drum.

"Proceed at your own risk," Neale snickered. Shrugging her hands into the pockets of her pink romper while she tried to keep her cool, she asked, "So do you want to look at the stuff on the walls first? Or her sculpture?"

"I think that corner over there is less crowded," Anthony said, leaning into her slightly as he navigated toward a large painting of stormy grays and deep blues, his nearness sending a shiver down Neale's spine.

Not trusting herself to speak, Neale nodded as she panicked internally. This was a terrible idea. As much as Neale had tried to deny it, she had a big crush on him. Like, if she were a cartoon, she would have heart eyes. Just acknowledging it made her want to crawl into a hole. She was not supposed to, under any circumstances, develop a crush on Anthony. Or anyone else, for that matter. The only thing that she was supposed to be doing was being New Neale, a woman who excelled at her job, kept a balanced budget, ate copious amounts of fruits and vegetables, and was regarded as reasonably well mannered and capable of making good decisions. A crush on a coworker—even one who looked good in khaki—was not, by any standard, a good decision.

"I really love the colors here. It's almost monochromatic, but not. Your mother is brilliant."

Neale's freak-out continued as Anthony happily chatted about her mother's choice in color, occasionally darting to one end of the painting or the other to look at something up close. The whole experience was so foreign to her that her head was practically spinning. This wasn't like Darin downing a beer and then asking her out. By contrast, this date felt wholly unique.

Not that she had any indication that this was a date or that Anthony wanted to date her. Outside of his showing up and noticing things about her, what evidence did she actually have that dating was on the table? As she reflected on his friendly gestures, it dawned on Neale that she didn't have to do anything about her crush. Hell, lots of people just sat around with crushes and didn't act on them at all. Surely that could be part of New Neale's modus operandi. New Neale would just wait for the crush to go away, then live her merry, complication-free life.

She exhaled a shaky breath and watched as Anthony darted back from the piece to take the whole thing in, his steps easy and graceful. She could totally wait this crush out. Sooner or later, he would smell funny or cover himself in pond scum or do something that would make him exponentially less appealing, and then she could just go back to being a secular nun without the threat of temptation.

Anthony returned to her side, still smiling. Drawing close to her, he said, "Can we go look at the sister painting in the corner?"

Neale's skin tingled as if he had just asked her if she wanted to get naughty with whipped cream, but she managed an "uh-huh" without responding inappropriately.

"Great," Anthony said, gliding toward another large, stormy painting, giving her a chance to check out his perfectly round butt, the kind that denim marketers everywhere dreamed of . . .

And now that butt would be in her dreams again. Giving herself a shake, she trailed after him, vowing to keep her thoughts and hands to herself.

CHAPTER FIFTEEN

"Neale, can you help me?" Billie called, forcing Neale to cut her aimless wandering through the Black Spot short.

"What's up?" Neale asked without making eye contact, secretly praying her sister would miraculously solve her problem herself.

"I need fresh eyes," Billie said, sounding frustrated as she dropped her head into her hands.

Sighing, Neale walked toward her sister, who was huddled over a table, staring at a stack of résumés, prospectuses, photos, and other miscellaneous papers. Over the past two weeks, Billie had blown off not one but two sister hangouts to spend her time in various galleries, coffeehouses, and church basements tracking down talent. In classic Delacroix fashion, when she found an artist she loved, she booked them without any real sense of a through element for how to make all the acts come together. Billie swore up and down that the confusion was part of her process and that overplanning drained the spontaneity that she wanted the audience to feel. Neale understood wanting the work to have an organic feel, but from where she was sitting, her sister's process seemed like more of a stress headache than it was worth.

"How can I help?" Neale asked, suppressing how irritated she was that Billie made time for a photo shoot with some never-heard-of-sup-posedly-up-and-coming art magazine but couldn't be bothered to ask how her day was going.

"How do they go together? I just have a bunch of unsettling art-ists. I mean, there is the poet, this person who does the Hula-Hoop contortion thing. I promise it's not as weird as it sounds," Billie said, holding up a hand at Neale's skeptical eyebrow. Even in a state of panic, her sister would never let her taste be impugned. "Anyway, then there is the person who does the real-time spray paint art in black, gray, and white. And that's only half the numbers. Plus, I still can't figure out the projector-lighting thing you said was brilliant."

"The projector is brilliant. It's not my fault you are creatively blocked. Did you try that mantra Dad recommended?" Neale asked over the sound of her sister snorting. "Don't laugh. His mantras can be really helpful sometimes."

"Right. Well, you let me know when I need to take my crystals out and under what moon, and I'll be sure to recite Dad's mantra."

"I think you are confusing two different concepts there—" Neale started, but she was cut off when Billie made a rude noise.

"Neale. Please."

Focusing on the papers in front of her, Neale said, "You have so many mediums here. What if, instead of looking for a common thread to string them together, you find a single act that does? Whatever ends the show needs to find a way to encompass movement, words, and visual art."

"Yes, but who does that?"

Neale squinted at the papers again. "No one, really. Maybe you could commission another piece?"

"I'm not made of money," Billie scoffed. "There is no way Marceline would let me commission another work. And what would I even say? *Excuse me, but can you make these ten acts fit into one hard-hitting four-minute piece? Yes, there is Hula-Hoop and graffiti, and no, it cannot be a remake of the 'Numbers' dance from* The Wiz?"

"Don't be grumpy at me," Neale said. To her mind, those instructions actually seemed like a good idea, but she could tell that her sister was not looking for that kind of feedback, so she kept her mouth shut.

"Sorry," Billie grumbled. Walking around the table, she came to stand in front of her sister, her head tilted to one side as she furiously chewed her bottom lip. "Question: What would you do to anchor this?"

"If it were me, I might find someone to produce a video that echoes some of the other pieces that could be run through the projector. Something gray like the graffiti artist, maybe the same reds that run through the velvet curtains outside. I know it's more than you want to add to your plate, but maybe you could collaborate with them and unveil a new painting at the end," Neale said, wandering toward the stage.

"Okay, but what is this person—that I can't afford—doing onstage?"

"Something like the *Cut Piece*."

"Yoko Ono?" Billie said, skepticism creeping back into her tone. "Way to swing for the fences."

"I don't mean hiring Yoko Ono herself. Just looking for something that has that same unsettling feel. Like, if it were my piece, I would splice in altered cuts of the footage from the gallery fire. Maybe even find a safer way to have a fire onstage again, like—oh! Like, I put the burn bin in a Hula-Hoop on one end of the stage, and I stand in another. Then the piece becomes about the distance from failure, or having flown too close to the sun, or rising from the ashes or something."

Neale remembered that Billie was in the room and turned to face her sister, who was squinting hard at her as if she couldn't decide what to think. Feeling exposed, Neale backtracked. "Okay, it's a stretch, but you get where I am going." She stopped her rambling explanation as Billie tilted her head to the side, the hypercritical squint still glued to her face.

"You would have something to say," Billie said at last.

"No. I don't have anything to say." Neale hesitated. Something in her sister's voice was making her nervous. "That is sort of what I'd want the last artist to say. They may want something else."

"But you could say it," Billie said, crossing her arms.

There was nothing inherently sinister about how her sister was standing, but the way she said the word *could* made Neale sweat. Taking a deep breath, she pushed back again. "No. Someone could say it. Not me."

"Why not you?" Billie shot back.

"Billie, we have been over this like six hundred times. And on top of the performance baggage, see this?" Neale asked, pointing to the white button-up sweater and navy-blue wide-leg slacks she had forever-borrowed from Dylan's closet and worn today. "This screams *I have a day job.*"

"Three-quarters of the people in this show have a day job on top of this commission. What's your point?" Billie said, looking unimpressed by Dylan's-turned-Neale's wardrobe choices.

"My point is, when would I have time for the workshops?"

"Neale. This isn't the Collective. We're not here to workshop each other's stuff. This is you bringing your polished work to the table. It'll be fun. We can build off of each other for the painting, have a couple run-throughs with the group so everyone can catch the vibe, and I can make adjustments; then it's showtime."

Her sister's tone was so utterly blasé that Neale wondered if Billie thought this was the same as waiting in line at the grocery checkout. She opened her mouth to see if words would come, then closed it again when they didn't. The back of her neck felt hot and cold all at the same time, and Neale wondered how long it would take her to sweat through Dylan's cardigan.

Billie continued to watch Neale as if they were in a staring contest. After thirty seconds of silence, she must have gotten tired of listening to the low hum of the HVAC system, because she said, "The Collective was about some amateur-hour bullshit. This is the big leagues, and I want you as my pitcher. Please, Neale."

"No, Billie. Find someone else," Neale said, happy to have her words back and even more pleased that her *no* sounded like she meant it.

"Why are you being such a chicken about this?" Billie asked, stomping her foot.

"I'm not being a chicken. I'm moving on," Neale shot back.

Neale let the HVAC system quietly whir away in the silence between the two of them again as she tried to stare down her sister. Finally, Billie said, "I don't believe you. You aren't passionate about spreadsheets. You aren't Dylan. This job just keeps you busy."

"I don't need to be passionate about spreadsheets. I need to feed myself." The sound of the truth echoing around the theater shocked Neale. She had never admitted how she felt out loud before, but the truth was, she didn't hate her job. She just wasn't in love with it either.

"Feeding yourself and creating art are not mutually exclusive. I waitressed for how long?" Billie said, her big voice filling up the space between them as she shook her head. "No. This isn't feeding yourself. This is cowardice. When did you become afraid?"

"Not afraid. Just not interested," Neale said, her voice sounding closer to a shout than she would have liked.

Billie picked up on the volume change, too, and a ghost of a smile crossed her face. Her sister knew she'd hit a nerve. "Look. You can move on, but I am not letting you cower away. You're doing this show. Then, if you're still over it, you can give up, or whatever vocabulary you want to call sulking away, and I'll never say anything about it again. Deal?"

"No deal." Neale shook her head violently as she said this. "Billie, I'm not negotiating with you. Find someone else."

"Honestly. I need your help. It isn't like you have a lot else going on besides your job."

"A new job is a lot going on," Neale said, trying not to be offended. It was easy for Billie to say she wasn't doing anything. Her day job days were behind her. Plus, she didn't have the specter of internet notoriety hanging over her head every time she stepped out in public. Two weeks ago, someone had actually recognized her in the grocery store. They'd even sung the stupid song remix to her.

Billie rolled her eyes like she was talking to an unreasonable teen. "This is absurd. Have you told Mom you are too scared to try again? Because she and Dad really think you are going to get back into it."

"Mom and Dad already know. They are the ones who kicked me out and told me to start supporting myself, remember?"

"Key phrase being '*supporting* yourself,' not '*losing* yourself.' They didn't mean for you to run and hide."

"I have a new life now. End of story," Neale said, sighing heavily and picking up her bag. There was no point in her hanging around when it was clear the only thing Billie planned on getting done today involved working on her last good nerve.

"Do you want me to talk to Mom?" Billie asked, as if she were genuinely doing Neale a favor. Like they were little kids and Neale still needed her to break bad news to their parents.

"No, Bill. You don't need to talk to Mom for me. My answer is no," Neale said, facing her sister head on so she knew she was serious. "Look, I'm happy to help you think through the stage and organize artists or whatever, but I'm not doing this."

"I'm going to talk to Mom about this. Seriously, I don't want you to live with regret." Billie crossed her arms, her eyes narrowing as she dug in.

Neale tilted her head back and looked up at the rafters, letting the sound of her strangled whine echo around dramatically. Looking back at her sister, she said, "Go ahead and tell Mom. It won't change my mind. Now, if you are done, then I'm going to go get a burrito. Coming?"

"Have it your way." Billie shrugged, the big black frames of her glasses wiggling as she wrinkled her nose. "I've got more work to do, but we aren't done with this."

"I will have it my way. Thanks," Neale said, feeling childish. Of course Billie would skip dinner after calling her a coward.

"All right, then," Billie said, her tone relaxing too much for Neale to feel like her sister was really letting their argument go. Looking down at her paperwork and then back up at Neale, she asked, "Are you going to TLF? If so, can you put an order in for me and tell them I'll be by to pick it up in forty-five minutes?"

A small part of Neale wanted to make her order her own stupid burrito. A bigger part of her knew that if she ordered Billie's burrito, she could put her dinner on her sister's tab and save her hard-earned dollars for her coffee habit.

"Fine. But you are paying for my burrito too." With that, Neale turned and marched out of the theater, doing her best to keep her posture just the right amount of moral-high-ground straight. Billie could make all the threats, skip every last one of their plans, and buy all the burritos she wanted, but this time Neale wasn't backing down. She would not be in the show.

~

"So . . . good news and bad news," Neale said, spinning around in her chair to look at Anthony.

"What's up?"

"I've been looking into the cost of licensing songs, and because it's a small run of cards, we wouldn't be able to get the rate our big clients usually get for a song." Ignoring the fluttering in her pulse as he turned to face her, she anchored her gaze to the corner of his jaw so that her eyes wouldn't rove in any un-colleague-like ways.

"Oh," Anthony said, his lips sinking into a frown. Not that Neale noticed his lips. She was looking at his jaw. Taking a deep breath, he said, "So what is the rate?"

"For us, they are willing to license the songs at the low, low price of triple what our competitors pay for it."

"Are you kidding? That is like two dollars a song."

"Yup. Do you want more bad news first, or are you ready for the good news?"

Anthony snorted. "How can it get worse?"

"Just printing the thing and licensing the music makes this card retail for roughly nine dollars, and that is before we look into the actual device that produces the sound."

"Ouch. We can't sell a twelve-dollar greeting card. No one is buying that," Anthony said, slouching slightly in his chair as disappointment set in. "Did you tell Rich yet?"

Neale hesitated. She had intentionally avoided giving Rich an update on the project this morning, namely because she suspected he would pull the plug without a second thought if she told him the cost projection had gone from $7,000 to $9,000. Rubbing her forehead, she said, "Not yet. I want to try a few other things before he puts the brakes on any of this. I did say there was good news, remember?"

Anthony perked up slightly. "Good, because I just handed him my sketches this morning. What was your good news?"

"I have an idea. What if we commissioned a piece?"

"You want to commission a Halloween song?"

"Well, it doesn't have to be a song, per se. It could just be a door creaking or someone screaming or evil laughing. But yes, I want to commission it."

"That sounds expensive. With licensing we only pay for what we use," Anthony said, sounding skeptical.

"Maybe not," Neale said, holding up a hand. "If we commission the work, then we know what the per-unit cost is long before it hits the shelves. Similarly, we can use it year after year, so the cost of song ownership comes down over time."

"Okay, but with licensing, we don't have to come up with all the money up front. They bill us back, and we pay off of what we've manufactured."

"What if we could find another smaller music-production company looking to crack into the game?" Neale said, sounding way too upbeat for the office's fluorescent lighting.

"Crack into what game?" Anthony asked, half smiling.

"The random-tech-that-needs-music game," Neale said, flat-out grinning as she began laying out her master plan.

"That's a game?" Anthony laughed.

"Oh, it is," Neale said, clicking to open a window on her computer and pushing away from her desk so Anthony could see her screen. Pointing, she said, "Behold, the Burgeoning Licensing Technology Conference. Or as I like to call it, BLT."

Anthony chuckled at her corny joke, shaking his head as he wheeled his chair into the walkway between their cubicles to get a better look. "It seems like it's for databases and home speakers."

"Okay, yes. But (a) it is a super affordable conference, so Rich won't say no, and (b) I checked, and they have a whole room for display booths, including musicians and recording devices."

Anthony tilted his head to the side and nodded, hemming and hawing as he thought. "It seems like a long shot. But we may as well try."

"That's just what I wanted to hear," Neale said, her voice bubbling over with excitement. "I'm going to register us for the Friday session, because it's the cheapest day, and who doesn't want to spend Friday outside of the office?"

Anthony's face split into a slow smile as he said, "Spending next Friday with you at BLT. It is going on the calendar."

Inside, Neale's whole entire heart expanded as she thought about spending Friday with him, a silly grin creeping across her face. She just hoped he would attribute the smile to BLT and not her potentially disastrous crush on him. Reminding herself that she had no intention of acting out any of her more exciting fantasies, she forced herself to focus. Wheeling back toward her computer screen, she said, "All right. I'll email you the confirmation page."

Deciding against asking Susan for the company credit card, Neale dug around in her purse to find her own new credit card. It would be easier to send an email with a receipt requesting a reimbursement from her least favorite coworker than to have to try to interact with her. As she typed in her card number, Neale's excitement built. When the licensing problem had first come up, she'd been convinced it was the end of the road. Yet here she was, getting creative and finding solutions to make this whole singing greeting card thing happen. Hell, she had put more energy into making this card than she had into half of the pieces she'd workshopped for the Collective . . .

The thought made Neale pause. She loved art, but she hadn't always worked hard at it. Not that she didn't want to. Sometimes, she just got overwhelmed by everything, from deciding which mediums to use to standing in her parents' shadow. And while she liked Anthony, and as grateful as she was to Rich for hiring her, greeting cards were not her passion. She knew what her passion was. She felt it in her bones when she sat down to write her thoughts or stood behind a camera. She didn't feel anything like that with greeting cards. Not even the cute ones with glitter gave her that feeling.

Maybe Billie was getting to her. After all, her sister and her parents had been pelting her with text messages and phone calls for the last few days. Was her sister right? Maybe she should try one more time?

Nope. Neale thought the word so hard she was pretty sure she had mumbled it. A fact that was confirmed mere seconds later when Anthony asked, "You okay?"

Neale forced her expression to relax as she looked for a way to explain that she was quietly having an existential crisis and decided on, "I'm fine. Just thinking about my family. They want me to do some art stuff with them."

"And you don't want to do it?" Anthony asked, his eyebrows creeping toward his fresh haircut.

"It's not that I don't want to. It's that I can't. I have a . . ." Neale paused, casting about for a way to explain a thing she didn't fully understand and landing on, "Conflict."

"If I were you, I'd cancel whatever else I was doing. Hanging out with your family is fun. Your mom's a riot." Anthony's expression relaxed.

"Believe me when I say that she wasn't joking and that she hides from people all the time," Neale said, shaking her head. "Actually, so does Billie, and she is terrible at it. It never works. But she keeps trying."

Chuckling softly, Anthony said, "If anyone else in your family has a show, you should text me. I definitely want to be there for the next one. Even if it is just your dad telling bad jokes."

"Duly noted. You'll regret it, trust me." Neale felt her big, stupid, goofy grin return as Anthony turned to face his computer. She decided she was going to have to work a little harder on the whole no-crush plan, or at the rate she was grinning, within forty-eight hours the whole office would figure out she liked him. Fixing her face, she finished filling out the conference form and drafted a confirmation email to Anthony without so much as a single heart emoji and with only one exclamation point in the text. Hitting send, she smiled. Operation No Crush was officially underway.

CHAPTER SIXTEEN

Have you reconsidered helping your sister?

You would be GREAT in Billie's show.

Honest, don't hide your talent away forever. You can do this.

Dropping her phone, Neale let out a mangled cry of frustration. How many of her mother's text messages did she have to ignore before Bernice took the hint? Pulling out a pair of bright-yellow oversize sweatpants, she huffed. She had been looking forward to Friday night all week, and now that she finally had time to relax, she was being hounded by her family.

Yanking a billowy T-shirt that she'd won at a Classical KING FM concert over her head, she reflected on how she'd gotten here. She couldn't believe Billie had actually told their mom on her. Getting Bernice involved? That was a low blow, even for her diabolical middle sister.

Ignoring me won't make me forget you exist, but nice try.

Neale rolled her eyes as she picked up the phone and pocketed it. Stopping by the bathroom, she grabbed a silk scrunchie and pulled her hair into a messy knot at the top of her head, acknowledging that her roots had grown out considerably and she probably needed to either bleach her hair blonde again or dye it back soon.

From over on a floor cushion, Corinne called, "Could you grab me another spritzer, please?"

"Sure," Neale said, walking toward the kitchen, feeling herself finally getting into the spirit of TV night. Sometime around Wednesday, she and Corinne had discovered they were both having difficult weeks and decided that the best plan was drinking wine spritzers, eating ice cream, and watching *Rhoda* until they had fully recovered. As far as Neale was concerned, she had never heard a better end-of-the-workweek plan.

Grabbing two spritzers, she felt her phone buzz and instantly regretted the day she'd asked Corinne for the Wi-Fi password. Now she couldn't use no cell phone reception as a reason to ignore her mother. Shifting the drinks to one hand, she took her phone out of her pocket and stared at the name flashing on the screen. *Darin.*

"Ugh," Neale grumbled, sounding like an exhausted cow.

"What happened?" Corinne called.

"Nothing. It's just that dude I used to hang out with."

"The one with the sad idea about being a janitor or whatever?"

"That's the one." Neale laughed at Corinne's interpretation of what Darin's piece was about. In sum total, she actually wasn't that far off; it just sounded funny when she said it.

"What does he want, you to come to his DJ set?"

Neale snorted as she handed Corinne her spritzer. "I haven't opened it yet."

"Well, jump to it. I'm living vicariously through all your mess."

"All right, all right. You little voyeur," Neale joked, looking at the sensor on her phone.

Hey! Did you get my last text about coffee?

"*Pfff.*" Neale fluttered her lips and shook her head.

"What did he say?" Corinne asked, impatience tingeing her voice.

"Something about working our miscommunication out over coffee."

"Hard pass," Corinne chuckled as she popped the tab on her can of spritzer.

"It's only funny because he used to ignore my texts all the time. But now that I am doing it to him, all of a sudden he just seems to always have his phone around, like he is waiting for an answer."

"Of course he is." Corinne shook her head. "Buddy, take a hint. You are not interested."

"I already gave him the polite brush-off too. I don't know why he wants to stay friends, but—" Neale's phone buzzed, and she looked down midsentence.

"What is it?"

It took a moment for her brain to stop short-circuiting. Then anger flooded her so fast she wondered if steam was coming out of her ears. Neale looked up at her roommate, who was leaning forward, waiting for her to fill her in, then back down at the offending text.

I heard your sister might be staging her show at the Black Spot.
Do you know if she'd be open to my audition? ;-)

"Oh."

"What? What did he say?"

"I guess we know why he wants to stay friends now," Neale said, holding up her phone so Corinne could read the text.

"He has to be kidding."

"I don't think he is." Neale's blood was practically boiling at this point. Some small, misguided corner of her brain had hoped his messages were overtures of friendship. She didn't want to talk to him now, but if she was honest with herself, she'd hoped that in six months, she would run into Darin at the grocery store or the Swedish bakery and they could laugh because Neale was successful in her new job and had moved on. Then he could text her, and maybe she would get coffee with him, just to rub in the fact that she now had money for parking on Market and was that special, saintly kind of person who really could stay friends with her exes.

For a split second, Neale wondered if there was an angle that she was missing. Some sort of code that Darin had embedded that meant she was important to him. That the squeeze she had felt on her heart every time she'd thought about him wasn't one sided. In her quiet moments, she really wanted to believe that somewhere in all of this, she did mean something to him.

Neale shook her head. That was her old way of thinking. Just another one of the daydreams that Darin had made fun of. She'd outgrown those kinds of ridiculous fantasies. In front of her eyes was the obvious reason he had bothered to contact her at all. He wanted access to Billie. Neale couldn't control whether or not Billie gave anyone an audition, but she could control whether or not she ever spoke to Darin again.

"Tell him to eat shit," Corinne said, her cheeks flushed with anger.

"Yuck. That's gross." Neale wrinkled her nose and laughed through clenched teeth.

"He's gross," Corinne said in her best disgusted voice.

"You do have a point there," Neale said, tilting her head to the side as she thought. After a moment, she began typing.

I'd rather eat glass than have coffee with you. Stay away from Billie.

Hitting send, Neale held up her phone so Corinne could see. Her roommate had just finished nodding in approval when the phone vibrated. Corinne saw the text before Neale could turn the phone around, and her jaw dropped open.

Don't be like that Neale. I thought we were friends.

"Can you believe this guy?" Neale said, flexing her fingers.

"Now can we tell him to eat shit?" Corinne asked, shaking her drink at Neale.

"No. That's still gross." Neale cackled as that afternoon in Darin's room replayed in her mind. "I have something better than that."

We are friends, Darin. And like you said, friends have to separate their personal and professional lives. Good luck out there.

"Boom," Neale said, hitting the green send button and dropping her phone on the floor.

"Taste of his own medicine. I like it." Corinne slurped the top of her can, where she had managed to shake a precarious amount of spritzer.

"The sad part is, if he wasn't the world's biggest dickhead, I would just give him my spot," Neale said, shaking her head. "Then Billie would stop bugging me about joining the show."

"Wait. Why won't you be in your sister's show?" Corinne asked, pivoting away from the laptop screen they had set up so she could look at Neale fully.

"Because I don't want to go through all that again. Billie wasn't there. She didn't see how bad it was," Neale said, sighing.

"But your mom was there. And from everything I've heard about your mother, she definitely wouldn't encourage you if she thought you could bomb like that again."

"Thanks," Neale said, shooting her roommate a look.

"What? It's true. You literally said yesterday that your mom was the most blunt person in the universe. And before you question me, that was a direct quote from you," Corinne laughed.

Neale actually remembered saying it as she'd poured her coffee before work. At the time she'd thought it was harmless to complain about her mom bugging her, but now that her words were a weapon, she wished she'd kept her mouth shut. Shaking her head, she said, "True. It's just, I don't think I'm ready to go through that again. Like, emotionally."

"When do you think you'll be ready?" Corinne asked, swigging at her drink too casually for the question not to feel loaded. Looking Neale in the eyes, she said, "Like, somewhere between when pigs fly and capitalism dissolves, or what?"

"Pigs flying is a big ask. But capitalism could happen." Neale smiled at her half-hearted attempt at a joke.

"Here's the thing. I have been studying your star chart, and it is all starting to make sense. I feel that this is a sign you should do the show. You can't give your spot to that Darin asshole."

"I mean, I wouldn't actually give it to him."

"You know what I'm saying." Corinne glared at Neale over the rim of her can. "You gotta put yourself out there again."

"Last time I put myself out there, it nearly ate me alive."

"Did it, though? 'Cause I feel like StarsSign told me that you guard a corner of energy. That way if you fail, you can say you didn't really give something your all."

"Are you sure you have my time of birth right? Because that was not in my daily notifications." Neale wrinkled her nose as Corinne grinned and nodded. "Also, how much time are you spending on that horoscope app?"

"Enough to know that you are deflecting," Corinne cackled, then took a sip of her drink before adding, "Seriously, though, have you thought about joining the show? I mean, for real thought about it, not just thought about different reasons to say no?"

"I actually really did consider it today." Neale sighed.

"See! I knew it," Corinne shouted, setting her can on the floor and pointing at Neale. "I could tell. Something about your energy when you came home told me that you needed me."

"We've had these plans for days," Neale said, trying to resist the idea that Corinne had had some sort of psychic premonition about her.

"Yeah, but that was just the universe lining us up so that we could have this talk. Neale, I felt it in my bones when you moved in. You have to try again. I just know it."

"The day of the last show, fire was a do in my horoscope, so I'm not putting a lot of faith in that right now." Neale sighed and reached for her can of spritzer. If she was really going to have this conversation, she might as well do it with a drink in hand. "Billie says I'm just scared."

"You probably have the app's time zone wrong or something. Also, Billie is right." Corinne scowled at her. "Seriously, look at the evidence. You consider going back to art for the first time in what, months? Then Billie offers you a place, then this bitch-made Darin tries to take your spot, and I read your sad energy. You need to do this in order to heal."

Despite everything that Neale knew about the way the world worked, she had to admit that Corinne's reasoning made sense—except the Darin thing; that made no sense. If the world didn't want her to do this, then why was she getting so many signs that she should?

Again, the word *coward* floated through her mind. This time, Neale didn't flinch away from it. Taking a deep breath, she said, "Corinne, am I being a coward? Like, is my energy cowardly?"

"Hmmm," her roommate said, closing her eyes for a moment. "It's not cowardly. Just more conflicted. You gotta make a choice, though, or you could end up with some fear hovering over your head. And, friend, I do not want that bad energy in my house when I turn twenty-eight. So you gonna do it or what?"

Neale laughed despite the churning feeling in her stomach. Either she was going to heed the signs of the universe, or she was going to bring bad vibes into their collective dominion.

When it came right down to it, Neale was going to feel torn until she found a way to make peace between Old Neale and New Neale. As much as she wanted to be Neale who was good at her desk job, wore boring clothes, and felt nothing toward coworkers, she kept finding herself doing things like noticing the way sound moved through space and having inappropriate crushes. Corinne was right; she had cognitive vertigo. Billie's show was the solution. If she did this, she could give Old Neale a final goodbye party. Prove she wasn't a mess anymore and walk away from everything with her head held high, not her tail between her legs. She'd told Darin off tonight. That had to be a sign that she was on her way to being New Neale for good. As long as she kept Old Neale in her lane, giving her creative self a little room to fly off wouldn't be a problem.

After taking a slow sip of her spritzer to heighten the drama of the moment, she said, "I'll do it."

"For reals? Because if you say yes, then turn around and change your mind and bring that gnarly energy back in this house, I swear . . ." Corinne shook her fist at Neale. The gesture was meant to be threatening, but it had the exact opposite effect.

"For reals," Neale chortled, then added, "This is my last hoorah. A moment of potential redemption so I can hold my head high and walk away."

"That a girl. Now, text your sister. Your phone going off at all hours is killing me." Corinne giggled as she angled the computer toward them and began pulling up *Rhoda* in her browser. "So what are you going to say to Billie?"

"I'm still thinking about it," Neale said, her voice sounding hazy as she tried to concentrate.

"It doesn't have to be a sonnet. You could literally text *You win*, and she'd get it," Corinne said, clearly ready to get roommate night underway.

"Never. I can't give Billie that kind of satisfaction." Neale snorted and shook her head as she began to type.

So, I have been thinking about your show, and I have decided I will help you out.

"Send," Neale said, shutting one eye and holding her breath as she hit the green arrow. She sort of hoped that Billie was busy doing something cool or important and that she wouldn't see the text. That way Neale could be another spritzer in before she had to deal with the reality of trying to reconcile her two selves. In fact, now that she thought about it, maybe she should be three spritzers in before trying to unbifurcate herself.

"Good," Corinne squealed, then took a sip of her drink. "Moving to the next item on our *Fixing Neale's Energy* list, we are watching the episode where Rhoda throws a New Year's party after she sees her ex-husband on a date, so we can get inspiration for my party."

Neale laughed, settling into her cushion and pulling a blanket over her legs. "You want your party theme to be *desperate*?" she said, waving her hand through the air as if the word were on an invisible marquee.

"I have all the phone numbers I need. Every girl in Seattle who is interviewing for the position of Corinne's girlfriend will be at my party. You, on the other hand, need some phone numbers."

"Nope. New Neale is focused on her career and getting herself together. She may be dabbling in art in order to fix whatever weird energy is hanging around her, but New Neale is not dating anybody."

"Maybe the energy was about your love life?" Corinne suggested as she hit play.

"Nice try. That is only going to work once." Neale laughed.

As the evening went on, Neale found the stress of the workweek slowly melting away. In between laughing at Rhoda's antics and coming up with plans for their own party, Neale had nearly forgotten that she had texted her sister until she felt her phone buzz in her pocket. Holding the device up, Neale opened Billie's note.

> Delighted you have had a change of heart, sister. I can't wait to work with you.

Of course, this would be the one time Billie is gracious about winning, Neale thought, rolling her eyes and dropping the phone onto the cushion beside her with a muffled thud. As much as Neale didn't want her to gloat, faux-gracious Billie was almost more annoying.

Looking over at her, Corinne asked, "Do you want some ice cream?"

"Yes!" Neale said, forcing herself to focus on the fun she was having. Whatever she felt about Billie and the show was tomorrow's problem. Right now, Neale was focused on food, party planning, and laughing with Corinne.

"All right," Corinne said, hitting pause before pushing herself up and dashing off to the kitchen. Over the banging of cupboard doors, she called, "So who are you inviting to my incredible Glitter Cat–themed extravaganza?"

Neale wondered if the theme needed a little finessing if Corinne was really going to land the girlfriend of her dreams, but she decided that her roommate was getting her ice cream, so now was not the time to mention it. Instead, she said, "Maybe a couple of friends from high school who you haven't met, but they are chill. My sisters, who will likely not come because Dylan goes to bed at ten thirty p.m. and Billie is literally too busy being cool. And Morrigan, obviously."

"Morrigan is on my list already," Corinne said, coming out of the kitchen with a salad bowl of ice cream in each hand. "Anybody cool from work?"

"I mean, my office is so small. I only really have one friend: Anthony. He's cool, though. We eat lunch and stuff."

"Invite him." Corinne grinned, reaching into her sweatpants pockets to produce another spritzer, then passing it off to Neale.

"I don't know. It's not that I don't want to invite him," Neale said, as Corinne flopped down on the floor next to her. "I probably shouldn't."

"Why not? I'm inviting my coworkers."

"Yeah, but I low-key have a crush on him, and I want that to go away. Like, I don't think it's a good idea to encourage it."

"Why?" Corinne shrieked, sounding so much like one of her sisters that Neale began to wonder if maybe she was a long-lost Korean Delacroix.

"Everyone knows you shouldn't date coworkers."

"Oh my God, Neale. Are you going to overthink every aspect of your life? You are inviting him to a party to get to know him. You aren't asking him to marry you," Corinne said, shaking her head and attacking her ice cream with a soup spoon.

"Yes, but I don't need to get to know him. I need to get some distance from him."

"Maybe you will invite him to the party, realize he wears weird shoes, and get over it that way," Corinne giggled.

"I already know he doesn't wear weird shoes," Neale said, taking a bite of ice cream. "And that's the problem."

"I'm over your boring angst. Would you please just text the guy?"

"It's not angst. And it's not boring." Neale's voice cracked with indignation.

"I'm over here planning to invite every crush I have and see how this plays out *Bachelorette*-style, and you are waffling about one dude? It's boring," Corinne said, scooping up another bite of ice cream. Only after making sure her mouth was full did she start chanting, "Text him. Text him. Text him. Text—"

"Okay, okay, okay." Neale waved her hand at Corinne to get her to stop. Setting her ice cream down, she reached for her phone. "He gave me his number, but I still don't really text him. Is it weird that the first thing I send him in weeks is an invitation to a party at ten fifty-two on a Friday night?"

Corinne banged her spoon against her bowl. "For the love of God, just text him."

"All right. Unbunch your panties," Neale said, tapping at her phone.

"Joke's on you. I don't wear underwear."

Neale snorted.

"What? They give you underwear lines in scrubs," Corinne said, shaking her head. "What are you gonna say to Anthony?"

"You're so in my business. Did my sisters put you up to this?" Neale said, finally locating Anthony's number. Maybe it was the spritzer or the sugar rush, but Neale felt like Corinne might have a point about Anthony too.

"No. But if you want, I can text them afterward," Corinne shot back playfully.

Neale laughed, then began typing.

Hey! My roommate and I are throwing a party for her 28th birthday on Saturday, the 26th. If you don't have plans, then save the date!

Immediately after hitting send, she panicked. What if he didn't know this was her number? Taking a deep breath, she quickly typed a follow-up.

This is Neale Delacroix by the way.

"That's so smooth," Corinne said, sarcasm dripping from her as she leaned over her shoulder to read what she had written.

"Thanks. So glad to have your thoughts after I sent the message."

"I mean, if I had known how bad you are at texting, I wouldn't have encouraged you to jump in there without backup."

"Whatever. You probably just text pictures of a unicorn and think that's game," Neale said, tossing her phone aside and scooping up her ice cream bowl again.

"Oh, it is game when I do it," Corinne said, snorting.

"Sure. That's why we are both home on a Friday night," Neale laughed.

"Well, maybe after this party we won't be," Corinne giggled, reaching over to hit play on their show.

CHAPTER SEVENTEEN

As Neale's phone buzzed, she couldn't help but think that she had made a mistake. She looked down to read the latest text message from Anthony. Sure, it was a mistake that she was enjoying, but a mistake nonetheless.

I just saw Rich leaving the grocery store . . . wearing a fanny pack.

Did you get photographic evidence? Melissa and Travis won't believe you without it.

They had been texting little things back and forth all week. As far as Neale was concerned, most of his texts were innocuous, friend-type texts, but they were having a catastrophic effect on her heart. At this rate, Neale was never going to get over her crush. Worse, she couldn't even reasonably say that she was trying, since she responded to every single joke about dogs, coworkers, and traffic with a speed that suggested she believed her life depended on it.

Sadly, no. Following him around QFC seemed like a bad idea. And he had his puppy in the car with him, so sneaking up on him in the parking lot was out of the question.

I've heard French bulldogs are pretty vicious. You made the right choice.

Okay, she had to stop texting him, or she'd be grinning like a fool all night. Pocketing her phone, Neale pushed herself out of the car and toward the rec center where Billie was holding rehearsal.

This was another mistake. In fact, she was pretty sure that last Friday night was shaping up to be one giant impetuous mistake. How big a bonehead was she that she'd let Corinne, two spritzers, and some ice cream talk her into doing every single thing that was bad for her? Thinking back on it, if Neale had said she wanted to take a bath in Jell-O, Corinne probably would have encouraged her, and she would still be trying to rinse red food dye out of her hair.

Taking a deep breath as she reached for the Plexiglas doors, she willed herself to think positive thoughts. From the hallway, she could hear Billie's voice making strongly phrased suggestions to someone else, and Neale was struck by just how quickly Billie's indecision had transformed into confidence. Not three weeks ago she'd been panicking about a projector, and now she was in the driver's seat, going a hundred miles per hour as if she had never met an insecurity in her life.

Neale sneaked into the room and settled into a chair by the door, careful not to let her purse—okay, Dylan's purse—make a sound as she set it on the chair next to her.

A short, copper-skinned person with an undercut stood in the center of a circle of chairs holding a notepad, furiously scribbling as Billie spoke. "So here is what I am loving about all of this. The undercurrent of the piece is totally raw and unpredictable, and you have used that to create a sort of structure for the audience. It feels subversive and thoughtful."

"Thanks," Undercut said, half smiling as they continued to write.

"But I'm a little worried that the third section takes that subversiveness to an almost cartoonish level. It's okay to be raw and to play with the sounds of consonants and paint cans, but I don't think you want to lean so hard into the idea that it feels overdone. Do I have that right?" Billie said, putting a hand on her hip and causing the fringe on the sleeve of her black crop top to shimmer.

"Totally." Undercut looked up. "So is it just the fact that I'm enunciating the p sound that hard, or is it word choice that you think is going too far?"

"I think that is for you to explore. My goal isn't to dictate your art but just to suggest alternative ways of thinking about it. Why not play with both solutions and come back to the next rehearsal with your preference?"

"Works for me," Undercut said, their shoulders relaxing with Billie's approval.

"Great. I think my sister is running late," Billie said, sounding irritated, which in turn irked Neale.

She was just about to say something to her sister when Undercut pointed at her and said, "Is that your sister?"

Whirling around, Billie grinned. "Oh, hey, Neale. Guess you're not late."

"Nope, just quietly watching you talk shit."

Undercut's features went pale as the two sisters looked at each other; then Billie began to cackle. "I earned that. Don't take it personal, Neale. You're always late."

Neale grinned. "Not as late as you." The joke made her sister snort, and for a moment, the weeks of missed hangouts and intense interactions melted away. It felt like they were back to their old selves. Neale stood and walked toward Undercut with her hand outstretched. "Hi, I'm Neale."

"Callen. Nice to meet you."

"They are the number before yours," Billie said casually.

"Oh! Good thing I was early. It sounds like you are working on a percussive piece?" Neale said, stressing the word *early* just so she could get one more jab in at her sister. Billie snorted again and wandered back to a set of chairs in the center of the room that she was using as some sort of desk.

"Yes, exactly. Are you working on a multimedia piece?" they asked politely. Neale hoped Callen wasn't closely following the Seattle art scene, or the fact that she was anchoring the show would probably send them running for the hills.

"Yes. I'm hoping to work in some elements from each act, so I'm super glad I caught a little bit of what you are doing."

"Sounds exciting. I can't wait to see what you come up with," Callen said, grabbing their bag by the door. "See you next week, Billie. Neale, nice to meet you."

"See you soon," Billie said, half focusing on Callen as they made their way out the door.

"Nice to meet you," Neale called as they left.

Billie waited exactly four seconds after Neale was done speaking before she said, "So, sister, what do you got for me?"

"Well, I figured we could talk through some of what I'm thinking for this round, then next time I can show you some stuff?" Neale said, taking her time as she walked toward the chair opposite Billie.

"Oh. I guess that works." The surprise in her sister's voice made Neale look up sharply. What had Billie expected her to bring to a first rehearsal? It wasn't like Neale was one of the other artists, who'd auditioned with a piece specifically for the show. She'd been coerced into this on Friday, and it was now Wednesday.

Trying to get a lid on her irritation, she sat down and looked at her sister. "I only committed to this like five days ago; it isn't exactly like I've had tons of time to execute on a vision."

"Sorry," Billie said, holding up her hands. "I just thought you would start working on what you talked about at the Black Spot. I totally get it if that isn't the way you want to go. We still have three weeks before the show."

Logically, Neale knew that her sister meant the apology to be reassuring, but somehow the mention of the timeline made her all the more stressed out. A month was not a lot of time. Stuffing her fears about execution aside, Neale admitted, "It's okay. In the Collective, we had a lot of time to workshop our ideas and really feel what was right for the piece. I'm not used to a tight deadline."

"Welcome to the world of commissioned art." Billie grinned, spreading her arms wide as if she had been waiting to drop that little truth nugget on Neale since she'd realized her sister didn't have a plan.

It took all of Neale's considerable adulting skills not to point out that Billie had basically "commissioned" this piece for free, since Marceline wouldn't shell out more money up front for another artist. All Neale was getting was a measly 2 percent of ticket sales, so if Billie's show wasn't a knockout, Neale was out of luck. However, arguing with her sister when she was trying to be nice wouldn't help her case right now, so she simply nodded to show Billie she was paying attention.

"Right. So listening to what Callen is doing got me thinking about the sound spray paint makes, and what if we played with unusual percussion over poetry?" Neale asked, shaking off her earlier trepidation.

"That could work. We also have someone doing a sort of rhythmic dance. You could work that in," Billie said, pointing one sparkly, onyx-colored acrylic nail at her with a smile.

"Then I was thinking that my actual spoken piece would be about fear," Neale said, mostly to herself now. After all, she was officially terrified of this whole process, so why not do something with that?

"Okay. What kind of fear?"

"I'm still playing with that." Neale shrugged. It wasn't that she hadn't tried to think of something, but she just got overwhelmed when she thought too much about her piece. If she had anticipated Billie asking so many questions, she would have pushed through the fear of a Collective repeat and spent more than twenty minutes on the drive over brainstorming something to put in front of her.

"All right, well . . . let me ask you this," Billie said, shifting in her chair and looking Neale dead in the eyes. "I get how you might incorporate others' work. But how are you making this personal to you?"

"What do you mean?" Neale asked, shifting uncomfortably.

"I mean, you are what makes your art unique. How is your fear going to be reflected in the piece? What personal fear do you want the audience to experience in real time?"

If she was honest, outside of critters in her hair and going viral again, she wasn't even entirely sure what she feared. Everything? Old Neale, New Neale, losing her phone, any guy who parked his car near hers with weird bumper stickers . . .

Biting down on her lower lip, she kicked the idea of her fear around for a second or two. Finally, she said, "I could probably work in the Fire Incident."

"But is the Fire Incident your actual fear?" Billie jumped in with the question almost immediately. "Or is it just a by-product of another, truer fear?"

"Yeah . . . I'm not sure," Neale grumbled, feeling like Sister Work Time was turning into Sister Judgment Time.

"Okay, well . . . ultimately the choice is up to you. But I think you want to ask yourself if the piece will feel truthful without that level of honesty from you." Billie's words were gentle, but Neale's face must have shown exactly how much she did not like that idea, because her sister jumped to add, "These are just thoughts. It is entirely up to you what you share. As long as the piece feels authentically Neale, it works."

"I'll think about what an authentic fear could look like," Neale said, trying to force a smile onto her face.

"Good." Billie reached over and squeezed her sister's arm. "I think you've given me enough of an idea that I can start filling in the painting. For the next rehearsal, could you have an actual draft of what you are thinking ready?"

"Sure." Neale sighed.

"Great. Our next rehearsal is in the Black Spot, so it will be good to actually run everything and feel the energy in there," Billie said, releasing her arm, then grabbing her papers and shoving them back in her bag. Turning to her sister, she said, "Will you help me put the chairs back? We have to be out of here by nine, or I pay the rec center for overtime."

"No problem," Neale said, a small spike of anxiety kicking in as she thought about rehearsing in the theater. Picking up a surprisingly heavy chair, Neale realized just how big a commitment she had made on Friday. Not only did she have Anthony in her phone, chatting away like an adorable possible boyfriend, but she had Billie expecting her, in a week, to put together a draft of a video, a free verse poem, and whatever lighting, sound, and movement she wanted to accompany it. Any one of her commitments was enough to make someone's mind feel chaotic. But all those elements? She had no idea how she was going to navigate this.

Dragging another chair into place, Neale looked up at the ceiling, hoping to bargain with whatever god or alien being that was listening. In exchange for surviving all of this, she would happily (a) never listen to Corinne again, (b) never make another impetuous decision in her life, and (c) recommit to secular nunnery and perfect order. Old Neale was officially done if the powers that be would just give her a *second* second chance.

CHAPTER EIGHTEEN

Neale's heartbeat raced as she rushed toward Seattle University's campus. The university grounds weren't even that big, but after a series of mishaps that had involved Neale's sleeping through her alarm and missing her streetcar stop, she was more than a little frazzled by the time she reached the unassuming front door of the Casey Commons. She had texted Anthony that she was going to be twelve minutes late about thirty-three minutes ago, a fact she hoped he didn't notice.

Giving the door a hard yank, she stepped into the cool, air-conditioned hallway and stopped to get her bearings. Fishing her phone and wallet out of her bowler-hat tote bag, she walked toward the guest check-in. Smiling down at the sleepy-looking undergrad sitting at the section marked *A–M Last Name*, she said, "Hi, sorry I'm late. I'm Neale Delacroix."

"Welcome," the student said with exactly as much pep as Neale expected for 9:32 a.m. Locating her paperwork, the sleepy student added, "You're just registered for today, correct?"

"Correct." As exciting as she was sure sessions like "Voice-Activated Speakers: Invasion of Privacy or Innovation?" would be, she was not about to pay an extra thirty-five dollars to listen to the panel. Although, if they made the recordings available for free afterward, she might—

"Great," the student said, attaching a lanyard to her name badge and interrupting Neale's thoughts. Passing her the badge and the day's schedule, they said, "The first session is just down the hall. The exhibitor booths will be in the commons, and there is coffee and tea in room 220. The reception will be in the atrium starting at four thirty p.m."

"Thank you." Neale smiled as the undergrad pushed an unruly lock of hair off their face before turning to chat with another student working the *N–Z* section. Neale turned toward the coffee room, then stopped. "Sorry, but can you tell me if someone has already checked in?"

"Happy to," the other student said. Obviously, the sophomore working the *N–Z* check-in was a morning person.

"Anthony Williams." Neale suspected he had already checked in and was happily sitting in some session.

"Oh, he's here," the perky student said without so much as looking at the list in front of them.

"How do you know? You didn't even look," Neale laughed.

"Five tenish, jacked, sleeve tattoo, in a yellow polo?" The sophomore smirked and arched an eyebrow. "I remember him. Pretty sure he went to the 'Surprising Sounds: Advances in Speaker Technology' panel in room 515."

Neale laughed again. There was no way that she could argue with the student. This was a completely accurate description of Anthony. "Thanks. You saved me a text message. Where is the coffee, again?"

"Room 220," the sleepy student said, pointing in the direction of the beverage Neale was desperate for.

"Thanks," Neale said over her shoulder. Dashing into the coffee room and grabbing a cup, she began filling it, wishing there were a larger size available. After adding a drop of cream, she made her way toward room 515.

Cracking the door open, Neale saw Anthony's spotless yellow polo in the corner at the end of a row, next to an empty chair. Slouch-walking past a few of the attendees standing in the back, she tapped him on the shoulder and whispered, "Sorry."

"Saved you a seat," he said, moving his conference papers off the chair so Neale could slide in next to him.

"Thanks. I slept through my alarm."

"On an easy Friday too. Shame," Anthony whispered, a hint of a joke playing around the corners of his mouth.

"You're such a Boy Scout; I bet you were twenty minutes early."

"Only fifteen minutes. I like to live dangerously." Anthony looked at her and winked, causing Neale's mind to spiral into a fantasy.

She did her best to swallow a giggle as she watched him turn his attention back to the panel. The smell of her coffee mixed with whatever spicy soap he used was almost as delicious as he looked in that polo. No wonder the student at the front desk remembered him. When her mind began wandering toward what sort of "dangerous" things they could do alone, Neale checked herself. Hadn't she just made a deal with the alien overlords that she wouldn't do this anymore? One whiff of Old Spice and his pheromones, and she was ready to shove New Neale off the proverbial bad-idea cliff.

Sighing, she whispered, "Did I miss anything good?"

"So far it's been pretty tame. Although the guy from SpeakerPOW made a pretty good joke about Siri."

"Your definition of good jokes needs improvement," Neale whispered back, causing Anthony to chuckle under his breath, the sound sending warm shivers down her spine.

"You had to be here."

Neale was just about to respond when the blonde woman in front of them with too much hair spray turned around and glared. Anthony shrugged apologetically. But Neale felt no such remorse, instead whispering, "Apparently, some people take Siri very seriously."

Anthony laughed again, earning another silencing glare from the woman. As soon as she turned around, he took out his notepad and wrote:

We are going old school and passing notes.

Neale smiled at his tidy handwriting as she took the notepad. It required every ounce of her adulting skills not to draw something rude. Instead, she picked up his nicely weighted pen and scrawled,

This is a very nice pen and paper set.

Way to come prepared. I didn't even think about taking notes.

Do you like me? Check yes or no:

☐*Yes* ☐*No*

Neale smirked at her middle-school-boyfriend joke, secretly hoping he'd check yes. She'd just handed the paper off to Anthony when she again remembered her Wednesday-night pledge. Neale winced and took the paper from Anthony's lap to scrawl, *Joking!* with a little arrow next to her boxes. Hopefully that screamed *friend zone!* and not *horny!* She really meant the exchange to be strictly platonic, she reassured herself.

Passing him the pen and paper again, Neale tried to focus on what the speakers were saying. After all, Happy Hearts had paid thirty-five dollars for her to learn something here. But the harder she tried to focus, the more she found herself watching the way Anthony's left arm flexed as he wrote. The occasional smile creeping across his face, his skin dimpling ever so slightly just above his jaw. Neale had never noticed the dimple before. Maybe because she'd never spent this much time watching him.

Oh God, Neale thought, willing the crush butterflies attempting to batter their way out of her rib cage to go away. What if he checked no? She didn't think she could deal with another kick to her ego after Darin's texts. She really should have left this alone.

Neale forced herself to watch the stage, feeling nerves run up and down her spine. She refused to lean over and look at what he was writing. It would be in strict violation of her promise to the aliens, and it would absolutely signal to him that she was not, in fact, joking. A gentle nudge at her side pulled Neale's attention away from the speaker that she was barely listening to. Looking down, she saw the notepad with the *yes* box checked, along with a caricature he'd drawn of the blonde woman hugging a speaker box labeled *Siri*.

The only thing Neale could do was aim her gigantic grin at the notepad instead of flashing it at Anthony. Letting her hair fall in front of her face, Neale tried to hide her blush. If anything, she had to admit that she was well and truly stuck on Anthony Williams. The only thing she could do now was hope he didn't notice.

~

"Ooh! Free pens," Neale said, stopping at the table just outside the reception hall.

After the morning panel, she had done her best to navigate toward safer waters with Anthony, which meant sticking primarily to topics like preferred fabric softeners and where to get the best bagel. And, of course, making as much small talk as humanly possible with the random composers and conference goers they met. In the end, her avoidance tactics had paid off, since they'd managed to meet a few composers, listen to music samples, and pick their favorite person interested in the project. The composer had even agreed to meet them at the conference's cocktail hour to hammer out more details.

"No thanks," Anthony said, wrinkling his nose as Neale tried to hand him a free Burgeoning Licensing Technology pen.

"But they are free. And triangle shaped so they won't roll away."

"Yes, but they are terrible to write with." Anthony smiled, strolling a few steps closer to the entrance of the reception hall.

"What do you mean, 'terrible to write with'?" she asked, her eyes narrowing playfully.

"You know—the ink comes out all spotty and inconsistent. They've basically gone bad as soon as they're made."

"Again I say, they're free." Neale grinned, catching up and nudging him in his broad shoulder jokingly as she dropped both pens into her bag.

"Who wants free stuff when it is crap?" Anthony shrugged, then slid his hands into the pockets of his dark-blue slacks.

"Those are strong words," Neale said, watching his smile slowly progress as she teased. "I never pegged you for a pen snob."

"Oh, I am. It is possibly my greatest fault," Anthony said, the corners of his mouth turning up.

Neale laughed as her eyes roved around the room looking for the stocky figure of Willa, their potential composer. Not spotting her, she turned her attention back to Anthony. "Well, are you also a wine snob, or can you stand to drink whatever eight-dollar bottle the conference splurged on?"

"Pens are the only thing I'm snobby about."

"I doubt it. If you embarrass me by getting up there and trying to order a Domaine Louis Latour Burgundy, I swear I'll never be seen in public with you again."

"I wouldn't want to sacrifice your company. Not when everyone in the room is jealous of me." Anthony glanced at her out of the corner of his eye as they made their way to the bar.

"Why are they jealous? Did you enter that raffle?" Neale said, digging in her purse for a few dollars to tip the bartender.

"Because I'm with you."

Neale stopped what she was doing just in time to catch Anthony's mischievous look as they reached the front of the drinks line. Was this some sort of polite-guy flirting? She couldn't get her hopes up. In fact, she shouldn't get her hopes up. As it was, Neale had spent most of the day avoiding even bumping into Anthony, lest her infatuation send her into cardiac arrest.

Or was he joking? She wasn't super well versed in polite men, after all. Darin's idea of chivalry involved eating the biggest slice of pizza so she wouldn't have to get a knife dirty. Neale was pretty sure that being referred to as a catch when she had only recently set herself on fire meant he was joking.

"Ha. Ha," Neale said in a tone that made it very clear she didn't think the joke was funny, then turned to the bartender. "May I have a glass of red, please?" Returning to the search in her purse, she said, "Sorry, Anthony. It doesn't look like they have Dom here."

"Red is fine, thank you," Anthony said, his tone still light as he accepted the wine and dropped a few dollars into the tip jar, ending Neale's heretofore futile search right as she triumphantly found her wallet.

"Thanks," she said, dropping the wallet back into the depths of her bag, belatedly realizing that she would have to perform the same excavation in an hour when she needed to get on the streetcar.

"I wasn't joking."

"About what?" Neale asked, half-distracted by locating her wallet.

"About you. You are the best, smartest, and prettiest girl in the room." Anthony looked her right in the eyes as he said all of this, confidence rolling off him in waves that seemed determined to knock Neale off balance.

In that moment, she could have sworn that the entire cocktail hour could hear her blood pounding through her body at a million miles an hour, while her brain reminded her to blink and breathe. For his part, Anthony stood there with a half smile resting on his face, as if he didn't mind waiting for her to catch her breath and then respond.

"I . . . I . . . ," she stammered. Literally all Neale had to do was the verbal equivalent of checking yes or no. But which direction did she want to go? Anthony's dark eyes waited patiently for her to form some sort of coherent thought. She'd been happily clinging to the emotionally grounding idea of New Neale and nunnery for weeks, and suddenly the option to cram a stick of dynamite into the friend zone was standing in front of her, wearing a well-fitted yellow polo and looking as if he told women he thought they were smart and pretty all the time. Neale swallowed and tried again. "Thank you, I like—"

"Sorry I'm late." Willa's voice pummeled into them, causing Neale to jump at least six inches out of her skin.

Glancing over at Anthony, she was slightly relieved to see that he, too, had been surprised, his shoulders still up by his ears. He cleared his throat, took a deep breath, and said, "Don't worry about it. We just got here ourselves."

"Oh, good," she said, running a hand through her short dark hair as she took a sip from a can of Coke. After a few more moments of stunned silence on Neale's end, Willa asked, "So how did you all enjoy the conference?"

"Really interesting. Did you get to the 'Home Speaker Security' panel?" Anthony asked, graciously continuing the conversation as if the two of them hadn't just been discussing the opposite of an Alexa.

"I did. From a creator standpoint, I'm always torn . . ."

Neale spaced out as Willa and Anthony continued to chat. Sure, she managed to ask a few questions and nod at the appropriate times, but there was no way her mind could focus on boring conference small talk with a bigger issue at hand.

Anthony thought she was smart. And pretty. Obviously being smart was better. But though she would never admit it publicly, it was fun to have someone think she was pretty.

"Neale, did you think that the designer-headphones guy was right about the direction of wireless?" Willa asked, attempting to draw Neale's attention more fully into the conversation.

Unfortunately for Willa, Neale had picked up exactly none of the context. So she simply nodded and aimed for some sort of verbal no-man's-land answer. "It had its merits."

As Willa and Anthony continued on, Neale couldn't help but marvel at his cool. How was he not freaking out right now? Trying to carry on a conversation when you'd just told someone you liked them was the cognitive equivalent of rubbing your stomach and patting your head and then reversing the motion. The whole concept made her wonder if there was anything sexy he could multitask.

"We were so excited to meet you, because we are looking to do something kind of new with our greeting cards." Anthony said this a little louder than he usually spoke, giving Neale's focus a nudge in the process.

"Ah yes. Sorry, I could talk your ears off about all this tech stuff. So tell me more about the project?" Willa asked.

Anthony gestured to Neale, making space for her to join the conversation. Taking a deep breath, Neale tried to fight through the mental fog caused by the good-looking distraction standing next to her. "Right, I know we talked about some of this earlier, but I'm sure you have spoken to as many people as we have, so just to recap, we want to build a different licensing model than the way the big card makers work. Our hope is to find a partner to commission a song for our first card. Anthony, did you want to tell Willa about the card details?"

As Anthony took over, Neale did her best to stay tuned in to the conversation . . . only losing the thread once, when he smiled and she noticed his dimple again.

"So what timeline are you looking for here?" Willa asked without batting an eyelash over the idea that she would need to come up with forty-five seconds of "peppy" Halloween music and a "better" happy-birthday song.

"That's the thing. We'd need to have these things printed and ready to ship that last week of August so that they are on the shelves right after the back-to-school stuff clears," Neale said, pausing before she had to level the hard part. Exhaling, she added, "So really we would need it by the first week in July so that we have time to get it added to all the recording devices and built into the cards."

"Wow. That's like three weeks from now," Willa said, her eyebrows shooting toward her hairline. She nodded for a second but didn't say much as she chewed over her words. Finally, she said, "Look. I am willing to do this, but I am not trying to get roped into something that is like seven hundred hours of work for the equivalent of three dollars."

"Totally get it." Anthony nodded solemnly.

"Of course. We are artists too." Neale gestured between the two of them, hoping that Willa would understand how desperately they did not want to be part of the churn-and-burn culture that creative people were frequently subjected to.

"Look, I have to pay my bills, and a thousand dollars up front is good money. At least until it ends up taking all of my time for the next three weeks to complete the project." Willa balanced on the edge of her sneaker, wobbling a bit but holding her ground. If they weren't in the middle of a negotiation, Neale would have high-fived her. Talking about money could be tough, but she was right to guard her talent.

"It makes sense. Maybe we could work out something around the number of samples you are willing to produce. Our company is small, so we don't have to behave like a big corporation," Neale said, instinctively reaching out and putting a hand on Anthony's shoulder. For a fraction of a second, she could feel the muscle underneath the thin material of his polo flex at her touch. The movement was visually imperceptible, but the spontaneous response to her made her mind hazy with desire.

Releasing her hand from his arm, she returned her focus to Willa. Clearing her throat and her fuzzy mind, she continued, "Perhaps we could commission the piece, and maybe if it does well, we could agree to some sort of licensing or bonus structure after the initial run?"

Out of the corner of her eye, Neale could see Anthony's face shift in surprise. This wasn't something they had talked about before. However, she had the sense that it was the right thing to do. After all, if this were a big music publisher, they would be haggling over pennies, and the likelihood that the artist would see any of that was almost nil. Happy Hearts was created by people who loved art, artists, and being local. Surely they could find a way to do better than some big, faceless publisher.

"Okay," Willa said, drawing out the word. Neale held her breath and waited while Willa looked from her to Anthony. "Then I accept. Pending a contract review."

"Of course," Neale said, grinning all around.

"We'll reach out to you on Monday to get the details squared away. I look forward to collaborating with you," Anthony said, producing a business card from one of his pockets.

As she accepted the card, Willa's smile was so big that it seemed to take up half of her face. "Fantastic. Let me get you mine." Passing a card to each of them, she said, "I look forward to working with you too. Now, if you'll excuse me, I have to pretend to leave here super calm and collected so that I can call my mom and squeal about this."

Anthony tilted his head back and laughed, the musical sound filling up the entire room as they waved goodbye.

It felt like it took forever for Willa to walk out the door so Neale could properly talk to Anthony. As they turned to face each other, Neale said, "So much to talk about."

Right as Anthony said, "Cheers!"

"Let's start with cheers," Neale said, giggling at the word collision. Knocking their cups together, they downed the remainder of their wine.

Looking up from his empty glass, Anthony asked, "Do you want to get another glass, or do you want to leave here?"

"Let's go. I think our work here is done," Neale said, smiling over a successful negotiation as well as the fact that they might finally be able to talk without interruption.

"All right, then." Anthony extended a hand and stacked her cup in his before walking the few steps to set them both on a nearby clearing tray.

As they navigated the crowded space to get out of the door, Neale's nerves kicked in. They were going to be alone in like twenty seconds, and she had no idea what she wanted to say. *I like you too. But also, I'm a secular nun now. How does that work for you?* seemed like not the right approach.

As she pushed on the door that led outside, the thought hit Neale that maybe Anthony had forgotten all about what he'd said. It would explain how he'd managed to be so cool for the last half hour. If that was the case, maybe she didn't have to bring up anything at all. She could just continue to stew in her crush until she moved on or died. Whichever came first.

She stepped into the early summer evening, and the sounds of traffic and busy campus life soothed her whirring mind. Neale filled her lungs with fresh air, then turned to Anthony and said, "So did you drive?"

Anthony looked surprised by the question, but his expression recovered nanoseconds later, and he said, "I did. Did you drive?"

"I took the streetcar. So I guess this is goodbye." Neale shrugged as his eyebrows shot toward his hairline. She just had to stick to the ignore-it routine a little longer, and she'd be fine.

"Do you want a ride?"

"No, I'm good. I like to stretch my legs," Neale said, proud of how quickly she managed to think of an acceptable excuse to skip out of further conversation.

"Can I walk with you to the stop?"

"Oh. Sure," Neale said, panic shooting through her. She hadn't expected the plot twist where she couldn't actually get away from him.

"Great," Anthony said, turning at a leisurely pace toward the campus exit and the Broadway streetcar stop.

"It's a nice evening," Neale said, then instantly wished she had kept her mouth shut. Nothing said *I'm avoiding a topic* like old-lady small talk. What should she remark on next, the flower beds?

"It is." Anthony smiled over at her, maintaining his slow saunter, clearly in no hurry to get to either the streetcar or their next topic of conversation. Neale was just about to remark on the state of the red poppies when he asked, "So have you given any thought to what I said?"

It was such a polite way of phrasing the question that Neale almost laughed. Truthfully, she would have if she weren't busy sweating so hard that she was glad she'd borrowed a navy-blue blouse from her sister. Forcing air into her lungs, Neale decided to come clean. "Kind of. I mean, yes. But I don't know what I want to do about it."

Anthony tilted his head at her, and she couldn't tell if he was hurt or curious. She certainly didn't want to hurt his feelings. This might be the only actual, real-life case of "it's not you, it's me" in the history of relationships. He opened his mouth, but she cut him off, just in case her explanation would help. "You should know that I like you, but I have terrible judgment, and in order to get my life together, I recently committed to a life of secular nunnery."

"What does that entail?" Anthony laughed, his demeanor easing. "I'm not familiar with that religious order."

Neale snorted, the weight coming off her shoulders now that some of her cards were on the table. "To be honest, it's a complex belief system that basically says that when you have messed up your life as spectacularly as I have, you need to get your shit together."

"And you have to get your shit together by yourself?" Anthony sounded skeptical.

"Well . . . yes. I mean, my bad decisions got me to where I am."

"So your plan is to enjoy someone's company but not make any decisions about them at all?"

"It sounds worse when you put it like that," Neale said, watching the pavement to avoid the hard stare he was giving her.

"Neale, I can handle rejection. You can say that you aren't interested, and I'll be fine—"

"But that's the problem! I *am* interested," Neale shouted, interrupting Anthony and catching him off guard. Looking over at his exceedingly high cheekbones, she couldn't tell if he was amused or confused. Very possibly a lot of both. Now that Neale thought about it, everything she'd said was confusing. Future psychologists would want to study the emotional whiplash in this moment, Neale was pretty sure.

"Okay, so you do like me. You just don't know what to do about it."

"Exactly." Neale knew that her explanation sounded absurd, but to his credit, Anthony didn't make fun. Rather, he looked pensive, as if she had just given him a new obstacle course to work through.

After a moment, Anthony said, "Have you thought about what parameters might help you decide how you feel? Like, do you have a checklist or something?"

Neale barked a laugh that echoed off the nearby parking structure. "Oh God no. Checklists are my sister's domain. I'm more of an experiment-and-see kind of a person."

"Okay." Anthony eyed her carefully, then said, "Would you let me kiss you?"

It wasn't often that Neale found herself speechless, but here she was, short on words. She was also aware that her jaw had dropped and that all the butterflies had returned to her stomach.

"You . . . you want to kiss me?" she stammered, her gaze dropping to his full, sensual lips. "Why?"

"You are an experiment-and-see kind of person. Kiss me and decide if you like it," Anthony said, with all the casualness of someone remarking on the weather. In fact, if Neale hadn't been so focused on his lips, she wouldn't have noticed him worrying the bottom one for just a moment. Somewhere, buried under his manners and cool exterior, he was nervous.

Something about his mouth sent her over the edge. Who was she kidding? She would absolutely let him kiss her. And probably do a lot more if he asked. He didn't even really have to ask nicely, if she was honest.

"Okay." Neale forced herself to consent slowly, giving other red flags time to pop up. Not that it mattered; she would probably ignore those too.

Anthony narrowed his eyes, tilting his head slightly as if studying her. Finally, he said, "Okay, like enthusiastic okay? Or okay, like I-have-some-concerns-but-I-don't-want-to-say-so okay?"

Something about the question put her at ease, and Neale felt herself smile. "Okay, like I-know-it-is-a-bad-idea-to-kiss-a-coworker-but-I'm-gonna-do-it-anyway okay."

Anthony's expression relaxed, and he took a step closer to her, gently putting a hand on her waist before he spoke. "I can deal with that."

As she looked into his eyes, his gaze sent warmth through her like the sun was overhead. Enjoying the light pressure of his hand at her waist, she leaned in and closed her eyes, inhaling his spicy smell just before he kissed her.

At first, the kiss was slow and sweet, like he was giving her room to make decisions about how far she wanted them to go. That changed when Neale sighed against him. Deepening the kiss, his lips parted, and he ran his tongue across her bottom lip. He tasted like the wine and the cookies they had smuggled into the last panel of the day. A rush of sugar and the heady feeling of delayed gratification took hold, and she pressed against him, enjoying the way he responded to her. His arms slid around her back, pulling her in close so she could feel every inch of his body, letting her revel in the solid feel of the muscles that she'd been dreaming about for weeks.

Neale let herself get lost in the deliciousness of the kiss until the sounds around them began to change. Pulling away, she leaned her forehead against his and listened to their uneven breathing and the traffic creeping along. She focused on the sounds of cars and buses rolling by, trying to get her bearings.

"So?" Anthony said, letting his arms fall from around her and taking a small step back.

"So?" Neale echoed his question, not recovered enough to form thoughts of her own. Her skin felt cold where he was no longer pressed against her, the only consolation being the hand he left gently pressed to her hip.

"How do you feel about our experiment?" Anthony asked, a smile playing with the corners of his delicious mouth.

Neale wasn't sure how to put into words what she thought. Kissing him was altogether something else. It was unexpected, fun, and sexy. Incredibly sexy. Like, she wished she had kissed him somewhere in private, because kisses like that could go so much further and that could get them both arrested for indecency. As it was, she wasn't entirely sure she would be able to sit near him in a meeting and not think about that kiss or the way his hands felt or his body pressed against her.

Oh God, she couldn't even think about work without thinking about him. She was sunk. A terrible sensation began to slink over her, and Neale felt like a candy bar made out of edible gold, joy, and lust mixed with the nauseating sensation one got when an elevator hitched unexpectedly.

"How do I feel . . . ," Neale repeated. Candidly, she felt like she had just committed one of her favorite mistakes, and while she couldn't quite bring herself to regret it, she wasn't exactly proud either.

"I feel like this is my favorite bad judgment call," Neale sighed. "Kissing you is wonderful."

"Then have you gathered enough evidence to make a decision? I can kiss you again if it helps," Anthony joked, and she felt like a complete jerk for even entertaining the idea of this experiment.

"Oh no." Neale rushed to put a stop to the entire thing before he, or more likely she, made any more bad decisions. "I can't gather more evidence."

Anthony's smile faltered, and he put an extra foot of space between them. Quietly, he asked, "What do you mean?"

Neale winced, looking for the most honest way to explain herself. "I mean. Think about how messy this is. There is a reason you don't make out with coworkers. It was totally unprofessional of me. I should have thought this through better."

"Eh, two to tango on this one," Anthony said, shrugging and pointing at himself. "You are in charge here, but I do want to point out that we are both consenting adults. If it doesn't work out, we'll just be awkward for a little while; then everyone will move past it."

"Maybe for you. I just got this job, and now I'm all snuggled up on you," Neale said, willing the sidewalk to open up and swallow her whole. Anything to avoid the look on Anthony's face right now. "I'm still getting myself together. I screwed up my last career, royally. You know, the internet fiasco and all that."

"Like I said, you're the boss. But maybe the whole internet thing isn't worth defining yourself by. Just a thought," Anthony said, his expression hovering somewhere between confusion and exasperation.

"It's more than the video." Neale paused, and the past washed over her. She thought about the Collective and Darin and how losing one had ripped the other away from her, leaving nothing but a messy, gaping hole where her life used to be. She wanted to believe that she was different from when she was in the Collective, but could she really say that just two months into her new job? Hell, she was still new enough that she hadn't memorized how the locks turned on the mail room door.

This kiss was proof. She wasn't different; she was just in a different place. Same Old Neale, just in a new job.

Somewhere in the back of her mind, Neale realized she could hear the streetcar coming. It wasn't a sinkhole, but it was enough to get her out of there.

"I think the streetcar is coming," Neale blurted. Briefly taking in the shock on Anthony's face, she added, "This was a good experiment. Now we can be coworkers again, and we have all the answers." She was rambling and backing away, but she didn't care. Neale just needed to get down the block and away from him before he made any more observations about her or asked any more questions.

"Um. Okay. Do you want to talk about this later?" Anthony called as she continued to back up.

"No. We're okay," Neale said, bumping into a lamppost and giggling, more from nerves than because it was funny. In fact, she was pretty certain she was going to have a very unfunny bruise there later.

"All right. See you," Anthony called, sounding unsure about his next move, as if Neale's behavior were a physics problem and he had only taken geometry. Whatever. The goodbye was all she needed to be released from this wreck of her own making.

"Bye. See you Monday. Good job today!" she called before turning around and sprinting through a minuscule gap in the traffic as the streetcar came into view.

When she finally tapped her card on the streetcar, she dropped onto a bench to reckon with the worst part of that whole conversation. Slouching low in her seat and throwing an elbow over her eyes, she thought, *"Good job today"? Could you be less smooth?*

CHAPTER NINETEEN

"Sorry I'm late," Neale called as she rushed through the Tammi Nails salon door.

"Don't worry about it. Billie isn't even here yet," Dylan called over the edge of a gossip magazine from a pedicure chair toward the back of the room. Every syllable her sister said implied that she was, in fact, worried about it and annoyed that neither Neale nor Billie could use a clock. Neale stifled a laugh as she waved to Tammi.

Sliding her flip-flops off, Neale jumped into a chair next to her sister and said, "So how's opening up the new office?"

"Well, I managed to hire a real superstar admin, so my life has gotten substantially better." Dylan grinned as she flipped the page of her magazine. "I swear he knows my calendar better than I do."

"Uh-huh," Neale mumbled, stretching as far as she could without standing up to reach a magazine that another customer had left behind. She would need it once Dylan got going on assigning offices to her new minions or whatever productivity consultant nonsense she did all day.

"And I think I'm going to be able to hire an associate from Clayton—take that, Moira Whitman. She shouldn't have spilled her drink on me at that leadership summit last month," Dylan cackled.

"I don't know who Moira is, but I'm sure she deserves to be out an analyst. She sounds wretched," Neale said, flipping through the pages and trying to hide a smile. Unlike Billie, Dylan was rarely petty, so when it happened, Neale made an extra-special effort to pay attention and encourage it.

"Oh, she is. You know, she didn't even apologize. Talk about tacky." Dylan rolled her eyes, then took a deep, calming breath. Exhaling, she said, "Anyway, that is really the big stuff."

"Not true. How is Mike?"

"He is basically a kid in a candy shop with that new sensory room. You should see it. It's kind of adorable."

"I'll bet. What's he trying to do with it now?" Neale asked, before flicking past a series of face-cream ads, as her sister listed the different childhood-development theories her boyfriend was testing out at the children's museum where he worked.

"So yeah. All that to say he is super happy with the piece that Dad designed for—"

"Sorry I'm late," Billie shouted as she crashed through the salon doors.

Dylan grinned at Neale, telegraphing some sort of see-how-silly-you-look message, which Neale ignored. Besides, Billie looked way cooler than Neale, who had only just realized that she had thrown on clashing prints in an attempt to get out of bed and make the ridiculously early appointment Dylan had scheduled.

"No worries. Dylan was just filling me in on Mike," Neale said, setting her magazine down and pointedly ignoring Dylan's glances.

"Oh! How is life with the serial killers' son?" Billie asked, dropping into the chair on the opposite side of Dylan with all the grace of a toddler learning to use a fork.

"First, neither Linda nor Patricia have actually murdered anyone, so stop saying that."

"There is still time," Billie said, around the straw from the iced coffee that was likely the reason she was late.

"And they do live across the street from Mom and Dad. I mean, if ever there were a reason to kill . . ." Neale shrugged.

"Oh God. We are not doing this again, you two." Dylan rolled her eyes. Not that long ago, her sister had helped settle their parents' bitter, decades-long feud with their neighbors—Mike's moms, Linda and Patricia—in part by dating their youngest son. A sin no one in the family could ever really forgive. Helping her father toilet paper the Robinsons' speedboat was one of Neale's fondest early-adulthood memories.

"I mean, I wasn't here to do this the last time," Billie pointed out, hissing as she dunked her feet in the warm water.

"Trust me, Billie, you didn't miss out," Dylan said, casting a sideways look at Neale, who grinned at her exactly the way one would expect a youngest sibling who was intentionally starting problems to grin. Narrowing her eyes, Dylan said, "What I want to know is, what is going on in Neale's life that she would agree to ten a.m. pedicures?"

Leaning forward to look at Neale in her pedicure chair, Billie said, "Yeah, Neale, what happened? You usually only ask us to buy you food. Since when do you want to hang out at ten a.m.?"

"No reason," Neale said, shifting uncomfortably as her sisters waited. Demanding a sister hangout that wasn't a 6:00 a.m. workout had seemed like a good idea during the workweek, but now that she had the whole Anthony thing hanging over her head . . . not so much.

"I smell a lie," Dylan crowed, setting her magazine down.

"It's just stuff going on at work."

"Define *stuff*."

"I love work problems!"

Billie and Dylan spoke at the same time, then looked at each other and laughed. Billie would skeptically demand more detail while Dylan looked for solutions. It was hardwired into their DNA, and if they weren't talking about her, Neale also would've found it funny. As it was, she knew she couldn't fully lie. Her sisters would smell it a mile away. Maybe she could just omit certain details?

"Girls! It is so nice to see all of you." Tammi, the salon owner, walked over with several bottles of nail polish in hand. "How long has it been since all three Delacroix girls came in here?"

"I feel like maybe two years," Billie said, frowning a little as she tried to recall. "Neale, was Dylan here for that show Dad did at the trapeze school in SoDo?"

"No. I wasn't here for that," Dylan cut in, her brow creasing as she tried to think.

"Oh, I know when," Neale said, a little more loudly than she meant to. Luckily the place was mostly empty this early. "It was that Christmas that Grandmama drove from Louisiana to Texas, surprised Dylan, then made Dylan fly to Seattle with her. Remember?"

"I'd rather not remember, thanks," Dylan said, her voice only half-serious as Neale and Billie both descended into a fit of giggles at the memory of a haggard Dylan lugging their grandmama's cheetah-print suitcases through the door. Meanwhile, the diminutive woman had barked orders in a fur coat and only carried her rhinestone-studded cane, which she referred to as her "husband." Grandmama's shine was outrageous, and she made the rest of the family's Delacroix glow seem like a penlight.

"How is your grandmother?" Tammi asked, distributing the bottles of nail polish directly to their pedicurists without explanation.

"She's doing well. Last I heard, she had a new boyfriend," Neale said, wiggling her eyebrows around the room.

"She told me Rigoberto is not her boyfriend," Dylan said, rolling her eyes.

"Well, this guy was called Matteous, so I'm pretty sure that's why." Neale chuckled along with everyone else in the room.

As the laughter died down, Tammi said, "All right, girls. You all enjoy yourselves, and if you need anything, just holler."

All three of the sisters knew damn well they were not about to need a single thing. The salon was Tammi's kingdom, and everyone and everything in it would behave accordingly.

"So are you going to tell us about work or not?" Billie said, interrupting Neale's reminiscing.

"Fine. But you two can't judge me. Especially you, Dylan, because I know that your beloved Dr. Victoria Blake book would use this as a prime example of bad decision-making, and—"

"Neale, what happened?" Dylan interrupted, looking mildly concerned.

Wrinkling her nose, Neale squeezed her eyes shut so she wouldn't have to see her sisters' reactions before saying, "I kissed Anthony."

"What!" Billie shrieked, causing her pedicurist to jump in surprise.

"Oh my God!" Dylan said, her voice only two volume notches lower than Billie's.

Neale cracked one eye open to peek at her sisters. Their expressions were just as bad as she thought they'd be. Dylan's mouth was wide open, and Billie was grinning like a kid on Christmas.

After an initial moment of shock, Billie said, "Tell us what happened."

"Okay, well . . . per the terms of our experiment, technically he kissed me, but—"

"What experiment?" Dylan asked, shock still written on her face.

"See, all of this started at the conference," Neale said. She had hoped her sisters would relax once she explained things to them, but it seemed like the more details she provided, the more excited they became. By the time she got to the part where they'd actually kissed, both Dylan and Billie were practically falling out of their chairs. Worse, at some point Tammi had decided the story was too good to miss and had rolled up a padded stool to listen.

"Wait. So you said, 'Let's be friends,' and sprinted to the streetcar?" Tammi asked. The absurdity of the whole situation seemed so much worse when she repeated it.

"I mean, not in so many words, but yeah."

"I don't understand. Do you not like him?" Leanna, Billie's pedicurist, asked.

"No. I like him a lot. What's not to like? He is smart and cute and funny. And he has hobbies like art and parkour, which is—"

"I really don't understand this choice," Tammi said, standing up and shaking out her blonde extensions as she went to greet another customer.

"Tammi's right. I don't get it," Billie said. "If you like him, why'd you leave?"

"Because. That book Dylan gave me said workplace romances are a bad idea."

"But, Neale, you already kissed him, so isn't it a little late to apply Victoria Blake to the situation?" Dylan said, as if any reasonable person would have come to that conclusion.

"Better late than never!" Neale said, sliding down in her chair as her pedicurist began painting her toes. "Seriously, though. What if I messed up our relationship?"

"Oh, you did," Dylan said, shaking her head so hard her sleek ponytail bobbed like a cheerleader's.

Brushing Dylan off with a dismissive sniff, Neale said, "What I am trying to say is, what if I messed up our friendship? Like, what if he doesn't want to talk to me anymore? I'll miss him. Work is already boring. It would be so much more boring without him."

"That ship done been sailed." Billie laughed until Dylan silenced her with a look.

"If you feel like you are going to miss him, then maybe that is a sign that you shouldn't back away from him. You know, follow your heart,"

Dylan said. The advice was meant to sound placating, but her oldest sister still looked like she'd swallowed a bug.

Neale almost laughed. In fact, she would have if Billie hadn't beaten her to it. Dylan threw their middle sister a dirty look, and Billie tried to turn the laugh into a cough before earnestly adding, "Really, Neale. Think about what you just said. If you are going to miss someone and the only downside you see is a book, then maybe you need to think about this differently."

Neale bit the inside of her cheek as she listened to her sister. It was easy for Billie and Dylan to say she should follow her heart. Their hearts weren't traitors. Neale's heart, on the other hand, was basically a foreign agent waiting to sell her secrets to the enemy.

It would be so nice just to see where things go with Anthony, Neale thought. He seemed different, but she didn't want to mess up her life by jumping in too soon. If she could just get it together, then she could date Anthony. Maybe once she found a new, more interesting job or he opened his own parkour/art studio or something.

Taking a deep breath, Neale said, "I don't think my heart is meant to go in that direction."

"But you just said you enjoy his company," Dylan pushed back.

"I don't know why you two are so pressed. Science literally says that you'll live longer and be happier as a single woman. Y'all should just follow my lead and steer clear," Billie guffawed. "You want my advice, Neale? Get a vibrator."

"Neale can do both," Dylan said, and the three of them howled until the new customer at a manicure station turned around to give them a nasty look.

Clearing her throat, Billie said, "Grandmama has been single since like 1982, and she is still going dancing at eighty."

"That, and the Seagram's probably helps," Neale said, and the three of them burst into a fresh round of giggles.

"Neale, you can do what you want. Be a jaded gremlin, like Billie, or the picture of optimism, like me. Just be thoughtful about it. No more sudden moves," Dylan chided.

Billie rolled her eyes before adding, "Seriously, though—Dylan is right. Do what you want. Just be up front with him. The only requirement is that you tell us along the way."

"I can do that." Neale grinned and tried not to "help" her pedicurist put on her flip-flops, an urge that was nearly impossible to fight.

"Good. We have rehearsal at the Black Spot on Wednesday, so I'm gonna need a full update then."

Internally, Neale winced as she remembered that she hadn't really finished prepping for their rehearsal. Between getting the singing card off the ground, going to the conference, hanging out with Corinne, and kissing Anthony, she just hadn't had time for her art.

"Be fair," Dylan jumped in. "Don't talk about Anthony without me. Seriously, I don't care if I'm still at the office; I need to be the first to know."

"And you will be first to know . . . right after me," Billie said, and all three of them busted up again.

Neale decided not to say anything about not being ready for rehearsal. Instead, she would just make sure she busted her ass when she got home. She had the whole rest of the weekend to stress about the show, but right now, she was having fun with her sisters, and there was no place she would rather be.

~

Good luck tonight!

Neale looked down at the message from Anthony and grinned as she stood outside the Black Spot. She shouldn't text him back anything flirty. Really, the message did not require a response at all, but responding would be the polite thing to do.

Typing back a quick thank-you text, Neale sighed. Anthony had been true to his word. He'd been nothing but a perfect colleague all week . . . and it was killing her. Even when she'd confessed to working on Billie's show, he'd managed to be excited in the most thoughtful way, flattering her without pushing the compliments so far as to seem like he was fishing. He'd even drawn her a little Post-it with a cartoon of her onstage holding a fire extinguisher with a caption that read *Crash and Burn Part 2: Art with a Vengeance*. It had made Neale laugh so hard she'd ended up making a copy so she could pin one up at her desk and keep the other in her wallet in case she got nervous.

And boy, was she nervous. When she had first visited the Black Spot, all she could see was its amazing potential. The building practically vibrated with creepy, creative energy. But now that she was actually expected to perform in the space, it was more terrifying than inspiring. Throwing up a prayer to the god of creativity, she gave the door a hard yank and stepped into the dark hallway right as Callen was going out.

"Hi, Callen," Neale said, as they stepped aside to let her pass. "How's it going?"

"Pretty good. It is awesome to rehearse in there," Callen said, pushing the hair out of their face. "The acoustics sure beat practicing in my bathroom, I can tell you that much."

They both laughed, and Neale used the opportunity to study them for hints about Billie's mood. She had hoped Billie would be more available to bounce ideas off, but her sister had been short on time for her all week, and finally she'd just given up on hoping she would answer her texts at all. Callen looked both tired and energized, like those people who were about to win a long-distance race in the Olympics. If Neale had to guess, this was going to be an artistic workout. All she could do was hope that she looked like Callen when she left rehearsal.

"Awesome. I can't wait to check it out. See you around!"

229

"See you," Callen called over their shoulder as they walked away.

Neale waited until she heard the subtle click of the door before she let the smile fall from her face. As she slowed her walking pace, a wave of nerves washed over her. Seeing Callen reminded her of the performance videos Billie had sent over. She had started watching the videos but couldn't make herself do it all in one sitting. Every time she'd tried, imposter syndrome had hit her like a brick. Each artist was so good and so polished that she just couldn't watch everything without feeling like a fraud. Instead, she'd done a random sampling that she hoped would be enough to satisfy everyone. *Knowing Billie, she's either too busy to care or planning a pop quiz for me*, Neale thought.

"Hey, Neale." Billie's voice floated through the back of the theater.

"Hey." Neale watched as her sister poked around at something on the tech board, muttering quietly to herself until the houselights came up.

Billie came out of the booth and opened her arms to give Neale a hug. Feeling her sister squeeze her, Neale relaxed for just a fraction of a second. Forcing herself to take a deep breath, Neale envisioned herself exhaling her nerves as her sister let go of her.

"How's rehearsal going?" Neale asked, turning to set her bag in a chair.

"Oh, it goes," Billie said, humor lurking just behind the exasperation in her voice. "One of the performers wants to change from batons to ribbon dancing, so there is that."

In any other context, Neale would have laughed, but one look at Billie's face told her that yes indeed, switching to ribbon dancing was a real thing and not a joke from a mid-2000s Judd Apatow comedy. She shrugged. "There's always gotta be a plot twist."

"Sure does." Billie shook her head, then added, "Anyway, Nhi's tech person needed to leave early, but they asked me to figure out how you want your lighting. Callen is going to finish with houselights down, only red stage lighting on a dimmer, set super low."

"Lighting?" Neale asked, looking up from attempting to find her notebook in her bag. She hadn't thought about lighting. How could she have forgotten about lighting? It was such an obvious thing, and instead of figuring it out, she'd spent all week freaking out over the other artists' performances.

"Yes. How do you want to start?" Billie repeated herself. She channeled her irritation at having to do so by employing her favorite gesture, a hand on her hip. Neale could survive a one-hand-on-hip interaction, but experience had taught her that if Billie got to two, she should probably run for cover. Callen had not warned her that whoever the ribbon dancer was, they'd left Billie with a short fuse.

Just pick something, Neale told herself. Anything was better than working Billie up before she got onstage. "Um . . . I'll keep the house-lights down."

"Okay," Billie said, nodding with approval despite the quiver in Neale's voice. "And onstage?"

"There're pinks and blues in the video, so maybe we could soften Callen's lighting to pink and bring it up some when I get onstage."

"I thought you were doing black and white for the video?" Billie paused, arching an eyebrow. "I've been working on the painting for our piece under the assumption that this was black and white. Did you look at my email?"

"I did." Neale cast her mind back to the message she had opened but not fully read. It was so long that it had just made her a little dizzy to think about. Searching for an excuse, she said, "I just thought that since it was in black and white, I could use any colors I wanted and it wouldn't clash."

Billie opened her mouth, then closed it, giving her head a shake. "We can work it out later. Do you want pink onstage when the video plays?"

"Maybe?" Neale said, regretting her unsure answer when Billie's brow creased. Rushing to bring her sister's blood pressure down, she added, "Can you tell me what it looks like from the audience, and we can adjust it?"

Billie pressed her lips together and nodded. "Happy to. Forgive me, did you already reply to my email with your video file? I didn't have a chance to check over lunch—my promo-material review ran over."

Neale was quietly delighted that her sister hadn't had a chance to check her email, because if she had, she would not have seen the file. In fact, Neale hadn't really finished the file until eighteen minutes after her lunch break at Happy Hearts had technically ended. Really she had meant to work on the video sooner, but after watching everyone else, Neale's mind had gone blank. It had taken a few days, and she'd struggled to come up with an idea she thought was good enough until she and Corinne had gone to the party store.

"No worries, I have it on a drive. Just let me find it," she said, diving back into her bottomless pit of a bag. She was just beginning to regret not buying the glow-in-the-dark flash drive when she felt it brush her fingertips. "Aha!" Neale said triumphantly, holding up the drive.

"Awesome," Billie said as Neale dropped it into her outstretched palm. "I'll go back to the booth, and you can walk me through the tech cues."

Shaking out her shoulders, Neale grabbed her notebook and walked toward the door that led to the stage, trying not to panic all the while. Why had it taken her so long to come up with a good idea? She should have just picked something. Every other performer seemed to have an excellent plan. They had probably logged hundreds of practice hours by now, and her stalling had likely put her even further behind her peers. The idea that she could be out of line with her peers made Neale sweat.

"Whenever you're ready," Billie called from the booth.

"Okay, I think I want . . ." Neale stopped when she realized that her voice was being swallowed up from where she stood behind a curtain. She hadn't realized just how much she would need to project to fill the space. Why hadn't she asked for a lav mic or something? Clearing her throat, she tried again. "Could you give me a five count from when I hit center stage before playing the video?"

"Noted," Billie called.

Neale watched as the red stage lights became pinker, then walked out. Counting in for one, exhale, two, inhale, three, exhale—

The jarring light of a video being projected silently behind her shook Neale's focus. Billie's idea of a five count was clearly different from her own. *This is why people have rehearsals,* Neale thought, trying to calm herself down as the video flickered. Taking a deep breath, she began.

"Failure is my definition," Neale said, her tongue feeling thick with the weight of anxiety as she read the words from her notebook. It was discombobulating to know that her imagery was playing overhead without sound. She hadn't decided to strip the audio until this afternoon, so she had practiced her piece with sound quietly playing from her computer speakers last night. She hadn't realized it, but she had timed the rhythm of her speaking to the sound of her career going up in flames, and now she was struggling to speak without it.

Neale tried not to berate herself for failing to practice more as she moved mechanically to stage left. She managed to trip over her feet at least three times, which, on the upside, was far fewer times than she tripped over her words. Neale blamed the echo in the room. Every time she said the word *failure,* which was a lot, it echoed back at her like a vindictive shadow.

At some point on the drive over, Neale had assured herself that even if she started the run-through a little rocky, she would eventually find her footing. Unfortunately for her, that never really happened. When she finally reached the end of the poem, Neale felt like someone had crammed a wad of cotton down her throat as her sister stopped the video and brought the houselights up.

"Okay. Lots of potential here," Billie said in a tone with so much forced positivity that someone could have mistaken her for a wedding dress salesperson or a life coach. Whatever she could have been with that phony bright smile, she could not have been an actress. It was clear to Neale that Billie thought the piece was a wreck. "I want to start by asking you some questions about your artistic choices."

"All right," Neale said, hating the note of trepidation in her voice.

"First, I want to think about how the video ties to your piece. As it stands right now, you're not really interacting with it. So it feels a little bland and self-indulgent to have it just running in the background on a loop. That said, I know this is your first run-through, so I was hoping you could walk me through how you might more closely tie it to the rest of your performance.

"Second: Is reading off the notepad part of the whole failure motif?" Billie asked, leaving no time for her to respond to the first statement.

"No, I'm going to memorize it," Neale jumped in. Her sister was being harsh. Of course she was planning on memorizing the piece. She just hadn't had time yet.

"That's good." Billie exhaled, looking visibly relieved as she waved her hand in a dismissive gesture, her hammered-gold wrist cuff winking in the dim theater lighting.

Watching her sister, Neale felt her agitation kick up a notch. If her sister didn't like the reading, she should have just said so instead of asking all these questions. It wasn't like Billie had felt the need to coddle or lie to her at any other point in their last twenty-eight years together. And besides, Neale hadn't intentionally gotten stuck. Yes, this piece was rough around the edges, but she could pull it together, especially now that she had her sister's attention and a good idea. All she needed was more time.

"What about sound effects? I know you thought you might work in the Hula-Hoop-and-spray-paint feel at some point."

"You have an excellent memory." Neale meant the words to be a compliment, but her tone wasn't nearly as light as she wanted it to be, so they came out sounding more like the frustration she felt. The silence felt like the one truly creative choice she had made, and apparently it was the wrong one because Billie was fully committed to her other idea. Clearing her throat, she tried to push her vexation with her sister aside. Neale had to remember that Billie really thought she was helping. Even if Neale didn't feel like her help was particularly helpful. "I thought maybe the piece might have a higher impact if it were silent."

Billie frowned. "I think it feels a little sparse. Especially with the basic lighting and a simple loop video."

"Okay. Ouch," Neale said, surprising herself as much as her sister. She couldn't remember the last time she'd talked back to Billie. Then again, she hadn't needed to because they used to be on the same page. It occurred to Neale that she and Billie really hadn't worked together much. She had imagined her middle sister as a lot more laid back. As it turned out, Billie had a lot in common with Dylan when it came to working. That probably explained why the two of them got along so well now. They were in the same ultraperfectionist league. One that Neale clearly wasn't ready to be a member of.

"Sorry, Neale. I wasn't trying to be mean." Her sister crossed her arms. Billie didn't sound that sorry.

"I know you're trying to help," Neale said. Everyone always made it sound like working with your siblings was fun. But this was not going particularly well.

"No. It's my fault. I forgot how sensitive you are about your work."

"Sensitive?" Neale repeated, the word grating on her nerves.

"Sorry, I didn't mean it like—"

While her sister might not have meant to call her piece self-indulgent and simple, she was having a hard time buying that a third insult was an innocent mistake. "Billie, I like time to think about feedback. I'm not that sensitive."

"It was a bad word choice." Billie took another step so that she was almost directly under the stage and stared up at Neale, her otherwise smooth brow creasing as she studied her sister. "I really am trying to help. It's just that time is tight, and this needs work. We have two weeks left."

It wasn't as if Neale didn't know that the piece was imperfect. She'd just thought they'd be working together to fix it. As kids, they'd always been a united front against the tyranny of Dylan's order, school rules, and whatever misguided ideas their parents had occasionally thrown at them. But ever since Billie had gotten back from New York, her idea of supportive seemed to vacillate wildly between *do whatever you want* and *I know what is best for you*, another trait she and Dylan had in common now.

"I'm just struggling to see what you want from me here," Neale said, letting the anger in her voice fill the space for the first time since rehearsal had started. It was a sound she would have appreciated if her regret over agreeing to this stupid variety show weren't tripling by the minute.

"Umm," Billie said, looking around the auditorium for some sort of assistance that wouldn't come. "How about this. Did my initial questions about the video and staging make sense?"

"I'm not stupid," Neale huffed.

"No. Of course you aren't," Billie rushed. "I just thought that it seems like we're both tired. So if you got what you needed out of my notes, maybe we call this a day? You can go home and work on it so that you're ready for the full rehearsal next week. How does that sound?"

What Neale wanted to say was that she'd been working on it and it hadn't mattered. This was the best she had. *Dr. McMillan might have been right*, Neale thought. Maybe she wasn't meant to go further in the art world. For a heartbeat, she considered telling Billie she couldn't do this, but she knew Billie wouldn't understand. She'd think Neale just didn't want to take her notes or to put the work in. Her mother's words echoed in her head: *It's Neale. She's always fifty fifty when it comes to hard work.*

No, Neale would never admit she was afraid she couldn't pull it together. She'd managed to find a job and make rent despite what her family thought. She just needed to find a moment to think, and then this would be better.

Sucking in a deep breath, she said, "I think that is the best idea you have had all night."

CHAPTER TWENTY

Neale was still not in the mood for a party. She had spent the last few days vacillating wildly between getting as many Glitter Cat–themed decorations as she could and trying to work out how she felt about Billie's feedback. By Friday night, she'd calmed down enough to recognize that part of the reason Billie's words stung was that there was some truth to them. Without context, the video did look a bit like Neale was just reminding people she'd gone viral for all the wrong reasons. That didn't mean she was about to admit to Billie that she might have had a point, though.

Affixing a picture of a kitten over a rainbow to the bathroom mirror, she readjusted her cat ears and wiped a stray smudge of glitter eyeliner from under her eye. The gesture did little to fix the eyeliner and more to smudge glitter all over her face. Then again, she was dressed like a cat for Corinne's party. There was little the eyeliner could do to add or detract from the costume issue.

"Neale, can you help me?" Corinne called from the living room.

"Just a second." Neale gave herself a once-over in the mirror. Adjusting the seams on her brown leggings and pulling the zipper up on her faux-fur jacket, she took just enough time to congratulate herself on her Value Village finds, then popped out of the bathroom, saying, "What's up, birthday girl?"

"Important decision." Corinne bounced over with her hands behind her back. Unlike Neale, who had aimed for a literal cat costume, Corinne was dressed in a giant pink cat T-shirt and leopard-print bike shorts with a tail attached. Taking her hands out from behind her back, she produced two spritzers in Koozies and asked, "Which limited-edition, special, commemorative Corinne-is-twenty-eight birthday Koozie do you want?"

Neale did her best to swallow a laugh. The gesture was sweet, even if the cat pictures on the front low-key looked like the animals would claw her eyes out if given the chance. "I'll take the blue one with the stripy kitty."

"I thought you would. Thank you for helping me with this party," Corinne said, handing her the Koozie. "Cheers before people get here and we can't make our way to the fridge to get a cold spritzer for the rest of the night?"

"Yes, and cheers to the fabulous birthday girl!" Neale said, popping her can open.

"To the best roomie a cat lady could ask for!"

The two of them giggled and knocked their cans together, the sound muffled by the fabric of their Koozies. The bubbles from the can tickled Neale's nose as she went to take her first sip. For her part, Corinne was treating her spritzer more like a cheap beer that needed chugging, which was only interrupted by a pounding on the front door.

"Someone's early," Neale said.

"Neale, it is definitely eight fifteen p.m. No one is early. Everyone is late," Corinne said, checking Neale's sense of time as she sprinted toward the door, opened it, and squealed at the same time her sister yelled, "Happy birthday!"

"Aw! You brought balloons," Corinne said as the sound of someone fighting with latex filled the apartment. From the living room, Neale could see Chloe try to walk through the door with a massive bunch of balloons, an attempt that was doomed to end in an explosion given the volume of balloons and the angle at which she was approaching.

"Watch the R balloon," Corinne hollered as her sister took a step forward.

"I'm trying," Chloe shot back.

Fearing a balloon massacre, Neale dashed toward the door to try to help. With a little luck, the three of them managed to get all but two latex balloons into the apartment unscathed. Even better, the sparkly silver Mylar balloons that spelled out Corinne's name were completely unharmed.

"We need to set them up so they arch over the photo wall," Corinne demanded, referring to the wall in the living room that they had covered in Glitter Cat wrapping paper.

In Neale's opinion, this was going to be a visually painful social media photo op. But it was Corinne's birthday, so she dutifully arranged the balloons at varying heights while Corinne and Chloe helped art direct and greet other guests.

By the time Neale was done getting the balloons in line, there was nothing left to do but enjoy herself. Spotting Morrigan's signature shoulder-length, teased orange hair, Neale went to go chat with them. Her smile grew as Morrigan looked up and she saw the perfect Glitter Cat nose and whiskers that Morrigan had painted on their face. On any other white person, orange cat whiskers would have looked like a mess. On Morrigan, it was perfect.

"Hey, Morrigan." Neale waved as she approached.

"Neale! So good to see you," Morrigan shouted, causing the people around them to jump back a few inches as they spread their arms out wide for a hug. Releasing Neale, they said, "How have you been?"

Smiling from ear to ear, Neale began filling Morrigan in on her attempts to establish a musical greeting card program and her work with Billie.

"That's wild," Morrigan said, shaking their head as Corinne darted by, making her way toward the woman that Neale was 100 percent positive was the same woman who featured most heavily in Corinne's fabulous-new-girlfriend-at-twenty-eight plan.

"Yeah, it's been a strange few months, but I think it's a good thing," Neale said, setting her empty Koozie on the dining room table.

"I gotta say, Billie's show is all anyone is talking about at the house. You know she didn't take a single one of those Collective assholes?"

"Really?" Neale said, trying to keep the surprise from her voice. "I just thought they weren't interested in the show."

"Oh no. People are interested." Morrigan shook their head.

A small corner of Neale's heart twinged with guilt. She hadn't even been nice to Billie this week, and here she was quietly waging a petty battle against Neale's old colleagues. It just didn't seem like something her now-worldly, ultracool sister would do for her. Then again, maybe her sister wasn't holding a petty grudge for Neale. If she had learned anything about Billie, it was that her sister wanted to make a splash. It was just as likely that the Collective artists didn't have anything that interested her.

Deciding to examine Billie's motives another time, Neale shrugged. "Who knows why my sister does what she does?"

Morrigan laughed. "Everyone at the house is going to be so disappointed that you didn't say it was some grand scheme against them."

"Not to my knowledge. And something tells me not to Billie's either. She is too pragmatic for that."

They both stopped laughing to watch as Corinne floated by again, grinning wildly as she made her way across the room with a fresh drink in one hand and Plan Girl's hand in the other.

"I should go wish her a happy birthday before she is 'otherwise occupied,'" Morrigan said, putting *otherwise occupied* in air quotes.

"That sounds wise." Neale was twisting around to try to see where Corinne had gone when a red Tony the Tiger T-shirt caught her eye. Or, more accurately, Anthony in a red Tony the Tiger T-shirt caught her eye.

"Let's get coffee soon," Morrigan called as they made their way toward Corinne.

"Cool. I'll text you." Neale's chest tightened as her mind oscillated between excitement and dread. She'd half expected Anthony not to show up after the whole conference thing. Of course, if she was honest with herself, she'd still hoped he would, but Neale's concept of hope and her grasp on reality were often at opposite ends of the spectrum. How tonight managed to be the one time those two things aligned was beyond her.

Anthony stood in the doorway, looking for her, and she was suddenly aware of how warm the apartment had gotten. Or maybe that was just her body responding to the way he looked in those black, slim-fit jeans. Neale had to wonder if they were strategically tailored to show off what jumping around an obstacle course had done for his thighs. Or if he was simply unaware that the way he looked in them was basically robbing her of her senses and destroying her idea of what jeans were supposed to look like on men.

Neale was just working up the nerve to call out his name when he spotted her and waved, a big, bright smile spreading across his face. Turning sideways, he attempted to weave through the crowded hallway to get to her, and Neale's jaw dropped. If his thighs were out here committing crimes, that butt remained an existential crisis waiting to happen.

And just like that, with Anthony no more than ten feet away, Neale's mind started to spiral. How was she going to do this? Work was normal. Like, too normal for two people who'd just made out and then had to work together. It had given her a false sense of security, and now that she was in another social situation with him, Neale realized how absolutely foolish she had been to think—

"Hey, Neale," Anthony said, stopping in front of her. For a brief moment, he hesitated as if he couldn't decide whether or not to give her a hug, and Neale felt like someone had kicked her in the sternum. It hadn't occurred to her that someone as chill as Anthony might also be quietly spiraling until he was standing right in front of her, indecision written all over his body. It made her feel more comfortable in her own skin.

"Hey," Neale said, holding her fur-covered arms out for a hug.

As he stepped in to hug her, Anthony's smile increased ever so slightly, and she felt him relax in her arms. His familiar spicy smell wrapped around her, and she was thrilled to be hugging him and utterly destroyed by the idea that he would eventually let go. Before she had time to process the emotion, he released her, his friendly grin still in place.

"Did you find the place okay?" Neale asked, then almost kicked herself. In her rush to not have awkward silence, she'd managed to sound like someone's mom greeting a sleepover guest.

"I did." Anthony nodded, nerves tingeing the edges of his voice, then added, "I mean, I caught a ride over, so really I didn't have to do much of the navigating."

"Ha. That's the way to do it." Neale cringed as the words escaped her mouth. The sleepover mom was getting worse. Not that she would be opposed to an adult sleepover.

Anthony stuck his hands in his pockets and began to look around, and Neale's stomach dropped. Was this entire evening going to be this awkward between the two of them? They seemed to have plenty to talk about at work. But here and now? The only thing that could make this moment more awkward was if one of them said, *How about them Mariners?* Worse, Neale wasn't even sure if it was baseball season.

"Is that your roommate?" Anthony asked, inclining his head toward the impromptu photo session happening under the balloon arch. Leaning quickly around him, Neale grinned as she watched Corinne stage a multiperson hot-girl photo shoot, in which she and Plan Girl seemed to be the center of attention.

"That's her," Neale laughed.

"She looks like her new year is gonna be fun."

"Oh, that's the plan. Literally—she has it written down and everything."

"Are you serious?" Anthony asked. As soon as Neale started nodding, he laughed and added, "Is it written somewhere I can see it?"

"If you can fight your way into the kitchen, it's right there on the fridge."

"What's on the list?" Anthony shook his head and took his hands out of his pockets. It shouldn't have mattered, but watching him become more comfortable made Neale a little happy inside.

"Besides *get a hot new girlfriend*?"

"Which it looks like she has already achieved," Anthony interjected, laughing as Corinne licked Plan Girl's cheek for another photo.

"It does, doesn't it?" Neale laughed. "I think there is something about going to Switzerland and getting another vet tech certification. Maybe for exotic animals?"

"Like for elephants?"

"I mean, I hope not. I don't know if I'm ready for zoo energy in our apartment."

"Well, she already achieved one birthday goal, so I wouldn't put the rest past her," Anthony chuckled, the corners of his eyes crinkling.

"Did you ever have a list? Or like, an outrageous plan?" Neale asked, the question coming to her off the cuff.

"Ah." Anthony winced and rubbed the back of his head as if Neale had accidentally elbowed him.

"Oh, now I have to know," Neale said, leaning toward him. She hadn't meant to get closer, but the party was loud, and she wanted to make sure she heard his secret. Or at least that was what she was committed to telling herself.

"It is really embarrassing."

"Obviously. That is why I have to know," Neale said, fighting to keep a straight face.

"You cannot judge me," Anthony said, his wince slowly fading.

"I'm sorry, Anthony. I can't make that promise," Neale laughed. "If you were a Beanie Baby collector or one of those people who saved Coke cans, I will mock you."

"Well, when you put it like that, my list is very normal." Anthony took a deep breath, humor running across his face, and said, "From ages nine to thirteen I had a list of rock stars I wanted to meet."

"What?" Neale asked, surprised. "How is that embarrassing? I mean, a preteen magazine is basically just a list of pop stars people want to meet."

"No. Not like that," Anthony said, softly chuckling at whatever memory lay just behind his words. "I mean, I was determined to meet Eddie Vedder, so I kept a list of everywhere I heard people had seen him, and I would drag my mom or grandma out to that location looking for him."

Neale blinked at him for a moment, then began to laugh. "Wait— so you basically fan stalked grunge musicians?"

"Yes! And I made my grandmother an accomplice," Anthony said, hanging his head and laughing. "I'm pretty sure she ended up emailing the band, because one day we just happened to 'run into' him outside the grocery store before they played a show."

"That's amazing!" Neale said, her heart expanding as she thought about little-kid Anthony's joy.

"It is . . . until you see my grandma's face in the photo. There is nine-year-old me, smiling so hard it looks like I could float away, several members of Pearl Jam just being normal, and then my grandma, who looks like she is relieved to be over with the whole thing." Anthony began to laugh, struggling to get the next phrase out between giggles. "The worst part was, I just doubled down and did the same thing for other bands. She spent all that time trying to make the list go away, and it only got worse."

Neale began to laugh so hard at the idea of his poor put-upon grandmother trying to track down rock bands that her side began to hurt. Next to her, Anthony actually slapped his knee. The gesture was so pure and silly that it made Neale laugh even harder.

Standing up, Anthony sighed. "Anyway, so that is my embarrassing list."

"I get why you didn't want to tell me." Neale grinned, nudging him with her elbow.

"And now, you can never tell anyone. Or I'll be forced to deny it."

"Should have sworn me to secrecy before you told the story. It's too late, and there is photographic evidence. All I have to do is ask your poor grandma for it."

The pair devolved into giggles again, and Neale was suddenly so glad she had invited Anthony. He was easy to be around, and not just because of the fit of his T-shirt. There was something enjoyable and effortless about standing in her living room laughing at his younger self with him.

"Hey," Anthony said, drawing Neale out of her reflection. "I meant to ask . . . how did the rehearsal go?"

"Oh boy," Neale said, leaning her back against the living room wall with a heavy sigh.

"On a scale of one to I-took-a-photo-with-Hinder, how bad was it?"

"Hinder. Really?" Neale shrieked. Pearl Jam she could understand, but Hinder? Anthony was never going to hear the end of this.

"I was ten. And don't change the subject." Anthony grinned.

"I feel like you are the one changing the subject," Neale said, poking his chest with the tips of her fingers playfully. Anthony reached up and took her hand, pressing it to his chest, heat flashing through his eyes. Watching as he bit down on his lip, Neale's mind started to go hazy. Anthony's grasp was firm but not demanding, and she felt just like she had at the conference. That all she had to do was make a decision, and the whole just-friends concept could disappear. The longer he held her hand, the warmth from his skin soaking through his T-shirt and into her palm, the less she cared about friendship at all.

Anthony let a slow, sensual smile cross his lips, and then he released her hand, breaking the spell. Neale felt dazed as her skin tried to forget the weight of his hand pressed against hers. As she tried to pull herself together, his expression changed to a mischievous grin, and he said, "So how was rehearsal?"

"What?" Neale left off the rest of the sentence and swallowed the words *the hell* before they escaped her lips.

Across from her, Anthony looked pleased with himself. "Rehearsal? There was so much going on at work; we never got the chance to talk about it."

It dawned on Neale that he was being coy. Sweet, polite, thoughtful Anthony Williams was a tease. Part of Neale was shocked that he would do this to her. Whatever the female equivalent of blue balls was, she had them.

"It was a little rocky," she said, clearing her throat as if he hadn't just thrown her for a loop.

"Rocky how?" Anthony asked, his forehead wrinkling.

"Mostly it was my fault. I just couldn't come up with a decent idea until it was too late in the week, so Billie wasn't happy with the work. It doesn't help that my sister has changed since she moved to New York. She has less time now. Back in the day, she would have talked through this stuff with me."

"What did you think she would help you with?" Anthony asked, leaning into her slightly.

"I don't know," Neale admitted, crossing her fur-covered arms over her chest despite how warm she was in her jacket. "I wanted to incorporate elements of the gallery fire into a video. But I didn't do enough with it. She called it 'self-indulgent.'"

"Really?" Anthony said, lifting a skeptical eyebrow.

"Yes. I mean, I can see where she was coming from, but still," Neale said over Anthony's soft laughter. "Anyway, I have been reworking it, and it's getting better, but it's still not perfect."

"I'm sure it's not that bad," Anthony said, inching closer, ostensibly to hear her over the noise, although Neale was fairly certain that wasn't the only reason.

She smirked, an idea forming in the back of her mind. "Want to see it?"

"The video?" Anthony asked in surprise.

"Yeah. You're so convinced it is good. I have categorical proof otherwise."

"I'd love to see your work." Anthony sounded genuine, as if he was touched that Neale was trusting him with a preview.

"Follow me," she said, reaching out a hand and interlacing her fingers with his. A little voice suggested that maybe taking Anthony to her room was a bad idea. Neale was fairly convinced that voice did not have her best interests at heart. If it did, it wouldn't be asking her to be the first female victim of death by blue balls.

However, when she pushed the door to her room open, she thought the little voice might have had a point. Neale had never been particularly concerned with her surroundings. Her parents were wonderful people, but attention to housekeeping and home decor weren't exactly their strong suit. Unfortunately, this was hereditary. As she led Anthony into her room full of brown moving boxes doubling as dressers and her unmade twin air mattress, Neale experienced her very first pangs of shame.

"Obviously, I'm still in a state of moving," Neale said, now painfully aware that there was no actual furniture anywhere in the apartment that didn't require one to sit crisscross applesauce on the floor.

Anthony smiled, looking around the room at Neale's things strewed mostly in piles on the carpet. "When did you move in, again?"

"Three months ago," Neale said, holding her head up like a queen on her throne. "I just haven't had the time to go shopping. I have a very specific vision for this room, and that takes some serious dedication to thrift store hunting."

"Sure," Anthony said. His tone was skeptical, but humor was written all over his face.

"Well, someone is judgy judgy," Neale said, tossing her thick curls back and sitting on her air mattress with a rubbery thud. Picking up her computer from its corner on her bed, she patted the space next to her and said, "Are you too fancy to have a seat? I'm happy to let you watch this standing up."

Anthony snorted, then dropped down next to her. "I'm certainly not too fancy to sit with you."

"That's what I thought," Neale said, executing a series of clicks. She let her mind wander to the nearness of Anthony on the bed. It was almost impossible not to be distracted by his presence, his body pressing into her side, as she started the video.

Neale left the computer in her lap so that he had to move in even closer to see the tiny details she had superimposed on the footage. As the video wore on, she felt herself growing warmer. For a brief moment, she wondered if she was just embarrassed to be sharing such a rough draft with him. She had been working hard on her piece, but she still wasn't completely confident in it yet. Neale remembered the symptoms of shame from her last brush with the emotion and ran through those as Anthony watched. Humiliating surroundings, yes. Hot under the collar, yes. Sweaty armpits, yes. Horror-induced statue pose—Neale wiggled her nose—nope. She could still move freely. This was likely not shame.

Looking down at her torso, Neale grinned. This was the combo of her fuzzy jacket and his body causing her to overheat.

Neale leaned away from Anthony slightly as she unzipped the jacket, heat rushing off her in waves. She could sense Anthony watching her out of the corner of his eye as she peeled away the jacket, revealing a brown crop top to match her leggings. When Neale had gotten dressed this evening, she hadn't been thinking about him. But his hungry looks at her exposed skin made her very glad that she had decided to aim for matchy matchy instead of throwing on the oversize green cat T-shirt that her roommate had brought home from an animal-adoption event a few weeks back.

Tossing the jacket to the floor at the end of her bed, she leaned back into place, feeling the fabric of Anthony's T-shirt and the warmth of his skin on her arm. Neale's body tingled with the new sensation of someone else's skin and the electric hum of wanting. Her pulse jumped, knowing that Anthony must be as aware of her bare skin as she was of his. As she looked down at their arms, her eye was drawn to the tattoo winding its way up his left arm and under his sleeve. She desperately wanted to touch that tattoo. To run her fingers over the ink and feel the skin beneath it, to trace its line up his arm to wherever that tattoo ended.

As tiny speech bubbles with her internal monologue popped up on the screen, Neale watched Anthony's gaze jump from their legs pressed against one another back to the video. The tension built between them as they both pretended to focus on the reason that he was supposedly in her room. The longer the video went, the more she found herself wishing that she had cut the thing down to highlight-reel length. It needed to hurry up and end. She was dying being this close to Anthony without actually touching any of the parts of him that she wanted to touch.

Finally, the video faded to black, leaving the two of them in silence. Neale set the computer aside with one hand, refusing to place the machine more than a few inches away, lest it force her to break skin contact. Folding her hands neatly in her lap, Neale turned her gaze to face Anthony and held her breath. Trying to process all her brain signals, she waited while whatever instinct had said *colleagues* was steadily drowned out by an overwhelming urge to touch him. To kiss him. To know what the skin on the side of his neck tasted like. To feel the pressure of his hands on her.

"That was—"

"Can I kiss you?" Neale asked. It wasn't that she didn't care what Anthony thought of the video. It was simply that she cared a lot more about his body right now.

"Yes." Anthony's response was sure and quick, as if he had been waiting for her to come to the conclusion herself.

Neale leaned in, abandoning all pretense of cool as she closed the gap between them. Unlike their first kiss, this kiss was hungry. The feel of his lips against hers, the trace of his tongue along her bottom lip, the smell of his soap, all of him all at once. Neale sighed against him as his hands found their way down her back, past the hem of her top to her bare skin. She could feel a smile creep into his kiss as he wrapped his arms around her, pulling Neale in so close that the weight of her toppled them over, causing the air mattress to groan.

The new angle gave him access to other parts of Neale's body, her skin humming with desire as he ran a hand smoothly over her lower back before giving her ass a squeeze. Neale growled. She did not want the layers of fabric between them anymore. What she wanted was his hands on her. Not her leggings.

Breaking the kiss, Neale propped herself up on her elbows and was pleased to see that Anthony's rich brown eyes were as heavy as his breathing. Toying with the sleeve of his shirt, Neale let her fingertips graze the soft skin underneath and asked, "Can I take this off? You know, for science's sake."

Anthony blinked at her for a moment, clarity rapidly coming into his face as he worked through her question. Half smiling, he asked, "Are you suggesting we progress our experiment?"

"If by *progress with the experiment*, you mean *experiment with sex*, then yes," Neale said, feeling her heart begin to race with anticipation.

Anthony pushed himself up on his elbows, closing the gap between them again. Slowly, he leaned in and placed a single deliberate kiss just beneath her ear, sending tingles down her spine, then whispered, "That is exactly what I mean."

Neale desperately wanted to shout *YES!* and throw her hands in the air. Instead, she settled for a big grin as she straddled Anthony's legs so he could sit up and reached for the hem of his shirt. Without a word, he lifted his arms, helping Neale peel the unwanted item from his torso, finally giving her access to the tattoo that had occupied her dreams for months.

Sitting back, she took all of him in. She had secretly suspected that the man was made of muscle, but taking his shirt off proved at least one of her theories. He was lean and hard in all the right places, and her hands ached to touch every inch of his skin—starting with his tattoo. Neale had thought he had some stars running up his arm. But now that she was looking at it, she could see what it really was. The curve of his shoulder was a compass rose, carefully etched in black ink with subtle designs fanning out in all four cardinal directions. Looking closely, Neale realized that the delicate designs weren't just stars; they were constellations.

"This is beautiful," Neale said, her voice breathy as she reached out to trace the line of one of the constellations across his chest.

"Thank you," Anthony said, his eyes steady on her as she traced the lines. "My father was in the navy. It seemed like a good way to honor him."

"I can't imagine anything better." Neale smiled, watching his expression carefully. "It is one of a kind."

"The artist helped me work the whole family's initials into the stars too," he said, taking her hand and pressing it to the constellation near the center of his chest.

"I love that. How long did it take to finish the tattoo?" Neale asked. She was trying her absolute best to focus on his words, but the heat coming off his skin was making it difficult.

"All in? About fifteen hours."

"You sat still for fifteen hours?" Neale said, her eyes going wide.

"I mean, yes. But not all at one time," Anthony said, looking at her like the question had come entirely out of left field.

"Well, how many times did you go in there?"

"Four." Anthony laughed, then squeezed the hand he held over his heart. "You really want to talk about my tattoo right now?"

"Honestly, no," Neale laughed.

"Okay, thank God. Because I was willing to talk about it but—"

Anthony never finished the sentence, because Neale chose that moment to strip off her shirt, leaving just her hot-pink bra on display, her ego inflating as she watched his words fall away and his eyes rove over her. Clearing her throat, she raised an eyebrow and said, "You were saying?"

"Nothing at all," Anthony said, tracing his fingertips up and down the length of her spine.

"That's what I thought," Neale said. She leaned in to kiss him when a horrifying notion occurred to her. Easing away from him, she asked, "Please tell me you brought a condom."

"I . . ." Anthony's face fell as he thought. Sighing, he said, "I did not."

"Damn it," Neale whispered, eyeing her boxes. Bracing for humiliation, she reminded herself that needs must be met. Turning her attention back to Anthony, she said, "Well, then I guess we are gonna have to unpack some boxes."

"What?" he asked, his hand still resting on the small of her back.

Slowly, she untangled her legs from around him and rolled away from the air mattress before turning back to face him. "I have some condoms in one of these boxes. Either we are gonna find them, or we are both going to die of no sex."

Anthony blinked at her for a few moments, then laughed low and slow. "I'm not sure that people can actually die from not having sex."

"Do you really want to find out?" Neale said, half smiling as she opened the first box.

"Not at all."

"Good, then start with that box over there," Neale said, pointing to a box at the opposite corner of the room as she unceremoniously began dumping things on the floor.

"All right," Anthony chuckled, rolling off the air mattress and pushing himself onto all fours.

Neale watched him from the corner of her eye and nearly screamed. Unlike her, who was tossing stuff everywhere, Anthony was carefully folding her sweaters and putting them in neat little piles on the floor as he searched. They were never going to find condoms if he kept searching like this. Standing up to dump out another box, Neale growled, "Just throw the stuff."

Anthony looked scandalized. "But then all your sweaters will be everywhere, and it will take forever to get organized, and—"

"Death by no sex," Neale shouted, interrupting him. "At the rate you are going, we will be mummified before we find—"

"Aha!" Anthony said, triumphantly holding up a package and waving it at her. "Look what I found. What was that you were saying about us dying and being mummified?"

"Beginner's luck," Neale mumbled, as Anthony walked toward her.

"More like attention to detail," Anthony said, holding his hand out to her. After helping Neale to her feet, he pulled her close and said, "I like to take my time with important things."

The words sent hot shivers through her, as anticipation gathered between the two of them. Leaning in, Neale kissed him as she reached for his belt buckle. She'd unfastened his belt and begun on the button of his jeans when his hands stilled hers.

Neale looked up, a question waiting on the tip of her tongue, and Anthony said, "I know we just spent forever looking for these things, but before we go any further, anything that I should know? Hang-ups, holdups, dislikes?"

She didn't have a mirror in her room, but Neale was pretty sure that if she did, she would see herself smiling from ear to ear. Of course Anthony would take the time to ask. He really was the most considerate guy she had ever been with. Still grinning, she shook her head. "Nope. Anything that I should know?"

Anthony laughed. "Nothing on my end."

"Good. Now, can we finally start the experiment?" Neale said, desperate to get down to business.

"I'm all yours," Anthony said, laughing before kissing her once more.

"All right. Let's get started." Neale smirked, feeling cheeky as she began to work on the top button of his jeans again. "Guess we can lose the pants."

"Only if your pants go next," Anthony said, his eyes floating up toward the top of her head. Smiling, he added, "But you can leave the cat ears."

CHAPTER
TWENTY-ONE

Neale rolled over as the sounds of Corinne cursing at her alarm in the other room slowly filtered through the wall. If her roommate's night had ended anything like hers, she had no idea why she was swearing like someone had cut her off on the freeway.

The memory of last night brought a smile to Neale's face. After the two of them had finished "experimenting," they decided he should head home, agreeing that her twin air mattress likely couldn't take the weight of the two of them all night, especially after the activity they had just put it through. So Anthony had left, gently suggesting that if they were to continue experimenting, they might want to do it at his place on a mattress not made of rubber.

Wrapping her comforter around her, Neale sat up and began fumbling about for her phone, hoping it still had some battery despite the fact that she hadn't plugged it in. Locating the device, she smiled as a text from Anthony flashed across her screen.

Thanks for hanging out with me last night. Maybe we can talk about your video at lunch. :-)

Neale smirked as she tapped out a reply about wanting to learn more about his tattoo and saying that she hoped *getting lunch* was the new stand-in for *experimenting*. She managed to hit send before doing a seated happy dance. Sure, she wasn't exactly maintaining her secular-nun vows, but she'd had a lot of fun, and that counted for something as far as she was concerned.

Rolling off her bed, Neale grabbed a T-shirt from the pile of clothes she had left on the floor the night before and pulled it over her head before tracking down some oversize sweats. Tying the drawstring around her waist, she threw her phone in her pocket and began the shuffle toward the kitchen, trying not to notice the mess in the living room. She would make herself some coffee first, then deal with cleanup.

Pushing empty cans off the counter, Neale pulled the coffee down from the shelf and absentmindedly began spooning some into a filter, replaying her night over again in her head. When she looked back on it, everything had seemed to happen so fast that Neale really couldn't pinpoint the exact moment that she'd decided to abandon the whole New Neale plan and sleep with Anthony.

After hitting the button to begin the brew cycle, Neale opened a cupboard and took down one of Corinne's Glitter Cat mugs. *Hell, cat ears brought me good luck last night; I might as well try to keep the party going*, she thought, smiling.

Although how she would keep the party going at work was beyond her. Neale frowned as the idea of going back to work with Anthony crossed her mind. Now that she really thought about it, she was 100 percent sure that she did not want the party going at work. Or at least she didn't want people to know about the party. Of course, the thought occurred to her now that it was too late. Neale shook her head as regret started to push against her happy little postsex bubble.

Nope, Neale thought. She was not going to freak out about this. Really, she'd already had this freak-out, and she knew how it ended . . . with her backtracking and Anthony being reasonable about it.

"What is the worst that could happen?" Neale asked her cat mug, trying to slow her spinning mind as she reached for the coffee carafe to fill her cup. "Anthony is cool. Rich seems like he wouldn't care. At least not as long as it didn't impact our work."

The cat stared at her as if she were suffering from some grand delusion, its ceramic face skeptical.

"Don't look at me like that," Neale said, squinting at the mug before opening the fridge to find some half-and-half. Locating the creamer, she shook her head and continued talking to her mug of judgment. "I know what you are thinking. That I was hasty and I shouldn't have rushed into anything. But it's too late now."

Neale picked up the mug and rotated its face away from her so she would feel less judged. Unfortunately, that didn't work, and she could practically hear the mug asking how she knew sex wouldn't affect their working relationship.

"Look, Dylan was the one who said I should follow my heart. I just took her advice," Neale said, sighing as she reached the kitchen table. Setting the mug down, she said, "I know it's not a good excuse."

Neale also knew that the personification of her subconscious in coffee-mug form was right. She should have talked to Anthony about the ramifications of their actions. Now she was stuck praying that sex wouldn't change or sabotage their work relationship. And really, when in the history of the world had sex not complicated something?

"What? I'm used to uncomplicated sex." Neale shrugged at her mug before taking a sip. Then she sighed. "Okay, fine. I know that isn't entirely true. But no need to bring Darin into this. Anthony is different. I'm different now too."

The mug's silence was overwhelming, and Neale's stomach sank. Could she truly say that she was a different person? The answer to that was obviously no. Otherwise, she wouldn't be sitting here at 10:23 a.m. talking to a coffee mug and trying to convince herself she hadn't fucked up.

But she had. And the ramifications of this were so much bigger. Sure, she wanted to believe that Rich was cool and that things would be chill between herself and Anthony, but what if they weren't? Unlike with Darin, there was no fallback here. She couldn't go back to her parents for money. And even if she could sleep on Dylan's couch, her name was on a lease. She had actual bills to pay now. As much as she might want to act like Old Neale, there was literally no way she could go back to being her. She had too much at stake.

Regret washed over her in waves, making the coffee in her cup seem more like ash than a beverage. What could she possibly do that wouldn't lead to the inevitable classic Neale hell storm of a mess?

Looking back down at her mug, she grimaced. "You were right, okay? Now, stop judging and help me get out of this."

The mug said nothing, and Neale had a sinking suspicion that she was on her own to figure this one out.

~

Hi Neale,

Thanks so much for reaching out. I went back to take a look at the numbers and there is just no way that we can make less than $2.03 work at 500 recording devices. That said, I think I could get my suppliers to knock the price per unit down on the speaker parts to $1.55 if you were to place an order of 1,000.

Neale felt like she might be sick as she did her best to focus on the email she'd received from the local recording device manufacturer. With just a few weeks left before these cards were supposed to go into production, nothing seemed to be coming together the way that it should, and it scared her. There was no way they could do $2.00 a part and keep the card affordable. Really, $1.55 was even pushing it, and Rich had made it clear that he didn't think they could move more than 350 cards. She was already stretching it asking for five hundred parts. But an extra five hundred on top of that? There was no way they could use all of those. The best thing that she could do would be to put the project on hold before it got any worse.

Dread crept over her as she looked at the clock on her computer. It was six minutes to 10:00 a.m., and Anthony's meeting with Travis would be ending soon. When she had walked into the office a little late this morning, the small reprieve from slowing things down with him had seemed like a gift from heaven. Now that she had been stewing in trepidation for an hour, she wasn't as convinced that she had been lucky. Any minute now, Anthony would step out of his meeting, and Neale would be forced to face the consequences of her impetuous decision-making.

Four minutes to go, Neale thought, looking back at the clock. She desperately did not feel like telling him that she'd made a mistake sleeping with him and that the cards weren't going to work out at the same time. But the idea of waiting until lunchtime to deliver breakup news seemed wrong.

Not that we are breaking up, Neale amended the thought quickly. As Darin had so painfully pointed out, she couldn't really break up with someone she'd never officially decided to date . . . further proof that she really hadn't thought through this decision.

The problem was that Neale wasn't entirely sure what she was looking for. With most guys she hung out with, she was super clear on what she wanted. But Anthony? He'd shown up to her party in a themed outfit, drawn her pictures, and remembered details about her art. He'd even met her family and not freaked out when her mother had yelled at strangers. That felt different. Serious, even. And Neale was a lot of things, but she certainly wasn't ready for anything serious, not when the one thing that she'd managed to do right was falling apart thanks to the pricing limitations of a vendor. Two weeks ago, New Neale had been on the come up. No struggling with art, no kinda boyfriends, no screwups. It was like she'd taken one risk and the whole foundation had started to shake. Now—

"Thanks, Travis." Anthony's voice startled her as he walked toward his desk. "Neale, did you want to meet in the conference room?"

Neale's stomach plummeted, even as she nodded in agreement. Of course he would be cheerful in his clean, white-and-blue-dotted trim-fit dress shirt. Somehow, it made Neale feel even worse. Her legs felt like lead as she followed Anthony to the conference room, each step of her bland ballet flats reminding her that she just had to be brave and get herself together. In the end, slowing things down was better for everyone. And sure, he would be sad about the card, but he'd get past that. Hopefully.

Reaching the room, Neale closed the door before she made eye contact with Anthony, using the time to gather the last of her courage from every corner of her brain. She turned to face him, and her heart hitched as he smiled. This already felt so much worse than what Neale had thought it would feel like. Why did he have to look so happy to see her?

Choosing a seat across from him, she tried not to notice the question in his eyes as she sat down. Splaying her hands across the table, she focused on her fizzy, sparkly nail polish and took a deep breath. "So before we talk about work stuff, I have been thinking . . ." Neale trailed off.

"Okay," Anthony said, his expression sobering as a wave of apprehension rolled off him.

Neale hated that expression. She hated the trepidation that threatened to swallow them whole. And she hated that Anthony was right to feel this way. Worst of all, she hated that she was the cause of it. Clearing her throat, she tried again. "I've been thinking that we should slow down."

"Slow down?" Anthony repeated.

"Yes," Neale said, her mouth feeling dry as three-day-old bread.

He nodded once and stared at a corner of the room as if it were helping shape his thoughts. Finally, Anthony said, "What do you mean by 'slow down'?"

"Like, be less intimate." Neale felt like her armpits were attempting to irrigate a field all on their own, despite the fact that her throat was parched. "And maybe we see less of each other."

The color drained from Anthony's face, and the air felt like it had been sucked out of the room right along with his joy. "That doesn't sound like 'slow down.' That sounds like 'break up.'"

"No. No, it's not a breakup. It's just a less-than," Neale rushed.

"So what would we be doing in this slowdown if we aren't intimate and we don't spend time together?" Anthony asked, his voice low and sarcastic.

"We'd hang out at work, get to know each other," Neale said, panic threading its way through her veins. He was not taking this as well as he had the last time she'd put the brakes on things.

"Can you tell me why?"

"I just . . ." Neale paused, searching for the words she needed. When nothing eloquent came, she started again. "Workplace romances are messy, and I feel like I'm not ready for anything serious. I'm still trying to figure myself out. Like I've said, I've made this mistake before, and I really should be working on me and trying to build a career."

Neale knew she was rambling, listing off every common excuse in the book for why she couldn't date right now. The good news was, most of the reasons had at least some truth to them. As she risked a glance at Anthony, her heart fell another inch. Even if there was truth in her pantheon of excuses, it didn't look like he was buying a single one of them today.

Blowing air past his bottom lip, he let his shoulders slump for just a moment before he said, "I think you may be throwing the baby out with the bathwater. If you are waiting to be a perfect, fully formed human with a CEO title before someone can date you, I feel like you might be waiting for a really long time."

"I know," Neale said, perhaps a little more quickly than she meant to. "Maybe in the future, when I'm where I need to be, we could try again."

Anthony's eyebrows shot up. "I'm a human being, Neale. You can't just stick me in the freezer for later."

"That's not what I meant," Neale said, her frustration mounting. It wasn't like she was asking him to take a vow of celibacy until she got it together.

"It's up to you. I like you, and I'd like to see where this goes, but I don't want to keep doing a seesaw thing. If we're done, then we are done," Anthony said, his brown eyes looking tired.

"I understand." Neale nodded. She had expected to feel relief once she got this off her chest. After all, done was what she wanted from him. Instead, she felt as exhausted as Anthony looked and exponentially more conflicted. She couldn't be in a relationship, but she hadn't expected him to close the door on being in one in the future. This all felt much more final than she had anticipated. Not that she could or would do anything about that now. Coercing her face into a half smile, she added, "Thank you. Want to talk about work?"

Anthony nodded but didn't say anything. His demeanor wasn't cold, but it wasn't the comforting presence that Neale had gotten used to over the past few months.

"I heard back from the manufacturer, and it isn't great news." She hesitated for the space of a heartbeat before letting the rest tumble from her. "They can't meet us anywhere close to one fifty per unit on the recording devices unless we order a thousand pieces."

Across the table from her, Anthony flinched, sucking air in between his teeth. Looking down at his notepad, he asked, "How much do they want to charge us for five hundred?"

"Two oh three," Neale said, her voice barely above a whisper as what was left of Anthony's pleasant facade melted away.

"That is a lot of money."

"Anthony, I don't think this is going to work," Neale said, finally letting herself speak the second set of dread-inducing words. "This card is going to cost us like six dollars to produce."

"I don't think we can change our minds now," Anthony said.

"What do you mean? We have to change our minds," Neale said, leaning back in her chair to try to escape the fatigued energy that was roiling off him.

"We're too far in. We already commissioned someone for the music. We have a printer lined up, and Rich already made calls to vendors," Anthony said. His tone had a veneer of patience, but underneath it, Neale felt like she was being lectured.

"What do you want us to do? Spend thousands of dollars we don't have?" Neale said, getting a bit testy in response.

"Spending money hasn't stopped you before. We are two weeks from starting to manufacture these things," Anthony pointed out.

"This could do real damage to Happy Hearts. We have to cut our losses. It's too big a risk." Neale's voice rose slightly as she gestured to the file folder with the card details in front of her.

"Now we are avoiding risk? Neale, less than two months ago you literally begged Rich to take this chance. You went out of your way to justify all kinds of spending. You were convinced that the ends justified the loss, and now that we are this close, you want to quit?" Anthony held up his thumb and forefinger to demonstrate how close he thought they were, adding, "You're ready to give up over what amounts to less than an extra thousand dollars after we have already committed to seven thousand dollars. This doesn't make sense."

Somewhere in the back of her mind, Neale could see where Anthony had a point. The extra $1,000 wasn't really much of a loss when looked at on its own. The problem was, it wasn't just the $1,000 for devices;

it was the extra $450 for printing, the extra $2,384 for assembly. Each extra cost on its own wasn't a big deal. It was the whole picture. Why couldn't Anthony see that?

Sighing heavily, Neale said, "All these extra costs are adding up. We can't deny that we are speeding down a road full of red flags. It's time to walk away."

"I disagree. This is what it looks like to do something new. There are going to be bumps in the road. At a certain point we have to buckle down and find a way to make it work," Anthony said. His words were not loud or hard, but they made Neale flinch just the same.

On the surface, she knew that they were talking about greeting cards, but suddenly the discussion felt like it wasn't just a disagreement around how to handle work. They were arguing over how to proceed with their relationship. The realization irritated Neale. She'd been down this road with Darin, and it had ended in her being brokenhearted and socially isolated. This kind of fight was exactly why she wanted to slow the relationship with Anthony down—so that they wouldn't be using petty work things to argue about their personal lives. She refused to repeat her previous mistakes with him.

Scowling, she said, "Look, I'm telling you that we can buckle down all we want, but that won't make this work. I get that you want this. But it isn't going to happen. You are being obstinate."

Silence hung in the air between them. Across from her, Anthony's eyes went wide with shock. Neale hadn't meant to say that last sentence out loud. Now she had to talk with a size 10 foot crammed in her mouth.

"I'm obstinate," Anthony repeated more to himself than to her.

"Anthony, I—"

"If we are name calling, then I'm saying you can't commit," he interrupted. The usual softness had disappeared from his expression, leaving only the severe bone structure behind. Anthony plowed on, his voice just a breath below its normal volume but its edge twice as sharp.

"What won't you quit when it gets complicated, Neale? So far you have quit art and me. Now it's this project. You are racking up quite a list."

"I knew this wasn't really about the cards. This is about us," Neale said, ignoring the stinging in her chest. How could he say something so cold? Yes, she had quit those things, but she always had good reason for walking away.

"Only inasmuch as there is a pattern," Anthony shot back, holding his chin at a defiant angle. "You want to quit this, too? Be my guest. But you are telling Rich. I'm still willing to work on the project."

"I will tell Rich, because I know when to cut my losses," Neale shot back, hoping she didn't sound as petty as she felt, like a petulant kid trying to prove a point. For a moment, they simply stared at each other, and Neale let the uncomfortable silence fortify her.

Finally, Anthony broke eye contact and cleared his throat. "Anything else we need to talk about?"

The question was phrased in such a mild way that it made Neale even more vexed. How dare he try to return to civility after a fight?

"No. I'm going to get an iced coffee. Would you like me to get you one?" Neale asked, standing up and trying to mirror his proud bearing. Her tone was not very inviting, but there was no way Neale could let him be more polite than herself right now.

"No, thank you," Anthony said, shaking his head and reaching to collect his notebook.

"All right." Neale nodded and turned to leave, already anticipating her comfortable seat on her high horse. Sure, her offer hadn't sounded particularly genuine, but she'd still gotten the last polite word in, and that was something.

She had just reached for the door when Anthony called, "Neale?"

All Neale wanted was to get out of the room and to take a slow walk around the corner for a watered-down coffee. *Of course, that just isn't how my day is shaping up*, she thought. Plastering a tight smile on her face before she turned around, she prompted him with, "Yes?"

Something in her tone hardened Anthony's resolve. Looking her directly in the eye, he said, "It doesn't have to be this card, or art, or even me. I just hope you find something that you want to do that you follow through on."

"I . . ." Neale stopped, her hand on the door as the wind went out of her sails. Breathing in sharply, she looked for a way to make his words feel more like a condemnation than a well-wish. But she couldn't find one, and she wasn't sure how she felt about that. Returning Anthony's gaze, she opened the door and said, "Thank you."

Stepping out of the conference room, she did not look back. She could deal with it after rehearsal, once she was safely at home with a cookie and a rerun of *Rhoda* playing in the background. For now, she just needed to get through the day.

CHAPTER TWENTY-TWO

Neale parked her car a few blocks away from the Black Spot, determined to use the walk to the venue as an opportunity to clear her head. After the day she'd had, rehearsal was truly the last place she wanted to be. But this was the final rehearsal, when all the artists, techs, and other staff ran through the performance, so there was no way that she could feasibly call in sick for this unless several eyewitnesses put her in the hospital. Otherwise, Billie would probably put her in the ER herself.

Drawing in a big breath of fresh summer air, Neale felt the sunlight hit her face and tried to reframe her day. Anthony had touched a nerve, whether or not she wanted to admit it, and she had spent the rest of the afternoon avoiding both him and thinking about his words. She did have follow-through. Following through with her life plan was exactly what she was trying to do. If Anthony couldn't appreciate that, then she had made the right call in cutting things off with him before it got any worse.

As for the card, she was lucky in that Rich had been on calls and in meetings most of the day, so she hadn't had to do all the hard stuff in one sitting. However, Neale had promised herself that she would work up the courage to tell him about their failed project first thing tomorrow.

Reaching the unassuming doors of the Black Spot, Neale pulled her shoulders back and gave the handle a tug. Unlike her previous rehearsals, this time the space was full of buzz and chatter as artists and performers darted from place to place, greeting each other and looking at Billie's paintings as they were being fitted to the walls. Other performers hovered and chatted animatedly while Nhi fussed with keys to unlock the theater doors.

"Neale, over here." Billie's voice cut across the room with such force that the wild, waving gesture she was making seemed utterly unnecessary. Her sister was practically glowing with excitement, surrounded by beautiful people that Neale didn't know. As soon as she was in earshot, Billie said, "Neale, I want you to meet a few of my friends who are visiting from New York. Marceline, my delightful dealer, and Kelsea, my manager extraordinaire. Y'all, this is my little sister, Neale."

Marceline smiled, her dark curly hair shining in the same invisible sunlight that gave her face a glow. As she moved her cane from one hand to the other, dozens of hammered-gold and onyx bracelets jangled on her forearm as she held out her right hand to shake Neale's. Beaming at her, she said, "So good to meet you. Billie has told us so much about you and how instrumental you have been in helping get the show off the ground while I was tying up things in New York and LA. This is like meeting a legend."

"Nice to meet you too," Neale said, before releasing her hand and turning to Kelsea, who was equally glamorous, her dark skin highlighted by her head-to-toe red suit and gray hair that managed to look fussy despite being in a buzz cut. Billie hadn't said much about either of these deeply hip-looking people except to complain when they wanted something. Then again, she probably told Dylan about them during their weekly calls or sister workouts, so Billie likely assumed Neale knew more than she did.

Taking a deep breath, Neale fished around for a convincing lie to make it sound like she and her sister were close enough that Neale knew all about her friends. "I hope half the things Billie said about me are as nice as what she says about you two."

The pair laughed, and Neale prayed it was because they were flattered and not because everything Billie said about her contained the words *hot mess* or *bail fund*.

Neale was just debating the best way to get out of the conversation when Nhi appeared at Billie's side. "Sorry to interrupt, but . . . Billie, the techs are here and ready whenever you are."

"Thank you," Billie said, radiating a mellow energy that Neale wished she could borrow. "Neale, can you help me get everyone inside?"

"Sure. Nice to meet you both," Neale said, nodding politely before she turned away. Wandering through the crowd, she felt her nervous energy start to kick in, no matter how many times she reminded herself that this was dress rehearsal, not opening night. Besides, this time she was ready. Her video was polished; her lines were memorized. She was only second-guessing herself because of her fight with Anthony. As she sat down in a chair close to the front of the house near where Billie was standing, she reassured herself that she was ready for this.

The space hadn't changed substantially since the last time Neale had been there, but it felt like an entirely different world with the way the stage had been dressed and lit. The gigantic three-paneled projector screen had been wrapped around the edges of the stage, and the formerly exposed wings were now covered in gauzy gray and red fabrics that fluttered in the air-conditioning like a sea creature. Someone had also taken the time to backlight the stained glass windows, and the aisle lights had been replaced with the same soft amber light, heightening the eerie ambience in the room. Overall, the creepy-church aura was mesmerizing and left Neale feeling small and on edge—just like the *New York Times* promised.

When it seemed like the performers were settled in, Billie took a deep breath and held her arms wide, saying, "Welcome, everyone. First, thank you for being here and being a part of this show. Each and every one of you has been a delight to work with, and I'm so excited to be sharing this stage with you."

Billie paused and smiled at the crowd before bringing her hands together at the center of her body and adopting a tone that sounded like she meant business. "So here is the plan. Tonight will be a bit long, but I think it is going to give everyone a real sense of what is in store. We'll run through the show twice—once with all of you in the audience so you get some sense for what your fellow performers are doing. In between acts, I'll give you any final notes that I have, although based on what I've seen from each of you, I don't anticipate giving out too many. From there, we will have everyone wait backstage and run it from the top just like it is showtime. All right?"

Billie paused and looked around, clearly waiting for a church response. After a moment, someone in the back shouted, "Yes, ma'am," which made the rest of them giggle as nervous energy crackled around the room.

"Let's do this," Billie said, clapping her hands together and half smiling conspiratorially. Dropping into an aisle seat three rows from the front, she said, "Belinda, you are up first. Charlie, you are on deck."

From the back corner, Belinda dashed forward in a massive, shimmering, fringe-covered black costume. Neale watched closely as she took her spot on the stage and waited for the techs to adjust the lighting. For a moment there was nothing but silence until the sound of a heartbeat came over the speakers, just once. Belinda's movement was nearly imperceptible, but it caused the entire costume to shiver, the sound of the fabric filling the silence. Eventually, the heartbeat came again, and Belinda truly began to whirl, hopping from foot to foot and moving lithely across the stage as the sound of another heartbeat was layered on top of the first. As more heartbeats were played, one on top of the next, Belinda's dancing became more erratic, and Neale found herself leaning forward, trying to catch each shimmy, the sound of the fringe and the sound of the heartbeats colliding and confusing her eyes and ears. It was terrifying, and she couldn't stop watching until suddenly the heartbeats stopped and Belinda dropped to the floor, silencing the percussive costume.

Neale didn't realize that she was holding her breath until Billie called out, "Looks great, Belinda; love the adjustments to the ending. Just a couple of notes for our friends in lighting, and then we can move to Charlie."

As Billie darted back to the tech booth and Belinda pulled herself up gracefully, Neale forced air into her lungs. She could feel the other performers getting excited, the hum of something untested and wild buzzing around them as Billie settled into her chair right as a replica of the painting that matched Charlie's number was projected onto the screen.

For the next hour and a half, Neale lost herself in the strange and delightful as each act built upon the last. Performers who on their own would have been odd were suddenly magical in the context of the theater and Billie's work. A baton twirler and ventriloquists were sprinkled in among the dancers, poets, and a woman who played the theremin, each adding a layer to the unsettling story being told. Finally, Callen took the stage, and Neale's brain began to wake up. Soon, she would need to get up there and tie all of this together into a bow for the audience. Even as she watched Callen nearing the end of their live painting, an inversion of the one her sister had created, Neale couldn't quite wrap her mind around how Billie envisioned Neale's work fitting into all of this. The idea of anchoring this performance made her stomach turn.

"Thanks, Callen. Just a couple of thoughts," Billie called as the houselights came up. Neale watched as Callen jumped down from the stage like a cat before sauntering over to talk to Billie while techs rushed out to move their supplies. There was nothing left for her to do but take the stage.

Finding her mark, Neale waited until her lighting came up and her new video began playing before she started to recite her words. The room felt too quiet; the only interruption was the occasional cough or a chair creaking as someone shifted their weight. Above her, the video flickered silently, but this time, Neale was ready for it. She didn't trip over the words in her poem or her feet despite the rush of blood to her head and the deeply disoriented sensation that came from attempting to suppress her nerves. From where she stood, with the lights trained on her, she couldn't really get a sense of how the other artists were responding. Eventually, her voice stopped shaking, and she found a rhythm. She just hoped it wasn't too late in the performance for people to appreciate her work.

A beat after Neale's piece ended, the houselights came up and Billie's voice rang out, causing Neale to jump.

"All right, now you all have a sense of how this fits together. It's eight thirty, so how about everyone take ten minutes and then head backstage for a full run-through," Billie said, twisting around in her seat so that she could look at the majority of the performers behind her. When it seemed like there was agreement, she turned around to face the stage and said, "Neale, got a minute? I have some questions for you."

The idea that Billie had more questions made Neale's heart sink. Easing herself off the edge of the stage and landing with a small hop, Neale walked cautiously over to her sister, trying to keep her tone light as she asked, "What did you think?"

Billie bit her lip and glanced from side to side as if checking to make sure the room was clear before she spoke her mind. "It's better, but you've got some issues."

"What?" Neale said, forgetting to keep her voice down. She had thought about all of Billie's feedback. "I did exactly what you said."

"I can see where you tried to, and you have added a ton of polish that really helps," Billie said, holding her hands up, her voice still quiet, as if the rest of the artists weren't already backstage or running to the corner for a snack.

"Then what's the problem?" Neale asked, her face feeling hot despite the air-conditioning.

"You followed the letter of the feedback but not the spirit. For example, you added the speech bubbles with your feelings, but did you ask yourself how you want the audience to feel about those feelings?"

"You don't tell people how to feel with art. You know that," Neale said, letting the edge hit her voice as Billie's eyebrows arched with indignation.

"Of course you don't tell people how to feel, but you do shape their perception. Right now, the speech bubbles make the theme of failure feel cartoonish. I can't imagine that Daffy Duck is what you are trying to lead the audience to," Billie said, holding her hand out as if the character were sitting in her palm.

"I don't think it's cartoonish," Neale said. Her voice wobbled, and her eyes stung. She had the nonsense urge to slap Billie's hand. However, she was pretty sure a mean-spirited high five wouldn't help.

"You know what I mean; otherwise, you wouldn't be upset," Billie said, her tone softening slightly. "Look, we have to start rehearsal again, but I think this could be an easy fix. Just spend the time backstage tweaking your verse a little so people are exploring that pain and that silly feeling with you."

"I don't want anyone to think I'm silly," Neale mumbled, torn between trying to defend her point of view and attempting to adjust to her sister's demands.

"Well, Neale, the show opens in a week and a half. I don't think we have time to fix the video, so you need to work with the movable objects." Billie sighed heavily, as if explaining something obvious. Putting a hand on Neale's upper arm, Billie gave her bicep a squeeze and said, "Head backstage and work on it, okay?"

Her sister's tone reminded her of when she was little. Every so often Billie would get a wild hair and try to pretend that Dylan wasn't really in charge. The result had always been her babying Neale to death and getting mad when Dylan still wouldn't let her decide what was for dinner. When they were young, this had been funny to Neale. Now, she just wanted her sister to back off and stop talking to her like she was a lost toddler.

"Fine," Neale said, her tone implying that there was nothing fine between the two of them.

"Thank you," Billie called, sounding as ungrateful as possible.

Blinking back tears, Neale made her way backstage and began looking for a quiet corner to think about her work as Belinda's heartbeat began to echo from the front of the house. Neale picked up her pen and notebook, going over where she could add either intentional cartoon energy to her monologue or play directly against it. The entire endeavor felt more hopeless and futile with each revision.

She did her best not to let her thoughts wander too far into the beginning of her day. Now that she looked back on it, Anthony's reaction to her at work had been an omen.

One by one the artists left the dressing room area, thanks to Nhi's expert calling, giving Neale a bit more space and a lot more quiet to think about Billie's critique. Last week she'd been self-indulgent; this week she was a cartoon. Neale's throat constricted as she thought through everything she had tried to do to make the show work. Flashes of light began to pop in front of her eyes as the very real idea that she could fail spectacularly danced to the front of her mind. This time would be so much worse. Not only would it look like her more talented sister had given her a job, but everyone would know that this was officially the lowest she could sink without finding herself in art hell, next to the woman who'd tried to restore that Spanish painting and turned Jesus into a monkey.

"Callen to stage left. Callen, stage left. Neale, this is your five-minute warning. Thank you." Nhi's voice floated through the near-empty room.

Neale looked up in time to catch Callen smiling at her and saying, "Break a leg."

She waited until they were fully out the door before exhaling and rushing to the bathroom. Turning on the cold tap, she splashed a little water on her face, grateful that she wasn't wearing much in the way of makeup for this dress rehearsal. Looking at herself in the mirror, she said, "Pull yourself together, girl. You have got this."

Splashing one more round of water on her face, Neale had just reached for a paper towel when Nhi's voice came over the loudspeaker again. "Neale to stage left. Neale, stage left. Thank you."

Tossing the towel in the little compost bin, she started her heavy walk to the stage, this time focusing on her breathing rather than her feet. Sure, she nearly fell down the sloped walkway when she didn't quite pick up her feet enough, but not hyperventilating seemed worth it.

Spotting the soft blue glow of Nhi's light over the call sheet at the edge of the stage, Neale walked over just in time to see the house go dark, and Nhi whispered into her microphone for techs to rush out to clear Callen's large canvas and spray paints. Turning to look at Neale, Nhi asked, "Ready?"

"Not really. But I'll go anyway," Neale said, trying to force a smile onto her face.

Nhi offered her a comforting nod and called the order for the lighting and video techs to be on standby, then nodded at Neale to take her place.

Neale walked onto the stage, breathing in slowly through her nose and out through her mouth, desperately trying to remember the different ideas she had for rewrites as the quiet and darkness enveloped her. Then the video flickered on and the stage lights came up, and all Neale could think was *oh shit*.

She was vaguely aware that her body was moving, and she was keenly aware that none of the words she had practiced were coming out of her mouth. Instead, it was a mix of her old monologue punctuated by "oops, no" and a series of other false starts. As the video flickered overhead, she could practically feel the other artists cringing or trying to hide laughter behind cleared throats and coughs. She couldn't decide if it was better or worse that she couldn't see everyone as she fumbled from one place to another, officially moving from cartoonish to flat-out cartoon. If she hadn't been onstage, she would have been crying, but as it was, she was forced to endure the imagined wrath of her sister and taunts of her colleagues for another full minute before coming to a flaccid stop slightly off her mark on center stage.

As soon as the house went dark, Neale was three steps into running for the door; then the lights came up with such blinding force that she had to stop moving and blink for a second. Glancing only briefly at the audience, Neale felt terror creep up her neck as Billie stood up to address the performers.

"Great run-through, everyone. I'm so excited for our opening." Billie clapped. Her tone sounded like forced excitement to Neale. Then again, maybe the rest of the artists were fooled by her pseudoupbeat handclap, which looked like her sister had been possessed by some sort of ultrachic cheerleader. "Anyway, it is after ten thirty, so check your email for notes, and I will see you all next week."

Exhaling, Neale continued her beeline for the exit until Billie's crisp voice drilled through the air, causing her to freeze midway through opening the door. "Neale, can you hang on a second?"

No, I can't, Neale thought as she took her hand away from the door, bitterness coursing through her. Unlike with her last telling off, this time Billie hadn't waited for the other artists to clear out, and now some of them had stopped packing up, ostensibly to listen to Neale relive the trauma of the Collective show, with her sister playing the role of Dr. McMillan humiliating her and her monologue assuming the role of her smoldering majorette hat.

"All right," Neale said, looking at the faces of the other performers. In the back, Callen was making meaningful glances at Belinda to hurry up and pack her costume, likely so they could leave before the fireworks got started. Unfortunately, not everyone was so invested in avoiding conflict. Both Kelsea and Marceline fully sat back down, and Kelsea even leaned in, forearms folded on the chair in front of her to better listen in.

"So I know you didn't have much time to make alterations, but I'm concerned."

Oh, Billie is concerned. That's rich, Neale thought, rolling her eyes.

"Don't look at me like that," Billie said, her voice low and hard as she crossed her arms in front of her chest.

"Billie, are you kidding? You demand a last-minute change, and then you are *concerned*?"

Neale felt her face getting hot as her sister narrowed her eyes at her. After a moment, Billie said, "Don't be like that, Neale. You know this is how it works."

"Do I? I mean, what am I even doing here? I don't belong on this stage at all." Neale felt herself deflate. Out of the corner of her eye, she saw Belinda freeze in the middle of packing up to listen.

"And yet here you are." Billie's voice rose in volume so everyone left in the auditorium could hear them.

Something about the change in her sister's volume rankled Neale, and she snapped, "Only because you had Mom wage an emotional blitzkrieg on me."

Billie's expression was murderous, and Neale kicked herself for sounding like a child. Who blamed stuff on their mom in public after the age of three? Clearly, Billie thought the same thing. Adopting an ultrastern tone, she said, "Oh, please. We did that for your own good. Everyone in the family thinks you need to try again. Honestly, I didn't think you would have said yes if some part of you didn't want to try. Besides, how was I to know that you would rather sulk over one failure than actually work? If I'd known, I would have let you wallow at that damn desk job."

"I know you don't believe me, but I'm a grown woman, capable of knowing what is good for myself. And I'll have you know that I'm good at that job." *Or mostly good at it,* Neale thought.

"Ah yes, so grown," Billie practically shouted, drawing out the *o* in *so*. "Frankly, thank God you are good at something other than being entitled. You're not the only one who has ever failed, Neale."

"I'm entitled?" Neale cried, fury making her blood pump twice as fast, filling her ears so she could barely hear herself think. "You were already on third base when you changed your mind about LA and decided you wanted to go home—not a real failure, by the way. You stroll around like you are really struggling and not some cooler-than-thou asshat who throws a minor tantrum when confronted with any shred of anything that differs from your point of view."

"I'm throwing a minor tantrum? What are you doing right now?" Billie fully shouted this, letting her hands fall to her sides with a loud slap. "All you do is whine and bury your head in the sand. Get over yourself. Lots of people want to be artists. Art isn't just a good idea. It's also the grind that makes it happen. Stop being a hack."

The pit of Neale's stomach dropped as she inhaled sharply. She could live with being called lazy or entitled, but a hack? That was just about the meanest thing that anyone had ever called her. Neale felt her eyes prickle as she looked at Billie, who was alternating between glaring at her and eyeing the floor with a scowl as if she couldn't quite decide how mean she wanted to look.

Biting back a sob, she looked at Billie and said exactly what she'd been dying to say since her sister had gotten back into town. "Screw you. You've been off in your own world so long that you don't even know me."

Realizing that the whole room would see her ugly cry in under five seconds, Neale made a dash for the door. Sure, running away was basically like handing over her last scrap of dignity, but then again, at least no one would get a second video of her crying on the internet.

CHAPTER
TWENTY-THREE

Neale made it exactly three feet outside the theater before she burst into tears. Not a month ago, she'd finally felt like she had some of life figured out. Now, she'd be lucky if no one from the show had filmed Billie shouting at her in front of God, everybody, and their dog. It was like the humiliation of the Collective show all over again, only worse, because this time she couldn't even hold on to a job that a family member had given her out of pity.

Sniffling as she walked, Neale looked down at the perfectly normal slacks she was wearing, and her sense of despair increased. Even when she was doing her very best to not be the kind of person who set a rented majorette suit and her career on fire, she couldn't seem to outrun herself. Here she was, shuffling along, still wearing someone else's clothes, disappointing her family, her coworkers, and her not-boyfriend boyfriend all over again.

A sob rocked Neale's body as she rounded the corner, reaching her car. How many times did she need to rip up her own life before she got it together? Her thoughts lurched as she searched for her keys. Breaking down, she dumped her purse onto the top of her car, barely catching her keys and phone as they attempted to roll off the hood. Cramming loose gum wrappers and receipts from the burrito truck back into her purse, Neale dived into the car and locked the door before she started sobbing again.

She needed to calm down before she could drive. She also needed a plan. Swiping at her tears, she reached for her phone to call the queen of planning and problem solving, a.k.a. her eldest sister.

Looking at the clock on her dashboard, she realized that it was 11:03 p.m. She was three rings in, so Dylan must be asleep with her phone off at Mike's place.

Shuddering out a sigh, she left a voice mail. "Dylan, it's Neale. I know you are asleep, but I just wanted to tell you that I had a really bad day." Neale hiccuped and paused to wipe her nose on the back of her hand before saying, "Billie yelled at me in front of everyone, and I quit. And then . . ." She hiccuped again and caught sight of herself in the rearview mirror. If she sounded as bad as she looked, there was no way Dylan wouldn't call her back.

Remembering that she was still leaving a voice mail, she continued, "And then, Anthony is mad. And I'm dying alone without art or love and only unicorns to keep me company." The last vowel of *company* sounded more like a wail than a word, but Neale was confident her older sister would understand. Unwilling to put additional energy into figuring out how to tie up her sad-sack voice mail, Neale said, "I'm coming to your house. See you soon. Love you. Bye."

Again, the word *bye* was more of a howl than a sign-off, but Neale didn't care. Forcing herself to take three deep breaths, she tossed her phone onto her passenger seat.

Slowly driving to Dylan's place, Neale was grateful that she still had her sister's guest key fob, despite Dylan asking for it twice. Sure, she felt like a loser in basically every other way, but at least she could be a loser sleeping on a comfortable rich-person couch tonight instead of her air mattress.

~

"Neale, did you eat all of the dried-cranberry-and-oat crackers in my bed?" Dylan's voice floated through her dreams. Neale cracked one eye open to see her sister staring down at her, clutching some gym clothes and looking perturbed. In her defense, there was no way Neale would have chosen to eat expensive health food crackers in Dylan's bed if her sister had kept any junk food in the house.

"What time is it?" Neale asked, shutting her eye, less because she didn't want to see her sister and more because she had a headache from crying so hard the night before.

"It's five fifteen. Are you sleeping in your clothes and a bathrobe?"

"You don't have any sweatshirts, and I was cold," Neale said, rolling over.

"Also, is that Mike's bathrobe?"

"Is his bathrobe green terry cloth?" Neale asked.

"Okay. Ew. You have to take off my boyfriend's bathrobe. And I swear to God, if you are still wearing your shoes, you will be changing my sheets."

"You were gonna change the sheets anyway. And I'm not wearing shoes." Neale meant to sound grumbly, but her words came out more wobbly. The threat of fresh tears pricked at her eyes, and she said, "Be nice to me, okay? I'm sad."

"I gathered as much from the voice mail," Dylan said. Then, pushing on her sister's hip, she added, "Scoot over, yeah?"

Neale half rolled, half scooted over to make room for her sister, who, in classic sister fashion, threw back the covers and crawled in with her. Throwing a protective arm over Neale, she said, "Do you want to tell me what happened?"

The word *no* was halfway out of Neale's mouth when she realized that she had literally broken into her sister's house just to be able to tell her the story.

"Okay." Taking a deep breath, she started from the night of the party and didn't stop until she reached the part where she raided Dylan's cupboards in search of comfort food. For her part, Dylan didn't say much, outside of giving a few encouraging hugs and passing Neale a tissue after she tried to wipe her nose on the duvet cover; she just listened.

"Anyway, Billie is an asshole, and I set another career on fire," Neale said, her chin trembling as she tried to suppress another round of tears.

After a moment, Dylan laid her head on Neale's shoulder and said, "Neale, can I ask a question?"

"As long as it isn't about if I got crumbs in your bed. Because the answer is yes."

"I figured," Dylan laughed, then stilled. "Neale, what exactly did you hope to gain by only putting half of yourself into all of this?"

"What do you mean?" Neale asked, although she was afraid that Dylan's answer might send her back into the sobbing-headache stage again.

"I think you know what I mean. You don't want the pain that comes with pursuing what you love, so you only put half of yourself into something. That way, if you fail, you can walk away and say you never really tried. You are half-in, half-out."

"I tried," Neale said, her muscles tensing as if they could shield her from her sister's words.

"No, you didn't. Look at the facts. You left literally every detail about this piece until the last minute. You only kinda reviewed the notes; you didn't attend the other artists' rehearsals or really watch the videos Billie sent. For that matter, you didn't even tell Billie when you made a change to your piece that might affect hers."

"I was busy. You, Mom, and Dad were all worked up about me getting a job. Jobs take time."

"I, of all people, know that jobs take time. Until three months ago, I was the only one in the family with a nine-to-five, remember?" Dylan countered without malice, but Neale still flinched as she continued. "But that's not the point. I think you know you are just using the job as another way to hide from potentially failing and getting hurt again. But—"

"You're wrong about the half-and-half thing. That was me in the past," Neale whimpered, and Dylan made some sound of approval, as if she'd expected Neale to concede that Dylan was right. Neale hated how pitiful she was, but at the same time, it wasn't like she could sink much further. As it was, she had nothing left to lose, and so she might as well be honest. Taking a shuddering breath, she said, "The thing is, I did try this time. I tried to be good at my job, to add value to the company and make it fun. Instead, I made it a stressful mess for everyone."

"Okay. But that's one example, and—"

"No. There's more," Neale said, cutting her sister off. Now that she was being honest, she couldn't stop herself, no matter how hard it made her cry. "I tried so hard with Billie's show. Literally hours of work at a time. And I still failed. I just choked. I looked at other people's stuff, and I couldn't do it. My ideas weren't any good, even when I put the work in. What does that say about me?"

For a moment, Dylan was still, and Neale was afraid that she had finally broken her older sister's problem-solving skills. She was on the verge of sobbing so hard that she started to shake, when Dylan took a deep breath and said, "It just means you're human. We all fail. Sometimes it is silly stuff, like when I failed to set the custard in that lemon chiffon before going to Uncle Luis's house."

"Just whipped cream and raw eggs. So gross," Neale croaked, her voice watery even as she laughed.

"Super gross," Dylan agreed, and Neale could feel her smile against her shoulder. "Anyway, sometimes we fail at the big stuff, and there is no way to make that funny. When that happens, there is nothing to do but dust yourself off. We fail, and we try again. That's how life works. It can't be lived in a protective bubble."

"I didn't want any of this. Not that job, nor the stupid show that Billie made me do." Neale sniffed and tried to roll out of her sister's reach.

The maneuver didn't work, and Dylan squeezed her tighter. "Stop it, Neale. This is why Mom and Dad wanted you to move out and get a job. You are a grown woman. No one made you do anything."

Neale froze for a moment, letting her sister's words turn over in her mind. Her reasonable self noted that Dylan might have a point. Luckily for Neale, her unreasonable self made the better argument that Dylan really didn't have all the facts. Otherwise, Dylan would have agreed with her. Snuggling deeper into Mike's robe, she said, "You weren't there when Billie yelled at me. It was humiliating."

"Okay, but what did you want her to do? Hand you a rattle and put you in a bouncy walker until you stopped acting like a baby? You wanted to spend time with Billie, and you agreed to do the show. Did you expect her to give you special treatment? Billie is a perfectionist at heart. Obviously, she was going to treat you just like any other artist throwing a fit."

"That's not . . . I don't . . . ," Neale sputtered as her throat tightened. Forcing air into her lungs, she tried again. "Billie has changed."

"This whole thing really isn't about Billie, but I will humor this diversion, because it is related," Dylan said, squeezing her as if the embrace would soften the blow. "Of course Billie has changed, Neale. No one can stay who they were at fourteen. That doesn't make her bad. It just means you have to learn to navigate her evolution, just like she is trying to navigate yours."

"It's not an evolution, Dyl. This is different. She used to be on my side."

"Did it ever occur to you that she was always on your side growing up because both of you weren't on my side? What you had in common wasn't likes or dislikes; it was a shared enemy."

"I'm sorry." Neale felt a hot tear run down her face and paused for a moment, her heart aching as she replayed some of her and Billie's greatest capers, including stealing Dylan's spelling bee prize candy. When she looked at it from Dylan's perspective, all the pranks at her expense must have made her feel even more like the family's black sheep.

"I'm not condemning you. I'm offering you a way to reframe your relationship with Bill so you see why it has changed. You and I grew up and learned how to be friends."

Neale let a sob run through her as Dylan's words turned over in her mind. She and Billie *had* built a bond on making fun of Dylan, but they no longer mocked their weird, orderly older sister. Over time, Neale and Dylan had become friends, but she and Billie hadn't put that kind of effort into developing a relationship as adults.

Dylan snuggled closer to her and said, "You don't need to cry."

"But it's sad. We were mean to you," Neale managed to choke out, wishing that she hadn't come to Dylan's house. This talk was making her head feel worse and driving a nail into her heart.

"And now you are not. Whether or not you knew it, we both made an effort to get to know one another as adults. Relationships are work, even the sister kind. Why do you think Billie and I have a weekly call?"

"She is such a bossy gremlin," Neale mumbled, still not quite ready to admit her sister had a point.

"Neale, I think you know I'm right," Dylan said. "Which means you need to apologize to some people, including Billie and Anthony—side note, I still can't believe a singing card is Anthony's career goal."

"I know. It's both hilarious and sweet."

"It really is," Dylan said, readjusting her posture so that she could sit up. Shaking her head, she said, "Anyway. Are you going to commit to finding a way to make all this work? Or what?"

Neale sighed. "What other choice do I have, really?"

"Nope," Dylan practically shouted, and Neale cringed. Her sister really was a morning person, and her lack of respect for the neighbors' hearing put that on full display. "Don't cop out. You could always quit your job, so either you want to finish what you started, or you don't."

"You are so hard core," Neale said, adding a bit of playful irritation to her voice. She waited until Dylan finished laughing before she said, "I'll find a way. I don't want to quit my job—or at least not until money from Billie's show starts to come in—I mean, it's a really good place to work."

"That's the spirit. So you're gonna roll in there, suck it up, apologize to everyone, and get it done."

"You make it sound so simple," Neale said, glancing over at her sister as she threw the covers back.

"Apologies are never simple. But if you can wear a flaming hat, you can do this." Dylan shrugged as she got out of bed. Ignoring Neale's incredulous look, she said, "Now, I'm going to make us some coffee."

"Thank you," Neale called as her sister headed toward the bedroom door. "Hey, Dyl?"

"Yeah?" Her sister stopped, her hand hovering over the main light switch, which would likely blind them both for a moment.

"Thank you for listening to me . . . and I'm sorry I ate all your expensive crackers."

"That's what I'm here for." Dylan smiled over at her, then hit the lights and said, "Now, do you want to go to the gym with me? It's five forty, and I have a six-fifteen TRX-band class. I'm sure I could get you in too."

CHAPTER
TWENTY-FOUR

Neale got out of the car, nostalgia washing over her as she looked up at her parents' home. In the few weeks since she had last stopped by, things had changed, gently reminding her that this was no longer her home. Her father had recently sold an enormous tiger sculpture that used to live on their front lawn. Once a major point of contention between the Delacroix and the neighbors, now all that was left of the Tiger and the feud was a brown patch of dead grass where the sculpture used to sit.

Not bothering to lock her car, Neale adjusted the strap on her purse and began making her way up the weed-strewed path toward the house, trying not to feel nervous. When she had decided to apologize to Billie first, she had convinced herself that this would be the easy apology. Now that she was standing on the doorstep of her childhood home, she wasn't so sure.

"Don't be scared," she told herself. Taking a deep breath, she twisted the door handle and walked into the house. Stopping to hang her purse up on a hook by the door, she peered into the living room and came face to face with Billie sprawled out on the couch, reading a book and using the family dog as a footrest. She was just about to say hello when both Billie and Milo noticed her. The dog was quicker to respond, tumbling off the couch and throwing a surprised Billie sideways as he hurtled toward Neale, furiously yelping, and launched himself at her.

"Hi, buddy," Neale said, bending down so the dog could properly pummel her with licks and paws. Somewhere over the dog's whines, Neale heard Billie's book slam shut and looked up from scratching the dog's ears in time to see her sister rolling off the couch with plenty of righteous indignation and almost no grace.

"Billie, please wait," Neale called out, standing up quickly. Her sister turned to glare at her, and her heart dropped. There, just behind all her anger, was the hurt that Neale had caused.

"What do you want?" Billie asked, her words hard and cold as granite.

Neale paused, not entirely sure where to begin. Somehow, when she had envisioned this moment, Neale had thought the two of them would be sitting at the kitchen table, smiling like old friends, the mistake already forgotten as soon as she walked through the door. Now that she was faced with her sister, she could tell that this particular fantasy was nowhere near reality.

Billie arched an irritated eyebrow, and Neale realized that she was running out of time. Either she was going to do this, or she was going to have to go back to Dylan and tell her she'd wimped out.

"I came to apologize."

"Oh." Billie's other eyebrow joined the first in surprise, which she quickly recovered from. Sounding put upon, she said, "Fine."

"Okay." Neale nodded. Walking over to the couch, she dropped onto one corner and gestured for her sister to sit.

Billie squinted at her like returning to the place where she had just been seated was some grand inconvenience. Finally, she marched back to the couch and sat down stick straight with her feet on the floor, as if she was prepared to run away at any time. "Go ahead."

Neale's blood pounded in her ears as she tried to begin what she had rehearsed. Forcing herself to make eye contact with her sister, she started, "Billie, I want to apologize for how I behaved at rehearsal. It was childish and unacceptable."

For a moment, all Billie did was blink, and Neale wondered if she had actually spoken or if she had just imagined speaking. As the silence stretched between them, she became more convinced that her apology had been in her head. Neale was almost relieved. At least, until she saw Billie's jaw tighten. "It wasn't just childish; it was humiliating."

"I know, and looking back on it, I can see that I ascribed a lot of motives to you that just weren't there. That wasn't fair of me, either, and I'm sorry."

"What do you mean by 'motives'?" Billie asked, wrinkling her nose as if Neale had tried to hand her one of Milo's more disgusting chew toys.

"I guess . . . ," Neale started, then stopped, looking down at her hands to collect her thoughts. "We used to be so close. And then you left, and I didn't hear from you much, but I guess I just thought we would pick up where we left off. Like two peas in a pod. But we aren't the same people anymore. You are so cool and put together now. And I'm not. Until like three months ago, I was a twenty-eight-year-old who still lived at home and had never really paid rent. I felt like you were judging me, and I just wanted us to be close again."

Neale stopped there and watched her sister's face. Her nose was no longer wrinkled, and the surprised eyebrows had been replaced with a carefully schooled neutral expression. But try as her sister might, Neale could tell she was listening, because she was still squinting ever so slightly, just like she had when they were kids.

"Anyway. I can look back on that now and realize how silly it was for me to think you weren't in my corner."

Neale let her sentence trail off and suppressed the urge to fidget with the safety pins on the edge of her shirt. Sending a signal to her body to unclench her stomach, she tried to remember to breathe as Billie sat incredibly still. Finally, Neale couldn't take the silence any longer.

"Again, I'm sorry."

"Oh, Neale!" Billie's voice burst over the top of her own as her sister cracked. Taking Neale by surprise, she bounced across the couch and grabbed her hand. "I didn't know you felt that way."

"How could you, when I didn't tell you?" Neale asked.

"It was never my intention to make you feel forgotten, less than, or unwanted. You were wrong about a lot of stuff, but you were right about one thing. I was caught up in my own life, and I didn't really make the effort I should have. I know I missed milestones for you and Dylan. And Mom and Dad too. And instead of just owning up to not being around lately and doing better, I was stubborn and tried to convince myself that maybe y'all hadn't noticed that I wasn't around," Billie said, squeezing Neale's hand and blinking back tears from behind her thick-framed glasses.

"Then your show happened, and I was at a crossroads, so I moved back home, and I railroaded my way into your life. I pushed for too much without taking your feelings into account. I shouldn't have pressed you to do the show, Neale. I was just overcompensating for not being around when you needed me."

Billie stopped and used the hand that wasn't squeezing Neale's to death to swipe at some tears, knocking her glasses slightly off balance in the process.

Rotating so that she was sitting across from her sister, Neale put her free hand on top of her own and Billie's, smiled, and said, "If by 'lately' you mean the last seven years of spotty calls, texts, and emails, then I forgive you. Even though you didn't actually say the word *sorry*."

"Don't push it," Billie said, looking affronted. "And I said sorry."

"You didn't." Neale smiled.

"Yes, I did."

"Nope. You said a lot of other words, but not *sorry*." Neale grinned.

"I could have sworn—" Billie froze, her mouth open as Neale shook her head. After a moment, her sister laughed and said, "I'm sorry, Neale. And if you accept my apology, I will accept yours."

"Okay, I accept." Neale nodded as her eyes prickled. After almost twenty-four hours of crying, the idea that she might cry because she was happy seemed exhausting, and she did her best to fight the tears. At least, she did until Billie started crying in earnest and pulled her into a hug.

"I'm so sad I hurt you," Billie half laughed, half sobbed into Neale's hair.

"I'm sad I hurt you," Neale said, wiping her tears on her sister's shoulder. "I wasn't nice to you."

"It's okay. I called you self-indulgent." Billie sniffed, releasing her.

"That was mean," Neale agreed.

"Oh, big mean. I remember thinking it was kind of harsh when I said it."

"It's okay. I called you selfish, and—"

"Maybe we don't need to relive every mean thing we said about each other right now?" Billie laughed, removing her glasses and wiping her eyes again.

"Good idea. Maybe we could get to know each other instead?" Neale said, watching as her sister attempted to clean her glasses with the edge of her shirt, which only smudged them more.

"I would like that. Any suggestions for where to start?" Giving up on the glasses, she returned her focus to Neale and said, "I promise I'll follow your lead this time."

Neale's chest filled with warmth. Taking a deep breath, she voiced the suggestion she hoped there was still room for. "I know I huffed off in a frenzy. But if you haven't filled my spot, maybe we could work on my performance for your show? Like, really collaborate this time?"

"I'd like that," Billie said, her entire demeanor softening. "And I would never fill your spot. You could have come back on closing night, and I would have handed it to you."

"Thank you." Neale felt another tear run down her cheek at the same time Billie started to sniffle again. The two of them looked at each other and burst into messy, wet giggles and another round of hugs. When they had pulled it together once more, Neale said, "I have my laptop in my bag. Want to see what I've been thinking?"

"Yes, please." Billie grinned.

Neale sprang up and dashed into the hallway to grab her purse, her joy so overwhelming that she felt like Milo knocking his tail into walls as she reached for the bag. She never wanted to fight with her sister like that again.

Smiling as she rounded the corner back into the living room, Neale pulled her computer out. Dropping her bag on the ground at their feet, she sat back on the couch, flipped the screen open, then said, "Let's start with the video."

~

Neale peeked around the corner of the building and then jumped back, her stomach twisting into knots. A small part of her had hoped that Anthony had decided to eat lunch away from the office so she could keep putting off her apology. Not that she was stalling, but she had arrived after him, and he'd seemed pretty engrossed in his conversation with Travis. Then she had wanted to send an email off to the vendor confirming that they could manage the recording device solution that she had thought up. Then there had been a meeting with Rich, and before she knew it, it was lunchtime. Or at least that was what she told herself. Really, she would have told herself that aliens were coming if it meant she wasn't scared.

"Now or never," Neale whispered to herself. Taking a deep breath, she ran her hands down the pleats of Dylan's navy-blue sleeveless blouse and stepped around the corner. When Anthony didn't look up from his lunch, Neale realized that the sound of the freeway didn't exactly make it easy for her to announce herself. Taking a few steps closer, Neale coughed loudly, causing Anthony to jump and throw bits of shredded lettuce out of his sandwich.

"Hi. Sorry to scare you," Neale said, her heart pounding in her throat.

"It's okay," Anthony said. His usual polite tone was flat as he brushed bits of lettuce off the table.

Neale had secretly hoped he would invite her to join him. Instead, she hovered awkwardly in front of him as he returned his attention to his sandwich with dogged determination. She forced herself to count to five as Anthony took a bite of his sandwich before she coughed again.

Anthony looked up. At this rate, he was either going to take the hint or think she had a nasty summer cold. Acknowledging that the coughing wasn't working, she said, "Is it okay if I join you?"

"The table is meant for everyone," Anthony said, although his voice sounded like he wished the table were reserved for him.

"Thanks." Neale slid onto the bench as quickly as possible so she wouldn't lose her nerve. Clasping her hands and setting them on the table, she held her breath for a second, waiting for Anthony to look at her after taking another bite of the sandwich, which he did not do. Exhaling, Neale made herself start just as she had practiced. "Anthony, I would like to apologize to you."

Neale watched as Anthony's shoulders dropped a fraction of an inch. Slowly, he set down his sandwich and reached his left hand for his napkin, thoroughly brushing away any crumbs on his hands before looking up. Training his dark eyes directly on her, he said, "All right."

"I'm sorry for the way I acted on Monday. I was frustrated with myself and the vendor, and I took that out on you," she said, giving her head a shake to clear her mind.

"Okay. Thank you for your apology." Anthony sounded like a robot. Nodding at her once, he looked back down at his lunch, and it occurred to her that nothing but manners was keeping him from cussing her out.

"The thing is," she said, watching as Anthony's hand paused inches from his sandwich. Neale's mind began to jitter as she anticipated the next part of her apology. "I have been thinking about what you said around making a decision and sticking to it. And you were right. I have been half-in, half-out on a lot of things. Including this card, my art . . . and you."

Neale stopped, hoping for some change in Anthony's demeanor to let her know if she should keep going or just shut up. Outside of his even breathing, the only physical change was his jaw clenching. Not the best sign, she decided.

"Anyway. I wanted to tell you that I reached out to the vendor, and I think I've worked out a deal. If you still want to do this, the vendor is willing to place a bulk order and store the unused devices for us—if we commit to producing two additional cards. We would have to pay for the devices we need now and pay for the second half of the shipment in installments for the next six months or until the other cards are ready to be printed—whichever is sooner. That should give us the time to earn our money back on the first set of cards, which we can use to finance the rest of the devices and possibly the next round of cards."

While her apology might not have gotten a reaction from Anthony, this news certainly did. Neale tried not to hope as some light returned to his eyes. She could tell he was a hair's breadth away from a smile when something changed his mind, and a fixed business-as-usual look crossed his face. Inhaling sharply, he said, "I think that is a reasonable set of terms. Thank you for working that out."

Okay, that wasn't exactly what she wanted to hear. In fact, if Neale had to put words to it, it was the opposite. However, Anthony's almost smile gave Neale reason to hope, and she pushed on with the next part of her plan. Fidgeting with the nail polish on her left index finger, she said, "Also, since I am working on my sister's show, I'll be making a percentage off of every ticket. If this show does even half as well as Billie's other show, I'll be leaving Happy Hearts at the end of the month. You were right about the follow-through thing. My heart just isn't in this job, and I need to commit."

After a beat, Anthony said, "That's great, Neale. I'm happy for you."

"Thanks," she said, although she wasn't all that thankful. It was hard to feel like she was having a meaningful conversation with someone whose poker face was so good that he could win national tournaments. Letting go of her index finger, she flailed her hands in a circular gesture and said, "I'm going to let Rich know this afternoon, but I wanted to tell you first."

"I won't mention it to anyone." Anthony blinked at her for a second, then looked at his sandwich.

Biting down on her bottom lip, Neale paused. She desperately did not want to take the hint that he preferred the company of turkey and provolone on sourdough to sitting with her. Not when she had come this close to making amends.

Taking a steeling breath, she exhaled the last of her pitch in one fast-moving sentence so she wouldn't lose her nerve. "Also, I've thought about what you said and about my hang-ups, and since we won't be working together anymore—well, anymore in like a month—but anyway, maybe we could try to date. Like, a real date. No back and forth. If it's not too late . . ."

Anthony looked up sharply, the rich brown of his eyes connecting with hers. Neale's pulse began to pound like her heart was trying to jackhammer its way out of her chest. She watched as he unconsciously flexed his hands, causing the tattoo that ran up his arm to ripple. Her skin remembered the way that his skin had felt as she'd traced the pattern of that tattoo the night of the party, and it made her heart ache.

For a moment, neither of them moved. In fact, Neale couldn't tell if he was even breathing. She knew she wasn't. Everything about Anthony seemed as though it were attached to a coil, waiting for him to make a decision about which way to release all his energy. She realized that she was squeezing her hands together so tightly that they were starting to lose feeling. Just as she made the decision to relax, she saw Anthony do the same, and she almost smiled.

Looking down at his now-crumpled napkin, Anthony took a deep breath, then met Neale's gaze without flinching. "Thank you for your honesty."

Neale's mind tripped over the words. This wasn't a yes-let's-try-again thank-you. This was more of a you're-dismissed-but-gently thank-you. She wasn't sure how to respond other than to go before she started to cry. She had missed her window, despite her best efforts, and there was nothing left to do but accept that.

"You're welcome," Neale said. Forcing herself to stand up, she walked away, her throat burning and her chest aching with each step. Reaching the glass door, she remembered that she would only have to sit across from her self-made heartbreak for another month. And if she was truly sorry, the least she could do was give Anthony his space. After all, he had done that for her.

CHAPTER TWENTY-FIVE

"All cast, this is your five-minute warning. Belinda to the stage. Belinda to the stage, please. Have a good show, everyone."

Chills ran through Neale's body as she put the finishing touches on her makeup backstage. Smiling at Belinda, who waved as she shimmered out the door, Neale set her lipstick down and settled into her quiet corner of the room. Despite the embarrassing blowout, the rest of the cast had been oddly chill about her return. Neale had been nervous about it, but when she'd mentioned this to Callen, all they'd said was, "Sisters fight."

Now she just had to hope that the fight was worth it. Somewhere overhead, the heartbeat of Belinda's music began to play. The disquieting sound simultaneously brought a hush over the dressing room and amped up the tension in each performer. As in rehearsal, Nhi's voice acted as a soothing balm, slowly beckoning each of them out of the room. With every departure, the nervous energy became more palpable.

"Hey, Neale."

"Uh-huh?" Neale said as Callen's voice interrupted her thoughts.

"Someone left this backstage for you." Callen extended a bunch of yellow, orange, and red roses with a little plastic **CONGRATS** sign peeking over the wrapping, along with a small square envelope. The neat, blocky handwriting was instantly familiar. Anthony.

"Oh, thank you." Neale did her best to smile at Callen as a new level of nerves coursed through her. Taking the fiery bouquet and the envelope from them, she waited until Callen was out of sight before she carefully undid the seal, her heart pounding as if it were part of this evening's soundtrack. Slowly, she removed the cream-colored card from the envelope. On the front, Anthony had drawn Neale in clean black ink standing under a spotlight, her arms held wide and a big smile on her face. Unlike his usual doodles, this was done in exquisite detail, as if he had memorized each line of her body, from the curve of her shoulders to the way she tended to stand slightly off center. He'd even managed to draw the strands of hair that seemed determined to go their own way, no matter how often she tried to tame them. Underneath the picture he had written *The Bounce Back*.

Neale felt her face shift into the same warm expression that she had on the front of the card as she stared at his work. Biting her lower lip, she opened the card.

Neale,

Being with you is a little bit like parkour. I think I know what the obstacles are and then you surprise me. Wednesday was a big surprise! But, like parkour, if an obstacle defeats you the first time, the best thing you can do is try another approach. I would like to try another approach with you. If it's not too late.

—Anthony

For a moment, all Neale could do was stare at the letter. It wasn't the mushy-gushy love letter that Victorian novels promised her. By those standards, this was barely a love letter at all. This was quiet, thoughtful, and true to Anthony. At least she thought it was. It wouldn't be the first time she'd misread a guy's intentions. For possibly the first time in her life, she desperately hoped her imagination wasn't running away with her this time.

When she flipped over the card to look at the back, Neale's eyes landed on a perfectly shaded little heart, flanked on either side by fire extinguishers, and laughed. She opened the card again and was rereading the message to look for hidden clues when Nhi's voice came over the speaker.

"Callen to the stage. Callen to the stage, please. Neale, this is your five-minute warning."

Looking up from the card, Neale turned to smile at Callen as they made their way to the stage, looking pale with nerves.

The sight of Callen anxious brought Neale back into the room. She was up next. The weight of this opportunity was almost crushing as she thought about the audience. Members of the press would likely be out there, along with her friends, family, coworkers, and, if rumors were true, Dr. McMillan.

Neale's mind hopped from one potential disaster to the next. But then she stopped herself. All she needed was five minutes of bravery. Five minutes to show the world what she could really do. To prove to herself that this was where she belonged.

"Neale to the stage, please. Neale to the stage." Nhi's voice floated through the empty room.

"Be brave," Neale said to her reflection as she pushed herself out of her chair.

She couldn't really feel her feet moving, but she knew she was walking toward the stage entrance because the sound of Callen's piece grew louder. Checking in with her body as she rounded the corner, she noted that her breathing was even, her vision was fine, and she could hear as she always had. This wasn't the panicked numbness of prior performances. This was as if her nervous system was dimming all the other inputs so that she could focus on what mattered.

Reaching Nhi, Neale watched as Callen put the finishing touches on the giant spray-painted work in front of them.

"Ready?" Nhi whispered to Neale, covering the mic on her headset.

"Like I was born for this." Neale grinned as Callen's set ended and the lights cut out.

"All right, then. Go kick ass." Nhi squeezed Neale's shoulder in the darkness, her faint smile just barely visible in the blue light of the stand that held her notes.

Nodding at her, Neale took a deep breath and strode onstage, letting the darkness and silence of the crowd's anticipation wrap around her like a blanket. Finding her mark, she waited until her lights came up. Overhead, she could see the flicker of her new video on a loop. She had redone it so that it was just close-up footage of her hands lighting images on fire, with the smoldering majorette hat interspersed at jarring intervals. Billie had suggested they lay a grainy black-and-white filter over the whole thing and loop it with the footage at an angle, which made the viewer feel like they were watching something sinister.

Neale gave the audience a moment to process the video before she began to speak. With the stage lights in her eyes, she couldn't gauge anyone's reaction. But she could feel their tension, and she let that discomfort bleed into her as she raised her right fist and knocked twice with force on her chest. The mic she wore picked up the sound, which was similar to the heartbeat that Belinda had used in her act. She let the false heartbeat rattle around in the silence for a moment before she spoke.

"What does it mean when someone fails?"

Neale hit her chest again as she stepped to the left, feeling eyes following her as she began to recite the actions and emotions that came with failure. "We jeer; we laugh. And oh, the schadenfreude."

Thump, thump: again she made the sound. "When we watch failure, what is it that we seek? To experience a grief we cannot know? Is it a collective social death? Perhaps a rebirth?"

Thump, thump. Neale reached the far-left side of the stage and turned around before asking the next question. "How was your failure? Was it cold? Were you alone? Was there fear? Rage? Are you still sitting in the bottom of the well? Or is it as they say, and you were reborn from the ashes?"

She struck her chest twice more as she reached the right side of the stage. She let the thumps echo around the room this time as she moseyed back toward center. Turning to face the audience, she said, "I have failed. Will you sit in the dark with me? Let's find out what happens in the ashes."

Suddenly, Neale was pitched into darkness, as the techs cut the lights and the video all at once. In the pitch black of the stage, she exhaled, knowing that her mic was off, and grinned as all the senses her body had been suppressing began to flood back. The audience was still sitting in darkness and silence. They hadn't realized the show was over, just like she'd hoped they wouldn't.

Scurrying toward Nhi's blue stage light, Neale felt like she might just float away. It was scary and exhilarating to think that right now, two hundred people were sitting in the audience trying to figure out their feelings. Neale couldn't control what they thought. But she had said exactly what she wanted to say.

Reaching backstage, Neale bounced up and down while Nhi waved and called orders into her headset. She was midway in the air when another body slammed into her and squeezed. Billie rocked back and forth, squeaking with delight as she hugged Neale so tight she couldn't breathe.

"You did it!" Billie said. The fact that she couldn't whisper was only saved by the techs, who brought the houselights up, revealing Billie's final painting projected onstage at that exact moment.

"No, you did it," Neale said over the sound of thunderous applause rushing at them.

"Okay, we both did it," Billie said, releasing Neale and flipping her long braids over her shoulder, then peeking out at the crowd. "Oh my God! They are standing up. Come on, we are taking a bow."

"No. We may have done it, but it's your show," Neale said, trying to dig her heels into the floor backstage as Billie yanked on her arm.

"Girl, if you don't get your act together and walk out there with me," Billie said, stopping just long enough to glare at Neale, "so help me God, I will have Grandmama kick your ass all the way down Broadway."

With that, she turned and pulled Neale onstage. Her sister, ever calm and collected, put her hand over her heart and grinned before waving directly at their family. Neale had just enough time to smile as Dylan stealthily accepted Grandmama's hankie and wiped tears before Billie pulled her into a side hug and forced them both into a bow. Releasing Neale's shoulders, Billie grabbed her hand and raised it in the air, then waved at various cast members in the wings, who took their cue to come out and join them onstage. Belinda appeared on her other side, smiling from ear to ear as she took Neale's hand, and they all bowed again. And again. And again.

Finally, Billie forced them offstage along with the rest of the cast so they could mingle with the opening night crowd. Giving Neale a close hug, she said, "Members of the press are here, and they are going to want to talk to you."

"They should talk to you," Neale said, trying hard to get her smile under control. She had no desire to talk to anyone with the capacity to review anything. The only thing she wanted to do was go hug her family. And maybe get a strong drink.

"They can talk to us both or no one at all. I'm so proud of you, Neale."

"Thank you, sister," Neale said, feeling herself get choked up. Fanning her eyes so that her mascara didn't run, she added, "For everything."

"I would do it again in a millisecond." Billie sniffled, and Neale thought her middle sister's cool exterior might crack. She watched as Billie formed an O shape with her lips and exhaled before schooling her features and saying, "Okay, let's go enjoy the party."

With that, she began unceremoniously dragging Neale through the side door into the lobby. Almost immediately, they were mobbed by a wall of people dying to get to her sister. Billie released her hand and began talking animatedly with Kelsea and Marceline, who seemed very excited by what they'd seen. Neale hoped this meant her sister would be raking in cash for her next project.

Carefully untangling herself from the group, Neale looked left, then right, for her family. When she spotted her grandmama's fur coat, her heart stopped. Not because of the fur or the fact that her grandmama was wearing it in July, but because next to her grandmother, smiling his quiet smile, was Anthony.

In all the chaos around the show, Neale had managed to put aside her feelings about him. Now they came rushing at her all at once, each feeling practically shoving the others to be processed first. Part of her was terrified that she had misunderstood his letter and he didn't want her. The other part was afraid she'd understood his letter exactly but would screw it up again, despite all she had learned about herself.

Biting the inside of her cheek, she took the first steps toward him. He was still chatting with her family, but she managed to catch his eye, his expression polite and unreadable. Resisting the urge to stop at the bar for some liquid courage, Neale continued to weave between people until she felt a hand on her shoulder.

Neale froze, looking at the face attached to the hand. After a tense heartbeat, Dr. McMillan inclined her head at her and said, "Congratulations, Neale."

"Thank you," she managed to say after getting over her initial shock.

Dr. McMillan must have deliberately ignored the look of horror that was surely plastered to Neale's face, because she continued, "This is exactly the kind of work I hoped you were capable of when you joined the Collective. A true tour de force. I couldn't be prouder to call you a Collective exile. Way to buck the establishment."

"I . . . thank you?" Neale said, confusion washing over her.

"Trust me. It's a compliment. Wait until the board of directors sees what you have done. They will be clamoring to have all kinds of arsonists join us." Shaking her head, Dr. McMillan chuckled. "People like you move art forward and make my job interesting. Jenna's probably weeping in the bathroom over it as we speak."

"Too bad I don't have a camera," Neale mumbled, as the idea that Dr. McMillan was poking fun at both the art establishment and her own students sank in. The joke made Neale smile in spite of all the pain that the Collective had caused her.

"Oh, I'm sure someone else does," Dr. McMillan laughed, then added, "I'll let you go celebrate with your family. But please know how delighted I am for you. And if you ever want to give a lecture to the next cohort of Collective members, give me a ring. I think it could be very instructional."

"Thank you, Dr. McMillan. I'll be in touch," Neale said, and she was surprised to find that she meant it. While getting kicked out of the Collective had felt like the worst night of her life, now that she looked back on it, it almost didn't matter anymore. Who she was then and who she was now were like two different sides of the same coin. She liked Old Neale, but she didn't need to dwell on her past self, except to thank her for bringing her to New Neale.

She watched as Dr. McMillan blazed a trail through the crowd, occasionally waving at other Collective members who Neale knew but didn't feel the need to say hello to. At least, not before she talked to Anthony. Glancing over her shoulder, she found him listening to what she could guess was her father's stand-up routine. Anthony was chuckling politely, but her father was practically rolling on the floor with laughter.

Looking to her left, Neale spotted Corinne barreling toward her, tugging Chloe and her new girlfriend, Jenny, behind her. Glancing fleetingly at Anthony, Neale decided he could probably take another three minutes of her father's jokes before she absolutely had to save him. Just enough time for her to hug her roommate.

"You were amazing!" Corinne shrieked, throwing her arms around her.

"Thank you." Neale coughed, wondering if it was possible for someone to collapse her windpipe with a hug.

"Here." Corinne reached back and snatched some hot-pink daisies from her sister. "These are for you. We are so proud. What did I say, Jenny? Tomorrow, we are gonna be able to tell everyone that we know one of the artists."

Neale's laugh echoed around the crowded room. "Maybe wait until the reviews are out before you tell anyone."

"Are you kidding me? I've been waiting to brag about you for weeks," Corinne said, her smile still wide.

"Well, it sure beats telling people your roommate was the fire-video girl."

"I would never call you that. Fire-video vixen, sure. Video girl? You are way cooler than that." Corinne nodded as if what she'd said were a categorical fact, and Neale was struck by how lucky she was to have a roommate who cheered her on. In a way, that was all she'd wanted when she'd dreamed up the artist-house idea. Now, she wouldn't trade her weirdo, unicorn-obsessed new friend for anything.

"And thank you so much for the tickets. The only opening night I've been to is, like, a Marvel movie," Jenny said.

"Of course. You are so welcome."

"Jenny doesn't know how fancy we are," Corinne laughed. "By the way, like my new dress?"

Neale studied the dress and was shocked to see that she wasn't wearing anything with a unicorn on it. Well, except for a small baby-blue hair clip, but that was barely noticeable. Grinning, she said, "I do. It's very chic and—"

"Wait. Is that the guy from the party?" Corinne interrupted her and started pointing. "It totally is him. Why are you talking to me?"

"Because you started talking to me," Neale said, with mock indignation.

"No excuses. Go talk to him. Your apology totally worked, didn't it? After you tried to tell me it didn't fix anything, too."

"Do you want me to talk to you or him?" Neale asked playfully.

"Oh my God. Go talk to him. We'll be over here. I'll get you a drink, so you can come find me and tell me what happened after."

"Okay. I'll come—"

"Go!" Corinne said, making a shooing motion with her hands.

"All right," Neale said over her shoulder as she turned toward her family.

Pulling her shoulders back, she tried to quiet her nerves and had just taken another step when Rich appeared, along with Melissa and Travis. Leaning slightly to the left to try to make eye contact with Anthony, she spotted Morrigan waiting behind her coworkers and looking put out by their company, who was none other than Darin. Suppressing a cringe, she leaned to her right, where she spotted Billie, who threw her a meaningful glance without breaking conversation with someone who Neale suspected was a journalist. Looking at the queue of well-wishers, Neale thought that if this kept up, it might take her all night to reach Anthony.

As if sensing her conundrum, Anthony looked up at her, then said something to her father before taking a step over to claim his place in the greeting line. He was letting her take the lead, giving her space to soak it all in and figure it out, just as he always had.

But this time, Neale didn't need space to figure it out. This time, she knew exactly what she wanted. One look at him, and everyone else seemed to melt away. Turning to her Happy Hearts coworkers, she said, "I'm so excited to see you all, but there is one thing that I have to do."

"Of course," she heard Rich say in his usual encouraging way. She had to give her boss credit; he'd taken the whole I-plan-to-leave-in-a-month thing pretty well, considering that he had just hired her. Of course, with her process improvements and the singing cards ready to launch, Happy Hearts really didn't need her full time. Although, dog dad that he was, Rich had offered her the chance to come back and do a little freelance scanning and spreadsheet work if she ever needed it in between gigs.

Smiling at the crowd, she stood up tall and did her best fake-it-till-you-make-it confident stride to where Anthony was waiting. Stopping in front of him, she said, "Hi."

"Hello," Anthony said, a hint of a nervous smile tracing his lips as he tucked his hands in his pockets. "The show was amazing. Congratulations, Neale."

"Thank you, and thank you for coming," she said, trying to get her nerves under control. Searching for where to start, Neale blurted, "I got your card and flowers before the show. They were beautiful."

Anthony's face fell a little. "You did? I asked the company to deliver them after the show so you could read it when I wasn't around and decide how you felt. I didn't want to distract you or—"

"No. I'm glad I got it." Neale rushed to cut Anthony off before he beat himself up any more. "Don't feel bad. I'm the one who should feel bad."

"You already apologized," Anthony said gently. "I just needed a minute to think about it, and I should have told you that, instead of 'thank you for your honesty.'"

"To be fair, you did tell me that you were done with the back-and-forth—rightly so," Neale said, holding up the hand that wasn't carrying Corinne's flowers, then added, "So I was kind of violating that to begin with."

"That's very adult of you. I felt terrible after saying it."

"Oh, I felt terrible hearing it. Don't get me wrong. It was brutal."

Anthony smiled, and some of the tension between them left the room. "It wasn't fair of me to take my frustration out on you like that."

"It's okay. I spoke to you with all kinds of frustration. I even made you an insincere coffee offer." Neale felt relief as Anthony laughed.

"Yeah, I didn't think you really wanted to get me a coffee. I went over to the office next door and used their Keurig machine after you left."

"Keurig. Yuck. I'm sorry I did that to you."

"It wasn't that bad."

"The man who won't use free pens is okay with those weird-tasting coffee pods?"

"Hey, everyone has their flaws." Anthony shrugged.

Her heart fluttered. She had missed joking with him more than she cared to admit. Letting the smile fall from her face, she asked the question she was afraid of. "When you said 'try a different approach,' did you mean, like, try a new way for us to be together? As a couple?"

Anthony smiled. "What else could I mean?"

Neale's head spun. She had finally gotten it right. The idea that Anthony truly did want to try again with her, despite the fumbles, bumps, and bruises she had managed to rack up for them, was almost too much. Grinning, she said, "Well, I hoped that was what you meant, but then I started to second-guess myself—which is a thing I'm trying not to do anymore, by the way—and anyway, then I just thought, *Best to communicate*, and so I was double-checking—"

"Neale, I know you're still trying to figure out a lot. And I won't lie—sometimes that is frustrating for me too. But here is the thing," Anthony said, running a hand down her arm. "You are someone special. You found out I wanted to design a singing card, and you made it happen. You helped Rich get over not spending money like it was no big deal. I watched you navigate Willa's fears and help find the best solution

308

for both her and Happy Hearts at the drop of a dime. You have great instincts, even if you don't trust them—yet."

"I think you could've solved that stuff if you wanted to," Neale said, dropping her gaze to the daisies in her hand.

"That's the thing," Anthony said. Noticing that she was looking down, he stepped closer and took her hand in his, drawing her eyes up with the gesture. "I wanted to make a singing card, but I didn't figure it out. You did. Hearing that you were leaving was a shock, and it made me think how much I would miss the surprising ways your mind works if I couldn't sit next to you. I want you to surprise me every day, Neale. Would you be interested in that?"

"I think I could be," she said, stepping toward him and savoring the moment just before his kiss. The way his smile looked, the warmth of him, and the comfort she felt being in his arms. Careful not to knock her flowers into him, she wrapped her arms around his neck, and then Neale leaned in close and kissed him.

The room melted away. All the sights and sounds and excitement dimmed in comparison to how this kiss felt. For the third time that evening, Neale's mind was clear. No fantasies or runaway thoughts were required, because she could never dream up a more perfect scenario. And she knew she wouldn't need to as long as she was with him. Tonight, the real world was far better than her imagination.

ACKNOWLEDGMENTS

Writing a book in 2020 truly was a group effort. About fifty million prayers had to be answered in order for me to type *The End*, and I am grateful for every single person who cheered me on. I could not have done this without you.

My first thank-you, as always, belongs to my incredible agent, Nalini Akolekar. Every day, I pinch myself because I get to say "I published a book." Those words would not be possible without you.

Similarly, I would not get to say "I published a book" without the incredible team at Montlake. Jillian, Lauren, Kristin, Jessica, and so many others are owed a debt of gratitude for their hard work whipping this book into shape and getting my books into the hands of readers. Another thank-you goes to Liz Casal Goodhue for finding a way to work pink into another lovely cover, Riam for such thorough copyediting, and Erica for your keen eye and thoughtful approach to cultural reads. Finally, a massive thank-you to my editors, Maria Gomez and Selina McLemore, for taking what I affectionately called "Struggle Book" and making it something worthy of some shelf space. Maria, thank you for appreciating my dedication to Post-its and enthusiasm. Selina, you are welcome to borrow my car anytime!

My next big thank-you goes to the Massengirls: Jodi, Josy, and Lena. Y'all are badass. My aunts, Bob, and Vik get a special shout-out for reading early drafts of my books and making sure that I hadn't gone too far down the stress rabbit hole. And, of course, my great-aunt Patti. You are the heroine in a cozy mystery that is just waiting to be written!

All my love goes to my cousin Joey, who was the inspiration behind the grunge-musician list. We miss you.

It is safe to say that I would not have written a single word if not for the Struggle Bus Crew. Pandas, K-dramas, and endless new book ideas remain the highlight of my week. I am deeply grateful to each of you for helping me bring this book into the world and for convincing me not to text Nalini that I am an imposter every other day. Thank you!

To my ride-or-dies, Angie and Ashley, I love you both to the moon and back. I also owe Natasha and Ashlee a massive thank-you. Without you two and your socially distanceable yards, I would have lost my mind. And, of course, thank you to Ann Thu, without whom opera night never would have happened. Thank you all for being my friends.

As always, my family deserves all my thank-yous and then some. Dad, thank you for the encouraging voice mails as I tried to power through each draft. Mom, thank you for literally sending food and flowers when I needed an extra push. CoCo, thank you for forcing me to Pomodoro my way through Thanksgiving break (no thank-you for Bamazon!). And Marshall, thank you for helping me decide if I was being too precious with my edits and misreading perfectly clear hiking trail signs with me.

Finally, a special thank-you goes to my grandmama, Dot Jean, and her sister, Jewel. Dot Jean could throw one hell of a curse, excelled at the red-nail-polish game, and needed no man, except her "husband." She danced with celebrities and on actual graves and taught me how to laugh, what it meant to be irreverent, and how to stand on my own. An equally big thank-you to Aunt Jewel. No one was more regal or better dressed, and she knew it. Aunt Jewel was always there when it mattered. She taught me what style, wit, and dignity meant. Y'all are the kind of women I hope I grow up to be. Thank you.

ABOUT THE AUTHOR

Photo © 2020 Natasha Beale

Born and raised outside Seattle, Washington, Addie Woolridge is a classically trained opera singer with a degree in music from the University of Southern California. She also holds a master's degree in public administration from Indiana University. Her well-developed characters are a result of her love for diverse people, cultures, and experiences.

Woolridge currently lives in Northern California. When she isn't writing or singing, she can be found baking, training for her sixth race in the Seven Continents Marathon Challenge, or taking advantage of the region's signature beverage: wine.